Secession

MW00945786

Joe Nobody & P. A. Troit

This is a work of fiction. Characters and events are products of the author's imagination, and no relationship to any living person is implied. The locations, facilities, and geographical references are set in a fictional environment.

Other Books by Joe Nobody:

Holding Their Own: A Story of Survival
Holding Their Own II: The Independents
Holding Their Own III: Pedestals of Ash
Holding Their Own IV: The Ascent
Holding Their Own V: The Alpha Chronicles
Holding Their Own VI: Bishop's Song
Holding Their Own VII: Phoenix Star
Holding Their Own VII: The Directives
Holding Their Own IX: The Salt War
Holding Their Own X: The Toymaker
Holding Their Own XI: Hearts and Minds
Apocalypse Drift
The Little River Otter
The Olympus Device: Book One
The Olympus Device: Book Two
The Olympus Device: Book Three
Secession: The Storm
Secession II: The Flood
The Ebola Wall
Holding Your Ground: Preparing for Defense if it All Falls Apart
The TEOTWAWKI Tuxedo: Formal Survival Attire
Without Rule of Law: Advanced Skills to Help You Survive
The Home Schooled Shootist: Training to Fight with a Carbine

Prologue

The man known as El General studied the oversized, high definition video monitors with an emotionless gaze as a specialist made final adjustments to the sound. Not to be hurried, the conference leader strode confidently, deliberately to the middle of the comfortable theatre seating area. After selecting a perch, he casually crossed one leg over the other and leaned back for a better vantage. Staring back at him were 12 faces, each separated by a thin, computer-generated frame. It was as if he were viewing a narco-photo album of some of the world's most powerful criminals.

Unlike traditional collections of family snapshots, this setup came complete with real-time audio and video and was protected by the planet's most sophisticated encryption technologies.

The impressive high-tech arrangement that enabled this secure virtual conference had been developed to thwart the United States, an unintended consequence of the superpower's global war on terror.

A series of leaks, whistleblowers, and defectors had resulted in headlines that had exposed the tremendous capabilities of the American intelligence community. Neither friend nor foe was safe from the vast arrays of supercomputers, satellites, microphones, and intrusive software hacks employed by the NSA and other clandestine U.S. government institutions. The Yanks could see and hear everything, everywhere, every second.

The world's best and brightest hackers suddenly found their talents were in demand from an entirely new clientele.

No one wanted the Americans knowing their business. Governments, terrorist organizations, and criminal syndicates paid far better than criminal activities like breaking into a bank's mainframe or stealing a retail giant's database of credit card information. Before long, there was an international hunger for software that could keep even the mighty NSA's nose out of the world's business.

The Mexican cartels were no exception.

The video conference, as opposed to a face-to-face meeting, was necessary for a variety of reasons. First of all, none of the 13 men attending the event trusted any of the others enough to reveal their locations. Such a breach of security would surely invite an assassin's bullet, or worse yet, capture by a competitor.

Even if that well founded distrust could be overcome, there was still no chance that the 13 criminal overlords would ever step foot on the same soil at the same time. An assemblage of wanted desperados would be more temptation than the pious gringos could resist. The U.S. would deploy drones within minutes, and those little flyers carried Hellfire missiles. Their military helicopters were always within striking distance. Their Special Forces were known to attack with deadly force.

The adoption of a high-tech solution was part and parcel of El General's reputation. His name hadn't been earned as a result of military service or training, nor was he known as a fearless combat leader. No, the leader of the Gulf Cartel had risen to the top of the potent criminal enterprise because of his meticulous planning, brilliant grasp of strategy, and creative thinking.

"We are losing money," El General announced, kicking off the meeting with a subject near and dear to all 12 hearts. "Since Texas now welcomes all of the sheep into her fold, my coyotes grow hungry. After the secession, the U.S. moved many of her border patrol resources to Arizona and California. Now, these agents intercept more of our goods moving north and seize our cash coming south. The Republic of Texas military creates havoc with our distribution channels along the Rio Grande. We have been forced to expand our operations into West Africa and Europe. And while those markets remain strong, the financial gains are far from what we have all enjoyed in the past."

As he scanned the dozen faces on the monitor, El General was pleased to see most were nodding their agreement. Only a few seemed reserved in their non-verbal responses.

"To make matters worse," he continued with conviction, "we seem determined to fight amongst ourselves. We waste valuable resources slaughtering each other, assets that could be used to expand international territories and increase profit margins. All of us ... myself included ... have devolved into nothing more than packs of wild, rabid animals who seek territory and dominance at any cost."

Again, he assessed the facial expressions staring back at him. Fewer agreed with him this time. He prayed that would change.

"How is it that we have arrived at this juncture? Why do we fall upon each other like ravenous wolves? We are all of the same blood. We all grew up breathing the same air, warmed by the same sun, and drawing life from the same land. Why is it that Mexican kills Mexican as if our lives were worthless ... as if we truly believe our race lacks value? Is inferior to others? Why do we turn on each other like this?"

No one answered El General's questions, and for a moment, the leader of the Gulf Cartel thought his passionate words were falling on deaf ears. Would they consider him weak? Would the truth make him vulnerable?

It does not matter, he thought. *We are all dead in a few years anyway. If these sharks smell my blood in the water, so be it.*

"Consider this, my friends. None of us were the heads of our respective organizations three years ago. Our own internal treachery coupled with the evil that calls itself our government has resulted in the demise of our leadership. The men who once guided us have all been captured, executed, or murdered one by one. Our organizations have been infiltrated and weakened. Our loyal employees die by the scores, either battling Mexico City's armies or each other. Do any of you really expect to live long enough to experience gray hair or grandchildren?"

No one spoke, nor did any of them show the slightest sign of emotion. Only the man everyone knew as Z-44 spoke, his tone thick with impatience. "What is it that you propose, El General?"

"Before I answer that, I ask one small favor. Could you explain to our comrades why you are called Z-44?"

The clean cut, military-looking man seemed both puzzled and angered by the request. Across the high-speed internet connection, El General noticed his competitor's head tilt slightly. "All of you already know why. Do you find the recent passing of my brothers humorous? Does it give you some sort of sick pleasure to hear about the death of good men?"

"No," came the instant, honest reply. "That was not my intent. I think it is important to this conversation that everyone has this information."

Z-44's sigh broadcast through the digital sound system as clearly as if he were sitting across the table. "Los Zetas Cartel was formed by 38 men who served with the Mexican Special Forces. Each member was given a radio call sign of Z-1 through Z-38. I joined the organization later, and thus, I was number 44."

"Of the original 38, how many still walk this earth?"

"None of them have survived. All are dead," stated the leader of the Zetas.

"And that, gentlemen, is my point," El General stated with a solemn tone.

After a pause to let his words sink in, he continued. "Not only has an independent Texas served to choke our primary revenue streams, but also the pool of available manpower from which we can recruit is shrinking. Our world is changing rapidly, and if we ... and I mean each and every one of us ... don't adapt, we will die like so many before us. It is for this reason that I propose we call an immediate ceasefire and end the hostilities between us. Furthermore, I have outlined a plan that I believe will bring all of us riches and control beyond our wildest dreams. I sit before you, gentlemen, convinced that together we are stronger. It will be difficult to eliminate the factors that divide us, but I firmly believe it can be done."

All 12 faces tried to speak at once, some of the voices angry, others loudly grumbling their protests. It was several minutes before the bedlam quieted, one of the attendees so frustrated, he left the call. El General sat calmly, observing the chaos and catching the occasional sentence here and there. The reaction of his colleagues had been anticipated.

El Teo from the Tijuana Cartel was using the forum to complain that the Sinaloas were trying to encroach on his territory.

The leader of the Knights Templar Cartel, Bolas de Toro, was frothing over a rival's supposed collaboration with the Mexican government.

On and on, the verbal sparring continued – accusations, threats, and promises of revenge.

Throughout the confusion, El General sat and observed as first one furious crime lord disconnected, then another. He smiled upon taking note that two of his competitors weren't raving like lunatics. After 10 minutes, the turmoil had quieted, and there were only six faces left staring back at the Gulf Cartel's honcho.

We have a beginning, he thought. *Only six, but it is a start. The others will either eventually see the light or wither in isolation.*

After an extended silent pause, El General began again. "Gentlemen, Texas is the primary source of our decline. I think it is only fitting that they provide the solution. This is my proposal...."

For over 20 minutes, El General delivered a high-level overview of his scheme.

When he had finished, he knew that at least three of the listeners were committed, the same number showing a strong interest in joining his consortium. All agreed to attend a second electronic conference in two days.

After the technician nodded to confirm the meeting had been disconnected, El General turned to a man sitting off-camera. "What do you think?"

The question was directed at the only non-Latino in El General's inner circle, an Arab who had only recently joined the criminal network. His malevolent reputation was the food for rumor and innuendo, so those who spoke of him did so in hushed tones, referring to him only as "Ghost."

"You did an excellent job. It's clear to me how you rose to the top of this organization," the Syrian replied.

El General waved him off with a gesture of humility. "It was your design that sold them. I merely repeated the words."

"Don't sell your contribution short, Jefe," Ghost countered.

"That's what I like about you," the drug lord nodded. "You don't seek fame, desire glory, or demand unearned respect," he paused as he stood to stretch and make eye contact with his collaborator. "However, I must tell you that after working side by side with you for over two months, I'm still not sure what motivates that devious brilliance that sparks inside of your head. And that does puzzle me."

Ghost spread his hands in innocence and smiled, "I want revenge, sir. I owe Texas a debt. Allah, through his grace, has allowed our paths to intersect. We are fortunate that both of our needs can be satisfied by the same campaign."

El General nodded his acceptance, but it was a feigned gesture of sincerity. Men in his position never took anything at face value.

He had found Ghost while shopping for arms in Pakistan, the character introduced by a mutual friend as the "most sophisticated strategist of mayhem on the planet."

After weeks of background verification, reference checking, and personal meetings with the Syrian, El General had invited Ghost to join his organization.

"You will have your vengeance, sir," the cartel boss stated with certainty. "And I will have Mexico."

Chapter 1

The captain lowered his binoculars and flashed a sly grin, "That has to suck, Gunnery Sergeant. They're earning their pay today; that's for sure. Good job on picking the location. I'll have to remember this little house of horrors."

It was the non-commissioned officer's turn to scan the canyon, the three stripes and crossed Garand rifles on his sleeve partially hidden as he lifted his own optic. "Yes, sir. That surely is one bitch of a hump. Don't mess with Texas."

The two Marines continued to observe the training exercise, watching a platoon-sized line of men slowly snake their way along a treacherous, nearly vertical wall of sun-bleached rock and yellowish sandstone.

Further below, the canyon's floor was littered with immense slabs of limestone protruding at harsh angles. The debris of erosion, massive sections of rock rested in haphazard, random heaps after being washed away and collapsing from the high walls. Some the boulders were the size of a single-family home.

Other formations appeared to be ready to join their demoted cousins at the bottom, their sharp, knife-like edges protruding from the cliff face, waiting for the next flood to send them tumbling down the wall.

"What's this place called again?" the officer asked.

"Eagle's Nest Creek, sir," replied the gunny. "I grew up in a town named Langtry that's just up the road. I remember climbing around these formations as a kid. I thought it would provide a worthy test for our little band of gung-ho raiders."

The officer whistled his approval, "You can say that again." The captain took his attention away from the column of struggling men and swept the surrounding area. To the south, only a few hundred meters away was the Rio Grande. Mexico was clearly visible on the far side of the river, the neighboring country's terrain looking just as foreboding. "Isn't Langtry where that famous hanging judge was from?" the officer asked, his eyes still tight against the binoculars.

"Yes, sir. That would be Judge Roy Bean, the only law west of the Pecos River … or so he claimed. There's even a museum in the town dedicated to him." Normally, the sergeant wouldn't have been so talkative, but it was well known that his commander, not being from Texas, was a bit of a buff when it came to local lore and legend.

The captain returned his gaze to the Marines below and then checked his watch. A glance at the setting sun seemed to confirm his thoughts. "Looks like it's going to be several more hours before they negotiate that canyon. The darkness will slow them down even more."

Wiping the sweat from his brow, the officer then had another thought. "At least it will cool off a little after the sun goes down."

The sergeant hadn't been asked a question or issued an order, so he held his tongue. Remembering how cold this part of Texas could get after sunset, a wisp of pity crossed his mind as he watched one of the trainees slide several feet down an embankment. *It will cool off all right*, he thought. *They'll be shivering in their own salt within an hour.*

After the secession, the border patrol had ceased to exist in the republic. While the new immigration policy implemented by Austin was supposed to eliminate the need for illegal crossings, the young nation's leadership fully understood that drug trafficking would still be an issue.

The solution proved relatively simple. Thousands of new soldiers, sailors, and airmen had relocated to the Lone Star nation as part of the treaty. They had to be garrisoned and trained. The vast, open spaces along the border with Mexico seemed like the perfect location. Two government birds could be killed with one stone.

New bases were hastily constructed, the effort reminding some historians of the massive military expansion the United States accomplished in the early months of World War II. The Rio Grande Valley was now dotted with installations ranging from live-fire ranges to schools for Special Forces and Marines.

The only immigrants rejected from the newly expanded ports of entry were those with a criminal record. Word quickly spread throughout South America and Mexico, resulting in far fewer individuals trying to sneak into Texas. Those that did make the attempt were either felons or smugglers of narcotics and other contraband.

The Texas military had all the high-tech systems and mechanical toys any soldier could dream of. Everything from drones to sophisticated radar as well as satellites and spy planes that circled the globe. However, all required training and skilled personnel. Why not deploy these assets along the border and give the troops a real-world 'sandbox' to practice their craft?

Eagle's Nest Creek was providing just such a test site at the moment.

"Let's break out those sandwiches, Gunny. Looks like we're going to be here for a while."

On the other side of the river, Juan shut down the engine powering his dilapidated 1981 Ford pickup and scanned the surrounding desert with a keen eye. Nothing out of the ordinary met his gaze.

Once a week, for the past six months, he'd driven the beat-up old truck to this very spot.

He always waited until the sun was almost down, the slightly cooler air making his task a bit more palatable. Pulling a machete from the passenger seat, he stepped toward the path that would take him down to the Rio Grande and the shoreline of high bamboo shoots that bordered the great river's southern bank.

Juan's village was just over 10 kilometers away. A small community of peasant farmers, the people were poor, mostly uneducated, and isolated from the rest of the world.

Bamboo was an important building material to the village, used for everything from roofs to fences. Adobe and stone walls were reinforced by the stout shafts that played much the same role as rebar in concrete structures.

Lately, there had been a bonus crop growing along the ancient waterway – cattails were plentiful this year, much to the delight of his neighbors and friends. Everything from bread to toothpaste could be made from the shallow-water crop, the nutritious tubers one of the local favorites.

A few weeks ago, another windfall had come Juan's way.

A group of strangers had arrived in the settlement's dirt square and had begun asking a lot of questions. Juan knew right away the new arrivals were "Soldado de la nacho," or night soldiers ... cartel shooters ... banditos.

The simple folk of the hamlet weren't overly concerned. They had nothing to steal other than the younger women of the community, and there were few of those who had not moved to the metropolitan areas to make money and find husbands. Many of the locals simply made the sign of the cross in hopes of banishing evil and went on about their business. They realized they lacked resources to challenge the visitors if they did decide to cause trouble.

When the group of compañeros began asking about activity along the river, Juan was thrust uncomfortably into the limelight. They soon put him at ease, however, offering American cigarettes and waving around handfuls of pesos in exchange for information.

Twice more they returned, each time seeking out Juan and asking about his ventures to the bamboo fields along the river. His answers were always honest and seemed to encourage the younger men. He never saw any activity along the gringos' side of the river. No hikers, policia, or military. Only the occasional small herd of cattle, and once, months ago, a rancher had waved to him from the northern bank.

Identifying themselves as brothers of the Gulf Cartel, they had made Juan an offer he couldn't refuse. It was a simple thing, requiring very little risk and offering an enormous reward.

Arriving at the edge of a sheer cliff, the old villager stared down at the Rio Grande as if gazing at a beautiful señorita. The great river had always provided for his family, and today, it was going to make him a wealthy man. At least by local standards.

Hefting his machete, Juan continued down the narrow path that led to the river below. The only thing different about today's trip was the whistle clasped tightly in his hand. His instructions were simple enough. If he saw or heard anything unusual, he was to blow on the device as loudly as his lungs could manage.

He kept a sharp lookout, scanning with more focus than usual, looking for anything out of the ordinary on the northern side of the waterway. There was nothing. Nada. Only the same barren landscape that had met his gaze for the last few decades.

Back at the pinnacle of the canyon, the bamboo covering the bed of Juan's pickup rustled with activity. Gloved hands pushed aside the thin layer of stalks, revealing five men hiding beneath the green screen. A few moments later, they were pouring over the ancient Ford's rusty fenders. Two more emerged from similar camouflage covering the small trailer hitched to the old truck.

The seven masked faces scanned right and left, Mexican military-issued FX-05 battle rifles sweeping the surrounding countryside.

Had there been anyone there to witness their actions, the onlooker would have surely thought he was seeing a small squad of Special Forces troopers readying for an operation. Such an observation would have been based on not only the body armor, load vests bulging with equipment, and heavy packs, but the coordination and controlled movements of the armed men.

That conclusion wouldn't have been in error. After the rise of the Los Zetas, all of the organizations that made up Mexico's patchwork of organized crime had begun recruiting from Mexico's elite Special Forces, or the Cuerpo de Fuerzas Especiales. Such men could make 100 times their military salary working for the cartels while at the same time enjoying better equipment, quarters, and leadership.

In less than a minute, the squad wound down the trail, moving swiftly for concealment. They would wait to cross the river after nightfall.

The lieutenant's ire was directed at the gunnery sergeant. While the captain had issued the orders designating Eagle's Nest as the training area, the younger officer was certain this particular hell on earth was the gunny's doing.

For 11 hours, his unit had struggled through the impossible terrain. With the blistering heat, leg-biting cactus, and jagged rocks, he'd been cut, gashed, poked, and burned to the point where he regretted ever joining the Republic of Texas Marine Corps.

The nightmare had intensified after sunset; his lead element slowed to a crawl by the low light conditions.

Now a new challenge was impeding their progress. The temperature had fallen like the stones that surrounded them, dropping 40 degrees in less than 90 minutes. Strained, sweat-soaked bodies began to shiver and cramp. Men had trouble maintaining their footing and handholds. The unit had suffered a twisted ankle and a nasty laceration in just the last 15 minutes.

For the tenth time, the LT considered calling over his radio man and throwing in the towel. He would broadcast his surrender to the captain and resign his commission in the morning. He was probably going to be given a reprimand anyway. His personnel file would be flush with negative entries that denoted how he'd failed to execute even the simplest field exercise. They were hours behind schedule. They had training causalities. He'd failed.

The young officer could just hear the captain's harsh words. "How can you lead men into battle if you can't even manage to move a small unit from point A to point B? There wasn't even anyone shooting at you, Lieutenant! How can the soldiers under your command possibly hope to survive a hostile encounter? What the hell are you going to do when high-velocity shit is flying at your head? Pick up your smartphone, call mommy, and tell her you want to quit?"

His mind, however, rejected the urge to give up. From some deep corner of his consciousness swelled a seething anger, a rage that provided the fuel to continue the struggle. He forced his numb, exhausted legs to take another step … to square his shoulders and hold up his head. He was a leader. He was an officer. He would set the example.

That wave of motivation had nothing to do with pride, honor, or reputation. Yes, he was a Republic of Texas Marine. Over and over again, it had been pounded into his heart, mind, and soul that quitting wasn't an option. Real fighting men didn't give up. The Corps didn't allow such thinking. He was an officer, sworn to leave nothing behind … to lay it all out … to carry on until the final breath was expelled from his aching lungs.

All of that sounded great on the parade ground, obstacle course, and in the classroom. Bravado and esprit de corps were attributes that had made the Marine Corps so attractive in the first place. He was a highly motivated individual who wanted to surround himself with like-minded men.

In a single day, Eagle's Nest Creek had evaporated all of the comradery, bluster, and starch from his core. None of it served to move his legs; none of it mattered anymore.

No, what did give him strength was more of a personal nature – he wasn't going to let that son of a bitch gunny win.

His thoughts were interrupted with yet another halt to the struggling column's forward progress. "Movement, ahead," came the whispered voice of his lead element over the radio. "Multiple contacts."

"Jesus Wilson Roosevelt Christ," the officer hissed, moving toward the front of the column. "Aren't the terrain and heat enough, Gunny? Now you've got to fuck with us some more?"

The first gunshots actually didn't surprise the LT. It was just like that three-striped old bastard to send in some of his buddies, armed with blanks, to mess with the trainees.

When the man beside the lieutenant fell to the ground clutching his chest, it was the first indication that something was terribly wrong.

The incoming volume of fire intensified – rock chips, sand, and zipping rounds creating havoc among the Marines. While they were carrying their weapons, only the LT's pistol had live ammunition … for snakes. This was a training exercise. His men were unarmed … as helpless as infants in their cribs.

Multiple weapons were now spraying the line of soldiers with deadly fire. Cries of pain and agony echoed off the canyon's walls, competing with curses and shouts of confusion.

Men were screaming, diving for cover, or frozen where they stood. No one knew what was happening. Why were people shooting at them? Why were their friends falling bloodied to the desert floor?

A few men shouted, "Republic of Texas Marines!" hoping the incoming hailstorm of bullets was a case of mistaken identity. Others stared at their commander, waiting with eager faces for his orders.

Suddenly, it all became crystal clear to the shocked officer. They had run into smugglers or criminals – armed intruders who thought his men were some sort of law enforcement patrol.

"Fall back! Fall back!" the officer shouted over the chaos as he reached for his sidearm. "Fall back!"

The lieutenant caught a glimpse of a muzzle flash right as another of his command was cut down. He was shocked at how calm his mind seemed to be. The muscle strain and exhaustion had disappeared from his body; his hands were steady.

The shadowy outline of the shooter was clear now. Centering the front post of his .45, he fired two shots and felt a sense of relief when the foe went down.

Movement drew the officer's eye, a strobe of muzzle flashes chasing another Marine as he scurried for better cover. The LT fired, again and again, his finger working the trigger until the enemy's body shifted its direction and dove for the ground.

The rock next to the LT's head exploded with stone-shrapnel and chips. The officer was stunned as he realized the shooter was the first man he'd taken down. *Body armor? These guys were wearing body armor!*

The officer knew his handgun wouldn't penetrate Kevlar. That meant his unit was completely defenseless. "Fall back!" he screamed again, turning to run. "Fall back!"

Searing, red-hot pain erupted across the LT's back, his legs no longer answering his brain's command to run. His last vision was the ground rushing toward his face, and then the world exploded in a shower of white, streaking light.

"What the fuck is that idiot lieutenant doing, Gunny?" the captain asked for the third time, scanning toward the last known position of his men. "Who the hell is shooting? I didn't authorize any live fire or dummy rounds!"

"I don't know, sir, but I think we'd better call in some help."

The senior officer hesitated, listening intently as the thunder of gunfire rolled through the matrix of canyon walls. There was another sound as well.

Finally, it dawned. "They're screaming like a bunch of schoolgirls, Sergeant. What the hell?"

The NCO heard the secondary noise as well, but his ear had the benefit of experience. After surviving multiple tours in two different wars wearing the U.S. uniform, he knew immediately that the training platoon was in serious trouble.

"Those are the screams of wounded men, sir. I don't think it's our people doing the shooting. Call for help, Captain. Right now!"

As the bewildered officer fumbled for his cell phone, Gunny was racing for the bed of the Corps-issued pickup. Pulling back a heavy tarp, he extracted an M4 carbine. In a flash, a magazine appeared in his hand, slamming into the weapon with an audible clank. That action was immediately followed by the mechanical racking of the rifle being charged. Gunny never left the base unarmed.

The sergeant appeared at the captain's side just as the officer's frantic phone call was answered by the base operator. In a rushed voice, "Get me the base commander… now… we're taking fire."

The Marine answering the phones was confused. "Who is this? Buddy, do you know it's a crime to prank call a military institution?"

By the time the officer had explained the situation, the distant gunfire had stopped just as suddenly as it had begun. The two Marines on the ridge exchanged worried looks. "I'm waiting for someone to find the CO," the captain whispered, blocking the cell's mic with his cupped hand.

Exasperated, the gunny reached for his own cell phone, punching 9-1-1 with enough force that he nearly shattered the smartphone's screen.

"Sheriff's Department, state the nature of your emergency."

Gunny did his best to explain the events of the last 10 minutes to the operator. To say the dispatcher was confused would have been an understatement.

At about the same time as the captain was finally connected to the new base's commander, gunny was transferred to a watch supervisor and had to start the entire explanation all over again. The frustration was evident in both men's voices as they pleaded for assistance ... any sort of help.

Both calls ended at about the same moment.

"Val Verde County is sending a SWAT team and a copter," the sergeant informed his commander.

"The base commander is sending armed MPs and scrambling some Blackhawks," the officer announced. "Can we get over there?" he asked, looking at the sergeant's loaded weapon. "How long would it take us to reach them?"

"There's no way, sir. There are two slot canyons between them and us. It would take at least two hours if the platoon made good time. I recommend we drive back up to the main road and wait for the cavalry to arrive. We can lead them in from there, maybe hitch a ride on one of the incoming birds."

The captain had never experienced anything like the frustration that surged through his being. The feeling of helplessness was bitter, filling his mouth with the foul taste of bile. Yet, he knew the sergeant was right. They would have to wait. There was simply no way for him to reach the men. It was maddening.

A minute later, their pickup was bouncing down the dirt path, neither man in the cab seeming to notice the jarring ride.

They made it to Highway 90 and turned to the southeast. It was only a short distance to the bridge that crossed Eagle's Nest Creek.

They parked alongside the road with no other course of action than to sit and wait for reinforcements. Clearly concerned about their comrades, their anxious glances constantly alternated between the land to the south where their men were likely wounded and the horizon where the military's birds were expected.

It was the sergeant who first spotted the blinking lights on the skyline. Both men watched with eager anticipation as the law enforcement helo diverted toward the coordinates gunny had provided earlier. A moment later, the flashing strobes of a squad car came into view as a deputy rushed toward their location.

The helicopter's searchlight switched on just as the police car pulled alongside the two waiting Marines. After a quick exchange, all eyes returned to the sky and watched as the helicopter began searching.

It only took the pilots three minutes to find the missing platoon, the discovery confirmed over the deputy's radio. "We're going to need medivac," the pilot's worried voice radioed back. "A lot of medivacs... and a lot of help. We've got bodies strewn all over the ground down there."

Chapter 2

Zach watched his partner rush into the diner, a thick newspaper and thermos tucked under Samantha's arm.

"You're late," he stated with a smirk. Nodding at the birdcage liner, he continued, "Get caught up in a good story?"

She ignored him, tossing the edition on the table and then holding out the thermos to an approaching waitress. "I need this filled with hot tea, please. And an egg … over hard … and two slices of sourdough toast with margarine, not butter."

"You seem a little flustered, Ranger Temple," Zach grinned.

"Your powers of observation are legendary, bordering on the supernatural, Ranger Bass," the female officer answered sarcastically. "I'm surprised somebody hasn't based a comic book on you," she continued, reaching for the chair. She paused as she sneered at her mental image of the Justice League's newest member, SuperBoy in Blue. Her mind's picture of Zach in cobalt tights and cape complete with silver star, boots and cowboy hat tickled her greatly. She covered her smile with her hand and coughed to disguise her amusement. "Hey, I'll be right back," she said, pivoting in the direction of the restroom.

After watching her disappear, Zach flipped the newspaper around. It was a two-day-old edition of the New York Times with a headline that read, "Texas Police Prepare for Bloodbath."

"What the hell is Sam doing with this rag?" he mused, tossing a glance again at the ladies room door. "I'm going to have a word with her later."

Tilting back the broad brim on his western hat, the ranger began reading:

In three days, the Treaty of Secession will celebrate its 2-year anniversary. As per the terms of the controversial agreement that created the world's newest republic, several grandfathered U.S. laws will expire.

One of the most controversial is the Federal Firearms Act of 1938, which among other things, restricts the general public from purchasing fully automatic weapons. Three days ago, after a lengthy debate, the Texas legislature passed a new law that will allow such weapons to be purchased by the citizenry.

Within the Lone Star Nation, there has been widespread pushback over the effectiveness and necessity of creating an equivalent of America's Bureau of Alcohol, Tobacco, Firearms and Explosives, or ATF as it is commonly known. The

ATF is the primary agency charged with enforcing the 1938 act in the United States and her territories.

"We're preparing our officers for the worst," stated Captain Anthony Morse of the Austin Police Department. "Every bank robber, gang banger, mental case, and violent felon will now be able to acquire weapons that can spray 30 bullets in a less than three seconds."

"Anyone can already acquire that category of weaponry," countered Jack Kimpel, president of the Texas Rifle Association. "Between illegal imports, homegrown modifications, and bump-fire accessories, the street's capability to shoot a lot of lead won't be significantly enhanced. Even in the US, with its thick reams of 20,000 pages of gun control laws, criminals can unleash a hailstorm of bullets."

The debate raging across our nation's southern neighbor extends far beyond Class 3 weapons. Gun control encapsulates the controversy that is tearing at the very fabric of Texas's fight for independence.

Terms such as "bloated government," or "authoritarian encroachment on individual liberties," were commonly spouted by Texas's elected officials who supported merely allowing the 1938 law to expire without any regulation whatsoever. Eventually, the "small government" factor won, arguing that the creation of such federal agencies as the ATF was a waste of taxpayer money and an infringement on the individual citizen's Second Amendment rights.

In fact, one of the few modifications made to Texas's version of the U.S. Constitution was a clarification to the Second Amendment. The vague wording originally penned by the Founding Fathers had resulted in numerous cases before the Supreme Court and led to countless hours of heated social discourse. The fledgling new republic vowed not to make the same mistake.

Yet, despite the much-touted clarification, there were still issues.

"We can't let every citizen possess nuclear weapons," commented one Senator. "There have to be limits. The term 'weapons of mass destruction,' is fine on paper, but what exactly does that mean? Where do we draw the line?"

Even those who strongly supported the Second Amendment were divided by the issue.

"Do we allow everyone to possess rocket launchers? Fully armed battle tanks? Caches of high explosives? Belt-fed weapons? Chemical or biological mortar rounds?" asked the Republican mayor of Dallas during a recently televised debate. "Active shooters in Texas won't walk into the theater with a handgun or rifle. They'll flatten the entire building using C4 explosives, or unleash a canister of mustard gas in the food court. If Austin doesn't do something, we will have complete bedlam in less than 60 days."

The controversy runs deep throughout the Lone Star nation and not just in the major cities or along party lines. From the arid west to the great pine forests of the east, the issue has long divided local governments, friends, and families, as well.

In stark contrast to her father's position on the issue, Carla Simmons, the daughter of the republic's first president, leads one of the country's largest gun control lobbies. "My dad and I normally agree on most things, but not this. I want our citizens armed and free, but there have to be limits and controls. We risk absolute anarchy if everyone has unlimited firepower."

In the end, the Texas legislature reached a compromise. Automatic weapons below a certain caliber will soon become legal, as will short-barreled weapons and noise cancelation devices, commonly called "silencers." A background check will be enforced, and safety training is required. But as long as a citizen doesn't have any history of mental illness or a felony conviction, purchasing machine guns is legal.

"It's a start," TRA President Kimpel commented. "Even in Texas, we have to compromise now and then."

Zach, sensing Sam's return, stopped reading. She was just in time for her eggs and toast.

"Why are you reading this liberal fish wrapper? I didn't know they were even allowed to peddle this crap in Texas anymore."

"You can sell anything in our great nation," she grimaced, pulling a knife full of yellow spread across her toast. "Including automatic weapons, hand grenades, and flame throwers."

Shrugging, Zach retorted, "Flame throwers have always been legal. Just saying."

Sam's butter knife returned to the table with just a little more force than necessary. "You know what I mean. Stop being a smartass for just one minute and listen to me. I'm worried about this. Damn worried. My mom has been calling me every day, sure that I'm going to go down in a barrage of gunfire at any moment."

"That could happen with or without a new law," he replied calmly. "Besides, we're Texas Rangers, invincible, above politics and corruption, fearless protectors of the innocent, and relentless pursuers of villainous humanity."

"I don't feel invincible, and sure as shit, I'm not fearless," she angrily retorted. "Maybe I shouldn't be a ranger."

Shaking his head, Zach said, "Now stop that. You're a damn fine peace officer. I couldn't ask for a better partner.... Well, maybe one that wasn't always so quarrelsome ... but a man can't have everything. Anyway, I'll bet you a cup of coffee that we won't notice any difference after the old law expires. Other than the occasional yahoo spraying a few magazines into the air on New Year's Eve, things will be just like they are now."

Sam didn't reply, her focus now on wolfing down the eggs and toast. After a quick glance at his watch, Zach understood her rush. Time to go.

Five minutes later, the two lawmen were rolling out of Alpine, Zach's government-issue pickup heading west. They were just accelerating up an entrance ramp when Sam pointed out the window, "Check out that gun store over there."

Zach glanced over, seeing a recently added banner draped across the front of the establishment. "Open All Night on Freedom Eve," it declared in bold letters. "Full Autos Will Be In Stock!"

"Ahhh, capitalism and free enterprise," Zach grunted. "Don't you just love democracy?"

"Once that genie is out of the bottle, there's no going back," she snapped. "I can't believe you're being so flippant about this."

"There's nothing we can do," he said. "Unless you want to resign and move to the United States ... or Mexico ... or wherever. I'm telling you, it's not going to be any big deal."

Sam thumped the newspaper still draped across her lap. "A lot of cops disagree with you on that."

"With all due respect to our brother peace officers, we both know they can be a bunch of Chicken Littles, running around shouting about a falling sky. I sometimes wonder why they choose to be cops. Do you remember a few years back, right before the secession, when the state of Texas passed the open carry law?"

"Yes," Sam replied, with vile, knowing where her partner was headed.

"Do you recall all the hubbub? All the police departments waiting for the avalanche of 9-1-1 calls? A lot of these same guys were predicting incidents out the wazoo, like accidental shootings, cops not being able to respond to legitimate calls because they were chasing down 'man with a gun buying ice cream' reports. All of the universities were shouting to the high heavens that anarchy was going to envelop our academic institutions. Do you remember all that crap?"

Sam suddenly found the truck's floorboard interesting.

"Do you?" Zach, on a roll, wasn't going to let her off the hook.

"Yes," she finally answered, but not willing to concede the issue. "But this is different, Zach."

"How?"

The debate was interrupted by the jingle of Zach's mobile phone. He glanced at the cell's display and then flashed the screen to his partner. "It's never good when the major calls before sunrise," Sam whispered.

"Ranger Bass," Zach greeted as if he was too busy to glance at the caller ID.

Sam observed as her partner listened intently, his face curling into a full-blown scowl after only a few moments.

"We're on our way, sir. We're about four hours out," Zach replied in a voice laced with both pain and anger.

Zach didn't need directions to find the scene of the crime. For the last 20 miles, he and Sam had watched a constant stream of helicopters coming, going, and orbiting the location.

"It looks like somebody kicked a hornet's nest," he informed the lady ranger. "And a huge nest at that."

During the drive down, they'd listened to police radio traffic, as well as a news station whose signal was picked up on the truck's satellite receiver. None of the information streaming across the airwaves was good. One reporter was already referring to the incident as the "Langtry Massacre."

The duo's first encounter on the ground was a Texas Highway patrol officer manning a roadblock designed to keep nosey civilians away. He recognized Zach before the ranger had rolled to a stop.

"Morning, officer," Zach hailed as he lowered the window. "Good to see you again, Trooper Reeves…. Well, sort of."

"I hear we've got one hell of a mess down there," the patrolman stoically replied. "Not good. Not good at all."

"I hear the same," Zach responded. "I guess I'd better go earn my pay … see if we can help."

"You've got plenty of company, Ranger. We've got military, civilian, LEO from three counties, and I even let some yahoo from President Simmons's office through a little bit ago."

"Thanks, trooper. See ya later."

They were stopped twice more, Zach's silver-peso badge quickly gaining them access. Since the secession, the rangers were the republic's equivalent of the FBI, technically the highest law enforcement authority in the land.

Finally, Zach maneuvered the pickup to the epicenter of the massive response. A huge, flat area outside of Langtry had been converted into a makeshift airport. Dust and exhaust fumes fouled the air, both a product of the near fleet of aircraft that had descended on the sleepy burg.

There were ambulances, ROTMC vehicles, and a sea of blue emergency lights - even a pair of battle tanks bordering the lane. Sam, noting the number of armed Marines running around and other war-fighting hardware observed, "My gosh! It's like we've been invaded."

"From what we've heard so far, that's probably not far off the mark. I just hope those guys don't get trigger-happy. I know they're itching for payback. Hell, we would be too if someone had bushwhacked a bunch of rangers. Still, it would be best if cooler heads prevailed sooner rather than later."

Again, the ranger's badge moved them to the front of the line. A few minutes after parking, Zach and Sam were airborne, riding in the next available Blackhawk for the short hop to the scene of the ambush.

As they descended, Sam pointed to a row of body bags lined neatly on top of the ridge. There were at least 20. "Oh, shit," the ranger commented under his breath.

After hopping off their shuttle, the duo rushed to escape the choking cloud of sand and grit blown into the otherwise clear Texas morning. Major Putnam met them at the edge of cleaner air.

"Ranger Bass, Ranger Temple," the company commander greeted. "Right this way. There's a temporary operations center just over the canyon's crest. We'll get you up to speed quickly, and then you can survey the crime scene."

"Sir?" Zach said over the drone of the helicopter, "Were all of those body bags our people?"

Putnam's grimace answered the question without any need for words. As the trio continued walking, he expanded. "Yes. The ROT Marines suffered 23 dead, another 8 wounded. They were on a training exercise and thus weren't carrying ammunition for their weapons. One of the survivors claims the lieutenant commanding the platoon returned fire, but we've yet to confirm that report."

"Who hit them, sir?" Sam questioned.

"Unknown. We're still interviewing the remaining Marines, but their stories vary wildly. It was dark. Their unit was exhausted, and the assault was a complete surprise. I've heard reports varying from 5 to 50 assailants. The truth is probably somewhere in the middle."

They arrived at a large tent, several folding tables having been placed in the shade. The state trooper at the roadblock had been accurate when describing the response.

Workers in a wide assortment of uniforms were hustling in every direction. A bank of radios had been brought in, as well as a small generator to provide electricity. Zach spotted military uniforms with insignias indicating the republic's military high command had gotten involved. The ranger didn't blame them.

Major Putnam led his two officers to a corner of the tent. After checking a small counter for the latest messages, the senior lawman turned and said, "Come on, I'll give you a tour of the crime scene... or at least, what's left of it."

Their commander led Sam and Zach down a steep trail where several MPs were working around the spray-painted outline of what had been the final resting place of a victim. Scanning the vicinity, Sam could see several similar groups processing a spot where a brave Marine had fallen.

Given her experience as a Houston homicide detective, the first thing the lady ranger noticed was the lack of shell casings around the deceased. The man who had died here had been shot from a distance.

Zach looked around politely, nodding to the MPs as they acknowledged the newcomers. After a bit, he glanced at Major Putnam and said, "Sir, I'd like to see where the shooters were."

The entire area was marked off with white, yellow, and red tape, denoting sections where it was "safe" to step and other patches where the scene had yet to be processed. Due to the size of the crime scene, quite a bit of evidence had been found and photographed but not yet collected.

Putnam led his team down a narrow path of white tape, occasionally pointing here and there at some potential clue. Finally, they arrived at a zone dotted with small, numbered cardboard markers. Each represented a spent shell casing resting on the ground.

A nearby crime scene tech noticed the new arrivals and immediately approached. "Please be careful where you wander," he warned. "This section hasn't been photographed yet."

Zach nodded and then asked, "Do you have one of the spent casings I could examine?"

"Sure," replied the tech. "They're all the same. 5.56 NATO boxed primer. I've seen the markings before. The shooters were using ammunition issued by the Mexican military."

"All the same lot, caliber, and type?" Sam inquired, a frown crossing her face.

"So far. We've only recovered about 200 out of what I would guess is close to 400 casings lying around. Every example I've seen so far has been identical to the others."

Zach rubbed his chin while exchanging worried looks with his partner. "How many rifles?"

"You're the hundredth person to ask me that, Ranger. We don't know yet. Until I can get this scene processed and examine all of the casings under a microscope, I won't be able to answer that question."

Putnam continued the tour that eventually concluded at the bank of the Rio Grande.

"We're pretty sure they came across here," the major announced, pointing at a group of officers snapping pictures and making notes on clipboards. "We found drag marks where some sort of boats or rafts were dragged up on shore. There are also footprints and other signs."

"How many boats?" Sam asked.

"We think two. Our preliminary analysis is that they crossed over, ran into the Marines, initiated the firefight, and then retreated back across the river."

Zach's attention was drawn to the southern side of the waterway where he could see a small group of Mexican authorities searching the shoreline. "Any word from our southern neighbors?"

"No," Putnam grunted with a hint of disgust in his tone. "Relations aren't the best right now. Our ambassador is waiting patiently for the Mexican authorities to communicate any findings. We've offered to send across some manpower but were politely reminded to stay on our side of the border."

On the way back to the command tent, Zach pointed toward a high outcropping of stone and asked, "Sir, would it be okay if I climbed up on that rock? I'd like to get a little better angle on the whole area."

"Sure, Ranger Bass. Knock yourself out."

Sam didn't want to be left behind. A minute later, she found herself scrambling up an incline, trying desperately to keep up with her partner's longer limbs.

Zach finally made it to the pinnacle, and after reaching back with a helping hand, he pulled Sam to the plateau.

For several minutes, the rangers simply stood and studied the scene below. It was easy to tell where the evidence was clumped together by the number of men processing each sub-scene. From the elevated perch, Zach started recounting what had happened the night before.

"The Marines' final objective was Pump Canyon," the ranger began, pointing to the northwest. "According to the map, that's less than a mile away. They were working their way down this draw, probably because it was the path of least resistance."

Sam nodded her agreement, "It's logical that the shooters from the other side were using it as well. It's about the only route north unless you're a mountain goat."

Zach pointed to a small group of deputies, closer to the river. "They ran into each other right there. You can reenact the battle if you follow the line of evidence north. Still, it all doesn't make any sense to me."

Sam flashed a perplexed expression. "Why? It all looks pretty clear to me. The people from the Mexican side were carrying drugs. They ran into the Marines by accident and shot it out with them. After it was over, they retreated. What's the big mystery?"

Zach pointed again, "Our friends from across the border continued to push into Texas after they knew the Marines were in the region. That doesn't fit with the typical dope smugglers or coyotes. Normally, if they had been hauling in weed or heroin or whatever, and they had run into a patrol, they would have scattered, retreated, or run like hell. These guys didn't. They kept pushing and pushing and pushing. It's like they were invading, not smuggling."

Following her partner's explanation, Sam surveyed the crime scene in a whole new light. "You know; you're right. They continued advancing into the main body of the Marine unit. There," she pointed, "and there and there. It's like they were out to kill as many of our guys as possible."

"But why?" Zach pondered. "Even the most aggressive of the cartels wouldn't just come across the river and shoot up a bunch of Texans for fun or sport. Why go to all that trouble, planning, organization, and effort? They could have broken contact and faded back across the Rio Grande without any issue. Why all the carnage?"

"Maybe they were running from someone back in Mexico?" Sam offered. "Maybe they had wounded people, or they just changed their minds."

"Look," Zach pointed, indicating an area further inside of Texas. "They didn't stop until the Marines were completely routed and scattered. You can see where they even chased a few down and mopped up. It doesn't make any sense."

Sam noticed Major Putnam staring up at them, their boss obviously growing impatient. "We'd better head back."

As Sam began crawling and sliding down to their supervisor, Zach paused to take in the scene one more time. "Were you protecting someone?" he whispered. "Someone really important? Is that why you didn't break contact and run for home?"

Shaking his head at the unanswerable nature of his own questions, Zach followed Sam down the treacherous slope, eventually joining his partner and supervisor. The trio of lawmen continued back to the command tent.

Putnam announced, "Here's your assignment, Rangers. While we're reasonably sure all of the invaders from the Mexican side retreated back south, we can't be positive. I want both of you working all of your contacts and informants, trying to fill in as many pieces to this puzzle as possible."

"Yes, sir."

The two lawmen were about to leave when a tall, wiry figure dressed in jeans and a western hat appeared on horseback. He dismounted at the major's corner of the tent, stretching his legs and slapping a layer of dust from his clothing.

Zach's face spread wide with a huge grin as he stepped closer to the older man and extended his hand.

"Ranger Baylor," Zach greeted. "I'm surprised to see you here, sir. Did they call you out of retirement?"

The older lawman nodded, clutching Zach's hand with a firm grasp. "The major asked me to come take a look at the area. How could I say no?"

Zach pivoted in Sam's direction, "BB, let me introduce you to my partner, Ranger Samantha Temple. This is Bartholomew Baylor, the absolute best tracker I've ever met and a legend among the rangers."

"Call me BB, ma'am," the man replied with a raspy voice, tipping his hat while extending a leathery hand toward the lady officer.

"I answer to Sam," Ranger Temple responded with a warm smile.

Sam was intrigued by Zach's reaction to the older officer. It was the first time she'd ever seen her partner enthralled by anyone or anything other than a short skirt or a new firearm.

BB, for his part, looked more the part of a rancher than a lawman. His denim pants were saddle worn and faded, a large but plain buckle securing an ancient, tooled belt. The knee-length duster hanging from the old ranger's shoulders had seen so many years its leather was worn shiny in places. As he stretched the saddle-time out of his frame, she spied the flash of a nickel-plated revolver on his hip. The man's boots had definitely seen better days.

He was as tall as Zach, ramrod straight with a slight bow in his legs. Sam surmised BB was the real deal, a man who spent as much time on horseback as on foot – tough as nails, and cynical to the core. Bands of salt-sweat stained his hat, the brim low and serious. Despite being at least 70 years old, she sensed the retired ranger was still a force to be respected.

"You all can catch up on your socializing later," Putnam interrupted. "What did you find, BB?"

"Seven men came north across the river, Major. Only two went back," came a steadfast proclamation.

Putnam was skeptical. "Are you sure? This entire crime scene has been trampled by hundreds of boots for the last several hours."

"I'm sure, Major. There was one pair of non-military issued soles that left this canyon to the north. They were fancy treads … like a high-end hiking boot. Those same tracks were down by the river in the mud where they came ashore. The owner's left foot turns in slightly. He's a slender man, probably just over 180 pounds. I'd estimate he's about 6" tall from the stride. He was carrying a pack, but it was lighter than the others."

"How far north did you track him, BB?" Zach asked.

"My guess is somebody picked them up on this side of the road," BB responded with a nonchalant shrug. "I followed the trail right up to the pavement, and that's where it ended. They never crossed the road, so I would assume their destination is southeast... heading for Del Rio or perhaps San Antonio."

Rubbing her chin, Sam said, "Must be a pretty 'influential' individual to warrant a heavily armed escort. Kind of makes sense, now that I think about it. The bodyguards were willing to shoot it out with our Marines to make sure their charge made it through. Somebody has a critical meeting or is on the run from Mexican authorities."

So you were protecting someone, Zach thought. *But who? Who is so important that you would kill 20 plus Marines?*

"His security team stayed with him until they reached the road, sir," BB continued. "Then, two of them hightailed it back to the river in a straight line and made off with the rafts. I'd also hazard a guess they had night vision or some other sort of fancy technology because I found this."

The old ranger's hand disappeared into his duster's pocket, emerging a moment later with a plastic baggie containing a battery. It was an odd size, with Spanish writing on the case.

Putnam accepted the evidence and then asked, "Where did you find this?"

BB nodded toward a table with a map and then moved to show his superior where he'd collected the evidence.

Zach picked up the old battery and realized that it was a size used in high-end flashlights, some cameras, military-grade optics, and as BB had stated, night vision devices. He had to agree with the old ranger's assessment. After an intense firefight, with dozens of Marines scurrying confused in all directions, it was unlikely any of the invaders was taking pictures or shining a torch. Night vision, however, made sense.

Putnam returned his attention to Zach and Sam. "Your assignment just had its priority raised, Rangers. I suggest you get moving. I'll put out a bulletin, but without a physical description, there's not much to go on."

Despite the urgency in the major's voice, Zach took a moment to shake BB's hand. "Thanks for the help, 'Old School.' Despite being a tequila-soaked old bastard, you're still the best."

For just a second, a hint of kindness flashed behind BB's eyes as he accepted Zach's palm. "Be safe out there, Ranger Bass. My gut says you're after a very, very bad hombre. Don't take that old saying of one riot, one ranger too far."

"One riot, one ranger," Zach repeated, invoking the phrase long associated with the organization.

As Sam and Zach left the command tent, she said, "You know that old saying about the riot isn't based on any sort of factual history."

"I know," Zach sighed. "Like most Western legends, time and the retelling have exaggerated the tale."

"Since I've joined our elite, little band of crime fighters, I've heard so many different stories on the source of that slogan. Which one do you subscribe to?"

"The Dallas prizefight was the one that seemed to be based on an actual event," Zach replied as they waited for a flight back to their truck.

Sam rolled her eyes, "Oh Lord, not another legend. What happened in Dallas? Who was fighting?"

"The story goes that in the late 1890s, Ranger Captain Bill McDonald had been sent by the governor to Dallas, the officer's mission to stop an illegal prizefight. The bout had been heavy publicized, with travelers from all over the territory in town to witness the contest."

Zach's retelling was interrupted by the roar of a landing copter. As soon as the noise died down, he continued, "Fearing a riot would erupt when the match was canceled, the very nervous mayor of Dallas had met Ranger McDonald's train. The politician had been shocked to find only one lawman aboard. When asked where the other rangers were, it's claimed that the grizzled, old captain replied, 'Hell, ain't I enough? After all, there's only one prizefight!'"

The lady ranger chuckled, nodding her head in recognition. "I remember that story now. From what I've read, just about every man with a badge was actually in Dallas for the contest. According to some accounts, most of the rangers wanted to see the bout for themselves."

"Yeah, I know," Zach sighed. "But the fight was canceled, and Dallas didn't burn. Nowadays, it's the spirit of the thing that counts. The rangers operated on their own back in those days. They didn't have radios, or backup, or computers. BB was only trying to warn us that we might be going up against long odds, and my gut says he's right about that."

Sam patted her pistol and grinned, "Can we change it to one riot, two rangers?"

Chapter 3

Sam and Zach made for San Antonio after leaving the crime scene.

"Why not Del Rio?" the lady ranger asked.

"Too small. Whoever came across was somebody important if BB has his shit in one bag. It would be too easy to be noticed in Del Rio, so I'm throwing the dice and guessing the larger town."

"Why do you question BB's findings? It seemed like you really respected the guy," Sam questioned.

Zach didn't answer right away, almost as if he was having trouble choosing his words. Finally, he said, "Something happened with BB back in the day. I heard rumors and tall tales, but nothing official. Most of the stories centered on the man having trouble with hard liquor and a bad temperament. Then, all of a sudden, he was gone. No retirement party, no goodbyes or farewells ... he just vanished. For a man who had over 30 years of service as a ranger, that's never good news. You'll find that when one of our own has issues; no one likes to talk about it. That's why I was stunned to see him at the crime scene."

"Maybe he's managed to get back into Major Putnam's good graces?" Sam speculated.

"I have been told he's living in Mexico," Zach countered. "I've heard rumors that he does some bounty hunting down there. No, I'd be more inclined to say that Putnam asked him to come across hoping BB knew or had heard something. Whatever the reason, it was good to see that old law dog. He looked like he had cleaned up his act. I sure hope so."

On the way to the Alamo City, both rangers started calling every source, informant, and "in the know," individual they could think of.

The route took them by two gas stations that ran side businesses cashing checks for those who didn't have bank accounts, often a prime source of interesting information.

They visited a couple of ex-gang bangers who'd seen the light after one or more jail terms and now preferred to work with law enforcement.

Word of the Langtry Massacre had already spread across the entire republic. Most of the people Zach and Sam contacted knew right away why the two rangers were beating the proverbial bushes. No one had any information of value.

Late in the afternoon, Zach steered the pickup into a convenience store parking lot and pulled into an empty space facing the street. He glanced over at Sam's khaki slacks, plain white shirt, and hiking boots. "Do you have anything more... umm... more attractive in your overnight bag?"

"Why Zachariah Bass! State your intentions," Sam responded in an innocent, alluring tone.

Snorting, the ranger knew a trap when he saw one. "Strictly business, Ranger Temple."

"Good. I'd hate to experience an accidental discharge of my weapon into your knee cap ... or perhaps slightly higher."

"So do you have something more provocative in your suitcase?"

Sam frowned, "Yes, I have a couple of more casual get-ups in my bag. Why?"

Pointing with his head toward a business across the street, he answered, "Because I need you to be a distraction for a minute after we go in that fine establishment over there."

Following his indication, Sam read the sign, "The Rio Cabaret, San Antone's Finest Gentleman's Club. Seriously, Zach? You want me to go with you into a topless bar?"

"Yes, I do. There's someone in there we need to talk to, but I need a diversion."

"Don't you think I'm a little old to be going undercover as a topless dancer?"

Zach couldn't help himself. "Those places are usually pretty dark inside, and we only need a few seconds."

"Pretty dark inside! Only a few seconds! Why you ... you thick-skulled...."

Zach clenched, anticipating a long-winded blast of foul language. Sam, however, stopped short and flashed the evilest smirk the ranger had ever seen on his partner's face.

On a roll, he threw the verbal dice again. "You can pull it off ... no pun intended."

"Pull it off? Ha, ha, ha, Ranger Bass. What a funny man you are. Start explaining, before I get really pissed."

It took less than a minute for Zach to expound on his plan. Without any questions or comment, Sam reached for the small bag in the truck's backseat.

He had chosen the convenience store so his partner could utilize the lady's room for a quick wardrobe change. Much to his surprise, after digging around in her luggage, Sam began unlacing her boots.

The ranger thought his partner was bluffing when she undid the top button of her slacks. A moment later, her eyes never leaving his face, Sam began wiggling out of her pants. "Dark, huh?"

She took just the right amount of time, exposing her thighs at a speed that fell somewhere between a shy schoolgirl and a seductive tease. Zach had to admit, the woman beside him had the longest damn legs he'd ever seen on a female. "Only need to distract them for a minute, huh?" she whispered.

Zach's discomfort increased exponentially when Sam began unbuttoning her blouse. Again, at just the perfect pace, she exposed one shoulder and then the other, leaving nothing but a pair of sheer white panties and an extremely thin sports bra covering her ample assets. "Pretty dark inside, eh?"

Zach pretended not to notice, but his peripheral vision strained for a glimpse of the show. "Why are you doing this?" he asked, shifting uncomfortably in the driver's seat. "This is very unprofessional behavior, Ranger Temple. And besides, you're just being mean."

Sam fluttered her eyelashes in innocence. "Obviously, from your earlier comments, you don't think I'm an attractive woman. So what's the harm? Surely a dedicated crime fighter such as yourself can't be distracted by something as innocent as your partner changing for an undercover op."

He started to reply but held it. Then he made a serious attempt to keep his face forward, pretending to scan the street. His tactic didn't work very well. While his eyes were cooperative, his testosterone level won out.

She took her time, tugging on a pair of stockings first, gracefully smoothing the nylon material along her legs. Next came a casual red blouse, and finally a skirt that didn't reach her knees. "Happy now?" she asked with a coy tone.

"Yes, you look professional. Excellent choice, Ranger Temple."

"Thank you," she replied, pulling up her skirt and strapping on a mid-thigh holster.

Then with a grin and a quick, "See you in a minute," she was out of the truck and strolling toward the street, an exaggerated hip-swing in her stride.

Sam could hear the club's massive stereo system long before she reached the front entrance. After pulling open the heavy, ornate wooden door, the thump of the bass was like a hammer hitting her in the chest.

Zach had been absolutely correct about it being dark inside. Sam hesitated at the entrance, trying to give her vision time to adjust. She finally could make out a smiling young woman behind a counter, a cash register resting next to the bored girl's elbow. Another female was standing nearby, her micro-miniskirt and skimpy top announcing that she was a waitress.

"There's a ten dollar cover tonight," the hostess shouted over the music.

"I'm here to apply for a job," Sam yelled back. "Is the manager in?"

The two girls, both in their early 20s, scanned the lady ranger up and down and then exchanged a look that clearly asked, "Is she serious?"

They, however, were well trained in the finer aspects of customer service and didn't voice their doubts. "No, the manager isn't here right now, but Butch does most of the interviewing anyway. Come on with me," the waitress said.

As Sam was being led through an inner door and into the main room, she asked, "Who is Butch?"

"He's the bouncer and the manager's right-hand man. He normally screens all the girls anyway. He looks mean, but really he's just a big, old, horny, teddy bear."

Ranger Temple's senses were suddenly assaulted by thick cigarette smoke, even louder music, and a visual orchestra of flashing, strobing lights.

She was led to the end of a long bar where a man with a shaved head sat scanning the stage and audience. A topless, rather appealing, young woman was gyrating seductively onstage, much to the delight of the mostly male onlookers.

Butch was the anticipated poster child for the bouncer's guild. After the waitress cupped her hand and informed the large gent of Sam's request, the behemoth slid off of his barstool perch and offered his hand.

Well over six feet tall and probably topping out at 350 pounds, Sam accepted the oversized hand while wondering what had happened to Butch's neck. It was as if that body part had completely disappeared.

"How can I help you?" he asked in a deep baritone that competed with the stereo's bass.

"I lost my job recently," Sam shouted her practiced response. "I'm not shy and heard that dancers can make some good money. I thought I would check it out."

The bouncer's eyes immediately moved to scan the lady ranger's body but gave no hint of his assessment. "How are your tits?" he asked, as nonchalant as if he was asking an old friend about his grandchildren.

"I've not had any complaints," Sam responded, subconsciously glancing down at her top.

Butch moved closer so as to be understood over the music. "Most of the successful girls here have implants. Have you had your boobs done?"

Before Sam could answer, movement drew her eye. Butch noticed it at the same time.

Zach was there, escorting both of the girls from the front. It took the bouncer just a second to recognize the tall ranger before he made a quick move for the bar.

Zach was quicker, catching the big man's arm as it stretched toward the button under the counter. "Don't do it!" Zach snapped, "I'm not here for that anyway. I only want to talk to one of your clients without being announced."

For just a second, Sam thought Butch was going to fight. She spotted the muscles across his back tense as he began reaching for his weapon. The lady ranger's hand moved for her own iron.

It was with no small amount of relief when she noted the massive fellow relax and nod at her partner. "If you say so, Ranger. You know we don't want any trouble with the law."

"I'm going to go up to the VIP room, Butch. I spied Chico's Mercedes out in the lot. I just want to talk to him. Understood?"

"Yes, be my guest," the heavily muscled bouncer continued, his voice dripping with disdain.

"If Chico gets any warning that I'm on my way ... even the slightest hint, then the rangers will come down on this club so hard you'll be lucky to get a bitch dog to dance in here. Understood?"

Again, the big man nodded. Sam could tell he didn't like it, but there was little he could do.

The Rio Cabaret was, as Zach had explained, a "player's club."

Like most similar establishments, the primary dance floor was an extremely controlled environment. "A guy could encounter more female skin at a church picnic than in the main area," he clarified for his female partner. "The customers can't touch the girls and would be tossed out on their ears if they even tried.

"Those fraternization rules, however, are completely ignored in the VIP room," Zach had gone on to explain. "It's on the second floor, and a few of the willing, young ladies are allowed to invite high rollers up the executive level for additional entertainment. The bouncer has a control under the bar. If he sees the cops come in, he sends a warning upstairs, and everybody gets their pants on real quick. While I could give a shit less about a vice bust today, if Chico is up there, his bodyguards will get real mean, real quick. They'll probably try to hustle him out the back door or hide him someplace. I want the element of surprise on our side."

As the two rangers ascended the stairs, Zach outlined his plan. "I want you to act like one of the dancers taking a John up for a little fun and games. Flirt me up. Rub around on my lap. Make it believable. You know the drill."

Sam paused on the first landing, turning to glare at her partner, "And just how would I know the *drill*?"

"Why Ranger Temple, you've never seduced a man?"

"Not like that," came the indignant reply.

"You've never seen a television show or movie that had a scene showing how the girls act in a strip club?"

The lady ranger had to think about that one. Finally, she nodded, but it was clear she didn't like her role in the upcoming drama.

Zach turned to continue his climb up the steps, but Sam stopped him again. "Hang on a second."

He watched with a mixture of fascination and desire as she pulled a bobby pin from behind her head and then folded up her skirt so that it barely concealed her panties. It was so short, she had had to relocate the pistol and holster to her clutch.

Then, with a series of swift movements, she unbuttoned her blouse and began twisting the tails, eventually forming a large knot right under her partially exposed breasts. Her stomach was smooth and flat, with a shadow of well-formed abs.

Zach was amazed. Shaking his head, he had to admit the woman was damn hot. "You don't need the low lights, Sam. You're the classiest woman in this place – bar none."

"I *do know how* to seduce a man, Ranger Bass," she grinned back. "The problem is finding one worthy of the effort."

"Of that, ma'am, I have no doubt. Ready?"

They continued up to the second floor, Sam draped on Zach's arm as if she was leading her prize to the Promised Land.

At the top of the stairs was another hostess, stationed at a small table so as to keep the riffraff from wandering into the restricted area. Ignoring Zach, the girl eyed Sam with suspicion. "I don't know you," she said with a hint of bitchy derision.

"I just started tonight," the lady ranger replied with a smile. Looking up at Zach with a sly grin, she added, "And so far I'm liking my new job."

The hostess seemed to accept Sam's explanation. Turning to Zach, she said, "Access to the VIP room requires a bottle of champagne or wine. Which would you prefer, sir?"

Zach, pretending to be slightly intoxicated, slurred, "Which costs more?"

"The champagne is $150 per bottle. The wine is only $100."

Zach knew he was probably buying a $10 item, but understood the game. It was how the club made money during this little transaction.

Sticking out his chest and smiling down at Sam, he responded, "The bubbly, of course. Only the best for this little lady."

"Go on in," the hostess said with a nod. "I'll have your refreshments delivered in a few minutes."

The duo entered through a plain door, finding themselves in a huge, open room. It was even darker inside the VIP lounge, the only light coming from a flickering, stone fireplace at one end. The music was far less dominant in this space. While the rhythm of the rock and roll tune still shook the floor, conversation was now possible. Sam assumed the volume was strategically arranged so that private negotiations could take place.

After giving their eyes a chance to adjust, Zach spied a series of leather conversation pits along one wall, the dim outline of men with their female companions barely discernable. Some of the patrons were simply sitting and talking, one man was receiving a seductive lap dance.

Along the other wall were a series of couches and end tables. The arrangement reminded the ranger of a furniture store with its wares grouped so as to resemble a series of individual rooms.

Sam, pretending to kiss Zach behind the ear, whispered, "How are we going to find your friend? It's cave-black in here."

"Easy," Zach whispered back, nuzzling in her neck. "Look for the bodyguards."

He felt her tense just slightly before the reply. "And just how are we going to get beyond armed security?"

"Don't worry," the senior ranger explained. "I've got a plan."

She bit his earlobe just slightly. "That's what scares me the most."

The couple began walking toward the far corner, negotiating around the seating and fixtures at a slow pace. There wasn't any acting necessary, Zach wishing he'd grabbed his night vision before leaving the truck.

Halfway across the room, they spotted Chico's likely lair. Two brawny men stood with their backs to one of the conversation pits, both of them homing in as Zach and Sam approached.

"This section is occupied," one of the thugs stated. "Move on."

"No problem, partner," Zach replied with the laid-back tone of a man out for a good time. "They need a little more light in here, so a fella doesn't break a leg."

Zach led Sam to a nearby couch, the seating providing the ranger a tactical view of the nearby pit and its guards. "We may have a problem," he announced with concern.

"What?"

"I busted one of Chico's thugs a few years back on a weapons charge, and I think he's one of the brutes here tonight. The way he looked at me ... he might be on to us," Zach worried.

After taking a seat, he pulled Sam close to straddle his lap. "Not to pressure you, or anything, but this needs to be especially authentic. Grind against me," he whispered. "Act like you're in heat."

The ranger was a little surprised at Sam's reaction. Without a snide remark or complaint, she caught the beat of the music and began a slow, exotic forward and back movement against his zipper, each pass accented by a tiny, torturous circle at the end.

It was difficult for Zach to keep his attention on their quarry. Sam smelled good, looked great, and her skin was soft and warm. He felt the familiar stirring in his groin and knew she would detect his arousal at any moment. He was also positive she would never let him hear the end of it.

Just then, one of Chico's henchmen took a few steps toward the two law officers, a perplexed look on his face. To Zach, it looked like the thug was trying to recall where he'd seen the tall cowboy before.

In an attempt to block the curious guard's view, Zach pulled Sam in tight, burying his face between her breasts. He braced for her to pull back in anger, but she didn't. Instead, she squeezed her arms forward to accent her cleavage and melted against him.

The bodyguard gave up, unable to see and evidently unwilling to interrupt Zach's pleasure. The ranger relaxed as the man returned to his post and shrugged at his co-goon.

"Damn, that was close," Zach whispered, moving from Sam's cleavage.

"You can say that again," she breathed, not sure what had just happened.

While Sam continued the bump and grind, Zach returned to his surveillance. The effort required supreme concentration.

As he focused on Chico's area, his eyes were able to make out a blonde head of hair next to the darker complexion of the Latino man. They were, it appeared, merely talking.

"He's only having a conversation right now ... nothing more. I hope we aren't too late," Zach relayed to his partner in a hush. "I need to catch him with his pants down ... literally ... for my little scheme to work."

Sam lifted herself off of Zach's lap, much to the relief of the stressed lawman. His reprise was short-lived, however, as she simply turned around and began the same motion, this time with her back against his chest so she could see Chico's lair.

A few moments later, Zach detected movement from Chico's love nest, the blonde headed dancer standing and removing her top. With the grace that accompanies a well-practiced motion, she dropped down to her knees and began to help her client with his zipper.

"Now we're talking," Zach announced.

Sam felt Zach rustle beneath her at the same time that the champagne arrived. After the waitress had left, Zach communicated the next phase of his plan. "Pour us each a glass and then 'accidentally' drop mine. We need a distraction."

"If you say so," she replied, leaving his lap and reaching for the bottle.

The next thing Zach knew, his partner seemed to stumble, and a frosty, cold glass of the bubbly was poured directly onto his crotch.

"What the fuck!" he shrieked, genuinely shocked by the icy awakening as he jumped to his feet.

"Oh, I'm sorry," Sam giggled. "Let me get you a towel."

As she backed away, the lady ranger nearly staggered into one of Chico's boys. Zach was right behind her, both of the guards distracted by the clumsy stripper.

In an instant, Zach's cell phone was in his hand, "Sam – close your eyes!" he ordered, the command immediately followed by several strobes of bright, blinding light as the camera's flash illuminated the completely dark room.

The camera's pulse accomplished two things. First, Zach now possessed a crystal clear image of Chico's shocked face, a head of blonde hair between his legs. Secondly, both of the bodyguards were paralyzed, unable to see a thing.

"Fuck!" somebody yelled, another voice growling, "What the hell! No pictures!

The bodyguards' vision finally did clear, and each goon discovered a pistol poking in one of his ears.

"Hello, Chico," Zach said calmly. "What's *up*?" he continued with a chuckle, nodding toward the criminal's now exposed manhood. "Not much, huh?"

"Who is that? Do you know what I'm going to do to you ... when ..." the angry voice from the pit snarled.

"It's Ranger Bass, Chico," Zach broke in with authority. "I need to talk to you."

"I got nothing to say," sounded the harsh response. "You can go fuck yourself and the horse you rode in on."

"Why so angry, my friend," Zach taunted back. "I just want to have a conversation. Why don't you order these two boys to hand my partner their pea shooters and take a seat over yonder?"

The blonde dancer decided she had business elsewhere, and with a dart, she scampered toward the door with a bundle of clothing under her arm. The other patrons, seeing the guns, decided to follow her.

"I ain't doing shit," Chico replied. "If you're going to arrest me, then do it. Otherwise, fuck off."

"Now, now," Zach said as if scolding a misbehaving child. "I think you should reconsider. You see, I have a rather telling photograph here on my cell phone. It's an image I am sure your wife … or her brother … would find disconcerting."

The once tough voice from the pit suddenly sounded rattled. "You wouldn't dare."

Zach glanced at Sam, the lady ranger's pistol still tight against the nearest bodyguard's head. "You see, Ranger Temple, our friend here is what is commonly referred to as an ambassador. He is a go-between the Gulf and Zetas cartels. A short time ago, the two sides finally realized they were killing not only each other but their profits as well. Someone with more brains than ammunition decided that talking was cheaper than murdering. There was even an arranged marriage of sorts. Chico's wife is Maria Botanize, the younger sister of Carlos Botanize, more commonly known as Carlos the Hammer. Now, Mr. Hammer is widely known as one of the Zetas's most notorious enforcers. The man supposedly favors a carpenter's claw hammer and believes in taking his time with the victim. Word has it that Mr. Botanize is also extremely protective of his younger sister."

"I see," Sam replied with a snicker. "I bet Maria wouldn't appreciate seeing her husband getting his knob polished by that little blonde-headed cutie."

"Just so happens I have Maria's cell phone number. Since Chico doesn't seem interested in talking with us, I guess I'll text her this picture."

"Don't. Please," sounded a rather weak voice from the pit.

The plea was immediately followed by Chico ordering his men to stand down and hand over their weapons to the rangers. A minute later, both henchmen were seated nearby on a couch, Sam's pistol covering their muscular, oversized frames.

Zach's voice dropped low and nasty. "Who came across, Chico? Who was trying to sneak into Texas and ran into our Marines?"

"I don't know."

If it weren't for the fact that she was covering two massive thugs while standing half-naked in a topless bar, Zach's next move would have caused Sam to burst out in hysterics. Like an old black and white gangster movie, Ranger Bass held up his cell phone with a finger hovering over the "trigger." The fact that he was threatening the villain with a text as opposed to a hailstorm of bullets from a Tommy gun was just surreal.

"Don't! Please! I'm telling the truth; I don't know who came across," Chico begged, his eyes bulging as Zach's finger started to descend on the send button.

Ranger Bass relaxed but kept up the pressure. "I don't think you're being straight up with me, Chico. Stop fucking around before I lose interest and move on to someone who won't waste my time."

"I don't know who came across. Really, I don't."

"Do you know why?"

"I've heard stories," the cartel go-between answered in a quieter, protective voice. "Ever since Texas started letting anyone cross the Rio Grande, the organizations have been losing money. There's been a rumor going around that new alliances have been formed."

"So? What's that got to do with the price of coffee beans in Guadalajara?"

Chico seemed really nervous now, his eyes darting right and left. Zach made another show of preparing to hit the send button and launch the incriminating text message along with the attached picture.

"Okay! Okay! Stop that!" the ambassador snapped. "I heard a few whispers that there's a coup in the works. The cartels are banding together to overthrow the government."

Again, Zach was cynical. "Pardon this stupid, old cowboy's lack of gray matter, Chico. But I still don't understand what some hair-brained, cockamamie scheme down south has to do with a guy sneaking across the border and killing a bunch of our kids along the way."

"They need weapons to pull off a coup. Lots of weapons and ammunition. Can you think of a better place than Texas to acquire such firepower?"

Zach now understood, the pieces of the puzzle coming together quickly. With an abrupt pivot, he turned to Sam and announced, "Time to change clothes. We've got work to do."

"Are you going to delete that picture?" Chico called as the two rangers made for the exit.

"Nah," Zach called over his shoulder. "A man never knows when something like that might come in handy."

Chapter 4

President Simmons sighed, frowning at the intercom while setting his glasses down on the baroque desk. "Send them in," he instructed his secretary.

Major Putnam and Colonel Bowmark were shown into the office, both men's expressions painted with several coats of seriousness as they removed their hats.

"What is so important that it can't wait for our staff meeting in the morning, gentlemen?" the republic's chief executive asked.

"Sir, we've received information concerning the massacre at Langtry," the ranger commander began. "While the source is somewhat dubious, the major and I felt the ramifications were serious enough to warrant your immediate attention."

"Go on," Simmons replied.

For the next three minutes, Putnam and Bowmark took turns briefing their boss on what Rangers Bass and Temple had uncovered. No mention of the specific methods employed by the officers was included.

Simmons stood, turning to gaze out at the Austin skyline through the large, curved window behind his desk. "Damn," the politician initially remarked, soon followed by, "The timing of this couldn't be worse."

"Sir, the obvious thing to do would be to delay or put a hold on the sale of automatic weapons until this can all be sorted out. I'm no politician, but I can't imagine it would be good for the republic to be providing arms and ammunition used to overthrow a neighboring government."

"I wish it were that easy, gentlemen. As I'm sure both of you are aware, the House and Senate have been vigorously debating that law, as well as the merits of a dozen major pieces of legislation due to expire, for the past several months. Texas was formed on the conservative principles that promised a small, non-intrusive government. The people want a federal presence that keeps its nose out of their business. Somehow, the gun control issue has become the litmus test to determine if we're going to keep our promise."

Simmons was pacing now, obviously deep in troubled thought. The two senior rangers watched, both knowing it wasn't wise to interrupt.

The president finally resumed, "This is a complicated issue, gentlemen. For example, I could sign an executive order delaying the new law by 30 days. That act, in my opinion, would lead to enormous public unrest, perhaps outright disobedience. Even the people who don't care about gun control would then be watching Austin with a suspicious eye. We have to keep the promises made before the secession."

"What if you informed the general pubic the delay was due to a credible, international threat?" Putnam offered. "Tell the people that law enforcement needs the additional time to round up some very dangerous men?"

Simmons waved off the suggestion. "We've had quite enough of law enforcement weighing in on this debate. If I were to sign such an order, a lot of people would proclaim we were stalling to keep the police happy and safe, all at the cost of personal liberties. There are about 100 police chiefs I wish had kept their mouths shut about this entire affair. All they've managed to do is gin up emotions on both sides of the argument."

The colonel weighed in, "Sir, if there is a coup in Mexico, it is likely to be an extremely violent affair with unprecedented amounts of bloodshed. Even if the cartels fail to overthrow the government, having a bunch of Texas weapons involved in the attempt can't possibly be good for the republic. There has to be something we can do."

The argument didn't seem to carry much weight with the Commander in Chief. "Even before the secession, Mexico constantly complained that the United States was arming the cartels. I remember one study that claimed over 90% of the weapons seized by the Mexican authorities were from America. I'm not convinced the Lone Star Republic's disallowing such devices would make all that much difference."

Putnam upped the ante, "If the cartels do win, many experts believe there will be a civil war in Mexico within a year. Perhaps more than one. I've seen models that predict our neighbor to the south will eventually end up like Europe in the 1600s, separating into a bunch of smaller, independent states that are constantly fighting amongst themselves. It doesn't take a Ph.D. from Texas Tech to see how such conditions south of the Rio Grande would spill over into our nation. The worst case scenario is that we would be drawn into those regional conflicts."

"Yes, I've read those same prophecies," Simmons nodded. He then began counting on his fingers, "First, Texas would be inundated with refugees trying to escape the violence. Then, the losing side would retreat across our border for sanctuary. They would be pursued by those with the upper hand, and our towns and cities would become battlefields. And that is just the first wave of contact; the forecasts continue with repercussions that last for years, perhaps decades. And yet, we can't impact the lives of our citizens based on the expectations, estimates, and the potential actions of another country. Believe me, gentlemen, I understand the ramifications. It's an extremely troubling paradox because there is no workable solution."

The three men sat in silence for some time, each running the private gauntlet of his own thoughts. The atmosphere in the president's office was fouled with both an air of foreboding and a deep-seated vein of frustration. All of them knew trouble was brewing on the horizon, the threat from their southern neighbor looming large in the new nation's path to prosperity. Yet, there wasn't any course of action, policy, or plan to avoid a collision.

"I feel like I'm stuck on a railroad track, and I can see the train in the distance," Putnam offered in a distant, monotone voice. "I know the engine is going to crush me. I can see the train's light, barreling my way. The only hope is that I come up with a plan before it's too late."

The colonel nodded, "I understand. I feel the same way. Yet, I was always a firm believer in the phrase, 'Hope is not a strategy.'"

Their words seemed to motivate the republic's highest official. Simmons stood again, his face brightened by a potential solution. "We'll close the border," he announced with a firm voice. "While I'm sure this decision eliminates any chance I have at a second term, sometimes a leader has to do what is right, no matter how unpopular."

"Are you sure, Mr. President?" the colonel asked, surprised by the abrupt turn. "A large part of our economy is exporting goods and services to Mexico. A lot of very wealthy individuals aren't going to be happy with that course of action."

"We can't be a catalyst for a civil war, gentlemen," the president stated. "All that I ask is that the rangers pull out all the stops to find any revolutionaries on our soil and bring them to justice."

Both of the lawmen rose to leave, each already thinking of the orders they would issue once back at headquarters. Simmons stopped them before they reached the door. "Hurry, my friends. I've just made our government the enemy of every factory, bank, rancher, and citizen along the border. If this situation drags on for too long, we may have our own civil war to worry about."

Four days had passed since the massacre, Sam and Zach working and reworking every lead, source, and potential. So far, they had nothing other than Chico's vague story. The ambassador had disappeared, the two rangers uncertain if his absence had been arranged so that he could avoid them, or Carlos the Hammer.

Chico's tale had sent hundreds of lawmen on a mission to find the who, what, when, and where of any mass purchase of weaponry. The task had not only been daunting, but fruitless.

There were "only" 112 companies manufacturing complete shoulder-fired weapons in Texas. While that number was manageable, it soon became clear to the various law enforcement organizations that they were facing a much larger beast.

Another 500+ firms manufactured or resold kits that would convert existing weapons to "fully automatic" blasters. That figure didn't count the unknown number of garage-based businesses with 3D printers, or the importers who were having trigger mechanisms produced overseas.

"Our friends in the cartels don't have to buy complete rifles," Zach informed his partner. "They can buy, make, or source small, inexpensive parts just about anywhere. We're looking for a needle in a haystack. It's a worthless endeavor."

The pressure on the two lawmen was made even more intense by the fact that it had been Zach's source that had initiated a rather large, extremely controversial ball rolling.

As promised, President Simmons had closed the border, and the outrage was quickly mounting on both sides of the international boundary.

The news was filled with a virtual parade of victims, everyone from human rights watchdogs to farmers and factory owners crying, bitching, threatening, and infuriated by the president's executive order.

It seemed like every broadcast was filled with folks from one side or the other telling a reporter their tales of woe. "My mother is dying in a Brownsville hospital," one teary-eyed woman claimed. "They won't let me across to be at her side when she dies."

One of the worst was a Texas woman who was obviously near term with her pregnancy. "I'm a citizen of Texas, born and bred," she sniffled into the

Mexican news microphone. "I came south to visit family before the baby came. My child is due any day, and if it's not born in Texas, I don't know what we're going to do!"

"Our business is going to fail if the borders are closed for much longer," claimed a nice looking man in a business suit. "We depend on exports to Mexico and Central America. Our product is sitting on trucks at the border while our customers are trying to find other sources for the parts they need. We will have to lay off over 90 workers if this situation isn't resolved soon."

On and on, droned the tales of the hardship and trauma being imposed by Texas's unexplained act. It seemed like every day new video of yet an even greater tragedy was broadcast over the airwaves.

Zach was just finishing his burger when the television behind the bar began another in a series of heart-wrenching reports. This time, it was a sobbing, older man standing beside a small truck overflowing with rotting vegetables. "I'm not going to be able to pay our mortgage to the bank," he wept. "The rest of my crop is decaying in the field. We're ruined."

The ranger peered at his partner, the discomfort evident on his face. Motioning to the bartender, he said, "Is there anything else on, Pete? That shit could ruin a man's appetite."

It took the barkeep three presses of the remote to find a channel that wasn't covering the situation on the border.

Sam, seeing her partner's scowl, repeated the same statement she'd already made several times during the last few days. "You didn't tell the president to close the border, Zach. It's not your fault."

Just like the half dozen times before, she braced for his moody, harsh response. She was spared by the ringing of Zach's cell.

The disgusted ranger glanced at the caller ID and then shook his head. "Not now, Cheyenne. It's not a good time," he whispered, returning the phone to rest beside his plate.

"You should talk to her," Sam advised. "As grumpy as you've been lately, a little personal time with your girl might improve that shitty mood."

Zach ignored the remark, stabbing a French fry deep into a puddle of ketchup.

Again, his cell buzzed, Cheyenne determined not to be denied. With a frown, Zach answered the call. "What's up?" he grumbled.

"I'm in trouble, Zach. I hate to bother you, but I don't know who else to turn to," came the rushed response.

The ranger's demeanor changed instantly, something in the woman's voice putting him on alert. "What's wrong?" he said, throwing Sam a look.

"I took out a loan… to consolidate my credit cards. And… well… the bank is getting really nasty with me, and I don't know what to do."

Zach relaxed, visions of someone breaking into her apartment or threatening her with a gun pushed from his mind. "I can lend you some cash if that's all it is," he said with a matter-of-fact tone. "How much do you need?"

Now it was Chey's turn to be frustrated. "It's not that. Not like that at all. I'm convinced this banker dude is up doing something very illegal. He's threatening my career, my family … everything."

"How much do you owe them?"

"I took out a loan for $65,000 Texas Greenbacks," she responded.

Before Zach could stop himself, a long whistle left his throat. "What on earth do you need with that much money, Chey? I know my birthday's coming up, but that's a ton of cash."

Her voice grew impatient. "I bought a new car and paid off all of my credit cards," she answered with a snarl. "The payments were supposed to be a little over $1,200 per month, which I can handle, no problem. After I made the first installment, the bank sent me a statement saying I owed $3,500 next month."

"Huh? That doesn't make any sense. Were you late with the payment or something?"

"No, not at all. I thought it was a mistake. When I went to talk to the banker, he got all shitty and then made me an … err … interesting offer. I think these guys are some sort of con artists or something. Given the proposition he made me, I have to wonder if this is a tactic to prey on unsuspecting women."

Zach knew Cheyenne wasn't one to overreact in most situations. This, however, was the first time financial matters had ever entered their relationship. Still, what she was describing didn't sound legit.

"Damn it, Chey, you know good and well that they don't bury bankers after they die – they screw them into the ground. They are all shysters, but legal ones for the most part. Where are you?"

"I'm in Abilene, sitting outside the bank. I needed to settle down a little bit after the meeting I just had. I'm shaking so badly I am afraid I am going to wreck my new car. These guys are scaring the crap out of me, Zach."

The ranger asked a few more questions, the answers more and more troubling. Finally, he decided Chey needed him, if not his badge. She sounded like a little moral support would go a long way, and besides, they weren't making much headway on the massacre case. "I'm about an hour and a half out. I can head that way. Let's talk this over in person."

"I don't want to interfere. I know you guys are right in the middle of a nasty situation... I just didn't know who else to call," she said, a sniffle punctuating the last sentence.

Zach's concern was growing. Chey didn't cry. He'd never seen her cry. These collection people must really be pushing her hard. "Meet us at the mall at that restaurant on the south side. You know the one.... We had a steak there a few months ago."

"Okay, Zach. And thanks. This really means a lot to me. I'll make it up to you; I promise."

The two rangers headed north, travelling mostly in silence after Zach relayed the pervious conversation. Eventually, they arrived at the lot of the specified shopping mall.

"There she is," Zach nodded.

Cheyenne saw them park at the same moment and began the process of uncoiling her gangly frame from the small, all-electric sedan. "I've got gun cases bigger than that car," Zach noted. "I wish she'd picked something with a little more meat on its bones. She's going to get herself killed in that cracker box."

Sam snorted. "You carry a weapon and chase down some of the most violent men the species has to offer, and you're worried about the sheet metal surrounding your girlfriend? I wonder about you sometimes, Zachariah Bass. How hard did that Middle Eastern ghost thump that noggin of yours?"

The reference to his arch nemesis was like a sucker punch to Zach's gut. "Not to mention the fact that some of my armed coworkers are the ill-tempered sort who threaten to shoot a man at the slightest provocation," sounded his snide comeback.

With her cheeks blushing red hot, Sam inhaled deeply, preparing to launch a significant verbal assault. Zach was saved by Cheyenne opening the truck's rear door and stepping up into the backseat. "Hi, guys! I feel so much better now that you're here," she sang with a cheery tone. "How are my two favorite white hats this afternoon?"

"Hey, Chey," Sam responded. Leaning toward the back and exchanging a quick hug with the new passenger. Zach was next, pivoting in the driver's seat to kiss the new arrival on the cheek. "I filled Sam in on the way up here," he began. "Why don't you start from the beginning, just to make sure we're both up to speed?"

"Sure," Cheyenne responded, instantly deflated by the need to relive past events. "This is kind of embarrassing. A friend of mine recently got a loan, and her interest rate was really low. She was saving all kinds of money, so I decided I would do the same thing … pay off my credit cards. Cut them up … and put back a little money. A girl has to think about the future, ya know."

Chey paused for a moment, collecting her thoughts before continuing. "A few months ago, I started checking around and came across a web page for this bank called Trustline. I was going to be in Abilene anyway, so I came in and filled out an application. At first, I only wanted to borrow about 20 grand, but the branch manager suggested I go ahead and roll in my car loan as well."

She went on to explain that one Mr. Carson, a distinguished-looking gent in his early 50s, had nodded, smiled, and seemed sympathetic to the beauty's dilemma. Cheyenne had left the branch an hour later, the proud owner of a 22-page loan document and newly funded account.

Chey had made her first payment. When the statement came in the mail for the second installment, the "minimum amount required," was quite a shocker, well over $3,500 dollars.

"I called the bank's customer help line, confused, slightly pissed, but sure it was all a mistake," the victim continued.

"What did they say?" Sam asked.

"The lady in the call center was very nice. She said that it was a brand new loan and wasn't in their computer just yet. She suggested I stop by the branch and speak with the loan officer. That's why I went by here today."

"And?" Zach said, not liking where the whole episode was going.

"I wasn't going to be back in Abilene for a while, so I first called Mr. Carson on the phone. It was as if I was talking to a completely different man. He scolded me like I was a child and kept repeating that I had agreed to the bank's terms … kept telling me to read the contract … told me it was only going to get worse if I got behind on the loan."

Continuing the story, Chey said she then began receiving nasty phone calls, threatening letters, and even a rather rough-looking goon at her door. The bank threatened to expose her as a fraud across the entire internet. "We know your social media accounts. We know where you work. We know your parents own land in West Texas. We're going after all of it and ruin you in the process."

Chey paused, noting the disapproving look on Zach's face. Anticipating his question, she offered, "Hey, I know I should have said something two weeks ago. I was just so embarrassed and wanted to try to handle this all myself."

The tension in Zach's expression eased and the model continued with her story. "Finally, yesterday, the once-again friendly Mr. Carson contacted me personally. I felt so much better when he said, 'Come into the branch tomorrow, and I'll see if we can work something out.'"

"Let me guess," Zach interrupted. "He tried to talk you into some sort of kinky, degrading sexual conduct. Probably something very nasty?"

"No," Cheyenne replied from the backseat. "Worse … I think."

"Don't tell me you think he has chopped up bodies in his freezer," Sam questioned, clearly growing upset. "I'll shoot off his balls if he tried to hurt you."

"Before I went to the meeting, I downloaded an app for my smartphone," Chey stated with pride. "I recorded the whole conversation, and now I'm glad I did."

Digging around in her pocket, Cheyenne produced her phone. After clicking a few buttons, the sound of footsteps came from the tiny speaker.

Listening intently, the two rangers heard Chey being shown to Mr. Carson's office. He voiced a friendly, professional greeting and then asked the aspiring model to take a seat. The entire conversation was clear as a bell.

"I'll come right to the point," the man boomed. "You're in default on your loan, and an avalanche of bad things are about to fall on your head. You seem like a nice girl with a great future ahead of you. I'd hate to see this situation spiral out of control and destroy your life. We need to address this immediately, before the fees do any more damage. As of today, Miss, we need $4,750 to bring your account current."

"I'm only late a few days. I can't believe the late fees are that high," Chey pleaded on the recording. "Look; if I couldn't come up with $3,500, you must realize there is just no way I can give you $4,750. I swear I didn't understand what I was getting into."

There was a pause, Zach visualizing the older man rubbing his chin in thought as he eyed Chey's spindly legs and short skirt. A moment passed before he replied. "I feel somewhat personally responsible for all this. Perhaps I should have explained the terms of the loan in more detail. Regardless, I can't have a black mark like this on my record here at Trustline if you default. It would ruin my career. So I'm willing to violate one of my strictest rules and get involved personally."

Zach and Sam exchanged eye rolls, the senior ranger whispering, "Here it comes."

"Go on," came Chey's timid reply.

"I have other clients … prominent, powerful, men who would pay fantastic sums to enjoy the companionship of a beautiful woman such as yourself. I'm sure the rewards would far, far exceed your monthly loan commitments."

The next section of the recording made it obvious Chey was growing angry. "You want me to sleep with men for money? So I can pay a loan? Are you crazy? What kind of woman do you think I am?"

"Oh, no…. Please don't misunderstand my meaning. The men of whom I speak are ultra-wealthy, very sophisticated gentlemen who respect and appreciate the company of elite, young women. They live in exotic locations, travel on private planes, own massive yachts, and have properties all over the globe. I'm sure they would be willing to help their *friends* with small personal debts, such as yours."

Now skeptical, Chey wasn't buying it. "If these guys are such wealthy jet-setters, why do they need to pay for anybody's *company*? It would seem like there would be lines of girls wanting to hang around and bask in the opulence."

"And that's the very problem my clients experience," Carson shot back. "They have to be careful of blackmailers, gold-diggers, and other nefarious types. They would prefer an established, professional relationship that was discreet and worry-free. The man I'm thinking of is someone of importance in a foreign government. I am sure you can understand his need to keep his activities out of the public eye."

Sam stared at Zach, surprise and exasperation commanding her expression. "He's not a pervert. He's a pimp. White slavery? Kidnapping?"

"I didn't see that coming," the senior ranger admitted.

"I don't know about this," drifted Cheyenne's voice from the recording. "I need to think about what you've said. Where would I be going? For how long?"

Zach's attention pegged at the banker's next words. "The man I have in mind is in Mexico at the moment. His yacht is docked there for the next few weeks," Carson stated. "I'm actually expecting him to visit our area very soon. Perhaps I could arrange a lunch or dinner between the two of you?"

"Mexico? Private planes? Government official?" Sam whispered. "Who the hell is this guy doing business with?"

Carson continued before Zach could respond. "Please, please think it over before the bank's collection efforts grow in intensity. And I must insist that you keep our conversation absolutely confidential. I'm going out on a huge limb here, and I'd like to keep my job."

"Okay," Chey responded. "I don't think this is for me, but I'll call you in the next few days – one way or the other."

The playback ended.

"And that's why I called you, Zach," Chey said. "This whole thing is so creepy. Is it legal for a bank to do that?"

Zach rubbed his chin, "Actually, I'm not sure. Technically, he wasn't trying to get you to have sex for money, nor did he make you a specific offer. Even if I stretched it a bit and said he was soliciting your services, the fact that the proposed activity would be outside of Texas serves to limit what we can do. First things first. I need a copy of that loan agreement."

Chey dug around in her purse, producing the original. "Here, you can make a copy and give it back to me when you're done."

As Zach began thumbing through the thick document, his girlfriend's ire continued to build. "I have this strong urge to puke *and* take a shower. I just can't figure out which I want to do first. What a slime ball. Can you just shoot him for me, Sam?"

"I can't think of anything else that would pleasure my trigger finger more," the lady ranger replied with an evil smile. "I wouldn't lose a minute's sleep."

After pocketing her cell phone, Cheyenne leaned forward to give Zach a peck on the cheek. "I need to wash off the sleaze that reeked from that guy," she stated. "After you peruse those documents, call if you need me to do something else. I gotta tell you, though ... I'm not going to sleep very well tonight."

"Where are you staying?" Zach asked, now concerned about the lady. She was trying to be brave, which warmed his heart, but he was still worried.

Chey told Zach the name of her hotel. "I've rescheduled today's photoshoot for in the morning, and then I'll be checking out and heading to Dallas. Let me know what you think I should do."

The two rangers watched her leave, both silent in their thoughts.

Zach set the contract aside. The ranger was clearly troubled. "This runs a lot deeper than we thought. I'm not sure whether Mr. Carson was more offensive as a pervert and potential serial killer or as a pimp. Either way, we have to take this guy down."

Sensing what Zach was thinking, Sam tensed. "You can't use her to get at this Mr. Carson. It's just too dangerous, Zach. We all know that if Chey crosses Texas's southern border, no one will ever see her again. They'll use her up in a few months and then kill her," Sam stated with a slight shiver.

"It's more than that," Zach said with a dismissive wave. "If there is foreign involvement of this sort with our banks, then we've got serious issues that no one is aware of. We need to talk to the major about this."

Zach strolled into ranger headquarters on a mission, his partner struggling to keep up with his lengthy stride. The place was bustling more than usual, the men and woman of the organization seeming to walk with a bit more purpose, their expressions and greetings shorter than normal.

"Everyone here seems to be wound up tighter than a $3 watch. I haven't seen so many grim faces since the president announced that the rangers were going to let females join the ranks," Sam noted after the elevator door had closed.

"If they're running into the same brick walls that we are, I don't blame them," Zach replied.

They exited into another busy corridor, Zach motioning toward an unmarked door down the hall. "Let's see if our legal consultants can make heads or tails of Chey's loan agreement. After that, we'll go visit the major."

"You're the senior officer," Sam nodded. "Lead and I will follow."

"Yeah? What if I have to go to the men's room?" he quipped.

Ignoring the question, Sam made for the door and entered a small reception area. A middle-aged woman sat behind the government-issued desk. "Good morning. How may I help you?"

"We're here to see Tony," Zach answered with a polite smile. "I have an agreement I was hoping he could review."

"And you are?" the receptionist asked.

"Rangers Bass and Temple," Zach replied, flashing his ID.

The screener reached for the large, multi-buttoned phone beside her. After a quick, hushed conversation, she pushed back her chair and rose. "Please follow me."

The two lawmen were escorted through an inner door, finally arriving at a small office that seemed completely overwhelmed with papers, folders, case files, and at least three laptop computers. A small, balding head appeared from behind the mess, examining the two rangers through thick glasses.

With a smile and extended hand, a short man traversed around the canyon of documents. "Ranger Bass, how are you?"

"I'm doing well, Tony. Let me introduce you to my new partner, Ranger Temple," Zach said, watching the two exchange a polite greeting. He then continued, "Sam, Tony is one of the best legal minds around. He's actually with the Attorney General's office, but graces us gun-toting primitives with his brilliance often enough that the colonel gave him an office over here."

Tony waved off Zach's compliment but didn't offer any verbal argument. "What do you have for me, Zach?" the lawyer asked. "I don't mean to be short, but we're completely buried right now with everything that's going on."

"Aren't you always trying to fit a size 10 head in a size 8 hat?" Zach teased, producing Cheyenne's loan agreement.

Pushing his spectacles up his nose, the attorney ignored the remark and began reading the contract. Sam noted the man didn't invite them to sit, and then realized it was probably because all of the chairs were occupied with paperwork of one form or another. The lady ranger had little doubt Tony wasn't a man known for social graces.

It soon became obvious, however, that the lawyer could read like a demon.

Sam watched as he flipped the pages at an astounding pace, the pudgy fellow's lips mumbling in a low whisper as he consumed paragraph after paragraph of the legal gobbledygook.

A few minutes later, Tony peered up and gave Zach a wide-eyed, blank stare. "This is very good," the attorney commented.

"How so?" Zach inquired, not expecting such a reaction.

Again, pushing his constantly wandering bifocals back up his nose, Tony responded, "A real pro wrote this." Then, thumping the pages with the back of his hand, he continued, "From a purely legal perspective, I'm actually a little jealous."

Sam was puzzled. "So you're saying there's nothing in that agreement that violates the Republic of Texas banking laws?"

"What banking laws?" Tony grunted, handing the contract back to Zach. "All of the old U.S. FDIC rules, banking regulations, and consumer protection acts have expired. They've not been replaced by the legislature ... just yet."

It was Zach's turn to sound surprised, "So a bank can do whatever it wants?"

Tony shook his head, "No, not *anything*. As a state, Texas had reasonably defined volumes of business and contract law, as well as a significantly detailed history of court decisions and interpretations. All of that case law is still on the books, and it applies to banks, as well as car dealerships, and even verbal contracts between two individuals. What our legislators haven't implemented are the regulations and codes that apply specifically to financial institutions or their interactions with the public at large."

"So any bank in Texas can fleece its customers, and there's nothing that can be done about it?" Sam asked, her voice sounding incredulous.

Tony pointed to the documents now in Zach's hand. "The bank's note is a masterpiece of legal doublespeak, shadowy clauses, and dependent requirements. I'm not sure how much could have been done even if the old rules and regulations were still in play. Regardless, I don't see anything in there that warrants the attention of the Attorney General. Sorry, Rangers, but that's just the way it is. The people of Texas wanted less government. There's a price to be paid for having fewer regulations or agencies to enforce them."

Zach went on to explain Mr. Carson's offer for services to be rendered.

"Now, you're going in a completely different direction. Like the loan agreement, you're venturing into some very complex legal waters. Prostitution is still illegal in the republic, but it doesn't sound like you have a clear-cut case of an offer to engage, an agreement to engage, or actual engagement in sexual conduct in exchange for a fee."

"So *we're* this ones getting screwed?" Zach stated, a look of disgust on his face despite the pun.

Tony sensed the frustration in the ranger's voice. Pulling a pen from his pocket, he scribbled a name and phone number on a sheet of scrap paper. "Call this number and ask to speak with Cecil. He works for the comptroller's office, auditing the banks for tax purposes. He might be able to shed more light on Trustline or its affiliates. That's about the best I can offer with what you have right now."

A minute later, the two rangers were back in the corridor, both of them frowning over what they had just learned. "That sucked," Zach offered.

"No shit," Sam spat. "What were you saying earlier about moving to the United States? I don't know which is worse – machine guns in the street or banks that can rip out your heart without fear of repercussions."

Nodding, Zach's next statement deepened the issue. "So now, the real question is do we go to the major with this?"

"It doesn't sound like we have a lot to go on. Other than Mr. Carson's mention of Mexican clients, there's not a whole lot of justification for our sticking our noses in. There have to be thousands of wealthy individuals matching the banker's description who aren't part of some criminal apparatus."

Rubbing his chin, Zach deliberated, "Still, the part about Carson's client coming to town is one hell of a coincidence. Don't you think? My gut says we need to dig a little deeper into our friendly financier's affairs."

Sam shrugged. "Maybe. Maybe not. Is this one of those situations where it's better for us to follow our instincts and ask for forgiveness later?"

Zach didn't seem to have an answer. "We got in a lot of trouble for not requesting backup on that last case. Not to mention the fact that Buck ended up dead. On the other hand, if Major Putnam orders us to cease and desist, I'll be leaving Chey hanging and ignoring the only possible lead we've got right now."

"You're the senior officer," Sam repeated. "Lead and I will follow."

Shaking his head, Zach sighed. "Somehow, I feel like I'm taking you someplace a whole lot worse than the men's room."

Chapter 5

The two rangers left Austin, Zach eyeing the phone number Tony had provided.

"Are you going to call?" Sam inquired from the passenger seat.

"Sure. Why not? How can it possibly make things any worse?"

Zach dialed the number, putting his cell phone on speaker so Sam could hear. "Texas Department of Treasury. This is Cecil. How may I help you?"

After identifying himself, the ranger quickly explained the reason for his call as well as Tony's recommendation.

Cecil was more than familiar with Trustline. "This isn't the first I've heard of Mr. Carson and the branch in Abilene. I've spoken with police officers from both El Paso and Lubbock in the last year. If you hold on a minute, I'll get you their names."

Zach threw his partner a questioning glance, not really sure where the bank inspector was going. A minute later, Cecil was back on the line, reading the names of two police officers and rattling off their phone numbers. Sam jotted it all down.

"What was the nature of those other two cases?" Zach asked.

"I'm not sure I am at liberty to discuss those matters, Ranger Bass. I wouldn't want to violate a confidence or interfere with an on-going investigation."

Shaking his head, Zach let it go. "I understand, sir. Let me ask you this; is Trustline in compliance with existing regulations? Are they financially sound? Is there anything you can tell me about the bank that might help me?"

"I can only tell you that they pay their taxes. I would suggest, however, that you contact those two law enforcement officers. I'm sure they can shed additional light on the subject at hand."

Zach could spot a government bureaucrat from the next ridge. Frowning at Sam, he thanked the man and disconnected the call.

The detective sergeant in Lubbock was out of the office. With building frustration, the Texan left a message.

It was with no small amount of relief that his next call to El Paso was answered on the second ring. "Detective Monroe."

Again, Zach introduced himself and provided his badge number.

"No offense, Ranger, but you understand I have to verify you are who you say you are. Let me put you on hold."

With his grip tightening on the steering wheel, Zach waited for over three minutes before Monroe came back on the line. "How can I help you, Ranger Bass?"

When Zach mentioned Trustline, the El Paso lawman's response was instantaneous. "Horseshit and bull feathers. Not another one?"

Zach liked the man instantly. "What do you mean, Detective?"

"We had a missing person case six months ago. A young lady ... apparently a nice girl ... just vanished into thin air. Her parents filed the report and claimed that Trustline had been threatening their daughter over a bad loan. I could never pin anything on the bank or tie their collection activity to the disappearance in any way."

"What made you think the bank had anything to do with the case?"

Monroe grunted, "We found on-line posts on the victim's social media accounts that were ... err ... harsh to say the least. We interviewed her co-workers, and they told us stories about collectors visiting the missing girl's place of employment. According to several eyewitnesses, these guys got very, very nasty with her."

Zach was seeing a pattern that would be obvious to a blind man. "When I first got you on the line, you said, 'Not another one.' Are you aware of other missing person cases associated with Trustline?"

"Yes, there was a woman out of Lubbock about five months before my case. I spoke with the sergeant over there a few times, and he described a similar set of circumstances with Trustline. We were both convinced that the bank had something to do with the missing women, but we couldn't prove a damn thing. Last I heard, both files are now cold."

Zach continued to question Monroe but learned little else. He ended the conversation with the detective's promise to email the file.

No sooner had the ranger disconnected, than a call came in from the sergeant at the Lubbock Police Department. The story was nearly identical. Missing person. Pretty girl. Bad debt. Vigorous collection effort.

"I wouldn't ever borrow any money from Trustline," the sergeant stated. "Even if Mr. Carson and his bank had nothing to do with the missing women, I saw what they were doing to this girl. Brutal is the word that comes to mind. Yet, according to the experts I spoke with at the prosecutor's officer, there was nothing illegal about their activities."

"Thanks for the briefing," Zach responded. "I'll keep you in the loop if our digging uncovers anything regarding your case."

Zach and Sam exchanged troubled glances. The predatory nature of the bank's operation didn't fall into the realm of the ranger's responsibility. Normally, such cases were left to the local authorities. This case wouldn't be the first time a loan shark set up operations disguised as a reputable banking institution. Probably wouldn't be the last.

Mid-level bankers had some percentage of perverts and predators, just like any other occupation. According to Monroe, the El Paso vice squad had storerooms stuffed with the files of such individuals. Banker Carson, however, had been "clean as a whistle."

The two rangers were back to the fuzzy recording taken by Cheyenne and the mention of the word, "Mexico."

They continued driving for some time, Zach's exaggerated sigh signaling the ranger had formulated a course of action.

"We have to bring Chey into this," he stated in a monotone.

"No, Zach. That's a bad idea," Sam protested. "We both know that if this thing gets away from us, she'll end up like those other girls … probably resting in some shallow grave south of the border."

"I don't see any other choice?" he countered. "Considering how the other two cases developed, there is just no doubt this situation is going to escalate and get very nasty. Even if we don't bring her in, she's already vulnerable to these parasites. Plus, we're getting nowhere on any other lead. We'll keep an eye on her … a really close eye."

Crossing her arms, Sam made it clear she was preparing to fight like a wildcat. "No. There has to be another way. Cheyenne has already been kidnapped once because of her ill-advised association with you. You can't ask that girl to endanger herself again."

Shooting his passenger an angry scowl, Zach spouted, "*Ill-advised*? Now where the hell did that come from? Besides, Chey called us – remember? If any other citizen of the republic had approached us with this situation, asking them to wear a wire to a meeting wouldn't be completely out of bounds."

"I don't know about how the rangers operate, but that would be extremely rare in most law enforcement organizations. Chey called you because she trusts us. And I used the word ill-advised because obviously you are not putting her safety first. What kind of friend even thinks of such a thing?"

Zach flashed hot, and for a second, Sam thought she'd gone too far. After a few more miles, the senior ranger mumbled, "We have a unique relationship."

Sam's response was softer this time. "That's none of my business. That's between the two of you. What is my business is how we conduct this investigation, and I will not support getting Chey involved at this point. There have to be other courses of action we can take."

"Such as?"

"We can lean on Carson ... subpoena his call records. We can get a court order to audit the bank. We can put the bank's employees under surveillance ... lots of stuff."

Zach shook his head. "Our chances of getting a court order are about the same as my being on Chico's Christmas list. You heard Tony. Besides, going after this guy via the long road means getting Putnam involved. I thought you decided that wasn't the best course of action right now."

"Then let's go talk to Carson. You can use that wonderfully persuasive personality of yours. I'll even dress up like a stripper again if it will help."

Again, Zach disagreed. "I'm sure the Lubbock PD and Detective Monroe worked our banker friend over reasonably well. He's obviously a pretty cool character under pressure. All that we would accomplish is giving ourselves away, and then he'd go down a rabbit hole for months or years. As far as your dressing like a stripper ... well...."

"Well, what?" Sam interjected, bracing for a full assault.

"No comment. I wish to remain silent, Officer. Exercise my Fifth Amendment right."

"Smart man."

"Look," Zach started, clearly wanting to change the subject. "We should, at least, talk to Chey about this. How about we leave the decision up to her?"

Sam was skeptical, "What decision? What are you going to propose?"

"I just want her to contact Mr. Carson, set up an appointment with his client, and wear a wire. He said the mystery man was going to be in Texas. We can protect her here."

The lady ranger didn't like it. Not one bit. "That sounds extremely risky, Zach. Seriously. You're going to have her meet, in person, with a potential mafia goon or cartel enforcer … a person who probably has more security than the president? What if he decides he likes Cheyenne … a lot? What if he decides just to kidnap her and tote her off south of the border?"

Zach nodded, "Yeah. I know. I don't like it either, but there's always a risk. Hell, that girl is in peril just driving to work in that little buzz-wagon she's piloting. But damn it, Sam, we've got missing persons, a banker that's out of control, and only one half-assed clue to solve the massacre. Besides, she asked for our help."

Sam didn't respond for a bit, her gaze focused out the window as Zach continued motoring down the highway. Finally, the female ranger retorted, "Okay. You win. Call her. I just pray that girl has enough sense to tell you to go jump in a lake."

Cheyenne's reaction didn't surprise Zach. It did, however, disappoint Ranger Temple.

"Sounds exciting," she stated without hesitation. "Besides, if that's what I've got to do in order to get these bloodsuckers off my neck, then sign me up."

The trio sat over cups of coffee and tea, a cloud of apprehension suspended above their corner table.

Sam's tone turned motherly. "Don't underestimate how dangerous this is. If Zach and I are right, Mr. Carson is in cahoots with some of the most dangerous men on gawd's green earth. Cartel bosses have zero mercy or concern for their fellow human beings. None."

"Ahhh … that's very sweet of you, Samantha, but I'm a big girl. I know things could go wrong … very wrong. On the other hand, these people are going to ruin my reputation, my credit … and maybe even get me fired. If they have anything to do with those other girls disappearing, then I want to help."

Sam's cell phone jingled, a quick check of the caller ID creating a deep furrow across her brow. "This is my mom," she hissed. "I'll be right back."

After the lady ranger had wandered out of earshot, Zach took his turn at trying to make sure Chey understood what she was getting herself into. "We don't know where this meeting will take place. We have no idea what kind of security Mr. Carson's client will have surrounding him. You know we'll do everything in our power to keep you safe, but even the Texas Rangers can't make any guarantees."

Cheyenne giggled, brushing her hand softly along Zach's chin and flashing the Texan a longing, seductive look. "Oh, I think I can motivate you to keep me safe, cowboy. You have to know I'm the sort of girl who would show her appreciation at being rescued from the evil villain's clutches. Where I'm from, heroes deserve the most *intense* rewards imaginable."

Zach shifted uncomfortably in his chair, trying to retain a professional demeanor and failing badly. "Please don't open that gate right now," he whispered. "It's been a long week, and I'm trying to stay focused on business."

With a wink, Chey removed her hand just as Samantha reappeared at the table.

"Everything okay?" Zach asked, not liking the look on his partner's face.

"Yeah. It's cool. Mom was watching President Clifton's news conference from Washington. She overreacts to those things."

Zach raised an eyebrow, an invitation for his partner to continue. Sam didn't take him up on it, instead returning her attention to Cheyenne. "So, are you still game?"

Now the senior ranger was really worried. Sam's entire attitude seemed to have changed since the call.

"It's okay if you've changed your mind," Ranger Temple continued, realizing how aggressive her last statement had sounded.

"Count me in," the leggy model replied without hesitation. "Let's take these rustlers out and hang 'em from a high oak tree."

Cheyenne arranged to meet the rangers first thing in the morning. She would call Carson early and agree to meet his client.

After kissing Zach on the cheek, the two lawmen watched her exit the coffee shop and enter her miniature, electric carriage.

She hadn't been gone more than two seconds before Sam turned and said, "Mom called to tell me President Clifton was closing the border with Texas. She's worried that she'll never see me again."

"The U.S.A. is doing what?" Zach responded with a start. "Closing the entire border?"

"That's what she heard the Prez say. Evidently, our neighbor to the north is pissed about a number of things, including the availability of unlimited firepower, our closing the border with Mexico, and the lack of cooperation between Texas and the United States."

Zach tilted his head, "Damn. That ain't good. If you think we were under a lot of pressure to solve this case before, wait until this shit hits Austin's fan."

The trio reunited at the coffee shop the next morning, Chey, as usual, running late. While he and Sam waited, Zach's attention was drawn to the wall-mounted television broadcasting a popular morning show.

The news, as anticipated, was dominated by President Clifton's decision to close the borders with the Lone Star Republic. From the sound bytes, it was clear the U.S.A.'s chief executive had her panties in a wad.

"This is a tremendous undertaking for our great nation," she stated. "The border with Texas encompasses four states and is actually several hundred miles longer than the previous international boundary with Mexico. It is a challenge that our law enforcement and border patrol communities assure me can be accomplished."

The commentators were all aflutter over the situation, no doubt motivated by the ratings boost sure to result from the strife.

Next came the opening bell on Wall Street, gloom and doom predictions aplenty as the world-famous index opened several hundred points lower. Uncertainty was bad for business. The billions of dollars' worth of trade normally flowing between the two countries would now be at risk.

The new Texas Stock Exchange, recently dubbed Harris Street, was experiencing the same negatives.

Chey rushed in, glancing at her oversized wristwatch and mumbling, "Sorry," as she made her way to the waiting officers.

Zach remained patient as the two women chitchatted over tea. Finally, he glanced at Chey and said, "Ready?"

"Willing and able," she winked.

Producing a cell phone from her bag, Chey started to punch in Mr. Carson's direct number, but Sam stopped her. "We want to record the conversation," the lady ranger explained.

"No problem. That software app I downloaded will do the trick. I can email you the file once we're done."

Sam threw Zach a questioning look, and after receiving an approving nod, said, "Put it on speaker so we can hear, please."

A minute later, the trio was listening intently as the familiar male voice answered. "Trustline National Bank. This is Mr. Carson. How can I help you?"

"Hi, Mr. Carson. This is Cheyenne. How are you?"

"I'm just fine, ma'am. Have you thought about my offer?"

Rolling her eyes at the two eavesdroppers, Chey responded with a pleasant, "Yes … yes, I have. I'm still sitting on the fence. I would like to meet your client before making any decisions."

There was a pause on the other end, Zach wondering if Mr. Carson was having second thoughts. That concern soon passed, however, the banker finally returning with, "Of course. I'm sure that can be arranged. From what I hear, he is apparently a very charming gentleman, and it just so happens that he's in Texas at the moment. Are you free this afternoon, per chance?"

Zach shook his head and mouthed a stern but silent, "No! Tomorrow at the soonest."

"I'm sorry Mr. Carson, but I have a photo session this afternoon. My schedule tomorrow is clear?"

"I see," replied the banker, apparently not troubled by Chey's busy calendar. "Let me get in touch with my client and arrange a time and place for you two to get acquainted. I'll call you back shortly."

Chey disconnected the call and then exhaled in relief. "Swoooo. That was a lot harder than I thought. Now I've got a bad case of the jitterbugs."

"You did great," Sam smiled, patting the girl's arm for support.

"Sure did," Zach chimed. "I'm damn proud of you."

The trio sat for nearly an hour before Carson called back. "I've got good news. My client is in San Antonio for a few days and would like to meet you. He will be dining at the Titus Steakhouse on the River Walk, and hopes you can join him at 5 PM sharp. Is that acceptable?"

Zach didn't like it. In order to buy time while the ranger thought it over, Chey said, "I've never been to that restaurant before. How should I dress?"

"Titus is extremely exclusive," Carson responded with a highbrow tone. "All of the dining rooms are private, and their wine cellar is known as far away as Paris. I would suggest something formal."

Now Zach really didn't like the meeting place, but there wasn't an alternative. With a reluctant nod, he signaled Chey to agree.

"Wonderful," she said with as much upbeat inflection as she could manage. "Tell him I'll be there at five. Whom should I ask for?"

"Don't worry about that. They'll be expecting you. Good luck."

Before Chey had punched the "End" button on her phone, Sam had already pulled up the restaurant's web page on her laptop and was studying the associated map. "This isn't going to be easy," she mumbled, looking at the eatery's location from a tactical point of view.

"The River Walk never is," Zach said flatly. "But we didn't have a lot of options. We're just going to have to bring in some help."

Zach watched Cheyenne drive off, the two rangers having spent the last hour doing their best to prepare her for tomorrow's meeting.

No sooner had her taillights vacated the coffee shop's parking lot, than the senior lawman turned to his partner and said, "You get to work on the equipment. I'm going to start making some calls for backup."

"Major Putnam isn't going to like this, Zach. I hope you've thought up a really good line of reasoning to convince him to pull personnel off the massacre case and point them toward a pervert banker."

"Who said I was calling the major?" the Texan smirked back. "I have a few friends that might be willing to help."

Sam wasn't pleased with where the operation was heading. "What the hell are you talking about, Zach? We need sworn peace officers involved in something like this, preferably Texas Rangers."

Zach shook his head, "Look, there's a distinct possibility that Mr. Carson's associate is just a rich dude that likes pretty ladies. Maybe he's into some weird kink, and the missing girls were too embarrassed to go home. Maybe they're still alive and enjoying the partying life on the man's private jet and private island. At this point, we just don't know what we are dealing with."

"Maybe. There's also a chance that the man is an ax murderer on a rampage."

"We're supposed to assume a person is innocent until proven guilty. Having the Texas Rangers come down on a wealthy man who is guilty of nothing more than being horny and having the money to satisfy his desires isn't the right move in my book."

Sam thrust her hands on her hips, a sure sign she wasn't going to give in quietly. "We have to protect Chey. And I mean *really* protect her. How are you going to do that without calling the major?"

"Let me make a few calls while you take care of the hardware. Afterward, if you're not happy with the team I recruit, then I'll call the major and plead our case."

Ranger Temple, after extended contemplation, agreed.

Zach pulled out his cell phone and dialed a number from his contacts. The call was answered on the third ring. "BB? This is Ranger Bass. I've got a little operation going on tomorrow in San Antonio, and I could use another man. Any chance you could get away and help out one of your old students?"

While he listened to the response, Zach flashed Sam an "I told you so," look. Shaking her head in frustration, she turned away and began working her own cell phone.

An hour later, Zach informed his partner that his team was in place. "We've got BB and Detective Gus Monroe from El Paso joining us in the morning. I think three rangers and a street-smart cop should be enough, don't you?"

"For Chey's sake, I sure hope so."

"How did your assignment work out?" Zach asked, wanting to change the subject.

"I've rounded up two micro GPS locator units, one of them disguised as a pair of earrings. The other we can put in her shoe. I also have two programmable button microphones with a 75-meter transmission range and encoded frequencies."

"Damn," Zach said, obviously impressed.

"The tech from Austin HQ is getting everything ready."

"Video monitoring?"

"We have two nano-cameras embedded in regular ink pens. They're older technology but will work. The tech at HQ said all the newer, smaller units had been checked out. We are going to have to get them inside the restaurant somehow."

"No problem. I can take care of that."

Sam's gaze drifted off for a moment as she mentally reviewed some stored checklist. "I think that's all we can do today."

"Agreed. Let's head for San Antonio. I want to scout the area around Titus and then get a good night's sleep."

"Lead on, oh, mighty fighter of crime," Sam teased.

As the two rangers drove toward the republic's third largest city, Sam noticed Zach seemed sullen and withdrawn.

"You worried about Chey?" she speculated.

"Yeah, but there's something else that's bothering me. Something about Chico's story that just doesn't make sense," the ranger admitted.

"Go on."

"The cartels are operating internationally; everybody knows that. We also know that there are places in the Middle and Far East where all kinds of heavy weapons are sold in open-air markets alongside slabs of beef and locally grown herbs. I've seen pictures of gun stores in Pakistan that offered everything from belt-fed weapons to Russian heavy mortars."

Sam didn't follow. "So?"

"So why take the risk of coming to Texas for firepower? The only thing we have to offer is automatic rifles, which wouldn't increase the cartel's offensive capabilities all that much. The whole scenario just doesn't make sense."

She contemplated his statement for a bit before responding, "I don't know about that. Having people able to spray all that lead surely scares the hell out of me, whether they bought the weapons here or overseas."

Nodding toward an upcoming exit, Zach said, "Let's stop and talk to an expert. You remember this place, don't you?"

Sam stared up at the sign announcing Florence, Texas. "Hell, yes, I remember. I spent several horrible weeks there while going through that boot camp everyone calls the academy. How could anyone forget?"

With a grin, Zach flipped on the truck's turn signal and maneuvered off the interstate.

The two rangers passed through the tiny burg of Florence, meandering south along Texas 195 until they reached a secondary county road labeled only with a small white sign designating it as 240.

A mile passed before a heavy, metal gate appeared across the roadway. Zach had to dig in the truck's console for his keycard.

The rangers were soon granted entry into the Department of Public Safety's Tactical Training facility.

Anyone wanting to become a trooper in the republic had passed through the same security fence, the location hosting part of the 23-week training program all such officers were required to attend.

The Florence facility, often referred to as simply "North," offered two areas of specialty training for the up and coming law enforcement recruit – driving and shooting.

Zach and Sam passed the main administration building and soon found themselves gazing across a huge open space consumed by what appeared to be a racetrack worthy of hosting an international Grand Prix. In addition to the extensive outer ring of pavement, the course was subdivided by multiple intersections and cross streets, all composed of different types of surfaces. It was one of the best premier, high-speed, driving facilities anywhere in the world.

As they continued, the two rangers soon approached what appeared to be three enormous, flat, empty parking lots. "That was my favorite part," Zach stated proudly, "the skid pads. That was a blast."

"Little boys love to play in the mud," Sam teased. "I suppose spinning a car around on wet concrete would be a dream come true."

They continued on, each remembering their own impressions of the academy. Next came the urban training area, complete with several blocks of streets laid out in a grid meant to mimic a common subdivision. Zach grinned when he noted the black stains on the white road-surface. He'd left his fair share of skid marks during the course, the sound of squealing tires and the smell of smoking rubber one of his fondest memories.

Finally, they arrived at the 40-acre firearms training facility. After parking, the two rangers made for the "clubhouse."

Once inside, Zach heard the booming voice of the man he was looking for long before he saw him. "I don't care if the bullets are made of kryptonite; the republic isn't paying that much for training rounds!"

The two rangers rounded a corner and found Captain Raymond Vickers bellowing into a cell phone, one arm spread wide in protest. "We don't need ballistic penetration! I don't give a horse's ass if the damn things will take out a battle tank. It only has to punch through paper. This is an educational facility, damn it, not a battleground."

Zach and Sam stood back, trying to let the busy man know their unscheduled visit wasn't any sort of emergency. They didn't have to wait long, the training officer ending his call with, "Fine. That will work. Yes. Yes, that's within my budget."

Vickers turned and faced the two rangers, his demeanor changing immediately. "Ranger Bass, Ranger Temple," he began with a hearty grin. "To what do we owe the honor?"

Zach extended his hand, the burly instructor vigorously pumping the tall ranger's limb. Sam received an identically enthusiastic greeting, the female ranger trying desperately not to show the pain that surged through her arm.

Captain Vickers was what Zach had once described as a "thick, steel-reinforced, brick wall" of a man. Barely six foot in height, the ex-Green Beret was powerfully built across the shoulders and chest. Yet, as he had demonstrated to countless cadets, the officer was extremely nimble and unbelievably quick. He was also one of the best shooters in the Western world.

"We're sorry to interrupt your day, Captain, but Ranger Temple and I are working on a case involving automatic weapons. We decided to seek the input of an expert … if you have a few minutes?"

"Sure," replied the training officer. "How can I help?"

The two rangers went on to explain the situation. "We assume most of the cartel's serious foot soldiers are ex-military. Recently, their operations have been planned and executed more like an infantry platoon than a bunch of street thugs. So would it be worth a lot of money and risk to upgrade to full auto blasters? Would it really buy them that much?"

Vickers nodded his understanding. "The short answer is no; it would not. Switching the average battle rifle to full auto may be fun, but the truth is that most professional soldiers rarely use that option. Back in the day when I served with the teams, we would have gotten our asses chewed for doing such a thing in all but the rarest of circumstances."

"What circumstances?" Sam asked.

"Suppressive fire is the most common. Trying to keep the enemy's head down while friendlies maneuver for advantage. About the only other good reason to engage the 'happy button' is if you're about to be overrun. Even then, it had better be a pretty dire situation."

Sam still wasn't convinced. "Why? What is the big drawback? It would seem like pumping a lot of bullets at a foe would be the smart thing to do?"

"Come on, I'll show you," Vickers grinned. "Let me get one of our carbines. The rifle range won't be occupied by a class for another hour."

A few minutes later, the trio was strolling past the pistol and maneuver ranges, Vickers carrying an M4 rifle along with a handful of magazines.

After adorning safety glasses and ear protection, the instructor handed Sam the weapon.

"Take lane one and put three shots into center mass," he commanded, pulling a timer from his belt. "I'll record the spread."

Having graduated from the academy a short time ago, Ranger Temple was up to the task. With smooth, graceful motions, she slammed a magazine home, racked the charging handle, shouldered the weapon, and fired.

Twice more the rifle roared, each shot less than a second apart. The lady ranger then flicked on the safety and glanced at her two male cohorts. "Well?"

"Nice shooting, Ranger Temple," Vickers grinned. "I can tell you've received some expert instruction," he winked. "You hit center mass three times in 2.2 seconds. Now, flip that weapon to full automatic and see how long it takes you to put three in the center on lane two."

Again, Sam repeated her well-practiced routine. This time, an arch of spent brass flew from the ejection port as she sprayed five, then six, then four more shots in short bursts. While the paper target was peppered with several more holes, there were only three in the kill zone.

"I see what you mean," Sam nodded, clearing the M4 and handing it back to Vickers. "The rifle vibrates against your shoulder and throws off your aim."

"It took you nearly four seconds on full auto, Ranger Temple," Vickers announced, checking his timer. "And you wasted half a magazine of ammunition inflicting the same basic hurt on the target. With a military unit that is engaged in battle, ammo is always precious. It goes so fast, and you never know when you're going to be resupplied. That's why the real pros don't flick that joy button very often. It buys you little and can cost you a lot."

"With an AK47, like the cartels typically use, spray and pray throws off your aim even more," Zach added. "The barrel on most of those weapons tends to ride up even higher with each round."

"Pretty soon, you're shooting an anti-aircraft gun," Vickers added.

"So why do so many people want fully automatic weapons?" Sam said, bafflement evident in her tone.

"People always want what they're told they can't have. Like I said before, there are some practical uses in a combat zone or when facing a larger force. But those circumstances are rare."

After taking a few minutes to thank their old instructor, Zach and Sam headed for the parking lot.

"Okay, I get what you're saying now," Sam admitted. "So what can the cartel possibly be after here in Texas? And even if it is automatic rifles, they can buy those just about anywhere and have them shipped in. What does the republic have that they want so badly?"

"I don't know," Zach replied, obviously troubled by the entire affair. "If I were going to try to overthrow the government, then heavy weapons like tanks or artillery would be what I'd want. On the other hand, Chico may have been completely full of shit. I'm beginning to think we've been barking up the wrong tree."

The drive to San Antonio added to the ranger's frustration. They hit Austin right at the peak of the afternoon rush hour, which equated to total gridlock.

The Texas capital had been experiencing enormous growth for nearly 30 years before the secession. High-tech companies had found a welcoming home in the centrally located city, some going so far as to refer to Austin as the "Silicon Valley of the Southwest."

At the edge of the Texas Hill Country, with a dryer climate than Houston or Dallas, the old state capital's booming growth had led to numerous infrastructure issues. The city struggled to expand highways, surface roads, sewage, and water treatment as the population kept increasing at double-digit rates.

After the secession, that frantic rate of growth nearly doubled, bringing twice as many problems along with it.

"How do these people deal with this every day?" Sam asked, peering around at 10 lanes of interstate that currently resembled a mall parking lot at Christmas.

"I ask myself that same question nearly every time we drive through here," Zach grumbled. "This reminds me of the few times I visited Washington, DC. I remember sitting in traffic and asking myself why would people choose this lifestyle? Is being so close to the seat of power really worth spending a quarter of your life stuck in gridlock?"

Sam pointed toward the distant skyline, which was monopolized by new high-rise office towers and dozens upon dozens of construction cranes. "Given everything they're building, I bet this is going to get even worse."

Grunting, Zach responded, "You know, I looked at housing down here not long ago. Unbelievable. It was like I was shopping for an apartment in New York or San Francisco. The prices have skyrocketed like crazy."

"And only because the political power base is here," Sam noted. "I guess Texas isn't all that much different than the U.S.A., no matter how hard we try to pretend we are different."

"Supply and demand," Zach nodded. "I hear Houston, Dallas, and just about every other larger town has the same issues. The cost of housing used to be one of Texas's primary draws. Before the split, we were always ranked among the best in affordability. Now, with all of the immigrants flooding in and the new construction, demand is driving the cost up everywhere. A lot of people are pissed about it."

"Maybe we should get out of law enforcement and into real estate speculation," Sam teased, trying to offset the frustration of the delay.

"Naw," Zach replied with a grin. "If I leave the rangers, I'm going to open a topless bar. That's where the real money is. You've always got a job, by the way," he winked.

"Thanks ... I think."

The next stop was ranger headquarters. Zach parked the vehicle, stretched back in his seat, and said, "You go in and fetch the equipment we need. I'll stay out here."

Sam thought it was odd. "You're scared you'll run into Major Putnam, aren't you?"

"No."

"Uh-huh."

Zach coughed and began his repartee, "The republic is in a state of crisis right now. I'm sure the major has more important things to do than hear about our conjecture and theories. The rangers were founded by men who acted independently, made their own decisions in the field, and exercised their best judgment. That's all we're doing, Ranger Temple."

"Uh-huh."

It was dusk when the duo finally arrived in the outskirts of San Antonio, and neither ranger was happy with the congestion and subsequent delay. "Damn it. I wanted to get a good look at that steakhouse in the daylight," Zach grumbled.

"I'm hungry. Are we there yet, Daddy? How much longer?" Sam whined, her imitation of a travel-weary child making Zach chuckle.

People from outside of Texas came to San Antonio mostly for the Alamo, which was the republic's single largest tourist attraction. Millions visited the historic mission and battleground every year, rambling through the gardens, small museum, and barracks where Santa Anna duked it out with Bowie and Travis. The Mexican general was to become the poster child for winning the battle but losing the war.

Texans, however, flocked to Alamo Town because they love the River Walk.

Residing one story below the downtown surface streets, the attraction is akin to an oasis beneath the city. For miles and miles, the San Antonio River meanders through the urban sprawl, flowing peacefully under dozens of bridges. The banks, lined with wide walkways, enormous bald cypress trees, and decorative landscaping, provide a cool, park-like atmosphere just beneath the hustle and bustle.

Built in the late 1930's with money from the Works Progress Administration or WPA, the River Walk was initially created to avoid deadly floods caused by the San Antonio River. Over the years and through several expansions, it had become the unofficial heart of the city.

Lined with theaters, restaurants, shops, and hotels, people came in droves to party, spend money, eat well, and stroll along the beautifully manicured river. There were even chauffeured boat tours and more extravagant dinner cruises drifting along the water.

Zach and Sam, however, had other reasons for visiting.

The two rangers checked into a mid-level hotel, an institution that always kept a few extra rooms available for government employees. Zach was ready to claim that they were food inspectors, but the clerk didn't seem to care.

Thirty minutes later, they met in the lobby, both ready to scout the area surrounding the meeting tomorrow. They crossed the bridge on St. Mary's Street and then descended two flights of wide, stone steps. It was as if they had been transported to an entirely different world.

The river wasn't wide, less than 70 feet across. Both banks were formed concrete, sometimes reinforced with various colors, shapes and sizes of limestone, granite, and bedrock quarried from the nearby Hill Country.

The sidewalk twisted right to the water's edge without any guardrails or safety devices that would have obstructed the openness or distracted from the view.

As the two rangers headed east along the winding waterway, they strolled past cafes, expensive restaurants, gift shops, jewelry stores, and practically every type of business they would expect to see on the city streets above.

Every so often, the duo encountered huge bald cypresses at the water's edge. Some were said to be several hundred years old, their massive canopies creating a tunnel-like effect of shade and cool air during the hottest of days.

Foliage and greenery were abundant, lush ferns often lining both sides of the walkway. Some of the bridges they passed under were completely covered in ivy vines, others sporting tasteful rows of hanging plants with carpets of flowers underneath.

The occasional fountain or statue added spice to the smorgasbord of hue and sound. In some places, brightly colored umbrellas lined the shores, providing additional respite for diners and those just wanting to sit and people watch.

Despite the seriousness of the upcoming meeting, both the lawmen couldn't help but feel some of their stress being absorbed by the tranquil surroundings. Zach was always amazed at how soothing the place was. The ranger couldn't decide if it were the water, vegetation, or some combination of factors beyond his reasoning. The "oasis within a city" just seemed to calm his nerves, no matter how taut or frayed.

They trekked for several blocks before Sam announced they had arrived at the prescribed address for Chey's meeting. Without being too obvious, Zach glanced left and right, but couldn't find any sign that advertised Titus. "You sure?" he asked, glancing at his partner.

"Yup."

The fact that the restaurant's location wasn't obvious didn't alarm the two rangers. Part of the River Walk's charm was the narrow stairwells, hidden nooks, and secluded plazas. In spots, it resembled a maze of Rome's back alleys passing through a matrix of 17th-century Spanish architecture.

It was Sam who spotted a gated, adobe brick staircase that led to an ancient-looking wooden door of Spanish design. Next to the heavy iron knocker was a small brass plaque that read, "Titus."

"Shit," Zach whispered, "That's not an easy place to observe. I was hoping for big, clear windows and lots of sidewalk seating."

"Let's walk around a bit," Sam suggested. "Maybe that's just the back entrance or something."

They returned to the surface level at the next bridge, the noise and car exhaust of San Antonio's streets greeting the two lawmen as if they had opened a door to a rock concert.

Ten minutes later, they had circled the block and cut through the only alley.

Like so much of the old city, Titus was sandwiched between two larger, newer structures. Part of its parent building had been converted to a street-view retail center while other sections had been divided into smaller shops along the river's bank. The result was a labyrinth of angles, corners, and a series of unmarked doors that could be anything from fire exits to delivery entrances. There was simply no way to be sure of the eatery's interior layout.

"This isn't good," Zach grumbled, stating the obvious.

"Should we have Chey cancel?" Sam pondered. "If we can't keep an eye on her, I don't think either of us will feel good about this."

Rubbing his chin, Zach reasoned, "If we knew there was only one way in and one way out, then I'd say it was worth a shot. Cartel boss or mafia Don, I don't think our mystery man is going to pull a gun and shoot her right in the middle of enjoying his filet mignon."

"How are you going to get inside without flashing a badge and forcing our way in? There's no way a judge would sign a warrant in time ... if ever."

"I've got an idea about that. I need to make a call first thing in the morning. Right now, let's find a sandwich, and then I need some sleep. We both need to be bright-eyed and bushy-tailed at sun-up."

Chapter 6

The next morning, the two rangers met early in the hotel's small restaurant for breakfast and coffee. Zach kept glancing at his watch as if waiting for the witching hour.

Finally, he reached for his cell and made a call.

Sam watched as her partner held the phone up to his ear. After a bit, he spoke, "Inspector Youngman, please." Then, apparently more time on hold before he continued, "Walt, this is Ranger Bass, how are you, sir?"

The lady ranger almost snorted a nose full of tea when Zach, listening to the droning response, rolled his eyes skyward and then stuck a finger-pistol to his head in a mock suicide.

"Sorry to hear that, Walt," Zach finally managed after nearly two minutes. "Hey, let me ask you a question. How long do you have before retiring? About two more years?"

Again, Inspector Youngman seemed to drone on and on. Zach was careful not to ask any more questions when the man finally took a breath.

"Say, I have to ask a favor for an ongoing investigation," Zach inserted. "I need to get inside one of your local restaurants and pretend I'm doing a health inspection."

Sam's eyes got big when her partner dropped that bomb. "Oh, you are a shit," she whispered. "And a damn creative one at that."

Another 10 minutes passed before Zach finalized arrangements with Mr. Walt Youngman. "He's going to call Titus and schedule the inspection in an hour. He said he's only been in the place once since issuing their permit last year. He found two issues with the fire suppression system, and the owners followed up less than 30 days later."

"That was very, very clever, Zach. I'm going to put that one in my repertoire of dirty cop tricks."

Zach waggled his eyebrows. "There's hardly a business that operates in any city that doesn't get visited by some sort of government employee at one point in time or another. A few years back, Walt was inside a new burger joint and saw some suspicious looking contents in the freezer. He called DPS, and I went with a couple of state troopers and checked it out. Sure enough, there were about 400 pounds of frozen weed mixed in with the hamburger patties and bags of French fries. I wrote the mayor a nice letter of appreciation from the rangers and gave Inspector Youngman credit for the felony bust. It pays to spread the joy."

"I bet he has it framed in his office," Sam grinned, reaching for the metal case at her feet. "Since you're going inside the restaurant, it would be good if you deposited a couple of our little helpers."

The lady ranger extracted what appeared to be two common ink pens. "These both contain a camera and microphone. They're the new models that use high-frequency burst transmissions ... just in case the bad guys are using electronic counter-measures. They have 120-degree views and directional microphones. The battery only lasts about two hours, but I can start them remotely once Chey is inside."

Zach took the devices and nodded. "I'll see if I can set these up in the right places. Anything else?"

"Not for the inside. I'm going to put two GPS locators and a microphone on Chey's person," she continued. "I will set up video recording on the restaurant's doors once we figure out where all of the exits are located. Other than that, it's typical cop stuff – mainly our eyes and ears."

The two officers continued discussing the surveillance package and the dozens of other details associated with the op. The fact that it was an untrained civilian meeting with the suspects made every little item far more complex.

After a time, Zach glanced at his watch and announced, "It's time to go meet with Walt. Ready?"

Inspector Youngman wasn't what Sam expected.

Anticipating a frumpy, older, slight-statue of a man with thick bifocals, she was surprised when Zach approached a middle-aged, slender fellow who was nicely dressed and quite good-looking. "So much for stereotypes," she whispered.

Not only was the city employee's appearance unexpected, so was his level of preparation. After introductions, he handed Zach a leather fold-over with a gold-colored badge inside. "Put your state ID card in the window, and no one will notice the difference."

Next, Walt produced a clipboard, complete with the city's insignia and several official-looking forms. "Try and take a few notes while we're inside," he advised.

The lady ranger watched from afar as the two approached Titus's front door and knocked with authority.

A distinguished looking Latino man answered, only taking a casual glance at both visitors' credentials. Youngman did all the talking. "We're here on a routine inspection for the city of San Antonio," he began. "We'd like to begin with the dining area."

Introducing himself as the maître d', the restaurant employee escorted his visitors to a small enclave that contained only one table. The theme and décor were obviously intended to remind diners of a hunting lodge. Expensive-looking art graced the wall, a fancy wine rack was located in one corner, and a large fireplace anchored one end. "There are five individual dining rooms," the fellow informed Zach and Walt. "What is it you wish to see?"

"Everything," Walt answered.

Zach knew instantly that he was in trouble. He only brought two cameras to plant. That would leave three seating areas unobserved. Those weren't good odds.

Again, Walt took the lead, surprising both Zach and the waiter by pulling out a chair and climbing to inspect a ceiling duct. It took one swipe of the inspector's finger to let their host knew he meant business.

Youngman stepped down from his elevated perch with a scowl creasing his face. He held up the nearly black finger to show the filth removed from the vent's grill. "This is right above the table, sir. I don't know about you, but I surely don't want such grime falling into my meal."

The maître d' was shocked, instantly stamping to the threshold and shouting harsh, Spanish instructions toward the rear of the establishment. Two younger men darted out, and in a matter of seconds, they removed and cleaned the offensive vent.

Walt ignored the efforts, his attention now focused on the dinnerware and place settings. Pulling a small device that resembled a flashlight from his jacket pocket, the inspector lifted a clear glass from the table and then flicked on a brilliant, blue-colored beam of light.

"I'm checking for detergent residue," the inspector informed the hovering, anxious waiter.

81

Zach casually backed out of the door and stepped quickly to the front reception area. There, residing on a small podium, was the restaurant's reservation book. "Maybe … just maybe," he whispered, reaching for the thick, leather-bound volume.

Scanning the pages, Zach found today's date. There was only one reservation for 5 PM. The name wasn't legible. The assigned dining room was. Chey would be meeting the mystery man in room #3.

Quickly closing the binder, Zach returned to find Walt inspecting the fireplace for some unknown code violation. The maître d' was sweating profusely.

Lifting his city-issued clipboard, Zach asked the waiter, "For our report, which dining room is this?"

"Number 5," the nervous fellow stammered.

"Thank you."

It took 20 minutes before the undercover duo managed to progress to what Zach assumed was the room where Chey would meet her dinner date.

Zach grunted when he entered #3, the ambiance obviously designed to mimic an Italian Bistro. Partially exposed bricks and raw plaster dominated one wall, the opposite sporting a well-done Renaissance mural. Like all of the previous enclaves, there was a small fireplace in the corner, the face and mantel adorned with an intricate tile mosaic. Chey would love it.

While Walt went through his routine, Zach was scanning for someplace to hide the cameras. The answer presented itself in short order.

Without the presence of natural light, the interior designers had little choice but to use silk ivy to accent the wall with exposed brick. The high-quality fake foliage was extremely thick and sturdy, covering a large section of the vertical surface.

While he was sure everyone's attention was focused on Walt's persistent search for code violations, Zach removed one of the cameras from his jacket, pretending to check the artificial vines for dirt or other nasties. A few moments later, the pen-camera was securely resting in the dense greenery.

It took a few cautious moves to properly align the barely-protruding lenses and make sure the device was aimed at the table. The ranger was confident no one had noticed.

He found a suitable hide for the backup device as Walt was turning over the plush chairs and examining the bottoms. *What the hell is he looking for*, Zach wondered as he strolled around the room. *Bubblegum?*

Above Zach's head was a bookshelf, complete with several expensive-looking, leather-bound titles. The backup camera was soon peeking out between two of the volumes.

The inspection continued for another 50 minutes, most of the remaining time spent in the kitchen. The food preparation area was where the ranger found the most important information of the entire expedition – the fire exit.

Pretending to examine the emergency release bar, Zach pushed opened the door and stepped outside into the alley. He quickly counted doors and got his bearings. They would have to make sure this exit was covered.

Walt informed their host that the establishment would be receiving his report via certified mail within 10 days. Since no significant violations were discovered, the restaurant would have 30 days to address any citations.

The duo left, walking briskly to Youngman's city-issued automobile and driving away. After thanking the inspector for a job well done, Zach shook his hand and climbed out at the next light. "I'll let you know if we find anything interesting," the ranger promised.

Returning to the rendezvous point, Zach found Sam sitting under a multi-colored umbrella, sipping on a glass of what appeared to be lemonade. Next to the lady ranger was a smiling BB and a steaming cup of coffee.

"Look who found me," Sam smiled as her partner approached.

"That didn't take much tracking skill at all," the old ranger grinned. "Hard to miss such a beautiful woman, especially one who's wearing a gun."

Detective Gus Monroe arrived a few hours later, the drive from El Paso encompassing several hundred miles of cross-republic travel. He was exactly what Zach had expected.

As introductions were made, Zach studied the one unknown member of his team.

Gus was in his mid-50s with a high-and-tight buzz cut of gray hair and the eyes of a man who had seen it all and was surprised by none of it. Zach judged the officer to be in pretty good physical condition and able to hold his own in a scuffle.

After everyone had settled down and played the "do you know so-and-so," game, Sam cleared her throat and got down to business.

Flipping her notebook computer around so everyone could see, she began by showing the satellite view of the restaurant and surrounding cityscape.

"There are only two ways in or out," Zach chimed in, pointing to where the two entrances were located on the overhead view. "Sam and I will pretend to be a couple enjoying the River Walk and cover the front. BB, you figure out a way to cover the fire exit and the alley. Gus, you're our quick reaction force. I want you sitting in your car on the street, ready to move to either door if there's a problem."

"Have you contacted San Antonio PD and let them know there is a surveillance op going on in their backyard?" Gus asked.

It was a fair question. "No," Zach replied. "While I know some good officers on the local force, what I don't know is how influential or connected our mystery guest might be. I wouldn't want any loose lips sinking Cheyenne's ship."

"Besides," Sam added, "We're not even sure our unknown person is even a worthy suspect."

Gus twirled his pen in thought, finally offering, "Look, I know you rangers deal with some high-profile cases and all, but speaking from my experience as a local cop, there have been times when I would have appreciated a head's up on activity in my jurisdiction. I know a guy on the local force … a captain. I trust this man completely. How about I give him a courtesy call and let him know we're partying on his turf?"

Zach and Sam exchanged troubled glances. "Might be a good insurance policy if things go really badly," she offered.

The senior ranger finally nodded his agreement. "No details," he said to Gus. "No location specifics, timelines or anything else. Just give our general operating area, team size, and act like it's no big deal."

"Agreed," Gus nodded.

The initial briefing took another 20 minutes, and then the foursome left Zach's hotel room in order to walk the perimeter.

It was BB who had the next recommendation. Pointing only with the brim of his hat, the old ranger remarked, "I think I need so go shopping."

Zach followed the old-timer's gaze to a second-story window, a large sign advertising Long Trails Western Wear and Tack Accessories. "You *are* looking a little seedy, BB. Maybe some new duds will spruce you up a bit ... help your chances with the señoritas."

Turning to smile warmly at Sam, the team's oldest member said, "Might help my luck with the local gals as well."

The four lawmen returned to the hotel to find a nervous Cheyenne pacing in the lobby.

Zach's stomach knotted when he saw her, the reaction a mixture of jealousy and nerves. The fact that his girl was decked out and gussied up to meet another man bothered the ranger more than he had anticipated.

She wore a royal blue dress that exposed her shoulders and left little to the male imagination as to the assets beneath. A sparkling necklace was draped around her neck, accented with hoop earrings and absolutely perfect makeup.

Although the dress hung to just above her knees, Zach couldn't help but notice the significant slits sewn into both sides of the garment. Chey's long, tan legs attracted the male eye like iron to a magnet.

Gus's reaction to the beauty was to be expected, the El Paso detective leaning close to Zach and whispering, "No wonder the suspect is interested in her. Hell, if I was a few years younger, I'd have to think about kidnapping that young lady myself."

Zach started to let his fellow officer in on the unmentioned detail that the leggy blonde was his girlfriend, but before the words came out, Cheyenne had rushed over and was kissing him on the mouth. "How's my favorite ranger?" she greeted with a flirtatious tone.

"I'm good. You ready?" Zach asked, trying to keep things business-like and professional.

A now red-faced Gus retreated for the elevator, closely followed by a grinning BB. "Do you feel as old as I do?" the retired ranger whispered to the embarrassed detective.

A few minutes later, all five were in Zach's hotel room. The lead ranger started again from the top, taking extra time to let Chey know where everyone was going to be stationed, and what she should do in case things went wrong.

Just 60 minutes before her designated rendezvous time, Sam took Cheyenne back to the lady ranger's room in order to hook up the electronics.

After a short time, the two women returned, the only noticeable difference in Chey's outfit being a different set of earrings. The model twirled with a giggle saying, "Do I look like a police snitch?"

Sam passed out the radios, each of the small transmitters looking like a Bluetooth headset commonly used with civilian cell phones. The team did a quick equipment check by moving down the hall and testing the device's signal.

After giving everyone a final chance to ask last minute questions, they gathered at the door. The team was eager to be in place early in order to study all of the guests arriving at the steakhouse.

Chey gave Zach a quick peck on the cheek right as the other cops strolled out of the room. "See you in a bit," he said, returning the embrace.

"Wish me luck," she said, clearly still on edge.

"Good luck, and remember – if it gets to be too much … if you feel like things are getting out of control, then just get the hell out of there. Just kick off those heels and sprint for the door like those foot races we had as kids."

"I used to outrun your skinny ass all the time," she teased, a hint of the old tomboy coming back into her tone. "At least until you were about 13."

Zach grinned, the short flash of memories helping both of them relax. "Trust your instincts, Chey. Run like hell if that's what feels right. This operation isn't worth a single hair on your beautiful head."

"Thanks, Zach. I'll try not to let you down. Remember, I want to hurt these jerks just as much as you do. See you at five."

With their arms hooked together, Zach and Sam strolled beside the river just like dozens of other couples enjoying a late afternoon walk.

Sam was the better actor, pointing at the sights and pretending to stop and window shop along the route. Zach had little trouble fulfilling his role as the boyfriend who didn't care about the dress on the mannequin.

The lady ranger made a big deal out of wanting to stop at the small café that provided a direct line of sight to Titus's front door. Appearing reluctant, Zach finally agreed to sit at one of the tables. Both rangers ordered a glass of iced tea from the attentive waiter.

"I'm in place," Gus's voice sounded in Zach's earpiece.

A few moments later, BB transmitted, "I can't believe the prices in this place. $600 for a damn hat?" The two riverside rangers grinned, both feeling a little better that everyone had managed their posts.

Zach spied the four men approaching along the river well before they arrived at the gate and stairs leading to the steakhouse. Something about their manner and dress raised the hair on his arms. "I bet that's them," he whispered to Sam, pointing only with his eyes.

Pretending to adjust her chair for more shade, Sam managed to get a clear view of the foursome. With a quick adjustment of her sunglasses, the ranger began videotaping the new arrivals.

After surveilling criminals for over a decade, Sam wanted to give whoever invented sunglasses with a built-in camera a huge hug. Practically unnoticeable, the tiny lenses appeared to be just another screw holding the frame together. The memory card was behind her ear. The microphone nearly invisible.

She didn't have to focus, adjust, or figure out some clever way to hide the camera while undercover. She simply looked at whatever she wanted to record.

The four men were dressed in very expensive-looking clothing, all of the gentlemen flashing freshly shined dress shoes and top of the line sport coats. The guy who seemed to be in charge was wearing a tie. Two of his "friends" were carrying Italian designer briefcases.

To the average onlooker, they appeared to be a small squadron of businessmen out for an after work cocktail. Zach, however, wasn't the average observer.

He immediately spotted several details that he referred to as "gangsterisms." The flash of bling. A bulge under a jacket that might disguise a pistol or sub machine gun. Just a bit too much bravado in their steps. But what really set them apart were their eyes.

As the foursome drew closer, Zach followed their eyes more than anything. No two of the men looked in the same direction, each taking a quadrant and scanning intensely for threats. The ranger noted they focused high and low, left then right. They were professionals. They were coiled for violence, looking for work.

When the obvious fifth member of their party came into view, Zach was almost certain he was surveilling the security team for a cartel boss of some very high rank. The trailer was 20 feet behind the main group, an extra precaution that only the most experienced units employed.

Sam spotted the sixth member of the detail, sitting only two tables away from the rangers. He had come early, scouting the route. After she made eye contact with Zach, the senior ranger studied number six and nodded to his partner. "We're in over our heads here," he whispered.

Sam pretended to receive a cell phone call, holding up her smartphone as she notified the rest of the team. "We have five serious security types and one primary," she stated into the microphone. "Stand by."

"Does the primary have a short limp from his left leg?" BB's voice responded. "Remember the tracks by the Rio Grande."

Zach focused like a laser, and sure enough, there was an odd hitch in the jefe's gait. "I'll be damned," he whispered.

The man next to the rangers stood suddenly. For a moment, Zach thought their surveillance had been detected. Reaching for his .45, the Texan was tensing for combat when Chey's blue dress entered the corner of his vision. The bodyguard moved to greet her, a warm smile on his face.

"Are you Cheyenne?" the man asked with only a slight accent.

"Yes," the model replied suspiciously. "And you would be?"

"I'm sorry for startling you, Ma'am. I am here to escort you to the steakhouse. My apologies, but my employer is extremely conscientious regarding security matters, and there are a few basic preventative steps that are required before you dine with him."

In one way, Zach was impressed. On the other hand, the high and mighty protection detail was having a conversation not six feet away from two Texas lawmen. Their bad.

Luck would appear to be on their side, and the ranger knew that sometimes good fortune was enough to carry the day.

Chey was politely escorted to the stairwell leading to Titus. At the top, outside the ornate door, another of the goon squad appeared, this time with some sort of electronic wand. As one man searched the model's purse, the other imitated an airport screener and ran the detector up and down the blue dress.

Then, without further issue, they opened the door, and Chey was allowed entry.

"I'm turning on the cameras now," Sam announced, reaching into her oversized bag for a laptop.

"No," Zach snapped. "These guys are very sophisticated. Wait just a bit longer."

"I've got one of the no-necks outside in the alley keeping watch," BB's voice informed them over the radio. "He's a big sum-bitch, too. Do I get extra pay if I have to work up a sweat kicking his ass?"

Sam's fingers were flying over the keyboard. "I'm sending the video we recorded to Austin. Let's hope we can get an ID on these guys."

Zach was worried. "We're out of our league here. I think we should call for help. I didn't expect a detail that large and that skilled."

"Want me to call Major Putnam?"

The Texan considered his partner's suggestion for a few moments and then shook his head. "We still can't be positive this guy is a criminal. He might just be ultra-wealthy and ultra-paranoid. Remember, innocent until proven guilty."

Sam didn't agree, her frown signaling the disapproval.

After a few seconds, Zach keyed his microphone. "Gus, can you call your captain friend and ask him to send over three or four of his better guys to our neck of the woods?"

"Sure," replied the detective. "On it right now."

The senior ranger's gaze switched to the ornate door and then to Sam. "Okay, turn on the hardware, and let's see what's going on."

Chey was cursing her wet palms as she was escorted into the darkness of Titus. "Right this way, Madam," the maître d greeted.

With her eyes still adjusting to the low light, she was shown into the Italian Bristol room, and for a moment, she was certain a whiff of Zach's aftershave lingered in the air. That one, brief connection helped settle her nerves.

A man was already seated. He rose sharply, smiled, and stepped closer as she was shown in. "My name is Vincent," he announced. "Thank you for having dinner with me this evening."

Chey offered her hand, which the charming gent immediately kissed. For a moment, she thought he was going to click his heels together during the act, but that didn't happen.

Their waiter held her chair and unfolded her napkin. "I've taken the liberty of ordering a pre-dinner wine. I hope you'll find a Montrachet Grand Cru acceptable."

Chey decided to be honest, "I have no idea what that is, Vincent. I'm afraid my knowledge of wines is rather primitive."

His response was an absolutely blank stare, and for a moment, the young beauty thought she'd blown the interview before it had even begun.

After a long pause, he smiled. "I like honesty. Someone with your charm has no need of pretense. I think you'll find the wine a wonderful experience."

With her eyes adjusting to the dimness, Chey took a moment to study her host. She estimated he was in his late 30s, early 40s. He had a lighter complexion than many Latinos, the kind that made it difficult to tell how much was suntan, and how much was genetics.

Her sense was that he was very fit, like a swimmer or runner. He wasn't nearly as tall as Zach, probably just a little over six feet. His teeth were almost too white, the man's haircut and mustache groomed to perfection. She could tell his suit had been custom fit, the cloth of extraordinary quality.

What drew the model's attention most were his eyes. They were dark pools of confidence, resonating with the self-esteem of wealth. Chey had seen plenty of well-to-do men in her career, and the man seated across from her was a prime example of the breed.

There was something else about his scrutiny, however, some trait that was unlike anything she had ever experienced. It took her a moment to identify the attribute, and when she did, the cold fog of fear entered her core.

Years ago, as a child, she'd gone hiking in Big Bend National Park. Cheyenne, always the rebel, had wandered off the trail, seeking a high formation of rocks visible in the distance.

Finally achieving the objective, she found a flat rock and reclined there, enjoying her victory and admiring the hard-earned view.

She'd been drinking from her canteen when some sixth sense alerted Chey she was being watched. Turning slowly to scan her surroundings, she encountered a mountain lion standing less than 20 feet away. It was an experience that she would never forget.

For over a minute, human and puma maintained eye contact. To the Texas teen, it had seemed like hours before the big cat had turned and vanished into the rocks.

Chey recalled the animal's eyes and the emotionless trance of the predator. To the cougar, she was nothing but a hunk of meat … a potential meal … a strange occurrence on the high formation. There was no anger, mercy, fear, or caring – only intensity.

Now, in the fanciest restaurant she'd ever visited, Chey sensed the same coldness in Vincent's gaze. She was nothing but a potential to satisfy a need. There was no compassion, intrigue, or disdain – only intensity.

Outside, less than 70 yards away, Sam and Zach were listening and watching intently. "Who is this guy? We need an ID … and quick."

The lady ranger was connected to multiple law enforcement databases, her hands flashing across the keyboard as she tried various searches. "I'm getting zero hits of any cartel bosses named Vincent. We need more information."

As if on cue, the two rangers heard Chey's voice streaming through the listening devices, "So tell me, Vincent, where are you from originally?"

"I was born in a small village that you've never heard of," he answered. "It is a settlement in the mountains, studded with juniper and white oak. As a boy, I would ride the high meadows on a 16-hand gelding who was sure-footed and always brought me home. The air and water were clean and invigorating. There are times when I miss that simple life."

By accident or design, the mention of horses was a lure Chey couldn't resist. For the first time that evening, the true sparkle of her eyes showed through. "What was the gelding's name?"

"Angel," came the quiet reply of a man drifting somewhere in his past.

91

Cheyenne wanted to change the subject, sensing something melancholy brewing in her host. Still, she was on comfortable ground talking about horses. "How long did you have Angel?" she asked innocently.

An odd smile pulled at Vincent's lips, the expression sending another chill down Chey's spine. That sensation soon became an outright horror. "Only a short time, I'm afraid," he replied, sipping lightly from his wine glass. "A drought struck our village, followed by an extremely harsh winter. There was no food. Angel fed many families."

The young model was shocked, choking on the mouth full of wine slipping past her lips. It wasn't only the tale, but the telling. Vincent showed no emotion, no regret or anger. Something about the delivery was cold, hollow, and frightening.

"I'm fortunate that I enjoyed her company for as long as we had together," Vincent continued. "She was very much like you – a beautiful image to behold."

Cheyenne managed to mumble a quiet, "Thank you," just as one of the bodyguards entered the room. "Excuse me, Jefe, but we have detected a disturbing signal."

"Turn them off!" Zach snapped at Sam. "Turn off the electronics – right now!"

Again the lady ranger's hands were darting across the keyboard as Zach watched the still streaming video feed. A man appeared on camera, holding some sort of electric device that looked like a miniature tennis racket strung with copper-colored wire. The picture went blank.

"Shit, shit, shit," Zach cursed, rising from the table and reaching for his weapon. "I don't think you turned them off fast enough. Let's go!"

Inside Titus, the security man stalked slowly around the room, scanning the walls, table, fireplace, and even the ivy. Chey was next.

A series of green lights illuminated on the device as the man passed them over her earrings. The bodyguard inhaled sharply and then stared directly at his boss, snapping a string of staccato Spanish.

Everything seemed to happen at once.

The room was flooded with Vincent's security team, muscular men hustling in all directions. She heard someone say, "Take her with us," and then her earrings were ripped from her lobes at the same moment strong hands pinned her arms.

"I've got movement in the alley," came BB's voice. "A large van just pulled up. Something's wrong."

"Gus! Gus!" Zach shouted, running for the front door. "Block the alley! Don't let them get out."

Zach and Sam, weapons drawn and badges exposed, were running for the restaurant's front door when a dark head appeared above them on the stairs. "El Rinche! El Rinche!" the guard screamed, using the Spanish slang for the Texas Rangers.

Another head appeared, quickly followed by the barrel of a gun. "Down!" Zach yelled, raising his pistol to return fire.

Zach spotted a Glock pistol, the magazine extending far beneath the meaty hand that grasped the weapon. "Oh shit!" the ranger managed to bark, diving hard. A hellfire of burning lead rained down on the stone stairs.

A seemingly endless stream of bullets flew at the two rangers as the man above emptied the 33 rounds through the Glock model 18 pistol. Rock and concrete splinters filled the air, and the 9mm rounds whacked and thwacked all around the two lawmen.

Then it stopped.

"He's reloading!" Zach shouted, centering his aim on the wooden door, sure that the thug was using it for cover. As his finger tightened on the trigger, he tried to calculate if the thick barrier would stop his .45 caliber slugs. There was only one way to find out.

The ranger squeezed off four shots, small white specs showing where his rounds were striking the ornate door. Before Zach saw her, Sam had come up beside him on the stairs and loosed another two rounds from her weapon.

"Get back!" he warned, moving to shove Sam to the safer side of the stone steps. He was too late.

Again the barrel appeared, a steady bright strobe of death spitting from the muzzle. Stone shrapnel and ricocheting lead filled the air as Zach tried to push Sam out of the way.

Sam felt like a power hitter's baseball bat struck her leg, and then a red pain like fire worked its way through her nervous system. She knew she'd been hit at the same moment the limb refused to answer her commands.

Zach felt his partner's body jolt from the impact as he flung her against the rock wall of the staircase. He knew she'd been wounded before her yelp of pain reached his ears.

"Where?" he shouted as he turned and began pouring rounds into the door above. "Where are you hit?"

"My leg! Oh, fuck that hurts! Damn it!"

Zach's pistol locked back empty. As he reached for a refill, Sam shoved her weapon at his hand. "Here, use this!"

They exchanged guns, Zach snap firing until Sam's blaster was empty. By then, she was handing him back his own weapon with a fresh mag. *What a woman,* he thought. *That's why she's a ranger.*

"How bad is it?" he yelled over the thunder of his shots.

"I'll live, but walking isn't an option," her brave voice announced. "I think the bone's broken."

Again, the maelstrom of lead rained down from above, the shooter exposing more of himself to get a better angle on the rangers. The shots were getting closer. Zach found himself pinned, wishing the man trying to kill them had slept through geometry.

"Officer down! Officer down on the stairway!" he remembered to broadcast over the radio.

Chey was a country girl, raised on a ranch and no stranger to physical labor. Yet, despite her excellent athletic conditioning, she found herself helplessly sandwiched between two granite-like walls of muscle. She tried to struggle, kick, and even bite one of her captors, all to no avail. "You scum sucking polecats.... I'm going to kick your sorry asses," she growled during the struggle.

The security men ignored her.

She was herded through the restaurant, Vincent's men hustling to get their boss clear of the now-constant roar of gunfire streaming from the restaurant's lobby.

Just as Chey and her two handlers burst through the back door, a strong voice yelled, "Freeze! Police! Drop your weapons!"

Chey was thrust against the side of a van, and then the roaring clap of a gunshot exploded by her ear. Another shot followed, the narrow, high brick walls serving to amplify the deafening assault. The alley erupted in chaos.

The man next to her went down, both of his hands flying to his face as a red cloud of mist filled the air behind the henchman's skull. Another weapon roared nearby, its sound reminding Chey of her father's chainsaw when it needed oil.

She watched another of Vincent's men fall, the fellow screaming in pain as he rolled on the ground. Voices were shouting in English and Spanish. People were moving in confusing blurs of color. Bullets whizzed and pinged off metal and brick.

Then rough hands were shoving her toward the van's open door. Instinct told Chey she didn't want to be inside. With a desperate grasp, she clutched the side of the opening and held on with an adrenaline-powered grip.

The van started moving, the noise of its revving engine now competing with the firefight all around her. Chey was being dragged, her feet bouncing along the pavement as her arms refused to let go of the door.

Then, out of nowhere, she spied Gus's face and arm reaching for her. Some portion of her brain identified the detective as a friend. He was running hard, trying to keep up. She let go with one hand, reaching for the safety of his outstretched arm.

She realized she was falling then, feeling suspended in midair as her forward momentum bled off. It was okay. She was calm. She was nearly in Gus's friendly arms.

Her finger touched his; then his strong grip was closing around her hand. She saw a smile form behind his eyes ... and then his head snapped back as his ball cap flew into the air.

Chey hit the ground hard, rolling like a rag doll as the rear wheels of the van passed right in front of her face. Then there was something else in her floundering arms. Something softer than the painful pavement and blacktop of the alley. Some cushion to diminish the beating her body was taking as she tumbled along the concrete and asphalt.

Finally, she stopped moving. Her brain raced to check her limbs and torso, trying to sort out the multitude of pain impulses that threatened to overwhelm rational thought.

Chey finally opened her eyes. Gus laid next to her, his eyes devoid of light, his skin the color of a white bedsheet. A pool of blood puddled where his dark hair should have been. The top of the detective's head had been disintegrated.

Cheyenne's very soul ached as she struggled to fill her lungs with air and shrieked in horror.

After making sure Sam's leg wasn't going to bleed out, Zach ascended to the top of the stairs when he heard Chey's distant scream.

A quick flash of satisfaction passed through the ranger's mind when he stepped over one of the Glock-shooters lying on a crimson-stained patch behind the splintered door. Obviously, the ranger's slugs had penetrated more than the thick wood.

It seemed to be taking him forever to clear the restaurant and its five small dining rooms. Then he was in the kitchen, scanning the frightened, huddled cooks and waiters who seemed in shock.

Zach could see bodies lying in the alley through the still-open back door.

There was one of the thugs. Another security man. Gus.

"Oh my God … Gus … no! Oh, Lord … no," Zach was mumbling as he forced his eyes away from the detective and back to sweeping the alley. He spotted Chey's blue dress, a look of sheer terror on his girl's face as she scooted and crawled away from the dead cop.

Seeing no threat in the narrow lane, Zach rushed to Cheyenne's side. "Are you hurt?"

She seemed unable to take her saucer-like eyes off of Gus. Her mouth moved, but no sound came from her throat.

Zach scanned her torn and soiled dress. He saw scrapes, minor cuts, and a couple of red welts. No bullet holes. "Chey!" he barked, "Look at me!"

Finally, his voice made it through the haze that controlled her mind. She looked at Zach, back at Gus, and then her eyes began watering. "Oh, Zach…. Oh, God…. He's … he's … Zach, he's dead."

Zach holstered his weapon and gently took her head between his hands. "You're okay, baby. It's okay. Help is coming."

Sirens were now echoing through the concrete canyons of downtown San Antonio, no doubt due to the hundreds of cells phones dialing 9-1-1 from the area surrounding the firefight.

It then dawned on the ranger that he didn't know the whereabouts of the remaining suspects. He pulled himself away from the distraught woman and said, "I'll be back in a second. Stay right here."

Again drawing his weapon, Zach sprinted toward the street where BB had been stationed. As he rounded the corner, he observed several people surrounding a man lying on the sidewalk. It was BB. He was trying to stand … alive … breathing.

Zach, scanned right and left, but couldn't see any other suspicious vehicle. He knew he was looking for a van, but had no idea of the color, make, model or year.

Holstering his weapon and flashing his badge, Zach scurried up to BB's side, finding the old ranger nursing a couple of serious-looking cuts on his head and arm. "You okay?"

"Yeah, damn it, I'm fine. They are in a white service van. I didn't get the plates. I think it was a Dodge. They tried to run over me."

Two San Antonio squad cars came to a squealing stop just then, both officers exiting with weapons drawn. Zach held his badge up high and informed the arriving reinforcements, "Texas Ranger! Texas Ranger! I need an APB right now … white van … damaged front end. Multiple armed and dangerous. Extreme caution."

One of the officers nodded while reaching for his radio.

"What the fuck is going on here?" questioned the other cop as another SAPD cruiser arrived.

Zach didn't answer. Instead, he waved the uniformed officer toward the alley. "Multiple causalities back here. All active shooters are in that van. We're going to need at least five meat wagons and two teams of EMTs. Direct the first ambulance to the steps on the River Walk side. There is an officer down at that location."

For Zach, the next two hours passed in the blink of an eye.

He watched Sam being loaded into an ambulance, thankful his partner's life was in no danger. Shortly thereafter, He repeated a similar scene with BB. The retired ranger didn't want medical attention, but the EMTs couldn't get the deep lacerations on his head to stop bleeding.

"At least, the scar from the staples will give me a good story to tell at the cantina," the old man told Zach as they were lifting him into the back of an emergency vehicle.

Chey was okay, surrounded by a virtual sea of uniformed SAPD. Zach had to grunt at the amount of attention his girlfriend was receiving, convinced the torn blue dress had something to do with the adoring, protective throng.

The worst part … the chapter that he dreaded most was the removal of Gus's body. As Zach watched the sheet-covered corpse being loaded, a million thoughts rushed through the ranger's troubled mind. He remembered the episode with Buck and the horrible experience of his friend's funeral.

The next hour was spent in a whirlwind of reports, investigation, interviews, and basically repeating his story over and over and over again.

Throughout it all, Zach kept asking the local cops about the van. After 15 minutes had passed without the suspects' vehicle being found, the ranger was frustrated. At 30, he was pissed. When one hour had elapsed, he was grumbling about the incompetence of the local authorities.

Zach's temper was beginning to simmer. He wanted to find that van, track down the men inside, and put an end to the entire affair. He was convinced Vincent was the man being escorted when the Marines were massacred. He was also confident that the suspect was up to something far more involved than just buying a few truckloads of automatic rifles and sneaking them back across the border.

Just then, Zach glanced up and observed Major Putnam walking his way. Alongside was a very unhappy looking SAPD officer wearing a uniform covered in medals, gold rank insignias, and more stripes than the ranger could count.

"Now, I'm in some serious shit," the ranger whispered, not really caring. "When the local boys bring out the dress blues, you know someone wants to chew ass all the way to the tailbone."

Putnam wasted no time getting down to business, "Report, Ranger Bass."

Zach did as ordered, recapping the events prior to the shootout. It was clear from both of the senior cops' faces that they were expecting more detail. The local honcho expressed his displeasure first, "Why wasn't my department informed of this operation, Ranger?"

"We did, sir. I ordered Detective Monroe to inform a local contact of his about our presence and location."

The comeback didn't work. "Yes ... yes, I've already heard about that half-hearted attempt to cover your ass. You and your little band of misfits just shot up this city's primary economic engine. Every businessman along the River Walk is raising hell about the negative impact this event will produce once it hits the press. They are afraid it will discourage tourism and hurt the city's image. The mayor is pissing venom and calling President Simmons as we speak."

Zach was at the end of his rope. He stepped toward the older officer and growled, "I am a sworn, active-duty Texas Ranger. That *little band of misfits* as you call them included two other rangers, plus a highly respected detective associated with the case. One of those *officers* lost his life in the line of duty. I suggest you show a little respect, *sir*."

The old cop wasn't used to anyone talking back to him. His jowls turning red, he pointed a finger at Zach and barked, "Respect? Why should I respect a bunch of cowboys coming in and shooting up my city? You had no authorization to do that. Even your boss here didn't know what you were doing in my town. If you want respect, son, you should learn to show a little. I think you wandered off the reservation. I think you are a loose and dangerous cannon."

Zach boiled over. He moved in close, almost touching noses with the local bigwig. "I don't care about tourism, or your mayor, or your public relations problem! That's not my job. I am trying to catch international criminals and potential terrorists. So pin that fucking ego on your chest with the rest of that junk and get the fuck out of my face!"

Putnam noticed that the confrontation had drawn the attention of several local officers, as well as the two rangers the major had brought from Austin. Wise and experienced, the senior officer decided it was best for all involved to de-escalate the situation. "Ranger Bass," he said, his controlled voice firm but calm as he stepped between the two irate men. "A word please.... Over there."

Zach was a good trooper and broke eye contact with his antagonist. When the two rangers were some distance away, Putnam said, "I know you didn't end up in this situation without good reason. Now would be a good time for you to explain that to me."

Nodding, Zach decided to play his ace. "Vincent ... the man in the restaurant was the man who crossed at Eagle's Nest. It was his men that shot up the Marines. I'm convinced of that, sir."

Putnam was stunned, and that wasn't an easy place to take the grizzled, old lawman. "Why?" was all the senior ranger managed to utter.

Zach recounted the haphazard investigation quickly, starting with Cheyenne's call a few days ago and ending with Vincent's limp. "These guys weren't some mid-level cartel thugs, sir. They were about the best I've ever seen, and that fits with the shooters that shot up the Marines. I think we're dealing with something a lot more serious than even Chico could have known."

"You played one hell of a hunch, Ranger," Putnam said after his man had finished.

For a moment, Zach thought he was in serious trouble, but then his boss nodded. "I've played worse hands and solved a case or two."

"We need to find that van, sir, and I'm not convinced the locals are giving it an all-out effort."

Again, Putnam contemplated his subordinate's words. "Let me work on that." Then the major turned to look at the red-faced cop behind them. "In the meantime, I suggest you finish your report and continue with the investigation … elsewhere."

The San Antonio police found the van 20 minutes later. It had been abandoned only three blocks away.

Zach rushed to the site, a public parking garage under a mid-rise office building. While the ranger was anxious to inspect the getaway vehicle, the search would have to wait until it was deemed free of any booby-traps.

The parade of frustration continued, the van identified as having been stolen from Houston the day before the Marines had been gunned down.

The license plates were another sign of the criminals' sophistication. Three sets of tags were found inside the stolen unit, each equipped with rare-earth magnets so they could be switched at a moment's notice. All of the numbers were registered to white vans of various makes and years. Zach assumed the trail would lead to junkyards or the owners of legitimate vans who hadn't noticed their plates being switched in the middle of the night.

The ranger was pissed, frustrated, and embarrassed. He'd underestimated his opponent, and now BB, Sam, and Gus had paid the price. About the only thing he'd salvaged out of the entire operation was keeping Chey out of the clutches of some clearly dangerous men. Even at that, the event had left the woman rattled and shaken. Zach didn't blame her.

Yet the investigation was progressing. The encounter along the River Walk had shaken loose dozens of leads. Already, Putnam was assigning ballistics experts to process the shell casings and recovered weapons. Zach had heard his boss order other rangers and troopers to begin running down a plethora of clues and possibilities.

Search warrants were being sworn out all over the republic. It was to be a dragnet of immense proportions – a massive undertaking all across the territory. Everything was subject to review – from the restaurant's phone records to dozens of video security camera recordings in the area.

Zach suddenly changed his mind. Rather than stand and watch the CSI techs pour over the van, the ranger decided to point his horse in a new direction. He wanted to talk to Mr. Carson. The banker knew something about Vincent, and Zach planned on "extracting" whatever information that was. Besides, given the level of professionalism the crooks had shown so far, it was doubtful any DNA samples, hotel room keys, or matchbook covers were forgotten inside the stolen vehicle.

Putnam was handling the public relations with the SAPD, which made Zach respect his superior even more. The gruff, old bastard was hardheaded, narrow-minded, and often lacking the slightest pinch of mercy, but the major did protect "his people."

"I'm going to find Mr. Carson and have a little chat with that banker," Zach informed his boss.

"I've already called the Chief of Police in Abilene and asked him to send a car out to detain the man. We don't want him disappearing on us," the major offered.

"That's a good idea, sir. Our escaped suspects might call and warn him, and now's not the time to let him drop off the radar," Zach stated.

"Be careful, Ranger Bass. And please, don't shoot up Abilene. I can only clean up one disaster at a time."

It was a relief to leave the mess in San Antonio. Zach hadn't wanted any trouble. He hadn't started it, but he would damn well finish it. He owed Gus Monroe that much.

It was just over 250 miles to Abilene, normally a four-hour drive through the Texas Hill Country and numerous small towns.

The ranger was pushing it however, eager to get back on Vincent's trail before it grew cold. That meant piloting the pickup at speeds well beyond the posted limits.

Zach had covered half the distance in just under 90 minutes when his cell phone chirped. The caller-ID informed the ranger that it was his superior. "Abilene PD can't locate your banker friend. He's not at home. They're keeping an eye on his place and will call you if he shows up."

The ranger drove another 20 minutes, various scenarios playing out in his head. Had Carson somehow gotten the word and gone on the dodge? Was Vincent helping with the escape? Could the banker just be out shopping or having dinner? Did Vincent decide to wrap up a loose end and kill the man?

There wasn't anything Zach could do at the moment but drive … or was there?

He dialed Cheyenne. "How are you managing?" he asked.

"I'm still a little shaken up. How do you go through life living like this?" she asked.

"Like what?"

"Having people shooting at you all the time … always being around the black hats that don't give a fresh cow pie about anybody or anything other than themselves. Oh, God, Zach. I couldn't do your job. It would drive me into the bottom of a bottle or put me at the business end of a gun," she stated.

"That happens to a lot of cops," Zach sighed. "A lot more than anyone wants to admit. As for me, I do the job because a lot of women find a man with a badge sexy as hell, and I need that to counteract my natural lack of self-confidence. It backfires some days, like today. Other times, there is a high level of gratification … like last Saturday when you stopped by the apartment."

The still-shaky model tried to laugh, but it was a forced effort, "Lack of self-confidence? Now I know you're pulling my leg, Zachariah Bass. Are you going to catch Vincent? Tell me you are. I need to hear that about now."

Zach hesitated, unsure that contacting her was such a great idea. The situation was, however, dire. "Actually, that's why I called you. I was hoping you might be able to help me – just one last time."

"Is anybody going to try and kidnap me or start shooting?" she asked in a tone that made it clear she wasn't joking this time.

"No. I promise. I need you to think back to Mr. Carson's office and your visits. Was there anything at all of a personal nature? Any pictures on his desk? Did he ever talk about his life away from the bank? Wife? Kids? Anything that might help me figure out where he is at the moment?"

Chey paused, her mind whipping back in time to the two visits she'd made to the bank. Finally she answered, "Hmmm … yeah, I think so. He had some trophies in his office. Golf trophies. There was a picture of him standing with a bunch of other stuffy-looking, old men on a golf course."

Zach thought out loud, "It's almost dark, so I don't think he's playing golf."

His comment made Cheyenne laugh. "Most country clubs have bars, Zach. Remember? One of my first jobs was driving around one of those little drink carts and letting strange men in terrible clothes flirt with me as I sold them expensive beer and peanuts. The bar inside the clubhouse was always packed, even after dark."

Smiling, the ranger commented, "You know, you might just be onto something. Thank you. I promise, as soon as the dust settles on this case, I owe you a nice dinner."

"Promise?"

"Yes, I do," Zach replied. "You've done great, Chey. I'm extremely proud of you. Texas is in your debt."

The compliment seemed to bolster the lady's mood. Zach chatted for a few more minutes as his pickup rolled away the miles. He felt better after they had talked.

Next, he dialed Sam, a little surprised when his partner answered on the second ring. "Where are you?" she asked immediately.

"I'm on my way to Abilene to question Mr. Carson. How are you feeling?"

Sam was all business, "They say the bullet nicked my upper femur, but the bone isn't broken. They also say I'm going to have a scar. There goes next year's bikini season. They claim I'll be walking with a limp in three weeks, and completely healed in three months."

"That's good to hear," Zach smiled. "I thought you were facing at least two months in a cast, and a lot of physical therapy. I was wondering how in the hell the medical staff was going to deal with your grumpy ass for that length of time."

"Grumpy? You're damn right, I'm grumpy. I'm not happy about this, not at all. One of the most important manhunts in history is going down, and I'm sitting here in this hospital bed being poked, prodded, and questioned. Can you swing by and kidnap *me*?"

"I'm already in enough trouble," Zach replied with a chuckle. He was relieved, Sam's temper indicating that she was feeling better. "And if we don't find Mr. Carson soon, I think my hot water is going to get a little hotter."

The ranger went on to tell Sam about his conversation with Chey. The lady ranger's response surprised him. "Hold on a second while I get my laptop booted up. They have pretty good Wi-Fi here at the medical torture facility."

A few moments went by before Sam's voice sounded over the airwaves. "There are four private country clubs with golf courses in Abilene. Hold on a second…. I'm looking up which one is closest to his house."

Zach could hear her fingers pecking at the computer's keyboard. "Oh, this is promising. He actually lives on the seventh hole of the Fairway Heights Country Club. That kind of narrows it down, don't you think?"

"Damn, Ranger Temple, good work. Give me the address. I'm rolling into Abilene now."

A minute later, Zach was punching the address into the pickup's GPS. He was close.

Back to Sam, he advised, "I'm not far away. Do me a favor and call the major. Let him know what you found. If you can't reach him, call Abilene PD and have them send me some backup."

"Will do. Be careful, Zach. These assholes are playing for keeps. My leg and I will testify to that fact under oath."

"I will," he promised. "I'll call you later and keep you in the loop."

Chapter 7

Zach arrived at the golf course a few minutes later, well after the last light of dusk had faded.

The grounds and clubhouse were fancy enough, well-manicured and plush just like he expected. There were a handful of expensive automobiles scattered around the parking lot. The Texan drove slowly up and down the rows, finding the Mercedes registered to Mr. Carson parked in the third row. "Gotcha," the ranger whispered.

Zach's first instinct was to march right in, flash his badge and ask for Mr. Carson. As he rolled the pickup into a parking spot near the main entrance, he decided a more reserved tactic might be a better fit for the circumstances.

Maybe he would saunter in, belly up to the bar and order a cold beer. He was sure the barkeep would be happy to point out the banker. It might be interesting to see who was a drinking buddy with Mr. Carson.

The firefight on the River Walk, however, gave the ranger cause for reserve. While Zach was reasonably certain Carson was nothing more than a meek, mild-mannered financier, he'd already been surprised once. That wasn't going to happen again.

He would wait for the local officers to arrive, place a couple of Abilene's finest in front, a couple more in back, and then step in and quietly ask for Mr. Carson to accompany him outside. From there, the next step would depend on the banker-pimp's level of cooperation and overall attitude.

As he sat waiting, two pairs of headlights entered the parking lot. The cars pulled into the row behind the ranger, and for a moment, Zach thought the local badges had finally arrived.

Instead, several people began exiting the vehicles, the party including a gaggle of children accompanied by adults carrying bunches of helium balloons and wrapped gifts. Someone was going to have a birthday party at the club. Wonderful.

Another, and then a fourth car moved in, all dislodging their contributions to the festivities. An oversized, chocolate sheet cake arrived shortly afterward.

"Shit," Zach mumbled, having counted a least a dozen youngsters and half that many adults. It was never good to have a bunch of little ones around. That was the worst-case scenario if someone got trigger-happy.

The next arrival caught the ranger's eye for a different reason. It was an expensive 4-door, Jaguar sedan that was clean as a whistle, including the brightly polished chrome wheels. Zach had always thought the brand produced extraordinarily good-looking cars. "Out of reach on a ranger's salary," he mumbled, admiring the sleek lines and fancy cat on the hood. "Maybe Mr. Carson would give *me* a loan," he grunted.

Unlike the previous arrivals, kids and presents didn't come bounding out of the Jag. No one did. The British sedan parked, turned off its headlights, and just sat in an eerie silence. Given the low light and tinted windows, the ranger had no idea who, or how many, were inside.

"This must be the hot spot in Abilene tonight," Zach complained.

Thinking to stretch his legs and run the Jag's plates, Zach reached for the door handle. Movement from the high-end sedan stopped him cold.

Two men exited, and they didn't look like golfers. Or did they?

In the lot's overhead lights, Zach got the impression of Latino heritage. His mind went into analysis paralysis.

Racial profiling was just wrong. Yet, cartel shooters were almost always Latino. Of course, there were wealthy individuals with darker complexions who could afford to join a country club. He was a ranger, not a racist.

By the time the two young, stout-looking men were entering the front of the clubhouse, Zach had gathered enough details that his threat alarms were screaming like air raid sirens. These two were displaying the same "gangsterisms" broadcast by the men who had just killed Gus and wounded Sam.

There was no sign of the local backup. The ranger had to make a decision and do so right now.

Reaching into the console, he palmed a handful of pistol magazines and dumped them in his jacket pocket. He had no proof of any wrongdoing or intent, so the M4 carbine, locked in the pickup's bed, wouldn't get an invitation to the party.

Exiting the truck, Zach hustled for the front door, whispering, "I wonder if you are here to kill, kidnap, or help Carson escape?"

He entered a large veranda with high ceilings and plush carpeting. A series of doorways lined the super-sized hall. Zach observed the broad shoulders of the two potential hitmen pacing toward the back of the building. They turned a corner and disappeared from his sight.

Walking briskly to close the distance, the ranger passed restrooms, an unmarked closet, the closed pro shop, and a banquet room full of singing children and birthday gifts. A sign with an arrow pointed toward Mulligan's Bar and Grill. Soft music and the sound of a woman laughing drifted down the main corridor.

As he surged to catch up, Zach pulled his cell phone and dialed 9-1-1. When the dispatcher asked about his emergency, the ranger's response was hushed, but urgent. "This is Texas Ranger Bass at the Fairway Heights Country Club. Please inform the patrol officers on their way to my location that I am inside the facility. Ask them to station officers at the front and back. Additional suspects in a late model Jaguar sedan have arrived on scene. I can't wait any longer."

Zach disconnected the call before the dispatcher could ask any questions or to confirm his identify. There just wasn't time.

The sounds of people eating, having fun, and enjoying a few libations grew louder as Zach made his way to the back of the facility. Another sign, identical to the first, pointed toward the watering hole. The ranger also learned it was happy hour, and that there was a special on pork chops with a side of mashed potatoes and a nice looking dinner salad.

Zach approached a wide, arched entrance. The opening was decorated with a small wooden sign that confirmed he had indeed arrived at Mulligans. The smiling young lady at the counter, next to the stack of menus and bowl of breath mints, confirmed that fact.

"How many, sir?" the hostess greeted with a warm voice.

"I was supposed to meet Mr. Carson here this evening. Could you show me to his table?"

"Sure," the young woman responded with the prerequisite smile. "You just missed the other gentlemen."

The hairs on the back of Zach's neck stood straight up. "The two men who were immediately in front of me?"

"Yes, I just seated them," she grinned. "Right this way, please."

Zach flashed his badge while dragging the girl out of the doorway. "I'm a Texas Ranger. How many people are in the bar?"

The hostess was stunned, her eyes darting between Zach's badge and his eyes. "Ummm … I … err…."

Zach didn't have time, "How many?"

She looked like a scream was forming in her throat, but then she got herself under control. In a voice three octaves higher than normal, she squeaked, "About 15 … plus the bartender and waitress … I think … I'm … that's it, I think."

Zach tried to make his face friendly, yet confident. "There are some Abilene police officers arriving out front. Tell them to get everyone out of this building right now, and do so quietly – especially those children. Got it?"

"Yes."

"Go! Hurry!" the ranger hissed.

"Okay."

Zach drew his weapon and entered the darkened interior. He popped his head around the corner, taking a mental picture of the main dining room.

After a second, quick snapshot, he not only knew the layout but also had identified Mr. Carson and his two guests. From the look on the banker's face, his visitors hadn't been expected.

Holstering his weapon, Zach stepped calmly to a nearby table that was close to the entrance, gave him a good angle of observation, and provided a clear field of fire.

One of the Latino men was seated beside the pale financier, the other directly across. The man closest to Carson was tight in the banker's face, and his expression wasn't friendly. The other guest kept his hands beneath the table. Zach was pretty sure the second man was holding a gun.

On a table next to the ranger was a nearly empty mug of beer. Zach noted it was a hefty container, built of solid-looking, thick glass. After casting another glance at the Carson party, he extended his arm and retrieved the heavy vessel.

With his pistol in one hand and his beer in the other, Zach rose slowly and walked toward the banker's little powwow. He was careful not to make eye contact, and even managed to pause half way there and look around as if he was trying to locate the restroom.

That was when he spied the gun pointed at the banker's stomach.

After two more steps, it was obvious Mr. Carson was being interrogated. Vincent, no doubt, was as nervous as a whore in the front pew. He probably wanted to know how the rangers had picked up his trail, and since it had been Carson's idea to hook up with Chey, the matchmaker was a logical place to start.

Three steps away, Zach could hear the frightened banker's voice whine, "But I said nothing.... I swear it."

Two steps away, and he heard the Latino say, "It had to be you! Admit it, and we will show mercy."

One step away, and the man in charge of Vincent's team nodded to his partner, "Kill this swine."

Zach lunged, swinging the mug with all of his considerable strength, aiming for the back of the gunman's head.

There was a sickening thud of impact, and then shards of glass were flying through the air. Zach knocked the man completely out of his chair, the gun rattling across the floor.

The man next to Carson was quick … damn quick. Before Zach could recover his balance, Mr. Mercy was drawing what appeared to be another of those fucking Glock 18s.

Still off balance and surprised by the speed of the henchman's reaction, Zach snap fired his .45 sending an ear-shattering wave of audible pain throughout the enclosed space. People began screaming, but no one could hear them.

The ranger's slug hit Mr. Mercy in the arm, just above the elbow. Before Zach could regroup, the target ducked behind Mr. Carson, spoiling the follow on shot.

The Latino enforcer rolled across the dark floor, coming up in the perfect shooting position. Zach was moving as well, trying to get an angle. A blistering stream of hot lead came pouring out of the Glock, six or more shots tearing into the restaurant's wall right where the ranger had been a tenth of a second before.

The sub-machine gun's rate of fire caused the cartel henchman's barrel to rise, giving Zach a blink of an opening to center the post and squeeze off two rounds.

A pair of dark spots appeared on the chest of the thug's white shirt, but he didn't go down. Zach, stunned, dove hard for the ground as another burst ripped through the air so close the ranger could feel the concussion of each 120-grain hunk of death.

"Body Armor!" Zach thought, rolling across the floor, chased by the incoming hailstorm of lead.

The gunman's burst missed Zach, but Carson wasn't so lucky. Caught in the line of fire, the banker fell, clutching his gut and howling like he was being eaten alive.

Zach finished his roll behind a table that had been overturned as the grill's patrons fled in panic. The ranger doubted the inch-thick surface material would stop the Glock's projectiles, and wasn't going to wait around to find out. No sooner than he had righted himself, he reared like a striking rattlesnake and fired two rounds at Mr. Mercy's head. Both missed. The ranger wasn't the only one who understood that constant motion was critical to surviving a gunfight.

Down to one round, Zach reached for a fresh mag, cringing in anticipation of the Glock's next outburst. Several shots rang out as Zach slammed home a fresh box of lead pills, but there was something different about the discharges.

Again, Zach rose from behind the table, sweeping for a target. The cartel assassin was down, jerking in sharp spasms of agony. Two of the bar's patrons stood nearby, both pointing smoking pistols at the dying man.

"Texas Ranger!" Zach shouted as both of the strangers moved their weapons in his direction. "Texas Ranger!" he screamed again, waving his badge above the table.

"Okay, Ranger," one of them answered. "We won't shoot you."

Not sure what was going on, Zach peeked and then ducked immediately. When no one fired, he rose quickly and moved to kick the dead Latino's weapon out of reach – just in case.

"Freeze! Police! Drop the Weapon!" came other voices, several uniformed officers rushing up with guns drawn, covering the two bar patrons as well as Zach.

It took a moment before the cops acknowledged Zach's badge. The two civilians set down their pistols and raised their hands, "We were helping the ranger," both of them started babbling as the cops moved in, screaming for them to get on the ground.

"They're okay," Zach shouted over the ruckus, moving to stop the Abilene PD. "They saved my ass," he continued, waving his badge for all to see.

After making sure no one else was going to get shot or arrested, Zach moved toward Carson. It was clear the man was close to his final breath.

"Who are you?" the banker managed between labored breaths.

"I'm Ranger Bass, Mr. Carson. I tried to stop them."

"I know," the dying man whispered. "I saw that."

Zach had to wait as a spasm of painful coughs racked the wounded man's frame, a small mist of red now staining his lips and chin. "College Station," the banker moaned. "It's all about College Station."

"What?" Zach frowned, not sure what Carson was trying to tell him.

"College…" he continued, the words requiring significant effort to form. "Go to…. Deadly," the now barely audible voice whispered.

"I don't understand, sir. What is in College Station?" the ranger asked.

It was too late. Carson's chest never rose again. Zach ripped apart the banker's shirt, prepared to do CPR until the EMTs arrived. One glance at the dead man's wounds told the ranger it was hopeless.

Pissed and frustrated, Zach stood and shook his head. "Damn it! Damn it all to hell!"

Did Carson have a kid at College Station? Was that where the banker's ex-wife lived … or his parents? What the hell was he talking about?

The ranger's thoughts were interrupted by raised voices rumbling from the bar. The two civilians who'd shot Mr. Mercy were growing angry. "What now?" Zach muttered, moving to check on his newest buddies.

"We played 18 holes this afternoon, and it was damn hot out there. We were thirsty, so my brother-in-law and I came in for a cold brewski. All of a sudden somebody starts shooting!" one of the Samaritans was telling a cop. "Those guys were going to kill everyone in here if somebody didn't do something. One of the bullets shot my beer right off the table. So we drew our guns and took one of them out. That's when we found out that second fella was a ranger."

The brother-in-law eagerly nodded his agreement with the statement. "So why are we in handcuffs? We have our concealed weapons licenses. We were defending ourselves. I want to go home. My wife is going to be pissed," his voice trailed off as he checked his watch. "Oh my God, that woman is going to kill me. I'm *so* late."

Despite the stress, adrenaline dump, and frustration, Zach had to chuckle. Only in Texas. Only here was a man more concerned about his wife being irate than being involved in a deadly shooting. Mr. Mercy should know better than to blast a man's beer off the table in these parts.

"There's no need to keep these men any longer. Is there, officer?" Zach asked the local sergeant nicely. "They did law enforcement a favor and should be receiving our gratitude, not our suspicions."

"Sir, the district attorney wants a full investigation into any situation involving the discharge of a firearm and the loss of life," the local officer countered.

"I'm sure these gentlemen aren't going to skip town, Sergeant. I'm also positive that they would like to go home, settle their nerves, let their families know they're okay, and probably throw back a good shot of strong bourbon. I know I sure would about now. You boys aren't going to skip town, are ya?" Zach asked, turning to face his rescuers.

"No, sir. Why would we do that?" responded one.

"I ain't leaving, no matter how mad my wife is," came the other.

"I didn't think so. Let 'em go, Sarge. They're the white hats in all this. I'm sure they'll be glad to come down to the station first thing in the morning and go through it all again … and again … and again."

The two civilians nodded eagerly, signaling their agreement.

The local cop didn't want to, but Zach held rank. "If you say so, Ranger."

Zach saw the EMTs arrive, one team heading immediately to the man the ranger had nearly decapitated with the beer mug. "I've got a pulse," announced the medic.

"That's about all we've got," said his partner. "Did this guy get shot in the head?"

The ranger moved over, kneeling beside the two paramedics. "He took a beer mug to the skull. Is he going to make it?"

"He's breathing. That's all I can say at the moment," frowned the EMT.

After they had loaded the unconscious henchman onto a stretcher, Zach gave strict instructions to the local cop who was escorting the prisoner during his ambulance ride. "If he wakes up, don't let him call anybody, speak to anybody, or even pass a fucking note. Call me at this number, immediately. If I don't answer, call Major Putnam at Company E."

An hour later, Zach was trudging away from yet another crime scene, leaving multiple dead bodies in his wake. Dreading the upcoming report to Major Putnam, Zach reached in his jacket and fished out his cell phone.

Peering down at the screen, he began a series of curses. The glass looked like a spider's web, and there wasn't any sign of life in the crushed device. "Now, I'm really in trouble."

Zachariah Bass was bone-tired, hungry, discouraged, and needing some down time to regroup and refocus. Sam was in the hospital, and there were a lot of dead men to be buried.

Detective Gus Monroe was one of them.

His instinct to dial Sam's cell phone, but his unit was out of commission.

He needed someone to verbally go over everything that had just happened. Cheyenne would listen, but she wasn't a cop and was probably still trying to figure things out herself. Major Putnam was a superior – and that didn't count.

He thought about BB. Sitting in his pickup, Zach remembered the first time he'd met the hard-nosed, old-school law dog.

There had been a homicide outside of Marfa, a local rancher found dead along a fence line.

"It was them damned illegals," the foreman had spouted to the responding deputies. "We see 'em all the time, crossing our spread, leaving trash and garbage lying around, and stealing anything that isn't nailed down."

Indeed, the dead man's wallet, watch, and rings were missing.

The deputies, however, weren't convinced. Yes, there was some illegal alien traffic in the area, and petty theft wasn't unheard of. That being said, none of the local lawmen could remember the last time any of the border crashers had committed murder.

The bunkhouse was in an uproar over the boss's death. A dozen capable, well-armed men were outraged and spoiling for revenge. A mob mentality was spreading to a couple of the neighboring outfits. Fearing a swell of violent backlash against anyone with a darker complexion, the county sheriff called in the rangers.

At the time, Zach was still like a new colt - a little shaky on his legs and unsure how it all worked. His captain decided the situation warranted some special help. "I'm calling BB," the superior had informed his newest ranger. "If you keep your mouth shut and your ears and eyes open, you'll learn more today than any class at Texas Tech or the academy back in Austin. Listen to the man. Learn from him. You'll be glad you did."

BB arrived at the crime scene pulling a horse trailer behind his state-issued pickup. Before long, Zach and his mentor were in the saddle, "Because the elevation allows you to see things from God's point of view."

BB didn't bother with the area surrounding the body. "That's polluted ground by the time I'm called in. Between the deputies, EMTs, witnesses, and everyone else tromping around, you typically won't find much there."

The two rangers began by circling the crime scene, riding slowly with eyes scanning the ground. A quarter of the way to the south, BB pointed at something that Zach couldn't see.

The old timer sat still now, his eyes seeming to examine every single pebble, stem, and a clump of sage. "Do you see it?" BB asked.

"No, sir. Sorry, but it just looks like hardpan to me," Zach replied honestly.

The lanky tracker dismounted, took a knee and pointed at a single, quarter-sized stone. "That rock has been moved at least a quarter of an inch. Only a boot would do that, not a paw or hoof. That little stone has been flagged."

BB then moved a stride away, again extending a gloved finger. "See that little indentation? That's the edge of a heel."

Zach had spent his fair share of time hunting and thought he knew how to track everything from coyote to jackrabbits. He soon realized his skills were like comparing a little league ball player to a seasoned pro.

Ranger Bass spent the next hour learning new terms, such as 'crying,' or the natural weeping of vegetation fluids after being squeezed by a footfall.

The old ranger was patient with his younger counterpart, explaining the difference between a "scuff" and "heeling," pointing out the "transfer" of material from one location to another.

The two mounted lawmen progressed slowly, partially because BB was teaching, mostly because he wasn't taking any chances on losing the line of sight.

"You have to imagine the man walking," BB explained. "Learn his direction and length of stride, and the clues become a lot more obvious. Ask yourself where the next step would land. Look for it."

After a few hundred yards, the two rangers approached an odd disturbance in the hard-packed soil. The older ranger grunted, "Now, we know that illegals coming across the Rio Grande didn't kill that rancher."

Zach didn't get it, staring at a small hole that looked like someone had fired a bullet into the ground. "Sir?"

"That's the mark of a motorcycle's kickstand, son. And over there, I bet you'll find tire tracks."

Sure enough, after spurring his mount, the new ranger found the pattern of a narrow tread.

They moved faster now, the machine's weight making the trail easy to follow. An hour later, the two lawmen crested a ridge and found themselves staring down on a small group of buildings constituting a neighboring ranch.

It didn't take long to find the matching dirt bike, the modern cowboy's choice to ride fence and count head.

The two rangers arrested a cowpoke a short time later. There had been a poker game a few nights before. The dead rancher had been a big winner, the guilty ranch hand the loser. The man was convinced he'd been cheated and had accidently bumped into his nemesis while chasing down strays. An argument ensued, quickly leading to a pulled knife and a dead man.

Now, sitting in the country club's parking lot, Zach reminisced about what he considered a simpler time for the rangers. "That was law enforcement," he grumbled. "That was solving crimes and locking up criminals. What the hell am I doing now?"

Overwhelmed, Zach's mind retreated to a time spiced with gratification and a sense of accomplishment. It had been so much simpler that day, riding on a horse in open country, searching for an outlaw. He could still hear BB's words as if they had been spoken yesterday, "Crooks can fool cameras. They can cover their financial tracks. But a man crossing the earth always leaves a sign."

The ranger glanced over at the Jaguar parked a short distance away. A CSI team was already pouring over the luxury vehicle, but Zach had little faith they would find anything of value for his investigation. It was most likely stolen. There had been no identification on the two shooters. Even the "hidden" serial numbers on their Glock automatics had been ground flat. The men he was chasing seemed to have found a way to get around BB's rule. They were crossing the earth without leaving a sign.

Or were they?

The Jag was inundated with a half-dozen roving flashlight beams. The trunk, hood, and all four doors were open, men and women poking and prodding the sedan in every orifice. The ranger's eyes, however, remained fixed on the windshield. There was a tollway automatic payment card next to the rearview mirror.

Zach exited the pickup and approached the woman obviously in charge of dissecting the Jag.

"I assume the vehicle is stolen?" the ranger asked.

"No, no report has been filed," came the stoic response.

Zach was stunned. Had the cartel goons finally made a mistake? "Who is it registered to?"

After flashing the ranger a firm, now-isn't-a-good-time scowl, the lady officer flipped two pages on her clipboard and answered, "A Dr. Myer Dattatreya. The license plate doesn't match the registration, but the toll card belongs to the doctor."

"And the owner lives where?" Zach fired, his energy returning.

"Says here Dr. Dattatreya is currently residing at 2404 West Pecos Street, College Station."

The ranger perked at the city's name. There it was again. The dying banker's last words rushing back into the forefront of his mind.

"We are trying to contact Dr. Dattatreya at the moment, but so far, the College Station PD hasn't had any luck," the tech added.

"Thank you, officer," Zach said with as much charm as he could muster. "You're doing an excellent job here; I might add. I'm very impressed with the Abilene PD at the moment."

The woman flushed for a brief second, obviously pleased to hear such words from the tall, handsome ranger.

With his warmest smile, Zach continued the flirt, "You wouldn't happen to have a cell phone I could borrow … would you?"

After a late night stop at headquarters in Austin, which included acquiring a requisition for a new phone and filing the minimal paperwork, the ranger caught a few hours of sleep and a quick, hot shower. He was on the road for College Station before dawn the following morning.

While driving east, Zach decided to call Sam on his new phone. The lady ranger was having breakfast. "How are you feeling?" he asked.

"Terrible. I'm going to go insane if I have to spend much more time in this place. They wake you up at all hours of the night, the food is terrible, and my nurse is Attila the Hun's great, great, granddaughter."

"Could be worse," Zach chuckled. "I bet you would be even more sleep deprived if you were on the road with me."

The two officers exchanged thoughts and theories on the case as Zach headed toward the small, central Texas town.

"Have the College Station cops found the doctor yet?" Sam asked.

"No, and that is troubling. Not only is he missing, but there is very, very little information regarding the man. He received U.S. citizenship after working as an academic at Texas A&M for 11 years, yet the campus police said he's no longer listed as being on the university's staff."

"What's so weird about that?" Sam responded. "He went into the corporate world or started his own business.… Could be anything."

"He hasn't filed any tax returns with the republic," Zach continued. "We've got a request into Washington for any records they have, but you know how long that takes."

"Let me know what you find out, okay? And Zach, please promise me you'll come bust me out of this place if they don't let me go home tomorrow?"

The thought of Sam fussing with the nurses and doctors provided Zach with some much-needed comic relief. "You got it, partner," he chuckled. "I'll tie a rope around your window bars, and pull them out with my horse."

"You don't have a horse."

"I'll use my pickup then. We rangers have to keep up with the times, I suppose."

The ranger arrived at College Station just after 9 AM, his first stop being police headquarters. A few minutes later, he was talking with the patrol supervisor who had been tasked with finding the missing doctor.

"His address is a rented home on the southeast side of town. My officers found no sign of foul play. The place was locked and tidy. We didn't go in, and I don't think there's enough probable cause to get a warrant. A phone call to the landlord this morning confirmed the rent was paid on time each month, and that Dattatreya was a quiet, trouble-free tenant."

Zach nodded his agreement. "No idea where this guy works?"

"Not yet. There is no social media presence that we can find, nor any relatives as far as we know of. We are positive he was a professor in A&M's veterinary school. One of my buddies on the campus force looked up his record for me. Single, no dependents. Resigned three years ago."

"Did he just retire?" Zach inquired. "Maybe he was enjoying the quiet life."

"Doubtful. He is only 44 years old. We also know that he travels back to India from time to time. We're trying to run that down as well."

The ranger rubbed his chin, "Who was his boss at A&M? Have you had a chance to interview anyone over at the school?"

"No, everything was pretty locked down by the time we got the call last night. I'm hoping to get someone over there this morning."

Zach offered his hand and said, "I'll take care of that for you, Sergeant. Appreciate the help."

It took the ranger some time to find the right building in the maze that was the massive university. Since the secession, the institution found itself in a constant state of accelerated expansion.

Two of the republic's new military academies, Texas's versions of West Point for the Army and Colorado Springs for Air Force, were being developed in conjunction with A&M. Corpus Christi was the new home for the Naval, Coast Guard, and Merchant Marine schools.

Once he'd finally managed to navigate the huge construction projects and found the right location, Zach had to show his badge three times before he was finally ushered into the office of an associate dean.

Dr. Herbert Womack wasn't a tall individual, nor did the intellectual appear to be athletically inclined. At just under 5'9", a good 40 pounds overweight, and sporting a billy goat beard, the ranger wasn't initially impressed. After experiencing a handshake that was wet, lethargic, and exhibiting the enthusiasm of a dead snake, Zach wanted nothing more than to finish the interview and get on with his day.

The ranger wasn't the only one, Dean Womack making it absolutely clear that he had far more important items on his agenda than talking with a cop.

"Do you know Dr. Myer Dattatreya?" Zach asked the rather stuffy gent.

"Yes."

There was more than a hint of apprehension in the dean's response, the ranger initially interpreting the fellow's attitude as unfavorable toward law enforcement. *He probably got a speeding ticket yesterday and is still pissed*, Zach thought. *Or maybe his daughter ran off with a deputy instead of that nice young man in the lab coat working on his Ph.D.*

"When was the last time you saw Dr. Dattatreya?"

"What's this about, officer?" Again, there was an edge.

"A missing person case," Zach replied.

The academic seemed surprised by the response. "Who is missing?"

"The doctor," Zach answered, mystified by Womack's obvious stonewalling.

The man across the desk was again taken aback by the ranger's statement. With a sudden case of fluttering hands, he said, "That's absurd. I just spoke with Myer yesterday morning. He was initializing an important phase of his latest research. He's not missing; he is sequestered at the lab."

"That's wonderful news," replied the ranger. "I will, however, need to speak with him immediately. A car registered to the doctor was used in a serious crime yesterday, and I need to investigate the circumstances."

The dean was now clearly upset. "I'm afraid that's not possible, sir. Dr. Dattatreya's research is extremely sensitive, and established safety protocols require complete isolation."

The ranger was now utterly confused. "I was told that the doctor was no longer employed by the university. Is that information incorrect?"

"Yes, that is accurate. He left A&M over two years ago to join the private sector."

"Who is his employer?"

Dean Womack didn't answer, his eyes darting right and left as if searching for a way out of his own office. He then started to reach for the telephone sitting on the desk's corner but stopped. Finally he responded, "I'm afraid I'm not at liberty to divulge that information."

In less than a second, Zach experienced a parade of emotions. First came a short eruption of anger, driven by the ranger's lack of sleep, one very dead El Paso detective, and the number of bullets recently fired in his direction. It took a considerable amount of effort to check his rage.

Then came frustration. Not everyone had voted for the secession. It was common for those against independence to focus their disdain on any government official who crossed their path. Law enforcement encountered such attitudes often.

Finally, the ranger arrived at curiosity. The dean was sweating now, small beads of perspiration showing on the man's nearly-bald head. *Why? What was this guy's issue?*

De-escalate, Zach thought. *Take down it down a notch. The man isn't a criminal. He's not stupid. Work with him.*

"Sir, I'm not sure what's going on, but I really, really need your cooperation in this matter," Zach began in a calm, even tone. "We believe Dr. Dattatreya's automobile was stolen by some extremely dangerous criminals. I only need a few moments of his time."

The dean's next move was completely unexpected. Reaching for the phone and staring hard into Zach's eyes, he waited for his admin to answer. "Get me the university's legal department, please. Tell them it's urgent."

For a moment, Zach thought that Womack was calling to get permission to answer his questions. The look on the professor's face, however, told a different tale – one that was soon confirmed.

"I have a law enforcement officer in my office," the academic stated into the mouthpiece. "I need legal representation immediately, please."

Zach shook his head as Womack disconnected the call. "Why?" he asked, not really expecting any answer. "I don't understand, sir? I just need to speak with the good doctor about his Jag."

The man across the desk folded his arms, his expression now set in stone. "I invoke my Fifth Amendment right to remain silent, officer. I have been advised not to speak with the police until I have an attorney present."

The ranger was now getting pissed. "That is your right, sir. Is your attorney on the way?" he growled.

The dean became smug, "I wish to remain silent, officer."

There were several options available to Zach. He could detain Womack for questioning. He could haul the frumpy, old goat down to the station. He could dream up any number of half-assed charges in an attempt to leverage or intimidate the fool. Obstruction came to mind. Hindrance was another option.

The ranger, however, didn't like operating that way. While a lot of hard-nosed cops would push the limits, Zach had always found such tactics distasteful. Long ago, he'd arrived at the conclusion that threatening to trump up charges was a method employed by lawmen of lesser skill and intellect. He was a ranger, a member of an elite organization, sworn to serve and protect. There was always a better way.

Again, the Texan pushed down his rage. Reaching to fish his new cell from a jacket pocket, it was the ranger's turn to make a call. "Major Putnam, I'm at Texas A&M and have run into an obstacle," Zach stated calmly. "For some unknown reason, the assistant dean that I'm interviewing has invoked his Fifth Amendment rights, and we are currently awaiting the arrival of his university-provided attorney. Would you be so kind, sir, as to call President Simmons's office and let him know that our investigation has been stalled due to this development?"

Zach listened as his supervisor acknowledged the request, and then read off the dean's full name and title. "Thank you, sir. I will inform you of my findings shortly."

For 20 minutes, the two men sat in silence, staring at each other across the dean's desk. The university's legal counsel arrived first.

The polite but cold introductions had just finished when Herbert's desk phone jingled.

121

Annoyed at the interruption, Womack picked up the headset and snapped, "Not now. No interruptions, please."

"But sir," came the admin's voice. "It's *the* chancellor on the line. He says it's urgent."

Zach couldn't control himself, smirking as the dean's expression turned sour.

"But, sir … but … the sensitive nature … but," Dr. Womack tried to protest into the phone. Even through the tiny speaker, Zach could hear a little voice shouting some very big words.

In the end, the dean's argument fell on deaf ears. After returning the headset to its cradle, the professor's expression registered total defeat. Glancing at the newly arrived lawyer, he announced, "Your services are no longer required, counselor. Thank you for coming by, but the chancellor has made his wishes quite clear. I'm am to cooperate fully with the ranger."

After they were alone, Zach asked again. "Who is Dr. Dattatreya's employer?"

"The U.S. government," the dean answered with a sigh. "More specifically, the Center for Disease Control and the Department of Defense."

The answer wasn't shocking. Texas had been a state for over 150 years, a republic for less than three. There were still entanglements at practically every level of business and government. Why should the world of higher education be any different?

"Where can I find Dr. Dattatreya?"

Despite the dean's boss's boss and the president of the republic being involved, the man across from Zach still hesitated. "He's working at a secure research facility, about 30 miles north of Bryan."

"An A&M site?"

"No … well … he's working on a co-op project started over 10 years ago. The facility is owned by a trust formed by the Department of Defense, the CDC, and two pharmaceutical corporations. The University is also involved, but I'm not sure of the actual contractual arrangements or legal formalities."

The ranger still couldn't grasp the reason behind all of the secrecy and vacillation. "In layman's terms, what is the nature of the doctor's research project?"

The dean grew pale, his upper lip quivering in fear. "Biological weapons research. More specifically, anti-biological weapons research."

Zach's color soon joined the dean's, all of the pieces of the puzzle falling into place. For the first time during the entire encounter, the ranger stood, his tall frame towering over the dean's desk in a clear sign of intimidation. "Call that facility. Right now!"

Nodding in terror, the academic fumbled inside of his desk drawer until he found a sheet of laminated paper containing columns of names and numbers. There was no answer.

"Try again!"

After the second attempt, the dean was now perspiring profusely, his hands trembling. "That's very odd. Normally, there are two or three lab assistants on duty at any time. Someone always answers the phone," he stammered.

Pivoting abruptly, the ranger nearly dropped his cell phone in his rush to dial.

"Major, we need a CBRN (*Chemical, Biological, Radiation, and Nuclear*) response team immediately. I think I know what the cartels are after, sir. In fact, they may already have it."

Five minutes later, Zach and the dean were scrambling for the ranger's truck.

As they sped through the campus and then the town of Bryan, the ranger continued to pump his passenger for information.

"What kind of biological agents are we talking about?"

"All of the common varieties," Womack responded with a matter of fact tone. "Variola, Yersinia pestis tularemia, Clostridium botulinum, Magnaporthe grisea – the usual cast of characters."

Zach frowned, "In layman's terms, please."

"Smallpox, plague, yellow fever...."

The ranger interrupted, "What the hell is that shit doing at A&M?"

"The university was one of the primary research centers in the U.S. government's efforts to combat agroterrorism," Womack explained calmly. "Dr. Dattatreya is one of the world's foremost experts in the field."

Zach had heard the term agroterrorism during one of the many briefings conducted by the Department of Homeland Security after 9-11. Biological agents, it was understood, didn't have to kill humans to be effective. Destroying crops, livestock herds, and other food sources would get the job done.

According to some, creating, packaging, and delivering this category of weapon would be much easier than attacking cities full of people.

Womack took Zach's silence as a signal to continue, "The university has been working with the CDC for decades in an effort to develop a series of vaccines, contamination procedures, and other proactive strategies to combat a potential terrorist attack against our food sources."

The ranger relaxed for a moment, wondering if he'd been a little fast on the trigger and the call to Major Putnam. "So Dr. Dattatreya's project didn't have anything to do with infecting people?"

"On the contrary," Womack countered. "It had very much to do with people. In the last few years, the advancements in DNA splicing led Myer to predict altered strains of various agents would be easy for terrorist organizations to manufacture. He believed it would be possible to infect humans, animals, and crops with the same weaponized substance. He also theorized that such an attack would quickly overwhelm any potential response by any government."

"Shit. Wipe out the crops, animals, and people? Isn't that a bit of overkill?"

Womack became the teacher, lecturing the student. "Even the worst of these compounds has some survivability rate, be it in animals, vegetation, or humans. If you strike at all three simultaneously, the results would be far more horrific."

The ranger didn't mind being schooled at the moment. "Is such a weapon possible?"

"Over the past few years, Myer's research indicated that it was not within the realm of current technology and knowledge. They did uncover, however, that two of the three potential targets were possible. More specifically, humans and livestock could be infected with the same genetically modified compound."

After maneuvering through a slight traffic jam, Zach continued, "And the results of that revelation were?"

"Myer was working on a way to manufacture a cheap, easily distributable vaccine. In that effort, he also uncovered a very economical method of producing the weaponized agents. That's when the university wanted out of the entire program. The Board of Regents wanted nothing to do with development, only prevention. The DOD and CDC were still engaged, however, and arranged for funding and an off-site lab."

Two military helicopters appeared at that moment, both of the birds zooming off in the same direction Zach was driving. "Those would be the CBRN teams from Fort Hood."

"Yes," the dean confirmed, watching the aircraft shrink into small black dots against the morning blue sky. "We're getting close now."

Following the professor's directions, Zach came to a gravel lane blocked by a high, stout-looking fence. The only signage warned of private property, electronic security, and the prosecution of trespassers. There were already four troopers parked and waiting at the entrance.

The two Blackhawks were circling overhead.

"I don't have a keycard," Womack announced.

"How close can we get without being infected - if there has been some sort of breach?" Zach asked, eyeing the gate with suspicion.

"We're okay for now; it is still over a half mile till we get to the lab."

Zach pulled his pickup so that the front bumper was pushing against the gate. "Forgive me, Major," he whispered, giving the powerful V8 a bit more fuel.

The back wheels spun, throwing up a small cloud of gravel and dust just as the hinges popped. Two of the troopers ran forward, lifting the remainder of the linkage away from Zach's paint job.

The ranger was then leading a small parade of official vehicles down the crushed rock path, just as the copters were landing in a nearby pasture. "Stop me before we get within infection ... or contamination ... or whatever you call it, range," he informed the dean.

"We're fine as long as we stay outside," the doctor promised. Regardless of his passenger's confidence, Zach found himself wanting to hold his breath.

They approached a small series of buildings, the largest a solid-looking structure about the size of an average barn. In bold, red lettering, the only sign indicated they had arrived at the TexStar AgroResearch Facility. The two vehicles in the gravel lot were soon joined by numerous law-enforcement units and would soon be surrounded by a sea of flashing blue and red lights.

"Don't go inside the large building," Womack warned.

"Oh, don't worry about that," Zach replied, eyeing the structure as if it were some sort of monster about to consume them all.

The troopers spread out, soon joined by a SWAT team from the local county. Zach was glad the extra manpower had been summoned by his boss.

Movement drew the ranger's eye, several men tramping across the countryside in what appeared to be spacesuits. The leader, and Army captain, carried a spare Haz-Mat unit under his arm. "I think it's a good idea if someone from law enforcement goes inside with us."

All eyes fixed on the ranger, given he was the senior man at the location. For one of the few times in his career, Zach wished he hadn't been on top of the authority food chain.

It took two of the military specialists 10 minutes to hook the ranger up. Zach found the outfit sizzling, suffocating, and restrictive. Despite the respirator humming in his ear, it was difficult for the lawman to breathe.

Zach couldn't remember ever being so scared. He'd faced countless criminals, evil men and women with no regard for human life and a special dose of vile when it came to the Texas Rangers. Most of them had possessed deadly weapons of one form or another.

He'd fought ISIS in the desert, survived riots in Istanbul, and arrested dozens and dozens of felons. Bombs, ambushes, assassins, mafia hit men, and rustlers were all on his resume. *Some of those sons-ah-bitches had been big mothers, too,* he thought. Most had been armed, and more than a few had been skilled in the arts of combat.

Now, facing a menace he couldn't see, smell, hear, or feel, the ranger was having trouble forcing his legs to move. The smallest foe he could imagine was filling Zach's core with the ice of fear.

In they went, six men in thick, one-piece spacesuits that smelled like cleaning fluid. The plastic shield in front of Zach's face provided little comfort.

The team's commander ventured first. Zach saw the officer hesitate one step inside the door, and it quickly became obvious why.

There was a body behind the receptionist's desk. At first glance, the young man appeared to be taking a siesta, his head bent backward, eyes pointing at the ceiling.

It was the small, black hole just above the bridge of his nose and the splatter of purplish blood and brain matter on the wall that froze the Army officer.

As Zach moved around the stalled trooper to examine the deceased, some minor flush of relief crossed through the ranger's mind. Until that moment, he hadn't been sure any crime had been committed here. Since calling the major, he'd worried that they would find Dr. Dattatreya hard at work over a table of bubbling test tubes, completely unaware that his Jag had been stolen from the parking lot.

In fact, they found Dattatreya next.

The door behind the dead receptionist was where the heavy-duty, caution signs began, all of them in bright, bold text and displaying somber language. Zach didn't have time to read them all but did take special note of the nuclear materials advisory as well as the skull and crossbones emblem which seemed to be a common theme with the lab's interior decorator.

The team progressed into what appeared to be a combination airlock and gym's locker room. There were benches along both sides, each wall lined with metal doors. Several spacesuits, similar to the one Zach was wearing, were hanging nearby.

After opening the heavy, sealed exit door, the team entered a room with tile floors and walls, a half-dozen water nozzles pointing from each side.

Another airtight door, and then they were in a large room that came closer to fulfilling Zach's image of a high-tech laboratory.

While there wasn't any forest of tubes and glass bottles, the ranger did spot several microscopes and other machines on the large, black working surfaces.

Dr. Dattatreya, or what was left of the poor fellow, was there, his legs and arms duct-taped to a heavy, metal chair. He had suffered badly before death's final mercy, the signs of brutal torture evident on the victim's limbs and bare chest.

Zach shivered when he saw the small propane torch lying next to the gruesome corpse, the tool most likely used to burn away large swaths of the doctor's skin. No doubt, he'd told his captors anything they wanted to know.

There was, however, a survivor. One of the soldiers discovered a young woman locked deep in a storage closet. She was hysterical, thinking the Army team members were the invaders who had come back to ensure her demise.

It took them a while to coax her out. Even then, her constant stream of babbling provided little to no useful information. The captain, after an approving nod from Zach, ordered his men to decontaminate the woman and get her outside to the waiting medical professionals.

The military team spread out, a variety of instruments, cameras, and tools in their hands. There was no way Zach was going to begin processing the homicides while wearing the heavy get-up. His nerves were too frayed, his mind overwhelmed by the events of the last few days.

The first hour passed quickly, the ranger watching as the specialists swabbed, scanned, and noted every nook, cranny, and surface in the lab.

It was another 15 minutes before the captain was in front of Zach saying, "There has been a small breach, but we've taken samples and sterilized the area. I want to run one more check, and then I'll declare the lab clean, and we can get out of these suits."

"Can you tell what, if anything, is missing?" Zach asked, wanting to know what deadly substance was in the cartel's hands and probably on its way to Mexico.

"Not yet. That will take a while. It looks like the researchers here did an excellent job of cataloging their work and inventories, so we'll figure it out soon enough."

"Is the public in any danger?" came the ranger's most important question.

"Yes," replied the officer without hesitation. "This place is full of some Class-A biotoxins … a virtual beauty pageant of the world's deadliest nasties. It's also evident that their work here involved some non-traditional manufacturing methods. Follow me. I want to show you something."

The captain led Zach to a far corner where the ranger hadn't yet ventured. The lawman was surprised to see what appeared to be a common meth lab used by criminals to manufacture crystal methamphetamine.

"Were they making crystal meth here?" Zach asked, having seen similar setups at more than one drug den.

"No. Worse. From the notes I've found, the team here was researching methods to manufacture large quantities of vaccines using primitive equipment commonly found in poor, developing nations. My guess is that the scientists knew crystal meth labs were a common fixture in those locales, and they were trying to turn a negative into a positive. According to the records, they succeeded."

Zach was confused. "So that's a good thing? Right?"

Despite the oversized helmet and Plexiglas mask, the captain's worried expression was clear. "Most vaccines are derived from the original bug. That means you have to be able to breed huge quantities of say, Small Pox, in order to extract the cure. What you're looking at is the poor man's version of a bio-weapons factory."

The ranger now understood another piece of the mystery. The cartels were probably the world's foremost experts on producing crystal methamphetamine on a large scale. Somewhere, the ranger had read an estimate that there were over 20,000 illegal "kitchens" operating in Central America, almost the same number in the United States. If even a tiny portion of those facilities could be converted to produce some deadly bug, the world was in for a very rough rodeo.

"We both know whoever did this wasn't just some jealous husband or petty thief. What did they take?" Zach asked, knowing he wouldn't like the answer.

"We can't be for sure," replied the military expert. "As I said, it looks like the lab was keeping excellent records. We'll have to compare what is still here versus what should be in stock. That will take someone above my pay grade to figure out."

Zach started to rub his chin but instead bumped his hand against the helmet. "Sounds like that is a time-consuming venture, sir. So let me ask you another question. If you were one of the terrorists who managed to get in here, what would you have taken, Captain? What do you think they were after?"

"Oh, that's easy. I would choose the pneumonic plague. It would be the easiest to manufacture and distribute. Just rent pressurized tanks and start spraying."

Zach wanted to be sure that he'd heard the expert correctly. "Pneumonic plague? I thought it was Bubonic plague?"

"They're cousins. From what I understand, the modified pneumonic version can infect animals and people. If I wanted to incite widespread terror and inflict as much damage as possible, I'd go for two birds with one stone of mass destruction, sir."

A soldier appeared just then, wanting Zach's attention. "Ranger Bass, there are two men outside requesting a report as soon as possible. One is a ... Colonel Bowmark. The other is Major Putnam."

Zach acknowledged the young trooper's message with a nod and then returned to the captain. "I've got to go earn my pay. Can one of your team help me get out of this monkey suit?"

Zach's spacesuit received a shower, chemical wash-down, and finally another shower. Then the ranger's ears were popped and unpopped as he progressed through the two airlocks.

He exited the building and found the entire area had undergone an amazing transition in the 90 minutes he'd been inside.

There were rifle-toting soldiers rushing around, blue and red emergency lights in every direction. At least six helicopters now rested in the neighboring pasture. Two more CBRN teams were suiting up, using a massive tent that had been erected at the edge of the parking lot. An additional canvas structure was under construction. Right next to the circus tents was the Department of Public Safety mobile command center, essentially a Class-A motorhome that had been equipped with military-grade communications, video monitoring, and a gargantuan amount of computing power.

Zach found his boss talking with the colonel in front of the converted camper. There was also an Army general, as well as Dean Womack in the huddle. The ranger could tell his boss was stressed, an unlit cigar being crushed and ground by Putnam's working jaw.

"Ranger Bass," the major greeted as Zach approached. "Your report, please."

Thank you for asking about my exposure to every fucking killer virus and germ on the planet, Major, Zach wanted to say. *It's always a morale booster to know your superiors are concerned for their officers' wellbeing.*

Instead, Zach reigned in his exhaustion, fear, and dread, providing a levelheaded, factual report to an attentive gathering.

"How long will it be before we are certain what substances, if any, were taken from the lab?" Colonel Bowmark asked.

"Unknown, sir."

"Do we have any idea exactly what we're looking for?" Major Putnam inquired. "Would it be a liquid? Crystal? Large container? Small? What can we alert law enforcement to start searching for?"

"Unknown, sir."

The interrogation was interrupted by the appearance of a trooper who obviously had something important to report. "Sir, we have the lab's external video surveillance system back online. The intruders destroyed the equipment used for internal monitoring, but the parking lot's camera is an independent unit. One of the techs has routed the feed into the command center."

The gaggle of law enforcement, military, and the sole academic shuffled inside the motorhome, gathering around a large video monitor.

The first episode of the drama showed grainy footage of two black-clad men working their way to the lab's entrance. Zach could make out battle rifles, masks, and load vests bulging with magazines. In a flash, the two assaulters were inside the reception area.

"I'm going to fast forward three minutes," announced the tech running the computer.

The next chapter displayed a white panel van rolling into the parking lot. Three more men exited, Vincent's face as clear as a wanted poster. "That appears to be the same van used in the San Antonio incident," Zach noted. "I'm certain that's the same man who was in charge at the steakhouse."

Again, the tech informed the gathering that he was fast-forwarding the video. "Nothing happens for two hours."

As the recording raced forward, Zach could see the shadows change position as the sun moved across the sky. When the operator resumed normal speed, the two masked gunmen exited the door first, their weapons sweeping the parking lot. A moment later, Vincent emerged, carrying what appeared to be a laptop computer under his arm.

Bringing up the rear were the final two henchmen lugging what looked to be stainless steel canisters, each about the size of a small fire extinguisher. After securing the containers in the back of the van, Vincent pointed toward the Jag and threw one of his henchmen what appeared to be a key fob.

No one said a word but Zach, who managed only two. "Holy shit."

Chapter 8

The gentle motion of the houseboat's deck was relaxing. The northern breeze was barely enough to disturb the lake's surface, let alone motivate the 22,000-pound hull of the 40-foot vessel.

Standing at the aft rail, Vincent welcomed the brief respite as he studied the twinkling lights in the distance. Since sundown, the air was cooling quickly. The weather was perfect for their task.

At just over 66,000 acres, Amistad Reservoir was the fourth largest manmade body of water in Texas. Of the 850 miles of shoreline, well over half was on the republic's side of the border.

The lake was the result of a joint water management treaty between Mexico and the United States, and quickly became a popular hub for fishing, water sports, and naturalists from both nations.

The double-decker houseboat was one of the dozens available for rent from the marinas that dotted the northern banks. With a full galley, the ability to comfortably sleep 12, and massive tanks storing fuel and fresh water, "Queen Ami" was a luxurious, floating condo.

Vincent's gaze was pointed south, toward home. He could clearly see Mexico, less than four miles away across the glass-like surface of the lake. "So close, and yet so far," he mumbled to the still night. "Soon, I will return. And I promise things will never be the same again."

It would seem a simple chore to ignite the big gasoline powered engines below and steer the large vessel south. After all, the border here was nothing more than an imaginary line across the water.

The experienced smuggler knew better, especially since his men had mangled the Marines 40 miles to the west of the spot where Queen Ami was now anchored. The border was now closed tight. No one crossed north or south – at least not legally. Lake Amistad was no exception.

There were at least four patrol boats in the area, two of which were equipped with radar and all of them commanding massive horsepower. Long ago, after being outrun by drug runners from the south, the Texas authorities had learned to buy the fastest vessels available. Vincent was sure a minimum of one helicopter was available as a backup to the surface patrols – just in case. Tonight, however, none of that mattered.

Austin's reaction to the massacre had been an unexpected bonus for the operation. For the first time since the secession, the cartel's coyotes were back in business. Thousands of people, stranded at the border and growing desperate, were lining up to pay his men for an illegal crossing. If the closure continued for a few more days, the resulting revenue stream would be extremely lucrative.

The whine of a speedboat gliding across the lake drew the drug lord's attention. Watching the vessel skim the dark water's surface, Vincent wondered if the authorities were reinforcing their already significant waterborne presence.

The go-fast boat raced past the cove were Queen Ami was anchored, the outline low and sleek in the dim light. Blaring rock and roll music drifted across the water, competing with the roar of powerful engines as the captain headed south. A few moments later Vincent felt the deck roll gently under his feet as the passing craft's wake spread across the surface. He reached for the rail to steady himself, unsure how long the disturbance would last – uncertain of its intensity.

The inlet, however, soon returned to a calm, placid state. It was as if the passing boat had never existed.

He wondered if the current state of affairs was similar. Was Texas the fancy, sleek speedboat that had just passed, making a lot of noise and disturbing the cartel's safe harbor? Was the impact of secession like the wake, rocking his boat, causing a reaction, but then lasting only for a few moments? Was unleashing the contents of the two stainless steel canisters really necessary?

Despite the open waters and the safety of Mexico being in such close proximity, Vincent had no intention of attempting to run the blockade. The risk was too high, their cargo too precious. Besides, it simply wasn't needed.

Glancing toward the bridge, he exchanged nods with the lookout and then watched as his trusted aide scanned their surroundings with a pair of thermal binoculars. "It's clear, sir."

A second man appeared on the deck, quickly removing a blue, plastic tarp covering a small section of the aft cockpit.

Two multi-propeller drones rested on the fiberglass deck, each looking like an oversized metal insect.

The cartels had been using the sophisticated flying robots for nearly two years, investing and experimenting as the commonly available technology improved with each passing month.

Initially, they had purchased expensive, industrial models most commonly employed by Hollywood movie studios for aerial photography. It hadn't taken the organization long to realize that carrying a three-pound camera wasn't any different than transporting three pounds of cocaine north – or three pounds of cash south.

While those payloads were insignificant compared to the tons and tons of marijuana moving across the border each week, the flying mules were nearly impossible to intercept. In fact, it was only the occasional malfunction that resulted in a loss of cargo. As far as Vincent was aware, not a single drone had ever been intercepted by the U.S. Border Patrol. An impressive, unequaled method of distribution.

Over the last two years, the reliability and payload improved at a frantic pace as the massive American consumer market fell in love with drones. Control software improved, GPS guidance systems became commonplace, and the flying machine's endurance was significantly extended.

Just a few years ago, a drone that could haul five pounds of cargo over a distance of 25 miles had cost more than $10,000. Now, the same weight could be carried for less than a tenth of the cost.

Not only had the prices come down, but the capabilities of the tiny flyers had also advanced by leaps and bounds.

No longer was their flight controlled by a human manipulating tiny joysticks on a battery-powered remote. Today's machines allowed the download of a map-based set of GPS waypoints, after which they could take off, navigate the route, and land without any human in the loop.

While most were still incapable of carrying more than 10 pounds, the cartels had found the inexpensive devices the safest method for conveying high-value cargo. Packages of cocaine and heroin were commonly flown across the border at low altitudes during the night, only to be retrieved well outside the normal operational areas of law enforcement or customs officials.

After a quick reprogramming and swap to a fresh battery, ten-pound bundles of cash would make the return flight. It was a trickle, but as secure as any method attempted so far.

Vincent grunted as he watched his assistant pre-flight check the two flying robots. The U.S. Border Patrol had been patting themselves on the back the past year, bragging to all who would listen that their war on drugs was close to victory. "We're not seeing nearly as many shipments of hard drugs coming across these days," one federal agent had recently boasted to a major news network. "We see this as a sign that the cartels are being weakened by our interdiction efforts."

In reality, the reason why shipments of cocaine and other high-value contraband weren't being seized at the ports of entry was because a fleet of unmanned aircraft now shuffled that expensive freight back and forth.

"I now control more aircraft than United Airlines," Vincent joked with his expert. "My father would be so proud of me."

After verifying the drones were ready for their trip south, one of the drug boss's crew crossed to the swim platform and began pulling up a thin line using a hand-over-hand motion. The two stainless canisters appeared from the depths. After a quick check of the seals, they were cleaned and dried.

Each container of deadly bacteria was carefully mounted on the undercarriage of a drone while another man punched a series of buttons on a laptop computer.

"The course is plotted and ready, sir. The diagnostics on both machines show all systems are operational."

"Excellent," Vincent replied. "Launch when ready."

The drone's programmer reached inside his pocket and produced a pair of tiny, button-like devices, each containing a single switch. After verifying both GPS tracking units were functioning, he attached one to each canister via a powerful, rare earth magnet. If the cargo was dropped or the drone malfunctioned, they would be able to locate the precious freight.

Vincent moved to stand behind the head technician, more out of curiosity than any concern. "Launching number one," the operator stated.

The propellers of the closest drone began spinning, quickly building into an annoying buzz. Like a rocket, the quad-copter shot straight into the air, rising 20 feet above the deck and then pausing in a steady hover.

The drug lord knew his man was performing another systems check.

The tech pulled a thick-looking set of goggles from his computer bag, tugging the bug-eyes over his face and adjusting the elastic strap. This man could now

135

see through the drone's camera, what Vincent's people called, "First Person Viewing."

The reason was simple. If the drone was about to be intercepted, the tech could take over from the autopilot and attempt to divert to another course. He could also ditch the cargo to be retrieved via the GPS homing beacon at some later time.

Sensing the boss was peeking over his shoulder, the tech punched a few keys on the laptop. Vincent could now watch the same show on the computer's screen.

Flight #1 tilted forward and was gone in a rush, the bothersome buzzing quickly fading into the distance. A few moments later, #2 was trailing its sibling.

Each of the propeller-driven robots could reach a top speed of nearly 50 mph, but the techs didn't push the machine's capabilities. They never knew when a few additional miles of flight time might come in handy.

There really wasn't much to watch through the camera. The darkness, combined with the featureless surface of the water didn't make for much of a show.

In the corner of the laptop's display was a small map, a tiny blinking dot showing the flyers' progress as they made for the south side of the lake. Before long, everyone exhaled with a sigh of relief as the cargo entered Mexican airspace.

It was only another few minutes before the image broadcast by the drone's high-resolution camera changed. A dim line appeared, dotted with more lights. The southern shore soon zoomed underneath.

The eventual landing zone was actually over a dozen miles south of the international boundary. All eyes aboard the Queen Ami watched as a tighter cluster of lights appeared on the horizon. Within moments, the flying courier was soaring over a small village of mud-colored huts and dirt streets.

Slowing to a hover, Vincent watched as the camera lowered its angle to show a courtyard next to one of the larger homes. A flashlight blinked on and off three times from inside the walled enclave, a signal that the coast was clear. "Landing, sir," the tech reported.

Everyone could see the ground rushing up as #1 began to descend. A moment later, the camera went black as the drone was retrieved by one of Vincent's trusted lieutenants. Within two minutes, the sibling drone had landed as well.

Turning away from his gathered crew, the cartel boss strolled back to his position by the rail and quietly exhaled. He couldn't let his men know of the liberation that surged through his soul. That would be a sign of nerves and would surely be interpreted as weakness. Yet the relief was deep and genuine. He had never been so happy to be rid of anything in his life.

Vincent despised what the microscopic contents of the canisters represented because they frightened him.

He had survived countless firefights, a handful of assassination attempts, and had faced more armed foes than he could remember. He had met each and every one of those situations with ice in his veins and a steady hand. He feared no man, armed or not. He was the predator, not the prey.

The bacterium in the canisters was different. It couldn't be killed with a weapon, beaten into submission, or bribed with cash. The germs had no loyalty or motivation. They knew no master. Vincent's combat skills were useless against such a foe. His armies were helpless in the face of such an enemy, and the cartel leader didn't like it one bit.

"I truly understand the meaning of the word 'terror' now," he whispered to the night. "Soon enough, those fools in Mexico City will feel the cold horror of its grasp."

Always the pragmatic thinker, Vincent's thoughts soon returned to the next phase of the operation. He would have to cross the border soon and return home. He had to pick a target to prove he now possessed a weapon of mass destruction. He had to somehow mold the cartels into an organized fighting force.

They were called flocks.

Long ago, the cartels had learned that the American, and later the Texas border couldn't be penetrated without developing advanced, creative tactics.

Through the late 1990's, the battle had been fought with technology. Night vision, thermal imagers, long-range cameras, and even ground-scanning radar had been implemented by both sides of the "War on Drugs."

When American military capabilities had been redirected to the conflict, even the wealthiest of criminal organizations couldn't compete. Multi-million dollar drones, Blackhawk helicopters, and computer-networked ground sensors were beyond the reach of even the cartel's deep pockets.

Realizing they couldn't win with silicon and software, the first decade of the 21st century saw the smugglers' emphasis change to a strategy involving maneuver, distraction, and sacrifice.

Tunnels, submarines, and even hot air balloons began to replace powerboats, private planes, and secret trails through the desert. If shipments couldn't go through, they would go around. If the Yankees intercepted airplanes and boats, the cartels would build submarines or dig their way under the border.

During this transition, the drug lords learned a valuable lesson about their foe to the north. The Americans operated on quotas and statistics. Their fiscal budgets were renewed based on the tonnage of illegal drugs seized or the number of migrant workers detained at the border. Promotions and advancement within the federal ranks were largely based on how much was captured.

The percentage confiscated from the overall illegal trade in substances and people didn't matter.

The U.S. Customs and Border Patrol was always touting the big stings, quoting the "street value," and bragging about how they had taken such a vast sum of money out of the cartel's pockets.

No one seemed to care that the profit margin on a pound of marijuana was over 400%, the markup on crystal meth almost 20 times its cost to manufacture.

"We seized a major shipment of cocaine today with a street value of $1,000,000," the government agencies would boast. The fact that the cartel had paid less than $50,000 for such a load was made to seem insignificant.

Even more misleading were the reports of the massive weights involved. "The U.S. Border Patrol today announced that it had intercepted over 400 tons of marijuana this quarter, up slightly from last year's record of 393 tons."

What no one mentioned was that the amounts being shipped had doubled.

The best criminal minds in Mexico soon learned that as long as the federal juggernaut could look good during its Congressional reports, the vigor and enthusiasm of the agencies working against them would wane. So they sacrificed small percentages of product in order to feed the beast protecting the northern border.

If a batch of crack cocaine was ruined at the factory, it would be offered in sacrifice. Low-quality marijuana and non-usable meth were deliberately sent through border checkpoints to be discovered. Often the mules were enemies or troublemakers who wouldn't be missed as they spent time in an American prison.

All of this had led to the development of the flocks.

It was U.S. immigration policy to return captured immigrants to Mexico if it were their first offense. It had been a simple matter for the cartels to offer a discount off of the typical $3,000 coyote fee to anyone who was willing to join a flock.

Scouts on the Mexican side would spot increased Border Patrol activity and stage a flock for crossing. The group of 10-15 first-time offenders would meander through the desert or across the Rio Grande, intentionally showing themselves to the agents waiting on the other side.

Helicopters and massive amounts of manpower would be dispatched to catch the crossers, the green and white trucks vectoring in from all directions to apprehend the handful of illegals.

Often a second, smaller flock would cross shortly after, just in case a few of the U.S. agents hadn't been dispatched to capture the larger group.

When they were sure all of the Border Patrol personnel were occupied running down the flocks, the real crossing would take place. They almost always made it through.

As Vincent sat in the passenger seat of a pickup and nibbled on his fast food burger, he listened as the first flock was being loaded into the rafts, preparing to cross the Rio Grande just 15 miles west of Del Rio, Texas.

The Spanish play-by-play was being broadcast over the latest digital encoded radios, using a model similar to that employed by the Texas Troopers. The communications were deemed secure.

His driver was a locally known guide who specialized in feral hog hunts along this section of the river valley. There was even a credit card receipt from Vincent's fake identity, $150 in payment for the excursion – just in case the authorities got nosey.

On the off chance they were stopped by any republic officials, Vincent's story would pass field-level scrutiny, and he would simply try again a few days later.

The men managing the flock eventually reported their landing on the northern bank. Their next update indicated that several Texas law enforcement vehicles were moving to intercept the 12 illegals. There was even a patrol boat now shining its spotlight along the bank, trying to help the agents on the shore with the difficult job of rounding up the scattering migrants. Four of his sheep were special – long distance runners recruited from a high school's track team.

The second flock was launched soon afterward, about 500 yards upstream from the first. There were only six sheep in this group, all of them aboard an inflatable raft and paddling with their hands.

Vincent and his guide listened carefully to the radio, the Texan's reaction to the second group critical to the crime lord's safe journey home.

"The first flock is keeping them busy," announced the cartel scout on the southern bank of the great river. That fact was verified by the distant thumping of a helicopter, its spotlight clearly visible as it moved away to the north.

"Agreed," echoed the second watcher who was a well-paid, legal resident of the Lone Star Republic. "Should we go, sir?"

"Yes," Vincent nodded. "I am ready."

The pickup was moving then, rolling down Highway 90. After a few miles, it made a sharp turn and headed down a farm lane toward the wooded bank of the river.

Ten minutes later, Vincent and his guide were hopping out of the truck and hustling for the bank. Three blinks of a flashlight guided them the final 100 feet.

Two shadows stepped from the brush, both pointing flashlights at the drug lord and his guide. "Stop! Freeze! Texas Troopers! On the ground! Get on the ground!"

Vincent knew if he was captured now, there would be no chance of escape. Despite his best efforts, his face was now well known to the authorities. After the debacle in San Antonio, his image had been plastered all over the nightly newscasts from El Paso to Brownsville.

He was so close to achieving his goals. There was no way he was going to be taken alive.

In a flash, he drew an automatic pistol from the small of his back and fired a burst of 9mm lead.

One of El General's rounds struck the nearest officer in the meat of his upper arm, ripping through the limb's flesh and entering the chest cavity via his armpit. It was a million dollar shot, penetrating less than a quarter inch above the cop's body armor.

The second trooper snapped two quick shots at Vincent's guide, the man twisting and falling to the ground in a tangled heap.

Again, the drug boss fired a spread of eight rounds, two of which slammed into the remaining officer's upper thighs with devastating effect.

Vincent was running again, his bad left knee screaming with pain as he made the final sprint for the river.

Unlike the makeshift, dangerous rafts employed to transport the average illegal, Vincent's waiting craft was equipped with a silent, electric trolling motor, life jackets, and even a GPS locator.

A few minutes later, he was being helped up the Mexican side of the riverbank and into a waiting SUV.

"Welcome home, sir," Ghost announced from the front seat. "You've done well."

Zach arrived at San Antonio General, a small batch of flowers sitting on the passenger seat. The bouquet had been Cheyenne's idea.

He guided the pickup around the circular drive, following the hospital's signs and eventually stopping in an area reserved for "Discharged Patient Transportation."

Sam's face soon appeared as the automatic door rolled open, the lady ranger being pushed by an orderly wearing sky-blue scrubs. Her smile broadened as the sunlight hit her face.

Zach opened the passenger door and waited while Sam was helped from the chair and handed a single crutch. "Afternoon, Zach," she greeted, obviously thrilled to be released.

The senior ranger moved to help her climb into the truck, but she shooed him away. "I can do this," she declared. "Get my stuff, would you, please?"

Knowing better than to argue, Zach turned and accepted a small suitcase from the discharge attendant, which he promptly threw into the backseat. "Where are all your flowers?" he asked, watching his partner struggle with the ascent into the cab.

"I donated them to a service that delivers them to senior citizens' homes," she announced. "They were beautiful and all, but I have enough memories of my time here at Guantanamo Bay Hospital."

After verifying she was secure in the passenger seat and as comfortable as possible, Zach settled behind the wheel. "Where to?"

The question seemed to take her by surprise. "Hmmm ... I was so enthralled with my freedom that I hadn't thought about that. I suppose back to my apartment ... unless you've got something critical going on with the case?"

There was a hint of hopefulness in her question, almost as if she was praying that the republic desperately needed her services. Zach hated to bear bad news, "I wish, but no, there have been no new developments in the last few days. Every lead has gone cold."

"Shit."

"I'll drive you home and help you get settled," he offered softly.

"Thanks. You're sweet."

As they left the Alamo City, Sam's thoughts returned to the investigation. "So, in summary, we lost a bunch of Marines, are missing a batch of deadly biotoxins, have a couple of dead scientists as well as a good cop. The republic is taking one hell of a financial and political hit with the borders being closed, and the cartels now hold a weapon of mass destruction. Maybe I should have stayed in the hospital."

Zach realized she left one thing off her list, "How's the leg?"

"I can't put any weight on it. The docs wanted me to stay and let Nurse Attila keep me company for a few more days. But it was getting to the point where I was going to shoot someone, so they let me out on bad behavior and time served."

Zach chuckled but then guilt fueled his emotions. "Are you sure it's okay for you to go home? I mean ... taking a bullet isn't like a head cold or a strained muscle."

"They told me to stay off of it for another week or so, which is fine," the female ranger explained, waving off his concern. "But I don't want to talk about my leg. I've done nothing but talk, talk, talk about my fucking bad luck and bullet wound for days. The boredom was going to kill me long before any blood clot or infection, so I want to change the subject. What happened to that guy you coldcocked up in Abilene, by the way?"

"He's still in a coma."

"And the lady they found in the lab?"

Zach shook his head, "She was shoved into the closet where she enjoyed listening to the doctor's tortured screams for mercy, and then after about 30 minutes, his death. She didn't see any faces and couldn't help with any sort of description. That, and the fact that she had been trapped in the dark for almost three days doesn't make for a coherent witness. All in all, she's been about as much help as the guy I waylaid at the golf course. Nada."

Sam gave her partner *that* look. "Remind me not to have a beer with you when you're in a bad mood. I've heard you can get a little carried away when your mug is empty."

"I didn't mean to cave his skull in," Zach replied in all innocence.

"Uh-huh. Any identification verified off any of the dead bodies you've left along the trail?"

"No, which in itself is a little odd. The Mexican authorities are cooperating all of a sudden, and they claim none of the fingerprints or DNA we've sent match any of their records. I think they're stonewalling us.... I think the shooters with Vincent were Special Forces types, and our neighbors to the south are embarrassed to admit that their highly trained military guys are defecting to the cartels."

"And Vincent?"

"Nothing. We've sent his picture and description to every country and police force globally. Nada again … zip … like the guy beamed down from some starship."

"Weird. Just plain weird," Sam mumbled.

"We know Vincent and his buddies took two canisters of fully enriched pneumonic plague and a laptop containing the instructions on how to expand their terror crop using little more than the same basic equipment as your average, everyday meth lab. We keep waiting for the bio-bomb to drop, either here or in Mexico."

"Nice. Do we know if the stolen variety of plague affects both humans and animals?"

Zach shook his head, "According to the experts brought in from A&M, Vincent made off with a batch that will certainly kill pigs and cattle. No one is sure how lethal the new strains would be to people."

"So what you are telling me is that we don't know squat. Is that right?"

The ranger was skeptical. "If you believe what the science dudes are saying, then yes, we are far from well-informed. The university, CDC, and the Pentagon are all being really, really close-mouthed about all this. Personally, I think they're hiding something, most likely that people are going to start dropping dead from a bug invented in Texas – by Texans. I wouldn't be surprised if the cartel figured out how to put a Lone Star tattoo on each germ's ass."

Zach pulled into Sam's duplex and shut down the engine. Trying to be helpful, he hustled around to the passenger side and stood ready to help his hobbling partner.

As anticipated, Sam wanted none of it. "I can do this, Ranger Bass. I'm not some schoolgirl on a prom date."

"That's no shit," Zach mumbled.

Slowly managing the descent, Sam was proud of her accomplishment when she finally got down from the cab. "Get my bag, will you, Jeeves?"

Using her crutch, she managed the door, but it was obvious she was hurting. "Damn, it will be good to sleep in my own bed tonight."

Zach followed her in, carrying the overnight bag and the small bunch of blossoms he'd brought along. His partner wasted no time in heading for the couch after the exertion of the short walk.

Zach put the bouquet in a drinking glass, giving the stems a couple of fingers worth of water from the tap. He then checked the refrigerator, expecting to find sour milk and furry yogurt – or worse. He started laughing when he found the interior completely barren. "Your fridge is in worse condition than mine, and that's saying something. Make a list, and I'll run down to the market in a bit."

"Why would I have food in there?" Sam's voice retorted from the living room. "I'm never here."

"Good point. I'll have to remember that excuse the next time Cheyenne gives me a rough time about my lack of supplies."

"I've seen your icebox, Zach. There's a difference between empty and gross."

Secretly, Zach was happy his partner was her usual feisty self. Still, he couldn't let it go. "Thanks for all your help and concern, Zach," he mocked in a horrible, high-pitched imitation of a woman's voice. "You're really a great partner and good friend. What would I do without you?"

Both of the rangers started snickering.

"I'm sorry," Sam said after they'd enjoyed the chuckle. "Seriously, I do appreciate your helping out. Before you go running off to the market, I'd love to take a nice, hot shower and take the opportunity to appreciate my own shampoo and soap instead of that tarry substance they had at the hospital. Can you hang around for a bit and help a girl out?"

The ranger's years of law enforcement training and experience kicked in, immediately wary of a trap. "Umm ... err ... what exactly do you want me to do?"

Snorting at his reaction, she countered, "Nothing dangerous. Just hang out and make sure I don't fall and crack my head open in the tub. Can you manage that, Ranger Bass?"

"You got it."

Sam made a show of closing her bedroom door as Zach flipped on the television. He kept the sound muted – just in case a thump sounded from a bathroom tumble.

After hearing running water, he began flipping channels, hoping to catch some baseball highlights. It was a futile effort, as all of the news stations were focusing on the border closings and the financial damages to Texas, the U.S.A., and Mexico. The ranger turned it off, settling on the couch and picking up an old *Texas Monthly* magazine lying on the end table.

Some minutes later, he heard the water turn off.

Heading to the door, Zach called, "You okay in there?"

"Yes, I'm fine. It takes me forever to do anything."

Grinning, Zach said, "I read one time that 95% of people masturbate in the shower and the other 5% sing. Do you know what song they sing?"

"No."

"I guess that tells us which group you're in!" he laughed.

"Ha. Ha. Ha. I just love high school boy-humor," she countered, her voice suddenly sounding tired. "But seriously, Zach, come in here. I'm bleeding."

The ranger didn't waste a moment, twisting the knob and barging in. "Where?"

Sam was sitting on the edge of her bed, her face a little pale, a towel wrapped around her hair, another around her torso. "On the exit side of the wound, I think. I saw the blood when I was drying off."

"Let me have a look," he said.

She was reluctant but nodded with a sigh. He helped her lie down and then roll over, moving the towel to cover as much of her bare backside as possible.

The tissue surrounding the wound was pink and healthy looking while the actual bullet hole was a black and purple area of dried blood about the size of a quarter. Sam had been right; her bikini would ride just above the scar. Given the length and shape of Sam's legs, Zach doubted most guys would ever notice, and fewer yet would care.

"You're fine," he pronounced. "You just scraped the scab a little. Looks like surface bleeding, nothing coming from deep inside."

She started to rise, but he gently held her firm. "Stay put, I'll redress it for you."

The ranger tore open a package of large bandages from the bedside table and placed one over the wound. Pressing it there, he directed, "Roll over just a bit."

Sam complied, her covering towel sliding higher than before, revealing the perfect upward curve of her buttocks.

Ignoring the exposure, with a square of bandage covering both entrance and exit, he began wrapping her leg with a long strip of gauze to hold the dressings in place.

The procedure required Sam to spread her legs to an unladylike width. "Easy there, cowboy," she whispered. Zach's movements were warming her heart, as well as some other sensitive areas.

"There you go," he answered, "just call old Doc Bass whenever there's a problem."

She didn't move to cover herself, instead rolling her legs over the edge of the bed to sit. With her eyes holding onto Zach's, she stood and wrapped her arms around his neck, letting the towel fall to the floor.

Zach's gaze never left her, his hands automatically moving to her waist. Her skin was warm and soft. She smelled wonderful.

Sam started to pull him to her, closing her eyes and tilting her head for a kiss.

The blood was pounding in his ears as her body pressed against him. Their lips were less than an inch away, straining for the touch. The gap between them was closing slowly, both of their faces burning hot.

Without warning, she tensed, paused, and then held back. "What am I doing?" she whispered, still unwilling to pull away from his embrace.

Not knowing what else to say, Zach whispered, "I don't know, but I sure as hell like it."

"We can't," she trembled. "Cheyenne. Our jobs. Working together…. We can't. Nothing will ever be the same if we do."

Zach nodded but didn't want to let her get away. A hunger had been ignited, sending the flame of lust flowing through his veins. He craved her. He would take her for his pleasure until both of them were exhausted puddles of satiated flesh.

Again, they locked eyes, Sam still tight, pressing against his chest.

Visions flashed through Zach's head, mind movies of lifting her in his arms, laying her on the bed and ravishing every inch of her gorgeous frame. The heat inside him was a savage beast, howling for release.

"Zach?" she said weakly. "We can't. I want to … but…."

It was a miracle that he got it under control, finally nodding and relaxing his grip. "You're right," he whispered. "Damn it all to hell, but you're right."

Then they were apart, Sam reaching for the towel while Zach pretended to straighten his shirt. He exited her bedroom in a rush, making for the kitchen and a desperately needed glass of water.

He stayed sequestered there for several minutes, trying to clear his head and wondering what in the hell had just happened.

The sound of Sam's uneven steps accompanied by the thump of her crutch made him look up.

"I don't think I should be taking a hot shower while on serious pain medications," she said. "Those pills they gave me at the hospital are strong enough to get a girl in trouble."

Nodding, Zach was happy to agree. "Oh, hell yeah," he said, realizing the excuse gave them both a way to save face. "Probably not a good idea."

Before either of them could think of something else to say, Zach's cell phone jingled from the living room. It was that special ringtone assigned to Major Putnam.

"What is your status, Ranger?" the gruff commander asked.

"I just gave Ranger Temple a ride home from the hospital, sir," Zach responded. *And I almost gave her a lot more than that, as well, sir,* continued his thoughts.

"Good. Her condition?"

She has an ass you could bounce a quarter off of, unbelievably long legs, and is hotter than a streetcorner Rolex, sir. "She seems to be doing well, sir."

Putnam didn't miss a beat. "Excellent news, Ranger. Let her know Company E looks forward to her full recovery and eventual return to duty. Now, I need you to make for Fort Hood immediately. They have some new information relating to the disappearance of those bioweapons."

"Yes, sir."

"They'll be expecting you at the gate. I want a full report after you've visited with the military."

"Yes, sir."

Zach disconnected the call, perplexity written all over his face.

"What's going on?" Sam asked, tucking a blouse into her jeans.

After Zach had relayed the major's orders, she seemed to perk right up. "I'm going with you," she announced.

"No, you're not. You're staying right here and healing that leg. If you don't get off those pain meds, we're both going to get in a lot of trouble."

She pouted, but Zach wasn't sure the reaction was genuine. "Please, Zach. Take me with you. I'm going to go off the deep end if I have to stay cooped up one minute more."

The ranger considered her offer. He hated to admit he missed having his pesky partner along. More than once, he'd wondered how the last few days would have turned out if Sam had been at his side.

"Okay … you can ride along," he responded begrudgingly. "But take it easy. You're not ready to return to full duty yet, and I don't want anyone pointing the finger at me if you fool around and have a relapse. Understand?"

"Thanks, Zach."

Chapter 9

The MP at the gate asked the two lawmen for identification. "I was told only to expect Ranger Bass," he stated, not sure what to do.

"This is my partner, Sergeant. If you need clearance, you're welcome to call Major Putnam, the commander of Company E."

The military cop made the phone call, eventually returning with a shrug. "Please follow that pickup. The driver will escort you to the proper facility."

The two rangers did exactly as instructed, both of them noting the thick cloud of stress that seemed to have settled over the base. "Ever since the massacre, the military has had its dander up," Zach commented. "I hope that when we catch Vincent, the president agrees to let him face a court martial instead of a civilian judge."

"That's not going to happen," Sam replied. "It's a nice fantasy, but there's no way."

"I don't know. Maybe we can build our own Guantanamo out on Padre Island."

The two officers were led to one of the huge base's newest buildings, the large structure another sign of the republic's rapid expansion from just a state to being a country that had to manage all of its own affairs.

After parking in a spot clearly denoted as "Authorized Visitors Only," Zach and Sam departed the truck and were shown inside a pair of double doors.

Again, both rangers had to show their identification, which was verified by a phone call to Austin. Zach thought the entire security procedure was a bit overdone. That sentiment was soon enhanced.

An officer appeared with a briefcase. After a quick handshake and introduction, he produced two non-disclosure agreements and asked the rangers to sign.

"We are sworn peace officers," Zach pushed back. "We have federal authority granted by the legislature of Texas. I don't understand why you're asking us to do this?"

Sam whistled while reading the agreement. "Treason? Sedition? I'm with Ranger Bass – why are we being asked to sign this?"

The officer was patient, "Because you're about to be exposed to information that could severely compromise the security of the Republic of Texas. Neither of you can speak a word of this to anyone, including your fellow law enforcement officers. Is that clear?"

Zach didn't like all the cloak and dagger shit, his initial assessment being that the military was being overzealous. "We have to inform our chain of command, just like you do."

"Major Putnam and Colonel Bowmark of the Texas Rangers have been cleared to receive this information as well," the Army officer pushed back. "But that's as far as it goes."

Giving each other a "what the hell," glance, Zach and Sam signed the papers.

"Thank you," the officer responded. "I'll have copies of these made for your records before you leave here today. Now, if you'll follow me."

The man rose and exited the room. Without looking back, he strolled down a long hall at a brisk pace, the speed challenging Sam and her crutch.

Eventually, they stopped at an unmarked elevator that didn't list any floors on the buttons inside. That's because there weren't any buttons. The officer swiped a keycard through a slot, and soon they noticed the sensation of the box as it moved down.

Zach had no idea how far underground they traveled, but when the doors opened, the two lawmen found themselves facing three, armed MPs and a sturdy-looking steel door.

For the third time, their identification was checked, and then the rangers were shown into a large room with numerous high-resolution monitors, rows of desks, and several military personnel bustling here and there.

Zach spotted a tall man approaching, his swagger signaling someone of importance. "Welcome to our new situation room, Rangers," he began. "My name is General Hopkins. I command the military intelligence and counter-intelligence units for the Army of the Republic. Please, be seated. We'll begin shortly."

Zach and Sam were shown to a conference table and took their seats. One by one, others began joining them, everyone in uniform and displaying a variety of different ranks and insignias.

Without further ado, General Hopkins arrived at the head of the table and launched the meeting. "As I'm sure both of you know, the Treaty of Secession granted Texas 9% of the existing U.S. military assets. Most citizens know about the naval ships, aircraft, and ground forces that changed flags and are now part of our armed forces."

The two rangers nodded.

"What many people don't realize is that we also were given 9% of the intelligence assets. These forces include space-based observation platforms, remote listening posts, and even a few spy planes."

Zach was beginning to understand all the security now.

"Without wading through the technical weeds, you both need to understand that our satellite assets can hear, as well as see."

Sam tilted her head, "Hear? As in actual auditory resonation?"

The general nodded toward a lady colonel sitting at the table. She answered, "In a way, yes. Let's just say our technology can detect sound waves at resolutions far beyond the human range of hearing."

Zach thought about the episode that had occurred in Sam's bedroom less than two hours ago. "How detailed of a resolution and resonation are we talking here?" the tall ranger asked.

The general chuckled, "No worries, Ranger. We're not spying on everyone and everything. I do, however, hope you now can understand our need for secrecy. The average citizen wouldn't have a positive reaction after learning that we can hear, and differentiate among voices, car engines, and even sounds that are beyond a dog's audible range."

"The system was designed to monitor battlefields and areas of operation for our troops," the female colonel continued. "We can not only identify individual truck engines but can tell if the vehicles need a tune up. We can also recognize the voices of enemy commanders and individual soldiers. I'm sure you can see how this would give our forces an advantage during a conflict."

Zach and Sam both nodded, but were still unsure how the military's disclosure affected them or their case.

The general cleared that up. "We can also identify individual firearms. Each rifle and pistol has a unique sound signature, just like a fingerprint or DNA sample. I can tell you with certainty that one of the weapons used during your recent gunfight in San Antonio was also discharged a few days later along the Rio Grande River."

Both of the rangers were stunned but for different reasons.

Sam jumped in first, clearly intrigued by the technical aspects of the information being shared. "So you can tell the difference between my .45 and my partner's? From space? Even if we're using the same ammunition?"

"Yes, because you don't use the same weapons," the lady colonel smiled. "Ranger Bass uses a full sized .45 with a five-inch barrel; you use a Commander model, with a 3.5-inch tube. There is a distinct difference."

Zach couldn't believe what he was hearing, "So you're watching … err listening to everything going on in the republic?"

"No," sounded the general quickly. "We are not spying on the people of Texas. Normally, our devices are utilized only during military combat operations or for training purposes. It is merely a coincidence that a few days before the events in Langtry, President Simmons had requested that we conduct some research for his office. The issue of the expiring Federal Firearms Act was hotly debated, and the executive branch thought our technology might provide for a compromise that would be acceptable to all sides. Their thinking was that Texas would legalize several classes of weapons, but the discharge of all firearms would be monitored by our equipment. If a crime was committed, we could identify exactly which weapon was used."

"So if somebody robbed a bank and sprayed the lobby with their newly legal machine gun, your space-ears would be able to tell law enforcement whose gun it was?" Sam asked.

"Yes," answered the colonel. "Every weapon – even when you compare samples from the same model, make, and lot – has unique audio properties, even more specific than the grooves left on a fired bullet. There are minor machining differences, sometimes less than a thousandth of an inch. Components used in springs, triggers, barrels, and even magazines all provide an identifying sound signature that we can store, catalog, and compare."

Trying to wrap his head around what he'd just heard, Zach probed, "So, say a man walks in a gun store and buys a new firearm. He'd have to shoot it, which in effect would register the weapon. Is that right?"

"Essentially, I believe that is what President Simmons and his staff were thinking. However, the Republic's Congress managed to work out a compromise, and our services will not be needed. We were in the process of retasking our equipment when the massacre at Langtry occurred."

Sam, not wanting to get sidetracked into a political debate, reverted to the general's previous statement. "You said one of the weapons fired at the River Walk was also used along the border recently?"

"Yes, the incident where two Texas Troopers were involved with some supposedly undocumented border crossers. I believe one of the officers was killed, the other wounded. That same firearm, a Glock 18, was also fired in San Antonio during your encounter there."

Everyone turned to peer at one of the large monitors. An overhead view of the River Walk area was displayed, and as the rangers watched, a series of several small dots was overlaid on the image.

Another of the military contingency described what was being shown. "The red dots are from a Glock 18 being fired. The blue and white are from Ranger Bass and Temple, respectively."

The demonstration continued, Zach able to follow the action as it led from the restaurant's front door back into the alley. He could see BB and Gus's shots, as well as the cartel henchmen firing back. One of the weapons being used only fired one small burst. That dot pattern, with an orange hue, was blinking."

Zach looked at Sam and mumbled, "Vincent made it back to Mexico. He was crossing that night the trooper was killed, not some random smuggler."

The general stood, "I hope you'll find this information useful in your investigation, Rangers. I'm sorry to put you into a position where you can't divulge how or where you acquired this knowledge. Given the circumstances and serious nature of recent events, President Simmons felt this clandestine brief was the best course of action."

The two lawmen sensed the meeting was over, whether they were ready or not. About then, their escort appeared, this time holding a copy of their signed agreements in his hand. He started to lead the two rangers out when the general interjected, "Just one moment, Captain. Ranger Bass, if you please?"

Zach stepped aside with the senior officer. The general leaned in close and said, "Of course, you understand that our neighbors to the south would be furious if they had even a hint that we were using our capabilities to monitor their country."

"Of course – who wouldn't be pissed?" Zach answered, still wondering if the general's staff had been monitoring Sam's bedroom.

"So given that, you should also be informed that I am strictly forbidden from monitoring Mexico."

Zach nodded. "Makes sense."

"Good. I'm glad that is clear. I would be risking everything, including my career, our program here, and perhaps even my freedom if I were to mention a city in Mexico by the name of Tampico, more specifically, the private marina located there."

It dawned on Zach what the general was doing. What he couldn't understand was why. He decided to ask.

"My son was a Republic of Texas Marine," the officer stated with a tone as cold as the north wind. "He was murdered in Langtry. I violated orders when I put two and two together and tasked some of our assets to follow a certain SUV – the same one that picked up a passenger along the river the night the trooper was killed. I will say it again, Tampico. I can only pray that information helps you bring the men responsible for murdering my son to justice. Good day, Ranger."

Zach returned to a curious Sam, but his partner didn't ask until they had left the base.

"His son was one of the murdered Marines," he informed her. "He was begging me to bring the killers to justice." For some reason, Zach didn't tell his partner the rest.

Sam frowned, "That sucks. It sounds like they're out of our reach now. What do you think Colonel Bowmark will do?"

"Other than invade a foreign country, I don't know what they can do. Nobody wants a war right now, so I imagine we will let our Mexican neighbors know what is going on and hope they catch Vincent and recover the germs before anybody else gets hurt."

Zach could tell from the expression on his partner's face that she didn't have much faith that was going to happen. To be honest, he didn't either.

Vincent scanned the facility, nodding slightly in approval. It was the last place the authorities would search for a meth lab, and that was one of the primary reasons why it was so special.

Funerales Crematorio Colon was a family owned funeral home that had served Monterrey, Mexico since the early 1900s, and the perfect front for one of the Gulf Cartel's most productive "kitchens."

On one side of the well-kept stucco and brick facility was the area's largest Catholic Church. On the other was the regional police station. "The Americans have a saying," Vincent explained to Ghost. "Location, location, location."

"Jefe?"

"Never mind," El General said, waving off the always-curious man.

Even if the local law enforcement hadn't been on the cartel's payroll, El General didn't think the cops would have noticed anything unusual. Funeral homes, and the grisly preparations that took place inside, were typically places avoided by the average citizen, as well as the nosiest of policea.

Such services required hefty doses of chemicals, masks, gloves, and other materials used in the trade. In fact, some of the substances utilized by Vincent's cooks were the same items used to prepare the dead for burial. Caskets were excellent containers to hide and ship product. Who would dare to look inside?

El General had selected the Colon site for other reasons as well. Cooking meth was one thing, manufacturing large quantities of plague was quite another.

Of all the tens of thousands of meth kitchens, cocaine refining facilities, marijuana-processing factories, and other assets under the control of the cartels, it was the morgue at Colon that had both the security and the equipment to safely accomplish the task.

When the 1918 Flu Pandemic had ravished this part of Mexico with influenza, the hospitals and city morgues had been overwhelmed. The government in Mexico City had licensed and equipped Colon and a handful of other private businesses with the necessary equipment to handle any diseases that might be carried, transmitted, or transferred from the dead. That capacity was still maintained to this day.

With a small security entourage and an oversized briefcase under his arm, Vincent entered the air-conditioned lobby and headed immediately for a non-descript door that led to one of several small, private chapels.

The sanctuary was furnished with two rows of padded pews. Sparingly decorated with religious artwork, it was equipped with an ornate bookcase filled with various titles advising how to cope with grieving, death, and dying.

Vincent placed his hand on top of the bookcase in a very precise spot. There, a fingerprint scanner powered up and quickly verified that the drug lord's prints were indeed in its database and made the electronic decision to allow him entry.

A metallic click sounded as the steel bolts holding the heavy, wooden structure were released. The well-balanced shelving became a door, swinging outward enough to allow Vincent and his men to pass through so they could descend a flight of stairs.

In reality, there were two basements.

One was used to prepare the deceased for entombment, or if desired, incinerate their remains. This was also the section of the building where the rare government inspector was allowed to visit.

The other subterranean chamber was slightly smaller, far more secure, and the location where Vincent and his security detail now stood.

Two men waited there, both dressed in bright white lab coats. The elder of the two was a recent university professor who had found the intersection of soccer and gambling financially unsustainable. His assistant suffered a similar, more traditional addiction. Amor de las Mujeres, or the love of women, had ruined the man after he was caught romancing a Mexican Army general's wife. He'd been in hiding ever since, only the protection of the Gulf Cartel able to keep the hombre alive.

Vincent noted a newly opened box of hazardous material suits in the corner. While the lives of the two men facing him were unimportant, having any sort of outbreak or accident might bring unwanted attention to the operation.

"Do you have everything necessary to begin production?" El General inquired.

"Yes, Señor, all of the equipment and supplies have been delivered. We have studied the files on the laptop, and are confident that we can safely accomplish the task."

"Good," Vincent responded. "And you're prepared to remain here for the duration?"

"Yes, Jefe. We have adequate food and comfortable quarters prepared. Your order that no one is to leave this facility until 20 kilos have been produced will be followed to the letter."

Well, of course, my orders will be followed, Vincent thought. *The alternative would be most unpleasant.*

"I will await your call then. Good luck, gentlemen. I will have your bonus ready in three days."

The mention of their cash bonus brought a smile to both men's faces.

Years ago, Vincent knew the cartels would never have honored such an arrangement. Before he had taken over, the two technicians would have been killed and buried in the desert after accomplishing their tasks. Such was the shortsighted, narrow-minded thinking that had so dominated the criminal organizations for years.

El General was sure such dealings had limited the cartel's growth and expansion. Who wanted to do business with such ruthless men? Who could trust any arrangement? As far as Vincent was concerned, those methods had done nothing but drive up prices, limit opportunities, and inhibit recruitment.

Even today, his inner circle had lobbied to kill the two technicians after they had finished manufacturing the deadly substance. "What if they talk? What if they're detained and questioned by the authorities?"

"Then even more people will know that the Gulf Cartel honors its commitments. Everyone will realize that we reward good work and pay top wages for skilled labor," he had informed his team. "Have the money ready when they finish the job. Let them enjoy it and tell everyone in Mexico that we are trustworthy people with whom to do business."

As he ascended the stairs, Vincent wondered if his men would ever understand. "If we succeed with this operation, then it won't matter. I'll be able to engage the best management team in the world. Harvard MBAs and Oxford lawyers will send me their resumes.

Men like Ghost would make the difference in the long run. Brilliant individuals who could think, adapt, and overwhelm competition or negative circumstances. "I won't have to spend my time surrounded by such dimwitted idiots forever," he whispered.

Four solemn men carried the casket to the waiting hearse, the pallbearers all dressed in respectful black suits, white shirts, and mundane neckties. Nearby, a grieving widow clutched a handkerchief smeared with eye shadow and tears, firmly supported by a few family members and a man sporting a priest's collar.

After sliding the elaborate casket into the back of the idling Cadillac, the director of Funerales Crematorio Colon gently closed and locked the swinging rear door and then approached the distraught relatives. "If you'll accompany me, we'll proceed to his final resting place."

Across the street, Vincent sat with his security team in an older model minivan, observing the proceedings through the deeply tinted windows. El General had to chuckle as the funeral procession rolled by. There was a police escort, complete with flashing blue lights, in front of the hearse. "That was a nice touch," he said to Ghost. "The devil is in the details."

After the last vehicle carrying mourners had rolled past, Vincent's driver pulled out to follow. The jefe was taking no chances, personally overseeing the transfer of the ultra-valuable cargo inside the sealed coffin.

They followed the procession to a graveyard well outside of the city, away from prying eyes of the townspeople. The minivan hung back to observe the short ceremony without drawing any unwanted attention.

As soon as the widow and her oldest son had each laid a single rose on the deceased's casket, the small group of mourners began disbanding.

Thirty minutes later, only the van carrying the drug lord's entourage and a pickup belonging to the gravediggers remained. "Retrieve the cargo," El General ordered.

Two of his men exited the van, stepping directly to the casket that remained suspended above the six-foot-deep hole. When they spotted Vincent's men approaching, the two gravediggers turned and walked away, both knowing not to look behind them.

There was a dead man in the casket, the widow and grieving family all unknowing characters in Vincent's grand deception. There was also a false bottom in the coffin.

Like so many times before, the two cartel henchmen quickly disconnected the thin layer of wood and began removing the hidden contents.

Rather than the typical bundles of crystal meth, they extracted two stainless steel canisters, each slightly larger than a man's forearm. Less than three minutes passed before the coffin was reassembled and the bodyguards were back with their boss. El General eyed the two containers with only a mild curiosity. If there was any sort of leak or breach, everyone inside the van was already dead.

As the old car headed north, it was joined by two other vehicles, each filled with the cartel's most skilled soldiers. Vincent was well aware of the dangers involved in the next phase of the operation. He hadn't risen to the top of the organization by taking unnecessary chances.

The caravan drove for two hours through the Mexican countryside before a sign announced they were approaching the village of Los Arcos, a small hamlet that his men referred to as a border town.

Los Arcos held the distinction of being located on the imaginary line that divided Los Zetas' territory from the region controlled by the Gulf Cartel. Unlike so many communities and cities located on similar boundaries, there hadn't been any battle to decide who "owned" the nondescript huddle of adobe homes and metal barns. There simply wasn't anything nearby worth fighting for.

As the minivan approached the settlement, Vincent lifted a radio microphone to his lips and broadcast, "Manuel, is all as agreed?"

A few moments later, a familiar voice came back, "Yes, Jefe, all is as agreed. The air is cool at this elevation, and the site has been inspected."

Vincent nodded, his scout having used the proper keywords to let him know that the Zetas were honoring the pre-negotiated terms. The Z-44 crew and with his own security detachment were waiting for them.

As Vincent's convoy pulled into the lane leading to a remote villa, apprehension filled the old van. A face-to-face meeting between two leaders of competing cartels was unheard of. Just a few months before, the Zetas and Gulf organizations had been at war, killing as many rivals as possible while yet another wave of violence rocked northern Mexico.

The opportunity to eliminate the top man of a competing organization was tempting. Vincent's people had pleaded and begged him not to attend personally, but El General had been stubborn. "We must start down a new road. We must establish trust if our plans and dreams are to be fulfilled," he had vigorously insisted.

The three Gulf vehicles stopped at the entrance to the villa, a single Zeta employee waiting there to verify El General wasn't arriving with a massive army. Just like Manuel, the soldier lifted a radio to his mouth after counting the number of men in Vincent's party. They were soon waved through.

The old farmhouse seemed like an unlikely location for two of the world's most powerful criminals to meet. Humble by even rural Mexican standards, the small adobe home and two dilapidated outbuildings hadn't been occupied for some time. There would be no unassociated witnesses.

Vincent exited after his men had taken up positions facing the three Zeta vehicles gathered on the far side of what had once been a corral.

After exchanging nods, El General and Z-44 began walking to meet in the middle. They even managed to shake hands, much to the surprise of their anxious security teams.

"This is historical, I suppose," greeted the Zetas leader. "Somehow I feel as though we should have photographers and reporters recording the event."

Vincent chuckled, glad his rival had chosen humor to break the ice. "If we succeed, I believe we'll have plenty of media coverage, as well as a host of historians clamoring for details."

Z-44 actually smiled. "I suppose you are correct. Did you bring the weapons?"

"Yes."

"And you trust me with such devices?"

"Yes ... as much as our circumstances allow. If you turn the bacteria against my organization, surely you know we would react in kind. What was it the Soviets and the Americans used to call it when their thousands of hydrogen warheads threatened each other?"

Z-44 laughed, "They called it MAD or Mutually Assured Destruction."

Vincent nodded, "Yes. I remember now. Let us hope it doesn't come to that between us."

"We have prepared the delivery system as per your instructions. We also agree with your choice of targets, although our friends in the Knights Templar aren't going to be happy with either of us when they figure out we've unleashed the plague in their territory."

Vincent shrugged, "We gave them every opportunity to join us. Instead of sitting and talking like civilized men, they attacked your people and mine. Perhaps they will listen the next time we make a reasonable proposal."

"Perhaps," the Zetas leader responded, his tone making it clear he didn't believe such a thing could ever occur.

El General turned and waved at his party, the signal sending a single man to the middle of the corral. Z-44 mimicked the motion.

A duffle bag was exchanged, the two steel canisters inside. After verifying the contents were not explosive devices, the Zeta man nodded at his boss.

Vincent extended his hand, which was accepted by the rival crime lord. "Until we speak again."

"I hope your travels are safe," Z-44 responded. "We will make the delivery tomorrow morning, just after dawn. We will discuss the next phase after watching the results."

"Agreed."

After departing from Los Arcos, Z-44 had ordered the two canisters repackaged. Special fire extinguishers had been prepared, and soon the deadly bacteria were wearing a disguise that would fool even the most vigorous searcher.

Not that such an event was anticipated.

As they drove west across Los Zetas territory, Z-44's convoy passed through a countryside that his organization controlled with an iron fist. Mayors, police chiefs, politicians, and even federal law enforcement were all on his payroll. The only real threat would be a surprise incursion by some units of the Mexican military, and even then, he would receive several hours warning.

Still, Z-44 didn't want to take any chances.

Of all the cartel leaders, he had been both the first, and most enthusiastic in forming an alliance with El General. The plan was brilliant, workable, and would bring Mexico out of the quagmire that had plagued his country for decades. He wasn't going to be the one responsible for any failure or setbacks.

As they drove through the state of Coahuila, the crime boss's thoughts roamed between the past and future, envisioning what he hoped would be the results of El General's devious plot.

He remembered joining the Mexican Army as a young man, his intelligence and athletic ability soon earning him quick promotions. Then one day, he'd been invited to see if he could make the cut and become a member of an elite unit of Special Forces.

Reeking of patriotism, full of invincibility, and wanting more from life than what his dusty village could ever offer, he'd gladly accepted the posting.

The training had been brutal.

Then, an event occurred that changed Z-44's outlook forever. He had been chosen for a special honor. He would be attending a Special Warfare class in America, the four-week program being hosted at Fort Bragg in North Carolina.

It was the first time the young soldier had travelled out of his native Mexico, and the experience changed him forever.

He and a handful of other troopers flew into Atlanta where a bus from Fort Bragg picked them up. Z-44 recalled his astonishment at the vast wealth that rolled past the bus's windows.

At first, he'd believed the American driver was simply passing through the wealthiest areas, trying to impress the foreign visitors. It was soon obvious that wasn't the case.

Sergeants lived in housing that was superior to that provided for brigade commanders in Mexico. The Americans used ammunition without any thought of the cost. Helicopters carried soldiers into battle rather than flying officers to visit their mistresses. Even the lowly privates had automobiles, mobile phones, and color televisions in their off-base apartments.

The food, medical care, equipment, and morale were all far and above anything the young Mexican trooper had ever experienced. As time passed, the realization dawned that he served a second-class nation, both economically and militarily. It was disheartening.

His feverish patriotism and loyalty wavered. For months, he tried to move on, but the same old internal debate raged. Why? Why was his homeland not a first-world power? Why did his people live in such poverty? Was it the government? Corruption? The cartels? Was America to blame?

Over time, the frustration welled up inside him. The eventual resolution to his mental conflict was a common escape. "Patriotism is an extravagance. It's obviously every man for himself," he realized. "No one is going to give me anything. I will only ever have what I can take, and I can take a lot."

When a recruiter for Los Zetas started buying rounds of beer at an off-base cantina frequented by Z-44's unit, the cartel pitchman had found it easy to lure the highly trained troops. "You have earned the benefits of free enterprise," he stated. "The rewards will be enough for you and your families to live a quality of life beyond your wildest dreams."

Four years later, Z-44 had found himself in charge of Los Zetas after his boss had been killed by Mexican Marines in a government raid.

The convoy finally arrived at the small town of Cordova, an agricultural village residing on the edge of Los Zetas territory. From here, it was only a short flight into the heartland of the Knights Templar cartel.

Waiting for them was a Polish built, M-18 Dromader, a frumpy-looking aircraft popular with crop dusters all over the world. To Z-44, the damn thing looked like a cross between a camel and a battle tank. One of his men, a private pilot, had stolen the plane less than two hours ago.

The Zetas hustled to install the canisters, paying special attention to the instructions provided by El General's men. The pilot kept his distance, watching the activity with a nervous eye.

Once the plane was ready, Z-44 approached the flyer and said, "You know the targets. Those tanks will only provide 20 seconds each of spraying, so the accuracy of your bombing runs is critical. We'll pick you up in a few hours."

"Yes, Jefe."

Sensing the man's apprehension, Z-44 patted the pilot on the shoulder – a rare display of compassion to a subordinate. "Wear the mask and gloves, and you'll be enjoying dinner with your family this evening and for many more to come. The bonus I am paying for this job will make you a wealthy man."

The Zetas crew watched as the plane rumbled down the remote dirt strip and then leaped skyward. A wave of panic shot through the men on the ground when the pilot banked steeply and flew by at a low altitude. "Is he spraying us?" someone shouted as the plane passed overhead.

For a moment, Z-44 wondered.

Staring up as the plane shot past, he could see the masked face of the pilot looking down, his white-gloved hand waving a friendly gesture.

They watched the aircraft turn to the west, its droning motor's hum fading into the distance.

For just a moment, Z-44 wanted nothing more than to stand and watch, unsure if his legs would move. It finally occurred to him what he had just done. For the first time in his adult life, the cartel boss experienced the deep frost of absolute terror.

What had he just unleashed? What sort of horror was in the crop duster's tanks? It was as if he had just launched a nuclear missile – a weapon that couldn't be called back. There was no radio in the plane. There was no recalling the germs.

For a brief moment, Z-44 wondered if the American President Harry Truman had experienced the same emotions when he'd ordered the atomic strike on

Japan. Did that leader have regrets? Did he wonder what hell he had unleashed upon his enemy? Did he ever sleep again?

Standing around, waiting for their boss's next command, the Zetas crew had no idea of the doubt and insecurity that rushed through Z-44's veins.

Z-44 began to rationalize. *For there to be the revolution my people need, some must be sacrificed. There are always casualties with change. There are always those who must perish for the greater good*, he thought.

The rhetoric helped push down the fear and trepidation that were building in his core. He couldn't make the negative emotions disappear, but he could control them. He wondered for a second if they would ever go away entirely.

Still, he couldn't let his men see his feelings. He had to be strong. Finally, when the black dot of the aircraft disappeared in the distance, he turned and said to his waiting crew, "Let's go get a cold beer. I'm thirsty."

Chapter 10

The stockyards outside the town of Amecia were packed, the border closure with Texas having an enormous impact on one of Mexico's most lucrative, legal exports – beef.

The few people who noticed the crop duster paid little attention to the tiny plane. The area was brimming with farms and orchards; family owned businesses that raised potatoes, blackberries, limes, and or course, maize. Such aircraft were a common sight during certain phases of the multiple growing seasons.

The vaqueros working at the yards were an exception.

"What is that idiot doing?" asked one weathered cowboy, leaning against a fence after just having separated two competing bulls. "He's going to spook the cattle!"

At 150 feet above the extensive facility, the pilot turned a knob in the cockpit and flipped a small switch. For less than 10 seconds he held down on the valve's control, allowing the odorless, colorless aerosol to flow from the canisters under his wing.

He made a wide turn, ignoring the waving hats, middle fingers, and clenched fists from the vaqueros below. The massive, compacted herds were already jumpy. If some of the stock were damaged or the fences were pushed down, all hell could break loose, and men could lose valuable jobs.

When the pilot made a second pass, a supervisor was calling the local police.

Before anyone at the rural station answered, the plane vanished to the east.

The pilot's next target nagged at the man's soul.

The Guadalajara metro area boasted the second largest population in Mexico. The pilot was thankful Z-44 hadn't ordered him to spray the city.

Instead, he was to follow the passenger rail line heading north and west to Tijuana. There, just outside the suburban outskirts, he would find a large train station.

As he flew toward the extensive cityscape, the roadways became wider and far more congested. "It's rush hour," he shouted over the drone of the plane's engine. "The train station will be packed."

As the miles went by, he began sweating. His family had ridden along that same railroad, a short spring vacation just a few years ago. He could still remember the packed cars and excitement in the air. His sister had been travelling to see the ocean for the first time. His father was going to take his sons fishing in the Pacific.

The pilot's chest began to hurt, and for a moment, he thought he was going to vomit in his mask. That thought led to even more distress as he realized his chances of being infected with the poison under his wings would greatly increase if he wasn't breathing filtered air.

He couldn't do it.

For a brief moment, he thought about returning with the second tank full and pleading for Z-44's mercy. He decided against that plan, as his death was practically guaranteed, and it would be a slow, painful demise. Los Zetas did not suffer incompetence, cowardice, or failure.

In a panic, he reached for the dash and dumped his cargo, paying no attention to what was underneath his plane. For 20 seconds, at 240 kilometers per hour, the deadly bio-toxin sprayed from the tank.

When his finger closed the valve, the pilot suffered his second panic attack. "What if Z-44 has people watching the train station?"

He decided to fly over the facility, just in case. Who would know? It wasn't his fault that the tanks malfunctioned. How could he be blamed for the bioweapon's failure?

Below the crop duster, Hugo Garcia and his family were traveling toward the coast on Federal Highway 70. Hugo, an assistant restaurant manager in Guadalajara, was already angry with his wife, and their vacation was less than two hours old.

She hadn't had the kids ready when he returned home. They had gotten a late start, and now he was gridlocked in a combination of weekend and rush hour traffic.

Hugo noticed the small plane flying parallel with the highway and welcomed the distraction. Anything was better than staring at the bumper of the oil burning, old Chevy he'd been following for the last 45 minutes.

When a slight mist blurred his field of vision, the frustrated motorist had scanned the sky, looking for clouds. "Where is that moisture coming from?" he asked his pouting wife. "The weather report didn't say anything about storms on the way."

He realized it wasn't raining when his windshield wiper smeared the substance. It required three blasts from the washer before his line of sight was clear.

"Whatever it was, there was a lot of it," he said, glancing in the rearview mirror. "I can see the cars behind us cleaning their glass as well."

Satisfied that his long-awaited holiday wasn't going to be ruined by hostile weather, Hugo's thoughts returned to the traffic, wondering how many more miles it would take before he was free of delays.

The disease spread through the stockyard like wildfire.

At first, the authorities thought the respiratory infection was merely due to the overcrowding. They did their best to separate the ill animals, including shipping some apparently healthy stock to neighboring facilities.

At the same time, the hospital at the resort town of Puerto Vallarta found themselves treating an unusually high number of cases involving what looked to be a resistant strain of pneumonia. Within 24 hours, the facility had identified patient zero as one Mr. Hugo Garcia and his entire family.

The first animal death was quickly followed by the demise of Mr. Garcia's wife. Within 48 hours, the World Health Organization was mobilizing a team to travel to central Mexico. Before they could board a plane, over 13,000 head of cattle had perished.

It was the death of the first cowboy working the Amecia stockyards that ignited a state of emergency throughout the Mexican healthcare system. It was extremely rare that the same bug infected humans and animals. Alarm bells were sounding in Mexico City.

That reaction, however, was benign compared to panic that ensued when a message appeared on several internet social media sites. The same video was delivered to every major news organization in the country and was soon being broadcast all over the world.

A handsome young actor, dressed in a conservative silk suit, appeared stately sitting behind an expensive-looking, mahogany desk. Staring square into the camera, he began: "My countrymen, it is with the greatest urgency that I come before you. We have become aware of the most horrible, despicable act being unleashed on the Mexican people. I speak to you as a representative of the organization commonly called the Gulf Cartel. I say to you with confidence that members of the federal government in Mexico City, as well as the leaders of the Knights Templar and several other cartels, have unleashed a terrible weapon on our citizens. We have undeniable proof that the slaughter of cattle being reported in Amecia and the sickness spreading along the Pacific coast are the results of a biological weapon that was developed in Texas."

The announcer paused, giving his words time to sink in before continuing. "Agents working for several key elected officials, in conspiracy with certain criminal organizations both in Mexico and Texas, have banded together in an attempt to overthrow the government in Mexico City."

The narrator became angry, his voice showing the first emotion of the well-rehearsed presentation. "I know that our organization is often lumped into the same category as many of the criminal gangs that operate in our great nation. Not long ago, much of this soiled reputation was deserved. Today, however, we come before you as concerned, common citizens. Today we are Mexicans … patriots who love our country … everyday men and women who wish to make our neighbors aware of this heinous act."

"I am here today to pledge to all of you that this corruption will not stand as long as my compadres and I draw air into our lungs. I promise each and every citizen of Mexico that we will use all of the resources at our disposal to fight this gang of megalomaniacs who will stop at nothing to consolidate their control over our lives."

The actor appeared as though he was close to tears, such was the depth of his apparent despair. "To the Army, I pray you remain vigilant. Those of you who do not join this rebellion will be attacked with the same weapons of mass destruction that have already been unleashed and are killing hundreds of innocents. To those in the government who are not involved in this treachery, again, I warn you to remain alert. The men behind these acts of terrorism will use every means at their disposal to destroy you and your families if you do not comply.

"To the people of Mexico, I ask that you join us in this crusade to eliminate this threat and restore peace and honor to our country. The government in Mexico City must resign. The military commanders and their corrupt infrastructure must resign. Our justice system no longer serves the people and must be replaced. It is time for a new revolution, my friends. It is time that the people took back our great nation and restored Mexico to her rightful place in the world community before these madmen kill us all."

No more than two hours after Vincent's video nearly overwhelmed Mexico's internet capability, Z-44 produced a similar online manifesto, pledging his support and decrying the holocaust that was poised on Mexico's door.

Before the end of the day, no less than seven cartel leaders had reiterated Vincent's message, all pledging their private armies to fight for the "cause" and put an end to the slaughter of the Mexican people.

The Chapultepec Forest was one of the largest city parks in the Western Hemisphere and had been inhabited since pre-Columbian era. It was often called the "lung" of Mexico City, the heavy foliage, and dense plant life deemed critical to filtering the air of the world's 10th most populated metropolitan area.

At just under 1,700 acres, "Grasshopper Hill" was not only home to numerous historical and cultural attractions, but also contained a section called Los Pinos (*The Pines*) - the official seat of the Mexican Executive Branch.

After receiving several calls from fretting state governors, President Salinas summoned his leadership to a special meeting to discuss the cartels' videos and their extravagant claims. Early signs of panic were being reported, resulting in numerous regional authorities beginning to ask troubling questions.

The cabinet members were all in their respective seats when the chief executive entered the conference room. As usual, it wasn't long before the different camps formed, each growing emotional and intense as the discussion matured.

"They are only trying to stir up trouble," the Secretary of the Interior informed the president. "There is a minor infection that has impacted a few unfortunate souls, as well as a virus reported in a single stockyard. We should not succumb to this attempt at extortion."

"It just goes to show how desperate they have become," added a general from the other end of the table. "The secession of Texas, combined with our forces killing or capturing their leadership, has them reeling. This is just a ploy to regain the initiative, nothing more."

The Secretary of Health, however, wasn't so sure. "The information I'm receiving is worrisome, Mr. President," she chimed in. "While we're still waiting for the official report and lab results, my people in the field are concerned."

A burst of conversation, protests, and side discussions filled the room, more than a few of the gathered officials trying to be heard at the same time.

President Salinas let the hubbub continue, but not for very long. Holding up both hands, he signaled for quiet. "I don't expect anyone to have all of the answers just yet," he stated calmly. "What I do need is a consensus on how to react to this provocation."

"Ignore it," snapped the man in charge of communications. "Do not give it the slightest bit of credibility by acknowledging their worthless propaganda."

Again, bedlam erupted, half of the room apparently agreeing, several others protesting the suggestion.

It took longer to settle the assembled officials, but once again, all eyes were focused on the man who had to make the ultimate decision.

"We will compromise," he stated. "We will use a lower level office to dispel their claims. We have a minor outbreak of an infectious germ – nothing more. The United Nations and other global agencies are here or on their way to Mexico to investigate. We will leave it at that."

The first riot erupted not out of fear or distrust of the government, but because a pharmacy in the suburbs of Guadalajara had distributed the last of its limited supply of antibiotics. Within an hour, shortages were being reported all across the country. Like a run on the banks during an economic downfall, long lines began forming outside of every hospital, doctor's office, and pharmacy outlet. In many locations, the police were dispatched to keep the peace.

The first indirect death was reported in Tijuana.

An older man, standing in a two block-line outside a health clinic, began coughing. The people waiting with him in the queue became concerned that the individual was already infected. They demanded that he leave. He refused. A fight broke out, and the victim was trampled.

News stations all across Mexico began reporting more and more cases of the severely contagious strain of what was being described by some as a "respiratory plague." No one was able to make any sense of the pattern of outbreaks and the rapid spread. The infected cars and trucks, stuck in the traffic gridlock when the pilot had dumped his load, had driven to a number of towns and villages throughout the western and central regions of the country.

It wasn't only humans that were suffering. Cattle were dropping dead by the thousands all over the northern states. Ranchers began to panic, rushing to diseased stockyards and demanding their apparently unaffected animals be returned, which only served to spread the airborne bacteria to healthy herds. The first case of a plague-ridden hog resulted in a wave of rumors, speculation, and inaccurate information to roll through the agricultural communities that fed the people of Mexico.

As the bad news continued to inundate the people, more and more credibility was being given to the cartels' accusations.

President Simmons glanced up from the report he'd just read, a deep frown crossing his face. "We need to tell Mexico City the truth, gentlemen. I know the consequences will be bitter and long-lasting, but it's time that we came clean."

Colonel Bowmark nodded, "Technically, sir, we had nothing to do with the development of those bio-weapons. The lab where they were being tested wasn't part of any Texas institution or sponsored in any way by our government."

Simmons shook his head, "Do you really think that's going to matter to President Salinas or the Mexican people?"

The Secretary of State, always the diplomat, cleared his throat, "If we do choose to go that route, sir, I strongly suggest that we downplay the entire affair. There is no proof yet that the strain in Mexico is the same one stolen from the lab outside College Station ... at least not any evidence that is likely to become public knowledge."

Simmons didn't like it. "Cover-ups and filtering the truth always comes back to bite you in the ass," he mumbled.

"The republic did nothing wrong. We had zero ill intent. We didn't even know they were researching such things," continued the man heading up Agriculture.

"But the United States did, sir," countered the republic's top diplomat. "If you go public with all that we know, it's going to make President Clifton and her administration look bad. That will serve little purpose other than to strain relations even further. Washington isn't going to like being designated as the villain here."

"But it's the truth," Bowmark barked. "Doesn't the truth matter for anything these days?"

The expression on the diplomat's face said it all. Bowmark was a cop who operated in a world of black and white, right or wrong. "I'm sorry, Colonel, but when it comes to international relations and politics, the truth is a many-splendored thing. Even if we stated the facts in an unbiased way, the Republic of Texas would still be open to legitimate, intense criticism. Why didn't we know what was being developed within our borders? How was it that Texas allowed such substances to be stolen right from under our noses? Why didn't we warn our neighbors immediately? Do you understand, Colonel?"

The old lawman nodded, but still didn't like it. "My apologies, Mr. Secretary. I should know by now to keep my opinion of political matters to myself."

The statesman smiled and then returned his attention to the president. "I would also suggest that you call the White House and discuss any release or statement with President Clifton beforehand. America is exposed in all of this, almost as much as we are. Clifton has some excellent people working up there – perhaps we can cooperate and manage the entire situation in a controlled fashion."

Simmons grunted, obviously not looking forward to having the conversation. Still, the secretary was correct as usual. "No time like the present," the president stated, reaching for the phone at the corner of his desk.

"Get me President Clifton, please," he spoke into the speakerphone. "Tell the White House that it is urgent."

"Right away, sir."

It was several minutes later when Simmons's assistant rang back. "I have the White House Chief of Staff of the line, sir. President Clifton is unavailable at the moment."

After exchanging approving glances with the secretary, Simmons said, "That will be fine. Thank you."

"President Simmons, it's been some time since we've spoken," the voice sounded through the speaker.

Only 15 minutes were required to brief the WHCOS, Clifton's right-hand man listening without uttering a single word.

"I had no idea such research was taking place in Texas, Mr. President. Evidently this is a program that fell through the cracks after secession, and has obviously developed into a problem for both of us," the Washington politician stated. "I will inform President Clifton immediately. Will you be available for a call this afternoon?"

For a moment, Simmons thought about barking at the man who was clearly acting as a gatekeeper. Ever since the secession, it had been "little you, big me," whenever the republic had business with the United States. The gravity of the situation, however, made him check the reaction.

"Yes, I look forward to hearing from Mrs. Clifton," Simmons said, hoping the subtle insult was understood on the other end of the call.

The second batch of product "cooked" in the basement of the funeral home was removed in the exact same way, but this time, the container was of a different shape and size.

Within a few hours, an unremarkable sedan was traveling from the cemetery toward the naval base at Veracruz.

The 90-minute journey along the coast was scenic and relaxing, the driver having no idea of what sort of cargo resided under the spare tire in his trunk. It wasn't unusual to pick up a little extra money as a courier. He never knew what was in any of the packages or envelopes and didn't care.

El General had selected Veracruz for a variety of reasons.

First and foremost was the fact that the Mexican Marines were the primary force used against the cartels. It was well known that the Army had been thoroughly infiltrated years ago, with everyone from field officers to members of the general staff on the criminal syndicates' payrolls.

The Marines had proven to be far more difficult to penetrate, partly due to their small size and isolated command structure, as well as higher standards of recruiting and training.

Unlike most nations, there was no integrated command between the Army and Navy in Mexico. Each organization had its own commander on the presidential staff, and competition for budget, influence, and political stroke was an everyday occurrence.

The other reason why El General chose Veracruz was the base's historical significance.

In 1914, the U.S. Marines had invaded the coastal town, Mexico's largest port at the time. The justification for the military action had been questionable at best, President Woodrow Wilson seemingly eager to become involved in his southern neighbor's ongoing revolution.

Ultimately, the vastly superior American forces overwhelmed the city's defenders, but not before the students at the Veracruz Naval Academy put up a heroic, if short-lived, defense.

Like the Alamo in Texas, the city holds a special place in the national memory of Mexico. The U.S. invasion and occupation are widely considered one of the ugliest deeds ever inflicted on the country. Later, in remembrance of the conflict, the port's name was officially changed to Heroica Veracruz.

It had been Ghost's recommendation to strike an iconic symbol that held meaning for the general population. In Vincent's grand scheme, that emblem of Mexican nationalism was the perfect target.

The courier arrived at the designated address, parking his sedan in front of a small commercial business advertised as G&L Mechanical. A few minutes later, after a busty, young lady had signed for the cardboard mystery box, he was on his way back to Tampico.

A truck soon left the business, the bright red and green logo of G&L Mechanical a common sight on the streets of Herocia Veracruz. The driver, a technician employed at the firm for over five years, made for the naval base.

He was passed through the security gate without much ado. The air conditioner atop the facility's main administration building had been experiencing issues for over a week. G&L was a registered vendor, the driver's identification already on file.

"The new part we ordered from Panama finally arrived today," the repairman informed the guard. "The base commander will be able to enjoy cold air soon."

"Perhaps it will improve his mood," the Marine sergeant chuckled, waving the van through the checkpoint.

Parking his company vehicle in a spot marked, "Service Units Only," the driver hefted his toolbox, pressure meters, and the cardboard container. He had been here several times before and knew exactly which entrance was closest to the misbehaving air conditioner.

Again, his identification was checked while his tools and the spare parts were scrutinized. All seemed to be in order, and he was allowed to enter the building.

He rode the elevator to the third floor, from there accessing a maintenance stairwell that led to the roof.

In less than 30 minutes, the reserve tank of "Freon," and new capacitor were installed on the building's primary HVAC unit. Using an ice pick, the technician then inflicted a small, pinhead-sized puncture in a tube leading to the main air induction ducts.

Holding his breath, he opened the reserve tank's valve and scurried for the door.

As he exhaled and breathed on the stairwell, he knew the reaction was silly. It would be at least 30 minutes before the pressure on the coolant tank bled enough to release the secondary's gas. While he'd not been told exactly what was inside the package, it wasn't difficult to guess.

Fifteen minutes later, he was leaving the base, happy to be done with the task, and looking forward to relocating to Brazil. The airline tickets were already in his glovebox, a bird to freedom that was leaving that very evening, well before anyone would come around asking difficult questions.

With his HVAC skills, a pre-arranged work visa, and the $100,000 U.S. he'd soon be paid, life was surely about to improve. *My portly wife will never find me*, he grunted, relishing the thought of the beaches and Rio's decadent lifestyle.

Aside from the money and a new start, the tech felt a strong sense of gratification derived from revenge. The Marines had gunned down his brother three years ago, an innocent bystander caught in the crossfire between the cartel and the government.

The money might be nice, a welcome, once-in-a-lifetime windfall. The arrangements to relocate even better. To live in a place with more opportunity and less violence was a Godsend. None of that, however, could compare to the satiation derived from the sweet taste of vengeance that rolled across the palette of his soul.

"I assure you that I personally had no knowledge that such research was being conducted," Heidi Clifton informed President Simmons. "I would never have supported such an endeavor."

The republic's chief executive was skeptical, but decided now wasn't the time. "I understand, Madam President. There have been numerous examples of government-supported projects that have been difficult to unwind post-secession. I believe it is in both of our nation's best interests to determine the path forward, not point fingers of blame over the past."

"I agree. What do you recommend?"

Damn her, Simmons thought. *That woman treats us like some backwater tribe until there's a catastrophe brewing. Then she is happy to stand aside and let us lead the way into the slaughter. I'm sure she'll be happy to arrive after the battle is over and bayonet the wounded.*

Clearing his throat, Simmons offered, "I think President Salinas needs to hear the truth – from both of us."

There wasn't an immediate response, almost as if the veteran Washington politician was having trouble choosing her words. Finally she answered, "There are many different ways to phrase the truth, Mr. President. We should be extremely careful how we present the facts to our mutual southern neighbor … and the world."

It was Simmons's turn to be coy. "How would you suggest we proceed, Madam President?"

"Before we get to that, I believe it's important for both of us to consider the ramifications beyond Mexico and Latin America. There are certain nations that would take extreme poetic license with any statement we make. North Korea comes to mind, as do Russia and China. If we're not careful, their propaganda machines will begin spewing tall tales that have both of us developing offensive biological weapons – and deploying them against peaceful neighbors. We'll both be reading headlines about a new arms race, something neither of us needs before the next election. Every treaty negotiation, peace conference, trade agreement, and diplomatic encounter for the next ten years is going to throw these events right into our faces."

"Go on," Simmons said, wondering where Heidi was going.

"I suggest we downplay the entire affair. I recommend we classify many of the details as secret and place the majority of the blame on over-zealous private enterprise."

Simmons didn't like it, but he had to admit President Clifton had a valid set of points. "And Mexico? The people?"

Heidi's response carried a dismissive tone, "We'll both send help ... lots of help. Between our two nations and the World Health Organization, we'll stop this thing in its tracks and end the crisis. Later, after the dust has settled, we will throw some juicy foreign aid at Mexico City to make nice. It's how things are done."

When the Texas leader didn't respond, President Clifton continued, "Let me have some of our best over at the State Department prepare a release. I will have it sent to you before we go public with anything. Agreed?"

Simmons didn't have a better solution, and he begrudgingly had to admit that Washington's diplomats had far more experience with such matters than his staff in Austin. "Agreed."

President Salinas scanned his senior advisors with an expression that managed to encompass fear, anger, and a deep sense of loss.

He found very few eyes meeting his own, most of the gathered secretaries and officials still fixated on the speakerphone that had just delivered news of their worst nightmare. The cartels had a weapon of mass destruction. They were deploying it. God only knew when or where they would stop.

"It is good that Presidents Simmons and Clifton have pledged their support," Salinas began, trying to muster bravado when in truth he felt none.

"The gringos unleash a tiger in our village, and then offer to provide U.S. bullets to hunt it down – after it has eaten the children," mumbled the Secretary of Interior. "With such friends, who needs the cartels?"

"Both of them were hedging," noted another. "They never tell the entire truth when they fuck up."

Salinas shrugged, "Would we? Have we been honest with our people and ourselves? The Americans didn't send the bio-weapon to our country. The Texans didn't invite the cartels to invade their territory and steal the germs. The blame doesn't rest entirely on their shoulders."

"Will any of that matter to our people?" grumbled the Secretary of Health. "There is a mass panic brewing in the streets. The pressure has been building like the magma of a volcano preparing to erupt. Our citizens have barely managed to tolerate the corruption, violence, and lack of justice that has commanded Mexico for generations. We've had outbreaks of vigilantism, a mass exodus of our most talented professionals, and now this ... this attack. I fear for our country. I fear for our people."

The president's gaze again canvassed the faces that surrounded him, giving all of them a chance for their voices to be heard. When no other comment was offered, he continued, "If Mexico is to survive as a sovereign nation, we must all pull together and summon every last bit of greatness in our souls. This crisis must bring out the best in all of us. We owe it to our people. We owe it to our great nation."

"What do you propose, sir?" a voice from the far end of the table queried.

Salinas pondered the question for only a few moments before he spread his hands and said, "We must give our citizens something to rally around. We must give them a reference point to focus their hatred and fear. Until we can bring this Texas-born death under control, we must provide a channel for the grieving, rage, and terror that will surge through our populace."

He had their attention now. For the first time since the foreign leaders had dropped the bioterrorism bomb, the leadership of Mexico was engaged. Their leader evidently had a plan, and in the vacuum of hopelessness that filled the room, any course of action would be welcome.

The president, sensing the momentum, continued, "I will go before the people and be forthright about the challenge we face. The blame, however, will not reside in Mexico City or with the cartels. We didn't create this horror.... This plague wasn't a product of our military or industry. If the United States and Texas hadn't been dealing with the Satan, his demons wouldn't have been loosed to ravage our countryside. The people need to know this."

Many of the officials grasped Salinas's concept instantly. They were educated people, well versed in a history that was ripe with examples where challenged rulers had redirected the ire, rage, and hatred of their citizens when faced with extreme challenges or external threats.

Hitler had used the Jews as a lightning rod, refocusing the German population's frustration with deplorable economic conditions. Stalin had used the West to rally the people to his cause. Japan had used the Chinese as they expanded their empire across the Pacific Ocean.

"We will put the blame directly where it belongs," Salinas stated without emotion. "We will point our people's pain and suffering to the north."

For the first time in his adult life, Vincent smiled while watching a national press conference. It was the only time he could ever remember cheering a Mexican President as he spoke to the people. He had to give the man credit; Salinas was definitely inspired today.

On and on, the politician droned, hammering home the message that the United States and Texas were doing what they had always done – treating their good-hearted Mexican neighbors like dogs.

El General had to admit, the man was doing a damn good job of bashing his fellow heads of state. Salinas didn't come right out and say that the gringos were deliberately trying to destroy their neighbor to the south. He didn't specifically point a finger at any single person, race, or political party. Yet the meaning was clear – the superpowers to the north had gotten sloppy, and now the poor, undeserving citizens of Mexico were paying the price.

When the speech arrived at the point where Salinas promised to lead his people out of the crisis, Vincent lost interest. When the president began promising a massive international response, the Gulf Cartel jefe turned off the television.

Turning to Ghost, El General sighed, "They are reacting just as anticipated."

"More inspired perhaps, but yes, El General, just as we predicted."

Vincent rubbed his chin for a moment. "As our gringo friends like to say, it's time to let the other shoe fall."

"Yes, Jefe. I'll see to it immediately."

An hour later, media outlets throughout Mexico began receiving a second series of video recordings from the cartel.

The release of professionally manufactured social media pieces had been Ghost's doing.

The rise of the Arab Spring, as well as the secession movements in Tibet and Scotland, had all used social media and the World Wide Web as their catalysts. "It is the most powerful weapon we can implement," Ghost had informed a skeptical Vincent. "Keyboards are the new ammunition and computer modems are far more deadly than AKs or M16s."

"The government in Mexico City is trying to place all of the blame on Texas and the United States," began the handsome, young actor reappearing in his role as a newscaster. "Salinas isn't telling the entire truth. The gringos didn't act alone. They had help from within Mexico. A coup is in progress, and the cowards that control our government are too ashamed or too afraid to admit it."

What followed was touted as "hard evidence." Point by point, Vincent's announcer began laying out the "facts."

A stack of documents was displayed on the screen, police reports with bold letters across the top. "Ballistics Report – Langtry Massacre." The camera then zoomed in as the smooth-talking anchor explained, "The incursion into Texas was performed by the Mexican military. We know for certain that the weapons, ammunition, and other equipment used by the men who stole the Texas Plague were issued to the Army of Mexico."

A red line circled the notation, "Ammunition casings found at the scene contained markings consistent with Mexican Military issued FX-05 Battle Rifles."

The face of the handsome young actor reappeared, his brow knotted in concern as he continued. "The men who fought a gun battle with the Texas police in San Antonio were from the Mexican Army's Special Forces, their identities are being kept secret by an embarrassed government in our capital."

Another document flashed, this one displaying the emblem of the SAPD. This time, the red circle highlighted the text, "No fingerprint or DNA match known. All international sources verified. Identity unknown."

The anchor again, "The banker involved in the scheme was working with government officials from Mexico City."

On and on, the evidence splashed on the screen. Somehow, the cartels had gotten access to the video footage recorded at the lab, which according to El

General's propaganda, clearly depicted a Mexican Special Forces Team exiting with bio-terror weapons under their arms.

"With the Texas border closed, we have to ask how such weapons of mass destruction could be smuggled back into Mexico without official cooperation and assistance?" the sham newsman questioned.

The final point, however, was the most damning.

"This is a photograph of Miss Elisa Velasquez, a Mexican national working on a doctorate at A&M University. Miss Velasquez was employed at the lab where the Texas Plague was being developed. Here is another image of her, along with the other scientists working at the facility. During the raid, every single person at that lab was killed with one exception – Miss Velasquez. Why?"

The actor paused perfectly, building a key point of suspense. "She was spared because Miss Velasquez is the mistress of General Ignacio Juan Perez, commander of the Mexican Army."

A grainy photograph filled the screen, the shot appearing to have been taken at one of Mexico's many oceanfront resorts. There was a handsome, middle-aged man walking through the sand with an attractive, much younger female on his arm.

Another picture was displayed, this one obviously inside of a nightclub, both the man and his attractive young companion holding cocktails while they exchanged a kiss. That image was soon followed by several more, each making the case that the pair was a romantically inclined couple despite the vast difference in age.

"So I ask my fellow citizens," the announcer continued, "how could all of these events have occurred if our own government wasn't involved in the tragedy that has befallen our nation? Mexico City is a principal in this cover-up. There is a coup taking place even as you watch this broadcast, desperate men trying to seize power illegally and turn us all into slaves. Join us, my friends. Come and stand with Mexico's only true patriots. United we can restore order … and protect our freedom and the lives of our families."

The television cameraman swept a scene that could only be described as chaos.

Armed men were scurrying in all directions, most of their faces covered in whatever type of mask, respirator, or covering they could scrounge.

Many of those wearing military uniforms were topped with ancient, WWII-era gas masks, the leather straps and old-style buckles pressing into their sweating mops of dark hair. Some of the ambulance personnel were stuck with mere painter's units, simple pieces of white cloth held over their mouths with rubber bands.

Sam had never heard of Heroica Veracruz, let alone the fact that one of the largest military installations in all of Mexico resided in the coastal town.

The fact that several senior commanders as well as over 1,000 Marines were apparently infected with the "Texas Plague," shocked the lady ranger. "We knew this was coming," she announced to the television, wondering why she was feeling such a strong reaction. It then dawned, "I might just as well be looking at a scene at Fort Bliss or one of our air bases."

Desperate first responders were scampering everywhere, some carrying medical kits, others hauling out men on stretchers. There were flashing lights throughout the video's background, as well as multitudes of people who were either blistering angry or staring at the ground with blank, hollow expressions.

Somehow, the reporter managed to corral an officer whose rank and position must have given him credibility. The Marine was obviously operating on adrenaline and rage, his blasting, poignant words sending a message long before the English translation rolled across the bottom of the newscast.

"This attack is the work of a highly organized, well-disciplined entity with access to secured areas of the base," the officer growled. "Our initial focus is on providing medical care for those exposed to the plague, but the investigation will eventually uncover who is responsible."

"Are there any preliminary indications who or how the bio-weapon was brought onto the base?" the reporter inquired.

"No, not currently," the Marine barked. "But who else could it be? The security at this facility is second to none. These murdering scum had to be insiders ... traitors with security clearance. We will find them and deliver justice."

The picture then changed to the city surrounding the huge base. A woman with three small children was attempting to herd her gaggle across a street. All of the little ones had towels taped across their faces, only frightened eyes peeking out in the small slits left for vision. When the mother looked up into the camera's lenses, Sam had never seen such terrified eyes on any human being.

It was an iconic image, one that would serve as the visual reference for the ongoing disaster in Mexico. When the broadcast finally returned to the anchorwoman, the desperate mother's face remained pasted on the background.

Sam turned off the boob tube, frowning at how quickly the situation was escalating just a few hundred miles south of where she sat. While Mexico had always seemed a world away, the connection with Texas and the involvement of the rangers served to draw the dire state of affairs closer, making each and every death seem more personal.

Bored, frustrated, and feeling sick over a looming sense of responsibility for the carnage, she considered calling Zach and demanding that the ranger immediately approve her return to active duty.

That initiative prompted a tinge of guilt to enter her mind. Zach had been so kind and attentive, constantly stopping by, going to the market, and picking up her prescription refills as needed. She was well aware that between her absence from the job and his babysitting duties, he was having to spend a lot of extra hours to keep up with the workload. Asking him to jump through the hoops of medical forms, evaluation reports, and the other bureaucratic nonsense just wasn't fair. Besides, she had her doubts if he would do it.

"I need to be an asset, not a liability," she said to the ever-smaller apartment. "Earn your keep, Ranger Temple. Step it up. You can still serve the people of Texas, gimpy leg or not."

It dawned on her that she had just hit on the crux of the problem. She hadn't made detective of the nation's fourth largest police department by sitting around on her ass and expecting people to wait on her hand and foot. She produced. She busted it. Lazy was not a word ever mentioned in the same sentence with Samantha Temple.

Pulling her laptop open, she decided to do something positive. During Zach's last visit, it had been discussed that one of her partner's biggest frustrations had been his lack of knowing whom he was dealing with. Vincent was a mystery, a complete unknown to every law enforcement agency in the world.

Around ranger headquarters, the smart money was on the assumption that Vincent headed the Gulf Cartel. Given that supposition, Sam was amazed that such a prolific crime boss was shrouded in mystery. Apparently, no one had been able to gain any Intel regarding the commanding criminal's background.

"We've wiped so many of them out; the middle management has been promoted faster than we can keep up. Most of these guys started as street thugs and mules. Hell, I know of two cartel bosses who never had a driver's license or a regular job. They are given nicknames early on so that the Mexican authorities or competitors can't identify their families. Remaining incognito means survival in cartel land," one of her old contacts in the DEA had shared.

Sam had access to numerous law enforcement databases, indexes, and file servers. She knew that the images their equipment had captured in San Antonio were a top priority at several different agencies throughout Texas. Yet, no one had been able to recognize the man widely assumed to be running the show.

The lady ranger decided to take a different approach. She would let everyone else chase the big cheese. She would start with the lower ranking rats.

Despite Hollywood's depictions to the contrary, facial recognition systems weren't foolproof or fast. There were a variety of standards that had been implemented over the years, some of the older software versions requiring a straight-on head shot, others being able to "see around," sunglasses, hats, different lengths of facial hair, and other cosmetic modifications.

All operated on the basic premises that human skulls had unique attributes, just like DNA and fingerprints. These features involved a set of measurements of different points on a person's face.

The most common method involved comparing two overlaid triangles, the three points being the distance between the pupils and one corner of the mouth. Other systems gauged the gap between nostrils, the width and height of a person's head, and even the depth of the eye sockets.

Sam started with the known inventory of faces involved in the crime spree. She had good images of the security team that had surrounded Vincent at the San Antonio steakhouse. There were the two men Zach had disabled at the golf course bar, as well as two more individuals who were recorded at the research lab outside of Bryant.

Of all the photographic evidence, it was the grainy images from the lab that were the lowest quality. Knowing that most of the people trying to identify the culprits would start with the best pictures, she would begin with the worst.

It was easy to eliminate the two exposed faces. One of those men had been killed by Gus in the alley, the other dead from Zach's .45 behind Titus's front door.

Sam replayed the recording three times before picking a frame with the clearest view of a masked man's eyes. It was when someone had tossed him the Jag's keys.

Her first comparison was with the morgue photographs of the shooter killed by the good Samaritans at the golf course's bar and grill. Within five minutes, she knew that the man who had caught the car keys wasn't the deceased.

Next, she eliminated the victim of Zach's beer mug assault. His eyes were far too wide.

Within an hour, she knew Mr. Mask had survived all of the encounters. She also discovered he was left-handed from his catch of the tossed keys and the side of the body where his weapon was slung.

In the primary database used by the rangers, there were 1,850 individuals with a similar distance between their pupils. Of those, over 500 were of Latino descent.

After cross-referencing another file provided by the Mexican government, she narrowed down the list to 54 males who were left-handed.

It took the lady ranger another two hours to filter that list even further. Who was dead? Who was in jail? Who was in the military? She ended up with six potential names, a very manageable number.

She was researching number three when Sam inhaled sharply at the image displayed on her laptop.

The Mexican Federal Police had been tracking down deserters from an Army unit and had been shooting surveillance photographs of a number of suspects. A quality snapshot of #3 was in the man's file, along with two other men in the background.

Sam reached for her phone, her fingers trembling as she punched Zach's number.

"How are you feeling?" he answered.

"I'm fine. I need you to get over here … right away!"

She heard her partner sigh, "Cabin fever striking again?"

"No, Zach, it's far, far more important than that. I've found a picture that I need you to look at. I think I've uncovered an old friend of yours, and I know you'll want to see this."

"An old friend? Of mine?"

"Yes," she replied, the adrenaline clear in her voice. "You do remember Ghost, don't you?"

"I'll be there in an hour.... Make that 40 minutes."

They rose from the ditch as one, 30 shadows moving in a line toward the gate.

Given the cartel's recent attacks and the outbreak of plague roaring across the country, the number of guards manning the base's front entrance had been doubled. Despite the early hour and lack of traffic, none of the assigned Mexican Army personnel were sleeping. It didn't make any difference.

Again, acting as if a single entity, the shadows moved directly in-line with the sentries' positions, flicked off their weapons' safeties, and fired.

A maelstrom of 5.56 lead slammed into the semi-fortified booth and guardhouse, a few of the steel-cored bullets managing to penetrate the thick, reinforced walls.

Three of the four guards were fast enough to duck below the blizzard of lead, their bodies reacting purely on instinct as their minds cycled rapidly in an attempt to rationalize why the night had just turned into a nightmare.

The attackers never intended on their initial barrage taking all of the guards out of the fight – that wasn't the purpose.

With perfect timing, the suppressive fire ceased just as the flanking shooters reached the hardened positions and dispatched the sentries – up close and personal.

Then they were inside the perimeter of the sleepy base, small teams fanning out in every direction.

For nearly 40 minutes, the Region IV Post outside Monterrey was a living hell for the soldiers garrisoned there. Well-coordinated fire teams first destroyed the communications center with explosive charges while another group of intruders sprayed hundreds of rounds into the enlisted barracks. The officers' quarters, as well as the base commander's apartment, received multiple volleys of hand grenades.

Eventually, a resistance formed, a few officers managing to rally a handful of shaken troops. They even succeeded in killing one of the attackers but didn't know it until dawn had broken several hours later.

Just as quickly and silently as they had appeared, the remaining 29 shadows faded back into the night. The base they left behind was in absolute bedlam, soldiers running in every direction, firing wildly at shadows and sometimes each other. It was over two hours later before the surviving leaders figured out that the intruders had left and demanded a cease-fire.

Shortly after daybreak, the remaining leadership found the lone enemy causality. He was wearing the uniform and equipment of the Naval Infantry – a Mexican Marine.

"This can't be true," a captain spouted, shaking his head. "Why would our own brothers attack us?"

"Sir! Sir, you might want to see this," shouted a nearby private. "This might answer your question, sir."

The officer stepped to the corner where the young soldier stood pointing. The captain's gaze followed the private's finger, arriving at the base commander's still-smoking home. On the side, spray painted in large, white letters was a message. "Army Bitches - Remember Veracruz!"

Four hours later, President Salinas had just sat down, ready to call his staff meeting to order. An aide appeared at his shoulder, bending to whisper a message into the chief executive's ear.

Salinas blanched white, glancing harshly at the messenger seeking to confirm the news.

Two men now seated at the large conference table then drew Salinas's attention. Both resplendent in their best uniforms, the president's eyes fixed on the general in charge of the Army and the admiral who commanded the Mexican Navy.

"Everyone else get out … immediately. I need a private word with my military commanders."

A wave of mumbling rolled through the gathered secretaries and ministers before they began shuffling out.

Curious why they had been singled out, both of the military men sat staring at their boss until the door finally closed behind the last straggler to leave the room.

"General," Salinas began, nodding toward the man who controlled the entire Mexican Army and Air Force. "You probably will want to turn on your cell phone and call your office in just a moment. There's been an incident."

The president began relaying what he'd just learned. "My aide informed me that there were over 50 casualties at the Region IV facility, including the base commander."

Fire filled the general's eyes as his head snapped toward the admiral. "Why? Damnit – tell me why!"

"I assure you, General; my forces had nothing to do with this cowardly attack. We both know that uniforms are easy to counterfeit and that the cartels use the same weapons as both of our forces. It wasn't our doing."

Mexico's two branches of armed services had always been in competition with each other. Throughout recent history, they had bickered and quarreled over everything from budget dollars to which honor guard would present the flag at the national soccer championships.

For years, both commanders considered the checks and balances imposed by the Mexican Constitution a positive for both of their respective services, as well as the country as a whole.

All of that had begun to change with the onset of the drug war. The larger branch of the Army had been far more vulnerable to infiltration and corruption than the smaller ranks of the Marines. While the senior officers in both services had done their best to keep the rank and file "clean," the cartels had still managed to buy, bribe, or influence key Army personnel. When dozens of Special Forces troopers had deserted to join Los Zetas, the government's faith and confidence in the Army had waned.

This had resulted in the Marines being used to hunt down and kill dozens of cartel leaders. Whenever the whereabouts of a wanted drug lord had been discovered, it was the naval branch that received the call. The situation was at best an embarrassment for the larger service, an insult at worst.

All of that frustration came to the surface when the general learned of the attack at Monterrey. Losing his barely-controlled temper, the senior army officer blasted away at his naval counterpart, "You son of a bitch. For the last five years, I've sat here and listened to you boast about your accomplishments and achievements. I've suffered in silence, listening as you've taken credit for the sun rising in the east and the rain falling from the sky. Wasn't that enough? Weren't all of the headlines and heroics enough? I'm beginning to think the cartels are right. I think you want to run the government for yourself and are too impatient to wait for an election."

The admiral wasn't a man to take such abuse calmly. "If you could control your own forces, our oversight wouldn't be necessary. I can't help it if your entire command structure is on the cartel's payroll. It's not my officers who warn those criminals when there is a raid on the way. It's not my men who sell their weapons and ammo to the cartel soldiers. You cooked up this septic stew, so stop whining like a schoolgirl about how the hot broth burns your mouth."

The general didn't rise to the insult, nor did he let his temper continue to run rampid. Instead, his intellect kicked in, overriding emotion with cool, logical, analytical thinking. Tilting his head in thought, his voice sounded with a cold monotone. "You think we had something to do with unleashing the plague at Veracruz, don't you? You sent those murderers to Monterrey for vengeance, didn't you?"

"We have no proof of any Army involvement at Veracruz," the admiral replied smugly. "If I did, I would approach the president with such facts, not launch some middle of the night raid on one of your bases."

"You are a coward and a traitor!" the general growled.

While the admiral and president sat stunned by the accusation, the general pushed back his chair with an angry motion and stood ramrod straight. "You won't get away with this coup. Not while I still walk this earth. I am loyal to the president and the republic, and I will fight you every step of the way."

"Gentlemen … please…." Salinas pleaded as the senior commander pivoted for the door.

It was too little, too late, as the Army's head honcho stormed out without another glance or word.

The convoy left Mexico City at dawn, rolling out of the base's gates with double the number of escort and security personnel. A platoon of military police, two companies of infantry, and a contingent of paratroopers were accompanying the column, assigned to protect the much-needed cargo from any threat.

Behind the lead element of Humvees was a string of 18-wheel, over-the-road semis, each filled to the brim with food, ammunition, and the spare parts required to resupply an army in the field.

The shipment was a regular event, Mexico's logistical supply line ruled by a doctrine that kept the vast warehouses of materials close to the capital, so the precious cargo didn't end up on the black market.

The destination of this morning's column was Reynosa, a city of over 700,000 residents, and the colonel commanding the resupply effort was on edge.

Residing just across the border from McAllen, Texas, the Mexican community had suffered over a decade of extreme violence as the government and various cartels had battled for control.

Since the millennium, the town had changed hands no less than four times as the Gulf Cartel and Los Zetas had fought each other in the streets. Whichever side managed to gain the upper hand would then have to deal with the Army and eventually a large contingency of Marines.

The entire community had breathed a sigh of relief when Z-44 and El General had called a truce. Seemingly overnight, the routine sound of automatic weapons and hand grenades had been silenced. Some of the more optimistic citizens held out hope that days of mass killings was behind them.

The plague hadn't reached this part of northern Mexico, and with the Marines in town, many of the border town's residents began returning to a peaceful lifestyle they hadn't experienced in years.

Not all was well, however. Since the attacks at Monterrey and Veracruz, the Army and Marine contingencies had been eyeing each other through the fog of suspicion. Rather than cooperate on patrols, checkpoints, and schedules, as before, the two branches of the Mexican military had been operating independently. Still, both sides had reached an unspoken agreement, mostly avoiding each other until the confusion in Mexico City and elsewhere died down.

The convoy would have to visit both contingents today.

They arrived at the Army's base of operations first, dozens of soldiers rushing to offload the trucks while clerks with clipboards shouted orders and kept counts. It was always a hectic exercise, sorting beans from bullets, separating medical supplies from laundry detergent.

During the controlled riot that was the unloading, no one noticed one of the base's civilian workers attaching a stainless steel canister to the underneath of a semi-trailer, nor did anyone catch the same man applying a second pressurized tank to a truck down the line.

After receiving an inch-high stack of signed inventory sheets and bills of lading, the convoy was rolling out of the gates, making its way to the Marine contingency stationed on the opposite side of town.

The Marines had moved into what had once been a regional law enforcement training center. The commander of the local garrison was a hard-nosed major, who, due to his heroic conduct in combat, had been nicknamed "Hellcat."

The resupply convoy was expected that day, but Major Hellcat wasn't absolutely sure when or if the Army would deliver. Rumors were sweeping both branches of the service, some of his fellow officers absolutely certain the country was on the verge of a civil war.

When the major's office phone rang, he was hoping it was the front gate giving notice that the convoy had finally arrived. Instead, a voice he didn't recognize warned, "The Army convoy is a Trojan horse. There are canisters of plague under the first and third truck. Beware."

Stunned by the statement, the Marine officer didn't immediately return the phone to its cradle. His inaction, however, didn't last long.

"Put the base on full alert!" he shouted to his assistant. "Sound the alarm! Don't let that Army convoy inside the gates!"

His orders soon produced results, the sound of shouting men and pounding boots resonating throughout the small facility.

Men in full battle loads were rushing in all directions, hustling for their designated defensive positions. Two up-armored Humvees, complete with .50 caliber, turret-mounted machine guns, raced for the front gate as reinforcements leaped into the sandbag-fortified nests that surrounded the perimeter.

When the convoy finally arrived, the Army colonel in the lead vehicle found himself staring at a multitude of gun barrels backed by a host of very frightened young men.

Initially, the resupply officer wrote it off to the incidents at Monterrey and Veracruz. "Marines," he whispered to his driver. "They are a paranoid lot. Let me get this straightened out so we can get out of here and back to Mexico City and our families."

The officer exited his Humvee and strolled casually toward the main entrance. He hadn't managed five steps when a voice shouted, "Halt! Approach no closer or we will fire!"

The colonel did just that, stopping in the middle of the lane and spreading his hands wide. "What is the problem," he yelled back with a sly grin. "Don't you want to eat?"

Major Hellcat and three of his men came through the gate, their weapons high, ready, and trained on the superior officer. When he was closer, the base commander said, "We've received information stating your convoy is carrying the plague."

Tilting his head, the Army officer replied, "That's preposterous. We just left Mexico City this morning and have only made one stop at the Army base. We aren't carrying the damn plague."

"Then you won't mind if we have a look before you're allowed inside the gate?"

Sweeping his arm wide to indicate the column of idling trucks, the colonel said, "Suit yourself. Have a look. We have nothing to hide."

Hellcat turned and made a motion with his arm, waving forward a contingent of men wearing gas masks. No one was for sure that the filters would protect against the germs, but it was the only option available on the remote outpost.

As the four-man inspection crew made its way toward the line of trucks, several of the troops assigned as convoy security began dismounting.

Stopping at the first semi, the leader of the Marine team took less than a minute to spot the shiny steel canister. Despite being muffled by the heavy mask covering his face, his shouts for everyone to get back could be heard clearly up and down the line.

Still thinking the entire affair was simply bullshit, the colonel headed for the now-freaking, still-masked Marines. "It's there, sir. A silver container that doesn't belong on the truck. I saw it!" reported the nearly panicked inspector.

Shaking his head, the colonel stooped low and scanned the underside of the semi until he saw the offending canister. While its surface was clean and looked new compared to the other equipment on the trailer, he believed it was simply a replacement part that had been recently added during the last maintenance session.

As he reached to touch the container, Hellcat thought the officer was trying to "set off" the device. "Stop!" the Marine commander screamed. "Don't touch that!"

The colonel didn't heed the order, his usually low-key temperament about full of the disrespectful junior officer.

The inspector, now certain the rumors about the Army trying to kill Marines had been verified, fired his weapon.

Three 5.56 NATO rounds struck the colonel across the back, their impact spinning the half-bent officer in a circle as his arms flayed wide, tossing the unattached canister at the gathered Marines.

Absolute pandemonium erupted.

Hearing the burst of fire and seeing their commander go down, the Army escorts assumed the reverse gossip was true – that the Marines were killing soldiers. The convoy troopers shouldered their weapons and began firing at the inspection team and Major Hellcat.

As more and more Army infantry jumped from their trucks, the two machine guns at the gate opened fire, spraying the convoy's riflemen as they scrambled for cover. Within 20 seconds, the two sides were fully engaged in an intense firefight.

In one of the rear-most trucks, a young lieutenant managed to push down the terror that filled his core and reached for the radio. In a voice filled with panic, he began broadcasting his unit, the convoy designator, their location, and a desperate plea for help.

At the same time, Major Hellcat's second in command was doing the same thing in the facility's communications room. "We are under attack! I repeat. The base is under attack!" he broadcasted over the Navy's emergency frequencies.

The Marine base housed a garrison of nearly 200 men, outnumbering the Army forces by 2:1. Yet, despite their superior numbers, they had been ordered to protect the base, not assault a convoy. Tucked into their defensive positions, the base's defenders were content to keep the interlopers at bay.

Strings of glowing tracers and a nearly constant rattle of automatic fire raged back and forth, both sides recovering from the initial shock of the fight. Two of the semis were now burning, their fuel tanks punctured by the blizzard of lead streaming from the base.

Inside the compound, a barracks suffered a similar fate as dozens of incoming rounds managed to set the structure on fire. The two sides now had to deal with a thick layer of smoke adding to the haze of civil war.

Major Hellcat barely managed to escape, geysers of dust chasing him back to the gate as he sprinted the fastest dash of his life. He was luckier than the rest of the inspection team. Their bloody bodies, lying in the open across the lane, served to motivate the barricaded defenders. The colonel's corpse had the same effect on the men in his command.

The first reinforcements to arrive were from the Army base the convoy had just resupplied. The commander of that facility had no idea what was going on. He was accustomed to fighting the cartels and sometimes even corrupt police. When he finally arrived at the scene of the battle, four trucks were burning, and the fire inside the base had spread to the enlisted head.

The Marines, seeing their foe reinforced, again began broadcasting a series of desperate radio calls for help. "The Army is trying to overrun our base! More and more of them keep arriving. We can't hold out for long."

All across northern Mexico, forces from both branches began responding. The regional Army commander, a general destined to become the supreme commander when his superior retired next cycle, diverted his helicopter and flew over the encircled base. Meanwhile, the Mexican Navy was scrambling every available man to come to the aid of its comrades.

The next encounter occurred less than two hours after the convoy's colonel had been gunned down. While the firefight raged at the outpost, a relief column of Marines encountered an Army checkpoint 20 kilometers south of Reynosa, and an extended gun battle left the roadblock in flaming ruins. There were causalities on both sides.

Mexico City scrambled a flight of two F4 Phantom fighter jets to overfly Reynosa. They encountered several naval helicopters rushing reinforcements to the besieged base and shot two of the birds from the sky after receiving direct orders from the regional commander.

The situation escalated rapidly, the command and control networks of the underfunded military quickly overwhelmed. Confusion, miscommunications, and panic led to an ever-deepening soup of war. Reports of skirmishes, ambushes, and outright battles were coming in from all over the country.

In some areas, the cartel joined the fray. Warned by El General and Z-44, the local drug lords were watching closely, waiting for the chance to use their extensive private armies to influence, incite, or execute a quick hit and run when an opportunity was presented.

It finally dawned on the Marines outside of Reynosa that they wouldn't be able to hold their outpost indefinitely. The Army was reinforcing at a much faster rate, and despite the heroic arrival of a few helicopters' worth of additional forces, they were outnumbered and outgunned.

In a maneuver worthy of a textbook example, the Marines freed themselves of the Army's noose, over 70 of the defenders breaking out and then executing a fighting retreat toward Reynosa. Major Hellcat's plan was simple – reach the city's airport, take control of a plane, and fly to friendly territory.

The Army quickly figured out the plot, moving forces to block the fleeing Marines.

Again, Major Hellcat found himself between a rock and an immovable object. Rather than get pinned down between two superior forces, the crafty officer ordered his men to enter the city proper, hoping to use the dense urban area to buy time and escape the trap.

All the while, less than a mile away, the Texas side of the border had no idea of the deteriorating situation unfolding on the southern shore of the Rio Grande.

That was about to change.

The pursuing Army units were using armored personnel carriers, giving them both superior mobility and greater firepower. The Marines fought like wounded, cornered animals, making their pursuers pay for every inch of ground. At one intersection after another, their rear element would execute a blocking action, using the office buildings, retail storefronts, and even residential structures as cover.

They would shoot up the lead Army units, inflicting as much damage as possible. Just as the chasing soldiers would bring overwhelming firepower to bear, the Marines would scurry to set up a few blocks away.

They were, however, running low on ammunition and room to maneuver. The Army was pushing them back. The retreating force had wounded, some severely so. Several of their Humvees and trucks had taken fire and were barely limping along. The outcome, Hellcat realized, was inevitable.

The major was about to order a desperate flanking attack when a green and white road sign caught his attention. "Texas - McAllen Port of Entry, 1 KM."

He ignored the sign at first, turning to scan the faces of his surviving officers. They were a filthy, desperate looking bunch, many down to their last magazine of ammunition, more than a few having a leg, arm, or head wrapped in a blood-soaked bandage. He loved them more than any brother or sister, his heart bursting with pride at how well they had fought.

It nearly brought the commander to tears when he realized that the Army wouldn't be taking any prisoners today, especially after the carnage they'd unleashed on the units pursuing them. The men around him deserved better. They had earned the right to live with their bravery and honor.

If he could only buy a little more time until help arrived.

It then occurred to Hellcat that there was a sanctuary, a place where the pursuing devils of the traitorous Army couldn't reach his men.

"Mount up. Make for the border. Move! Move! Move!" he ordered.

A few minutes later, the ragtag line of shot-up vehicles was rolling toward McAllen, Texas.

It hadn't occurred to Major Hellcat that the border had been closed for several days. Nor did it dawn on the exhausted officer that Texas wouldn't want him inside her country.

With several Army units in hot pursuit, the surviving Marines drove as fast as their rides would take them, busting through the first set of sawhorse barricades on the Mexican side of the river and sending the lightweight units flying in a shower of splinters.

Heavy machine fire followed the escaping Marines onto the International Bridge, the rearmost Humvee exploding in a spectacular ball of red and yellow flames.

With the border being closed, only a skeleton crew of immigration agents was manning the Hidalgo entry port. All of the multiple traffic lanes normally used to inspect cars and trucks heading into Texas were closed, concrete barriers and hydraulic steel posts blocking access into the Lone Star Republic. When the Humvee had exploded on the bridge, frantic calls went out to the local police departments, the few on-duty border guards screaming that Texas was being invaded.

None of that mattered to the desperate Marines. By Major Hellcat's way of thinking, the Army wouldn't pursue him across the river. Skidding to a stop in the paved area before the inspection lanes, he began directing his men to dismount and take up defensive positions. They were technically in Texas. The Army wouldn't dare cross the bridge.

The soldiers, hot on the heels of the fleeing Marines, did pause at the bridge. Two armored carriers stopped in the middle of the street, both commanders looking at each other and unsure what to do. Their superior, however, didn't hesitate.

Blind with fury over the losses the traitors had inflicted on his men, he ordered his lead elements to cross the bridge and kill the bastards – every last one of them.

From the Texas side of the river, sirens were sounding throughout Hidalgo and McAllen. Deputy Sheriffs, city cops, and even the local SWAT team rushed to answer the port's call for help.

Major Hellcat couldn't believe it when the Mexican Army personnel carriers began crossing the river. After a moment's hesitation, he ordered his men to fire their remaining ammunition at the approaching forces.

Out in the open and limited by the narrow concrete lanes, the leading Army units began absorbing serious punishment from the Marines. Hellcat still had one functioning .50 caliber M2 machine gun, its heavy, armor piercing rounds knocking out one and then another of the armored pursuers.

For the moment, the bridge was blocked by smoldering wrecks.

Given the reprise, the major turned and ran for the closest building, hoping to find someone in authority.

The Texas border agents inside were still in shock and keeping low, their .40 caliber service pistols seemingly of little value given the intensity of the firefight raging just outside their offices.

"We request political asylum," Hellcat spouted when he finally found someone in uniform. "We will be killed instantly if we are not allowed to enter Texas."

Stunned by the appearance of the bloody, desperate man standing in their doorway, none of the agents knew exactly what to do.

At that same moment, the blistering mad Mexican Army commander ordered the burning hulks blocking the bridge pushed aside. Well beyond any understanding of the potential repercussions of his actions, he demanded his forces charge across the river and kill "those fucking Marines."

Heavy machine gunfire now began raking the handful of survivors on the Texas side, the bridge quickly filling with charging troops and machines of war.

Out of ammunition, exhausted, and unclear where Major Hellcat had gone, the remaining Marines finally broke and ran like hell toward the closed port of entry, the nearby shoreline, and anyplace else that looked like it might provide sanctuary.

Several law enforcement patrol cars squealed up just then, the responding officers having no clue what was going on or why. They could only see men in green uniforms running away from the river while another group was firing volley after volley of lead toward the republic. More than one of the cops thought the retreating Marines were Texas border agents.

More and more police arrived, the on-site shift supervisor ordering his men to take up positions around the inspection lanes and to stop anyone trying to cross that bridge.

A moment later, a Hidalgo city officer was hit by a stray bullet fired from the Mexican forces now directly over the Rio Grande. The police opened fire with everything they had.

Less than four hours after it had started, the Mexican Civil War had boiled over into Texas.

Chapter 11

El General sat and watched news footage showing a line of Mexican Army trucks and Humvees rolling out of their base. The announcer's voice was near panic as he described the mobilization, reciting rumors that the Army was preparing a mission of revenge after the cowardly attacks outside of Monterrey.

"They are preparing to tear each other to shreds," Vincent grunted to Ghost. "Civil war will rage across Mexico by the end of the week. I think it's time we retreated to enjoy an extended stay on *The Rose.*"

La Rosa Roja (*The Red Rose*) had begun life with the Russian Navy as a 62-meter brown water patrol boat in the 1980s. Budget cuts had left hull number 18 rusting on blocks in the Almaz Shipyards just outside of St. Petersburg at 60% complete.

For the price of scrap, the German naval architecture firm Rienbolt Industries had purchased the military-grade vessel and towed her to their yards in Hamburg. There, the sparse, business-like blueprint was completely redesigned and revamped.

Steel bulkheads were adorned with exotic woods and surfaces. Italian marble was imported for the floors. No luxury or amenity was spared.

Less than 18 months later, she was listed on several yacht brokerages as a 205-foot pleasure vessel available to the world's wealthy elite.

A Chinese manufacturing mogul purchased the yacht less than two months later, claiming the steel hull would perfectly suit a lingering desire to explore the waters around Antarctica, as well as ply the often-stormy South China Sea.

A delivery crew was hired to pilot the vessel to Cancun, the cross-Atlantic voyage deemed a worthy shakedown of the $300 million dollar yacht.

In reality, the Chinese billionaire had no interest in boating. His investment portfolio had suffered badly as of late, and cash flow had become an issue for his global enterprise.

Supply met demand through a series of backroom interactions. The Gulf Cartel was always struggling to launder its excessive cash. The Asian firm needed hard currency. It was a match made in heaven.

El General had arranged for the straw purchase in order to keep nosey DEA and Mexican officials at bay. After one short voyage, just in case anyone was watching, the Chinese industrialist had found he suffered terribly from seasickness. He had been more than happy to hand Vincent the "keys."

La Rosa was the perfect fit for a drug lord. She was fast, strong, and had an operational range of nearly 4,000 nautical miles. Her steel construction was impervious to small arms fire. Her interiors had been designed for the uber-wealthy who wanted to sail in comfort for extended periods, with enough food and water to last for months without entering a port.

No detail was overlooked, and her list of pleasantries was extensive. A helipad allowed visitors to board her while marooned in the middle of the ocean. And her water garage encouraged guests to try a little water fun, offering two jet skis, a 22-foot launch, and state of the art scuba equipment.

Within two months of being handed over to Vincent's loving care, La Rosa had become a world-class headquarters for the multi-billion dollar criminal organization, with state of the art communications, military-grade radar, and even a small arsenal of shoulder-fired, anti-aircraft weapons.

"My beautiful red rose has thorns," the kingpin once joked to an associate.

She was also mobile, able to constantly motor up and down the Atlantic coast of South America or beyond. A moving target was always the most difficult for any hunter.

Vincent's caravan arrived in Cancun a short time later, rolling through the city's extensive section of resorts, seaside hotels, and impressive marina.

They eventually meandered to a pier lined with other such vessels, the private yachts of the world's rich and famous. There, tied to the concrete pillars, was The Rose's speedboat, complete with two large outboard motors and a man dressed in flawless starch-whites.

El General greeted the deckhand with a casual familiarity. Soon Ghost, Vincent and his most capable security men were speeding over the protected waterway, making good speed toward the open ocean beyond.

It took nearly an hour to reach La Rosa, the vessel's gleaming, white profile anchored exactly 13 miles offshore, just over the line in international waters. Vincent, seated at the launch's bow, seemed enthralled by his vessel's lines and stark contrast to the royal blue waters of the gulf.

After maneuvering the speedboat into the yacht's "garage," Vincent and his entourage were met by La Rosa's skipper. "Good afternoon, sir."

"Hola, Captain. Is everything in order?"

"Yes, Señor. We are fully stocked with food, fuel, and the other requirements for an extended voyage," replied *La Rosa's* master.

"Good. I wish to make for Tampico. Please dock *The Rose* at the warehouse along the Rio Panuo River."

"Yes, Jefe," the captain nodded. "The cruise will take approximately six hours."

After the skipper had hustled for the bridge, Ghost leaned close and asked, "Are you sure docking within reach of the government is the safest approach?"

For a moment, Vincent thought to reprimand his "employee" for questioning the order but then decided against it. After all, Ghost had proved himself well worth the significant deposits being made into the terrorist's European bank accounts.

"It is not the most secure mooring, which is obvious. On the other hand, we own the police and the Army in that district. I may need direct communication with our people. I will order the captain to keep *The Rose* ready to depart on a moment's notice. It is the best compromise available to us."

Ghost gave no indication of how much of El General's reasoning he accepted at face value. Besides, there were worse accommodations and far more difficult positions to defend. The Syrian knew – he'd spent most of his adult life in hellish, war-torn countries where sleeping in anything off the desert floor was considered a luxury.

The "consultant" as Vincent often referred to mysterious Ghost, watched his benefactor closely, his age and experience warning the Syrian that El General was beginning to drift toward an egotistical mindset that would ultimately lead to the man's downfall.

He'd watched the ISIS leadership become intoxicated with its initial success, the same with al-Qaeda in Iraqi and with the Taliban in Afghanistan. "Why is it that success can make a man forget what made him great in the first place?"

Ghost made a mental note to watch Vincent closely. When men like that began to fall, their impact usually crushed those around them.

They called her "Weekend," because simply looking at the dark-headed beauty put the weekend in a man's heart.

In heels, she barely nudged 5 feet in height and was tiny though the waist and thighs. With a Korean mother and father born in Puerto Rico, her skin projected a unique golden hue that drew the eye.

She was a petite woman, tiny all around with the exception of oversized breasts and a smile that seemed to dominate her girl-like face. With her dark, curly tresses and eyes the color of emeralds, she was an exotic beauty that kept any admirer guessing her heritage.

Weekend had been Vincent's favorite female companion for many months, the crime lord returning with the young lady on his arm after a business trip to Texas.

No one knew how El General had met the stunning girl, nor had the jefe explained how he managed to woo her into his fold.

Some of the crime boss's inner circle speculated that El General had kidnapped the woman, given her sultry attitude and uncooperative demeanor. Others thought Vincent had purchased her from some exotic locale where slavery was still in vogue.

Such gossip and speculation had reached a peak when Vincent had informed his security detail that Weekend wasn't allowed off the ship or to communicate with the outside world in any way, shape or form. "I don't trust her," he justified. "She might be a DEA agent, or worse."

She spent her days reading, sunbathing on *Rose*'s deck, and enjoying the expensive wine and culinary delights offered by the megayacht's galley and chef. Whenever El General was aboard, she seemed to grow even more withdrawn, often seen leaving his private stateroom in the mornings with red, watering eyes.

"She doesn't like it rough like the jefe," one of the bodyguards speculated, a knowing gleam in his eye. "He's using her well."

Still, Weekend hadn't tried to escape or run away. On the few occasions when she was allowed to go ashore, she had replenished her personal items and expanded her wardrobe without protest or issue.

In reality, Weekend was one of the missing girls who had made the mistake of borrowing money from Trustline National Bank, another victim of one Mr. Carson. She had agreed to become the plaything for the banker's wealthy client in exchange for the forgiveness of her debt. Her life at home sucked anyway, the combination of an alcoholic father and a mother who wouldn't stand up to the abusive bastard. Then there was the dead-end job and a never-ending string of men who treated her like a piece of meat. It all made the banker's offer much more palatable. Who knew – it might even be an exciting adventure.

Vincent and Weekend were taking in the sun on the pilot deck when one of the bodyguards interrupted the jefe's acute study of the young lady's perfectly shaped, bikini-clad bottom.

"El General, Señor Ghost believes there's something in the media room that you'll want to see," the burly man said.

Sighing, Vincent rose from the plush lounge chair and sipped his wine. Slapping Weekend playfully on the ass as he passed, the crime boss led the way down two flights of stairs and then entered *Rose*'s well-appointed theater room.

It wasn't a large space, one wall consumed by a massive Sony 4K television that was perfectly curved to allow excellent viewing angles from the two rows of cushy, leather recliners. Ghost was seated in the front row, the Syrian's gaze transfixed on the display.

On the screen was the face of a well-known Mexico City news anchor, the bright red banner at the bottom reading, "Special Report – Region in Crisis."

After watching less than a minute of the broadcast, El General handed his man the half-full wine glass and said, "Bring me coffee, please. Things are moving faster than anticipated. I need to clear my head."

The newscast switched to an image of a young man who was reporting live from Ciudad Juarez, just across the river from El Paso, Texas.

"There have been sporadic clashes here for the last two hours," the excited reporter blurted. "Gunfire can be heard throughout the downtown area as the Juarez Police appear to have sided with the Naval Infantry against the Army."

The reporter's eyes suddenly shot skyward, the shaky cameraman following the newsman's line of sight.

It took a few seconds for the video to focus on a small dot in the bright, blue sky. Another moment passed as the camera zoomed and then focused.

There was a helicopter in the distance, its dark green paint, along with the Mexican flag painted on the tail section, indicating it was a military bird. Any doubt regarding the aircraft's ownership was eliminated when the red exhaust of rockets began streaming from the two pods mounted below the fuselage.

Explosions rumbled in the distance, pillars of smoke and dust rising into the air as the cameraman struggled to keep up with fast moving projectiles.

"You can see how close the fighting is to the center of Juarez!" shouted the hyped-up correspondent.

The picture returned to the copter as it engaged in a slow, banking turn. Without warning, a throbbing white streak rose from the ground, the red plume of missile exhaust clearly visible across the airwaves.

The pilot evidently saw it, too, as the helicopter banked hard to change direction and pointed its nose in a dive toward the earth.

The avoidance maneuver was only partially successful, a small, dark cloud of smoke and shrapnel exploding near the aircraft's tail section.

"It looks like some sort of shoulder-fired missile has been used against that helicopter," the reporter's voice sounded in the background.

The picture then showed black smoke pouring from the wounded bird's bay as the pilot struggled to maintain controlled flight. After a few seconds, it was obvious the aircraft was going down.

The camera angle was good enough to show the helpless copter spinning around and around as it sailed through the sky, orange flames engulfing its frame as it lost altitude.

A skyline appeared at the bottom of the picture, a cluster of skyscrapers and streets now coming clear. "Oh my God!" the journalist screeched. "It's heading for El Paso!"

Six seconds later, the helicopter slammed into a tall, white building, a crimson and mustard-colored ball of fire blossoming as the remaining fuel and munitions exploded on impact.

"It's struck the bank tower in El Paso! It's hit the building!" the shocked newsman managed to report. "I can see flames…. The building is on fire! Oh, my God!"

Vincent grunted and then turned to his bodyguard, "Inform Weekend that business requires a change in our plans for this evening. Take her ashore for shopping if she wishes. It might be our last opportunity for a while."

After the protector had left, the cartel honcho turned to his trusted advisor. So, Señor, what is rolling around in that devious mind of yours? We are doing well, are we not?"

205

Ghost sighed, but not enough to embarrass the man who was replenishing his retirement plan. "Get Z-44 on a secure connection. We must accelerate the timeline."

Zach was on Samantha's couch and nursing a cold brew when the news of the spillover into El Paso flashed across the television screen.

The two rangers watched in silence as the images played, several ambulances surrounded by wide-eyed, scrambling men in every assortment of facemask and respirator imaginable.

The view then moved skyward, the blackened windows of the El Paso bank tower reminding the two rangers of 9-11. "I wonder if that building is going to collapse." Sam ventured.

The news then switched to Mexico City where a huge crowd of marchers filled the massive square in front of the National Palace. Many of the protesters were wearing masks, and Zach didn't think it was to protect them from tear gas or air pollution.

The cameraman made a point to show several of the homemade banners and signs carried by the throng, many of them in English. "Death to Gringos," was a common mantra.

"That mob is more frightened than angry," Sam commented. "Look at their eyes."

Zach had to agree, "Yes, I think you're right. I also believe that will change in the next few days. Fear has a way of manifesting itself into a rage."

The anchorman then appeared, his commentary sending a chill down both of the law officers' spines. "Our sources are reporting that the government offices in the Mexican state of Sinaloa have closed, the governor scheduled to make an announcement soon. We're also hearing reports of police and other first responders calling in sick or failing to report for duty throughout Mexico. More on this as it becomes available."

The lady ranger muted the broadcast, "Why hasn't our government said anything? Why hasn't Texas told Mexico who's responsible and what they're dealing with? Fort Hood and the military's secrets aside, you'd think Simmons would spill the beans before we have a hot war right on our doorstep."

Zach shook his head, "I have no idea. Decisions like that are way, way above our pay grade. Maybe Simmons has told them, and they're keeping it quiet for some reason. I mean, this is international politics – there's seldom any logic or common sense involved."

Grunting her agreement, Sam said, "I used to like being in on secrets and the internal workings of the republic, but not with stuff like this. It's frustrating as hell sitting here, knowing the truth and not being able to utter a single word of it."

Zach indicated the television with a nod of his head, "Chico said the cartels wanted to overthrow the government. I guess he was right all along. Mexico will tear itself apart if this keeps up, and you and I both know a civil war down there will leak into Texas if things get really, really bad. We've had two incidents already, and they're barely getting started down there."

"Why do I have the feeling that we are going to be pulled into this?" Sam pondered aloud.

The two rangers continued discussing the situation until Zach finally rose and stretched his long-limbed frame. "I should probably head into the Austin office and catch up on my paperwork. Do you need anything else before I leave?"

Before Sam could answer, Zach's cell phone rang with "*Hail to the Chief*," the familiar tone assigned to Major Putnam.

"Ranger Bass," barked Putnam. "We have a situation brewing in the capital city. The colonel is calling all hands on deck. Report to the executive branch offices. Now."

"Right away, sir. What's going on?"

"There is a demonstration in progress, and the colonel is concerned that things might get out of hand."

Zach rolled his eyes at the curious, eavesdropping Sam while mumbling, "I am on my way, sir."

After disconnecting the call, Zach filled his partner in on the so-called emergency. "You called it. From what the major just said, we're already involved. You don't have any riot gear in your closet, do you?"

"As a matter of fact, I do. But God help me if my gear is large enough to cover your sorry ass," she grinned. "Seriously, though, I do have some leather and lace if you are the kind of guy who can improvise," she added with an eyebrow waggle, trying to break the tension that suddenly filled the room.

Zach ignored the suggestion, his expression all business. Out of habit, he pulled his sidearm, dropped the magazine and verified the contents. "I'll call you later," he said, pivoting in a rush toward the door.

"Be careful," she whispered too late. He was already gone.

The march had started at Austin's House Park, the organizers using social media and sympathetic news outlets to spread the word.

Details of the protest rolled like wildfire across the nearby campus of Texas Tech, many of the 28,000 plus undergraduates already seething over the news that their country had been involved in the research and development of biological weapons. The fact that the plague-genie had escaped from the bottle simply added fuel to the fire.

Every Hispanic political organization in the city jumped on the bandwagon, many of the members having family that resided in Mexico. Even the Catholic Archdiocese got involved, informing parishioners of the event and decrying the catastrophe that was occurring south of the border.

To say the northern Latino community was in an uproar would be an understatement. As in Mexico, rumors of conspiracy, racism, bigotry, and even a purposeful attack were zipping across the internet. Some of the most radical opinions held that the government of Texas had intentionally provided the weapons of mass destruction, others claiming that it was simply a matter of Gringo loathing Chicano.

After an hour of blaring megaphone speeches and a few dozen volunteers handing out flyers with a variety of inflaming messages, the parade of nearly 6,000 people began marching down West 15th Street toward the capitol building. This, of course, prompted a serious amount of concern from the Austin Police Department.

In addition to being the government center of the Republic of Texas, Austin was a college town and host to several large music festivals. This translated into the APD having some experience controlling unruly crowds. When patrolling officers saw the size of the mob forming in the park, the mounted units were hastily called into service.

At Lavaca Street, less than two blocks from the grounds of the capitol building, the demonstrators ran straight into a barricade of 20 police cars and a line of mounted officers. The message was clear - the protest would be allowed no closer. Behind the blue wall was the ominous presence of the Austin Fire Department's massive ladder truck, its water cannon pointed at the advancing throng.

This, of course, didn't sit well with the ginned-up mob. They wanted to take their message to the men who directed the republic. They demanded access to the capitol.

For 30 minutes, the march stalled, the crowd mingling, milling, and occasionally hurling a strong statement at the wall of police blocking the street.

A few hundred hardy souls decided to circumvent the roadblock and approach the capitol building from a different route. It quickly became apparent that a ring of police officers had formed around the entire perimeter.

Zach, along with a dozen other rangers, was assigned a secondary position in the building housing the executive branch's offices. Their orders were to deal with any stragglers that might manage to elude the picket line of law enforcement. If things appeared to be getting out of hand, they would evacuate President Simmons.

The main body of activists remained on 15th. Their numbers, however, were growing by the minute. The captain commanding the APD presence was just fine with conceding that single street but had orders to give no additional ground.

After an hour, it became apparent that the local cops had done an excellent job of containing the crowd. At 90 minutes, Simmons had finished with the day's government business and was ready to leave for a groundbreaking ceremony in Houston.

When the chief executive was safely on his way to the presidential helicopter, Zach found himself curious regarding what was happening at the primary site. After hiding his badge and replacing his western hat with his lucky baseball cap, the ranger meandered his way through the police lines to stand at the edge of the huge mass of protestors.

As with many such events, there appeared to be a variety of messages, demands, and points of view. Directly in front of the ranger was a large group of Latino women holding signs declaring "La Raza Lives Again!"

The ranger knew that La Raza was a political movement established in Central Texas in the mid-1960s. During an era when national headlines were controlled with stories of the Deep South's struggle with segregation and civil rights issues, Texas had faced similar challenges with its Latino population.

Jim Crowe laws existed in the Lone Star State at the time, their discriminating cross hairs primarily aimed at those born with brown rather than black skin. Throughout the Rio Grande Valley, many of the communities had been founded by people with names like Martinez, Garcia, and Briones. They were the Tejanos, and it wasn't uncommon for these early residents to own prosperous ranches and businesses that had been established decades before Texas was even considered for statehood. Yet discrimination ran rampant, society divided by creed and heritage.

Just as great leaders emerged from the oppressed African American population in places like Mississippi and Alabama, similar men arose from the Latino communities in Texas. By the end of the 1960s, the movement was gaining steam and making headway. A decade later, much of the inequality had been eliminated – at least officially.

While the intensity of the struggle in Central and Southern Texas wasn't as violent as the headline-grabbing campaigns of Dr. Martin Luther King and others, the conflict had been intense. They had rallied the people into a new political party – La Raza Unified.

By 1972, however, Hispanic sheriffs, school boards, mayors, and town councilmen were being elected throughout southern Texas. Finally, one citizen equaled one vote, and the result was representation that was proportional to the demographics of the population.

While a racial divide still existed throughout much of the West, the Latino civil rights movement lost steam during the latter portions of the 20st century. Some claimed it was the FBI sabotaging the leadership; others simply wrote it off to the progress that had been achieved. The Democratic Party played a role as well, making a concerted effort to integrate those with a Latin heritage into its fold.

La Raza Unified had faded as a political entity, but now the events in Mexico seemed to have reignited the concept – at least for the people directly in front of Zach's perch.

The ranger moved on, staying well away from the main body of protestors, but close enough to study the various elements that made up the crowd. It was like strolling through a shopping mall of discontented citizenry.

The next group he encountered was a throng of younger Hispanics, all donning brown berets. Again, Zach had to search his memory of high school history classes to pull up the meaning of the color-coded headgear.

In the decade before the secession, debates regarding immigration policy, the border fence, and an explosion of the Latino birthrate rekindled the movement for Mexican-American civil rights. Old terms began to resurface, some of the more radical elements calling for the creation of a new nation often called Aztlan. This new country would encompass much of the territory annexed from Mexico after the Mexican-American war.

University professors, state politicians, and numerous grassroots efforts had campaigned for the concept of Aztlan, calling for Texas, California, Arizona, and New Mexico to secede and began a separate country.

Organizations such as the Brown Berets, Nation of Aztlan, and others gained national headlines during the heated immigration debates that gripped the United States shortly before the secession. Their strategy was simple and undeniable – Hispanics were having more babies than white people. In contrast, the Angelo population supported birth control and 1.8 children per household.

At the time, one state official was quoted as saying, "California is going to be a Hispanic state. Anyone who doesn't like it should leave."

There was no need for protests, marches, civil unrest, or even the formation of a new political party. European whites were growing older and dying. The era of the Chicano would eventually arrive, driven by the birthrate of future voters. The momentum and energy that once supported Aztlan were severely deflated, or so mainstream America and Texas had thought.

Zach was surprised to see hundreds of the people wearing the brown berets. Their signs and banners were professionally printed, not some last minute effort with magic markers and poster board. Of all the sub-groups making up the crowd, they seemed to be the most organized.

The ranger kept moving toward the primary police barricade. As anticipated, the closer he got to the front of the protest, the more radical the marchers became.

Scanning the crowd, Zach's brain registered a familiar face. It was one of those fleeting images … a match from his memory … someone he just somehow *knew* he should pay attention to.

It took the Texan a few more passes before he identified the image. There, in the middle of the street, stood one of Chico's bodyguards.

The VIP room at the gentleman's club had been extremely dark. He'd only caught a glimpse of the man, but Zach was almost certain it was the same fellow.

There was something else suspicious about the guy.

As Zach watched Chico's henchman, it dawned that the heavily muscled gent was much older than any of the other protestors in the area. He was also better dressed and far, far more alert to his surroundings.

Zach moved into the enclave afforded by a small dress shop when he noticed Chico's friend was paying more attention to the surrounding crowd than any part of the protest. He was scanning the mob for someone – or something.

Chico had disappeared after the incident at the gentleman's club. Sam had speculated that the cartel ambassador had gone underground because he didn't trust that Zach would keep his incriminating pictures to himself. Still, the two rangers had monitored Chico's usual haunts – all to no avail.

Now, here in the capital, right in the middle of the largest protest on record since the Vietnam War, there was one of Chico's bodyguards. Why?

About then, the ranger noticed Mr. No-neck's attention was focused across the street. Zach followed his gaze and spotted Chico's second security man.

Now the Texan was certain. He'd busted #2 on a weapons charge.

"What in the hell are you up to?" Zach whispered. "Why are you here?"

The answer came a few minutes later.

Reaching inside of his jacket pocket, one of the bodyguards retrieved a glass bottle, complete with a white length of cloth protruding from the top. Zach knew immediately what it was.

The ranger pulled his .45 just as Mr. No-neck flicked a cigarette lighter. As the bodyguard reared to throw the Molotov cocktail, Zach aligned his pistol's front post on the target's chest.

But he couldn't fire.

There were too many people swirling around, both in front and behind the target. Zach stepped left, and then right, trying to find a clear field of fire. He screamed, "Police!" but there was no way his voice could be heard over the roar of the crowd. The ranger watched helplessly as the goon heaved the deadly gasoline bomb toward the police barricade.

A moment later, a second missile was launched from the throng, the ranger almost certain it had come from Chico's other playmate.

The first projectile landed in the street less than 10 feet in front of a line of officers standing behind an impressive bastion of riot shields.

With a loud whoosh, the gasoline ignited, followed by several terrified screams and countless excited shouts. Two of the horses added their protests to the disruption, rearing wild-eyed on their hind legs and nearly tossing their riders.

The cops closest to the pool of searing-hot fire backed away.

While Zach watched helplessly, the two cartel henchmen tossed more items at the police line as the crowd scrambled in all directions at once.

"They're trying to instigate a riot," Zach hissed, pushing his way through the swirling mass in order to reach the closest man. The effort was hopeless, hundreds of surging, screaming, panicked bodies blocking his way.

Before the ranger could even manage 20 feet, the police responded with a barrage of tear gas. In less than half a minute, 15th Street became a living hell.

Just as the hissing canisters of gas began enveloping the pavement with blinding, choking clouds of white fog, a young man picked one up and threw it back toward the police.

Inspired by their friend's bravado, a wave of projectiles soon filled the air, mostly composed of anything the protestors could scavenge from the trashcans lining the sidewalks.

The first storefront window shattered a few moments later, the breakage driven by the need for something to throw back at the cops rather than any desire for the goods displayed inside the hardware store.

Zach did his best to try to find the two cartel instigators, but the task was simply impossible.

Bound and determined not to let the now-violent multitude gain any momentum, the mounted officers charged into the center of the crowd, the 25 horse-wide wedge scattering any resistance. Behind the cavalry, a wall of clear, Plexiglas riot shields marched forward, the hawk-like helmets of the police peering over the top of the bulletproof barrier as they readied their batons.

Zach didn't want to hang around in the hope that his badge would provide immunity. It didn't look like the APD was checking IDs.

The ranger reacted like most of the surrounding crowd, retreating down an alley and then zigzagging through several side streets until the mob had thinned.

Well away from the isolated pockets of violence still raging on 15th, Zach circled the dispersing crowd several times, trying in vain to catch another glimpse of the two cartel enforcers.

Finally giving up the quest, he returned to the executive offices where he found Major Putnam milling around with the few remaining rangers.

"Why would the cartel want to incite a riot?" the senior lawman asked after Zach had relayed his recent experiences. "That doesn't make any sense."

"Unknown, sir," Zach answered honestly. "I suppose there's a chance they were legit protestors caught up in one cause or another, but it sure seems odd that they would come prepared for battle."

"And you never saw Chico?"

"No, sir. I did not."

Putnam scratched his head in thought. "Having a riot in the capital is not going to play well on the airwaves this evening. The general public is already uneasy over recent events. The closed borders and unrest in Mexico are sending economic shock waves through our economy, and a lot of very important people are nervous. Add in the fact that there's a large segment that is hopping mad that Texas was involved in bioterror research, and we're sitting on a tinderbox. Poke around, Ranger Bass, and see what you can find. But stay close to Austin. I have a feeling we're in for a rough ride until the situation resolves one way or the other."

Zach wandered back to the scene where the protest had turned into an insurrection, Major Putnam's words rolling around in the ranger's troubled mind.

His official reason for returning was the dim hope of catching a glimpse of Chico or his crew. At least, that's what he initially told himself.

In reality, Zach was deeply disturbed by Putnam's attitude.

The republic's leadership was being pulled into a game they could not win. The ranger conjured up images of Simmons and Bowmark on puppet strings, Vincent and Ghost manipulating the controls.

Zach believed both of his superiors were good, honest servants. He was also becoming increasingly convinced that Ghost and Vincent had them outmatched. Men like Bowmark and Simmons played by the rules of law and order, individual responsibility, and elected authority. It was their greatest strength, and now, their exposed vulnerability.

The ranger walked past a row of ambulances, many of the injured, young college kids holding bloody bandages against their heads. There were cops there as well, more than a dozen officers injured in the line of duty.

These are the people of Texas, he considered. *These are the same people that sit across the aisle from me at the restaurant or nod hello at the grocery store. These are my countrymen, neighbors, and friends. What the hell are we doing to each other?*

Just beyond the medical triage area, he began to see even more evidence of the violence. A car, overturned and torched by the mob, was still smoldering. It fouled the air with more than just the fumes of burnt plastic and charred rubber – the stench was a harbinger of the republic's future. It all sickened Zach.

He continued his stroll through the aftermath, past the looted store windows, litter, and a few other pedestrians who wouldn't make eye contract. All the while Zach searched for what was troubling him so deeply.

Mexico was embroiled in open warfare, the conflict already boiling over into Texas on two occasions. Zach couldn't conjure up any scenario where the fighting less than 200 miles to the south of where he stood wouldn't continue to escalate. He could foresee the republic being pulled further into the quagmire with thousands and thousands of her sons and daughters being shipped home in body bags.

Zach slowed to watch an older couple ambling toward him along the sidewalk. Just a few feet away, they stopped and stood speechless as they stared at a store that advertised itself as Moe and Betty's Dry Cleaners. The place had been badly damaged. The woman turned to her partner and began crying uncontrollably.

The ranger saw the man try and comfort her, his arm moving around her shoulder and pulling her close. All the while, a tear rolled down his cheek. "What are we going to do?" the lady managed to sob.

"We'll be okay, Betty. I promise. Things will work out – they always do."

Unable to take it any longer, Zach crossed the street and continued rambling through the aftermath. "This is my fault," he whispered. "If I hadn't let Ghost get away … if I'd just done my job."

His thoughts returned to Putnam's orders. "Stay close to Austin," his boss had commanded.

"That type of thinking won't resolve this conflict, Major," The ranger pretended to argue with his boss. "That strategy will only lead to more heartbreak and death. That's not the level of thinking required for Texas to win this thing. We need bold. We need ruthless. The republic must have strong, aggressive initiatives or the foes we face will destroy us. We need to battle evil with a greater evil, fight fire with hotter flames."

As the ranger continued strolling through the destruction, it dawned on him that Texas was now in reactionary mode. Simmons and the other leadership of the republic had to sit and wait for the opposition's next move. They were on the defense, and that wasn't how to achieve victory.

He turned to stare back at the capitol building, its 300-foot outline dominating the skyline. A column of smoke partially obscured the grand dome. The gray and black cloud of ash provided an eerie, apocalyptic essence, that when combined with the sunlight, made it appear as if the structure itself was on fire. Zach knew it was an optical illusion but wondered for a moment if such a vision was a harbinger of the future.

"Men like Ghost and Vincent would love to see you burn," he whispered, staring at the icon of the republic.

Zach pivoted, a determination spreading through his core. As he approached the capitol grounds, he paused for a moment to gaze up at the statue honoring Terry's Texas Rangers, a regiment that had served with distinction during the Civil War.

Zach had always admired the monument. A single man, on horseback, wearing a western hat with a repeating rifle in his hands. The sculpture captured the essence of the sacrifice and gallantry of the Texas cavalrymen while at the same time relaying the burden and fatigue that war placed on a man's shoulders.

His eyes zoomed in on the plaque where he read the words, "The Terry Rangers have done all that could be expected or required…."

"Have I done all that could be expected?" he asked the lone rider. "Have I done all that is required?"

It dawned on Zach that he could stop the madness. He could end this thing. Like the bronze cowboy above, he would take the fight to the enemy. It would require that he leave his beloved Texas, and perhaps the rangers, but there was no other choice. The lives of millions and the wellbeing of two different nations were at stake.

The next morning, Putnam seemed surprised by Zach's unusual request. "Sir, I'm requesting a few days of my accumulated leave."

"Now, Ranger Bass? Right when the republic faces its greatest challenge? This request doesn't seem like the actions of the man I've come to know over the last few years."

"I've not taking a vacation, Major. There are, however, some avenues of investigation that I would like to pursue in an off-the-record capacity. I know my request is unusual, sir, but I don't see any other option. I need to operate outside of official channels."

Putnam obviously didn't like. For several minutes he tried to talk Zach out of the request, but the young Texan wouldn't budge. The major had never seen his subordinate so resolute and determined. "Okay, Ranger Bass. Email me the vacation request form, and I'll put it through. I pray that you know what you're doing."

"That makes two of us, sir. A prayer may be all that can save us."

After disconnecting the call with his boss, Zach glanced at his watch and smiled. Sam was at a doctor's appointment and would have her cell phone turned off. It was the perfect time to call.

"Sam," he advised her voicemail, "I'm taking a few days off. All this is beginning to weigh on me, and I'm going to head up into the mountains for a little hiking, fresh air, and reflection. I won't have cell service, so I'll call you when I get back. Hope the doc says you're doing well."

His next call was to Cheyenne. "What's up, cowboy? Or should I say, are you *up*, cowboy?"

"I need your help," he answered with a serious tone.

His request caught her off guard. Zach never needed help. "You okay? What's wrong?"

"Nothing more than what you are reading about in the headlines. Do you think your dad would let you borrow his truck for a day?"

The model was clearly mystified by the request. "Umm … sure … Why do I need a truck? Don't you already have one?"

He didn't answer, instead firing another question. "Are you working today?"

"No, Mr. Texas Ranger Man, today is my only day off this week. I was going to call you and see if you were willing to offer this girl a little couple time. I just did this hot lingerie shoot and got to take home a few samples…."

"I wish, but believe it or not, that's not really what I had in mind. I need you to help me sneak across the border and not tell a soul that you did it."

Now Chey was really worried. "Zachariah Bass, what's going on? You're freaking me out."

"Get your dad's truck and meet me at my place, ASAP. I'll explain it all when you get there."

She wanted to launch a dozen questions, but she'd known him since they were kids. Something in Zach's tone warned her not to press. "Okay. It will take me a couple of hours, but I'll be there."

"Thanks, Chey. I owe you one."

Chapter 12

It felt odd to the Texan.

He'd carried a badge for so long, been in a position of authority for so many years. Now, here, he was just a regular guy – an average Joe. The fact that he was about to commit a series of crimes added to the peculiar sensations running through his mind.

For the Nth time, he reconsidered his plan. Wouldn't it be easier to sneak across to Mexico via a small boat? He was sure such craft could be rented in Brownsville. *But I don't know how to pilot a boat*, he reasoned.

Perhaps hiking across the border from Texas would be the smarter option? *No*, he came to the same mental conclusion. *Since the massacre and outbreak of civil war, the line between Texas and Mexico is now an armed camp. The military is shooting first, asking questions later. I don't blame them.*

After a long goodbye, he'd watched Cheyenne amble away in her dad's truck. Standing at the trailhead, he'd wondered if he would ever see her again. She was absolutely sure he had gone loco, and quite frankly, he couldn't blame her for thinking that, either.

Zach had worked the Texas-New Mexico border area for years. He knew every back trail and unmarked road. It had been child's play to cross. The U.S. Border Patrol, new to working an area between states, hadn't figured it all out yet. Chey had been able to cross the *Land of Enchantment* without issue, keeping below the speed limit and heading west using secondary roadways.

He hiked for two hours through the state park, following the marked trails with his heavy pack full of equipment. Primitive camping wasn't popular in Whitmire Canyon ... but not unheard of. Most outdoorsmen were too afraid of the border area and chose destinations further north. For Zach's purposes, it was the perfect locale.

"I'm just another backpacker, enjoying the dry air," he kept whispering as he made his way through the rugged, high desert terrain. The ruse was unnecessary. He hadn't seen another soul.

After an hour, he was second-guessing the adventure. The ranger's leg muscles were beginning to burn, the late afternoon sun draining his reserves. Blisters were in his future. "You spend too much time riding in a truck," he cursed, scanning the barren rock and hot sands. "This is good for you."

Two miles north of the Mexican border, the wilderness area ended, the boundary denoted by a common livestock fence.

Pausing to take a drink of water from the reservoir strapped on his back, Zach pondered his next move. As soon as he crossed the fence, he would technically be breaking the law as a trespasser. A few miles further on, he'd come to the international border where he would begin compounding his crimes.

But first, he'd have to get past the U.S. authorities.

Zach figured that his time spent working with the U.S. Border Patrol before the secession would come in handy. He knew their technology, tactics, and capabilities. These folks were very good at their jobs. It would take some doing to cross. *Old women with children did it all the time … surely a Texas Ranger could pull it off.*

Zach removed his pack and dropped it onto the private property. He didn't know who owned the land. It was most likely a cattle rancher who lived miles away and probably wouldn't care. There were no barns, wells, water tanks or other infrastructure in sight. Nothing to harm or steal.

There were, however, likely to be ground vibration sensors and perhaps even infrared cameras watching the area. The ranger had no idea where such devices might be located as they were often moved to keep the other side guessing.

He did know there was no fence on this section of the border. The Mexican side was just as devoid of population, towns, and roads. That, combined with the harsh environment and rugged landscape, meant this area wasn't a popular crossing point. Still, the ranger was sure it was monitored.

Climbing the 4-wire fence was easy, the Texan's long legs and thick-soled boots making the barb wire strands an ineffective detriment. After pulling on his pack, he began walking south, now more alert to his surroundings than before. Now, he was breaking the law.

According to the satellite maps, the only roadway between him and Mexico was actually more of a path. Two worn lanes of dirt served as a patrol route for the green and white trucks of border patrol.

Zach knew the odds were strong that they would be coming. Between the cameras, ground sensors, helicopters, and drones, there was very little chance he would escape their scrutiny.

He found himself crossing a respite of prairie grass and mature trees, the foliage and flat ground a welcome change from the harsh gray and red rock that had monopolized his journey so far.

The island of green was short-lived however, the environment quickly reverting back to scorched, barren surroundings seemingly devoid of all life.

Zach worked his way down a draw, wanting to follow the low ground as much as possible. Neither infrared nor light amplification devices could see through solid rock.

Down he climbed, the rock and stone walls growing steeper as he followed a dry creek bed along the bottom of what was turning out to be a rather deep canyon. The heat was nearly unbearable, Zach constantly depleting the water supply strapped to his back.

It was easy to understand how this part of the Southwest had claimed so many dead. Zach was in good condition, jogged and lifted weights on a regular basis, and had significant drinking water available to him – yet he struggled with the exertion, heat, and dry air.

He noted his body was using far more water than usual, every breath of the low-humidity air drawing critical moisture from his cells. His perspiration was evaporating almost instantly, making his body fight even harder to keep itself cool.

Eventually, his canyon led to a larger valley. Snaking through the bottom of the flatter ground, he spied the route traveled by the border patrol agents. The international boundary was another mile south.

For a moment, Zach was tempted to make a run for it. He could see a reasonable distance in both directions, and there wasn't any sign of human activity. With his heavy pack, Zach figured he could cross the uneven terrain in about 15 minutes if his legs and lungs held out.

He quickly dismissed the urge. The local agents probably had horses, ATVs, and 4-wheel drive trucks. They could be hiding in a thousand different places. Making such a run in broad daylight was just stupid given how much was riding on his safe passage.

If they caught him, his career was over, he would cause no small amount of embarrassment for Texas, and Mexico would most likely be torn apart. If the U.S. boys were in a vigorous frame of mind, he might even go to jail.

Zach scanned his surroundings again and decided the canyon was his best bet at concealment. Unless a drone or copter flew directly overhead, he would be difficult to spot. Dropping his pack to the ground, he leaned against a large boulder and again pulled a few swallows of water.

After resting a bit, he began removing the gear from his knapsack and setting up camp. There was an old tent, entrenching tool, a small butane powered stove, and a special package he'd prepared just for the trip.

The tent was a mess, complete with worn fabric, unworkable zippers, and a hole large enough for a good sized scorpion to make a nocturnal visit. Zach didn't care – he wasn't going to be sleeping tonight.

The fire pit required special care. There was enough dried mesquite and scrub oak lying around to provide fuel. The ranger was careful to dig the pit extra deep on three sides.

He made coffee and heated a camping meal, shoving the last spoonful of the extra-salty beef stew in his mouth just as the sun sat in the west.

Dusk was the perfect light to run the wire and dig his hole.

There was only one way up the small draw to his camp. Zach quickly secured one end of the thinnest fishing line he could find and began unwinding the spool. The first time he tried to test his equipment, he broke the thin, plastic string. The second attempt proved workable.

It was much darker by the time he started digging the spider hole.

He knew the BP would be using night vision and infrared equipment. The light amplification units weren't his primary concern. It was the infrared that worried Zach the most, and it wasn't just the agents on the ground that he had to bypass.

Aircraft and fixed position cameras also were equipped with similar technologies.

Moving as close to the mouth of the canyon as he dared, Zach selected a semi-exposed shelf of rock. After picking the best example, he began hacking, scraping and digging out a burrow large enough to conceal most of his oversized frame. It was hot, filthy work.

Next, he unfolded a sheet of radiant barrier material used to insulate houses. The metallic fiber was similar to the thin, Mylar "space" blankets commonly found in emergency kits. According to the manufacturer, it would reflect 95% of the heat generated by his body.

He draped himself in a cloak of the shiny metal fabric and then did the same with his leather duster. Zach knew his two-layered approach wasn't a long-term solution, as his body heat would eventually bleed through. "All I need is 30 minutes," he whispered, wishing there had been more time to test his gizmos.

When his spider hole and thermal suit were ready, Zach threw a large bundle of firewood in the pit, connected the wire to his special package, and darted for his hide.

The ranger knew the fire's signature would point the local CBP toward the canyon. He was hoping it would draw them in like moths to a flame.

Zach was also well aware that the typical border crashers didn't build fires. He was putting a lot of faith in the never-ending game of cat and mouse played along the international boundary and the continuing creativity of the smugglers. Everything from tunnels to ramps and even catapults had been used for illegal border crossings. He was reasonably sure something unusual, like the flames, would be sure to lure in the agents.

Sliding under the rock and then draping his enhanced duster over the opening, the ranger waited. It was less than 15 minutes before he heard the first engine noise.

Zach was tempted to peer out, but he knew any exposure of his skin could be detected on an infrared reticle. Before long, he could hear several sets of boots working their way toward the camp.

There were at least four of them. Once he was sure they had passed his hide and were approaching his fake camp, Zach felt safe chancing a look through a narrow slit in his heat shield.

With the fire backlighting their approach, he could make out five agents spreading out to approach his lure.

When they were within 20 feet of his fire, he pulled hard on the fishing line.

The thin line tightened, pulling Zach's package into the flames. Inside the paper bag was what the lady at the fireworks stand called a "multi-stage artillery shell."

Zach closed his eyes and covered his ears.

It took the fire another few seconds to burn through the paper.

A throbbing white fireball erupted in the canyon, the strobe of blinding light accompanied by an ear-splitting crack of overwhelming noise. The rock surrounding Zach vibrated for a moment, the searing flash visible through his clenched eyelids.

The fireworks had been designed to be launched skyward and then explode in the brilliant spread of white, thunderous starbursts, quickly followed by secondary poppers and fizzling streaks of color. When the nearly two pounds of powder exploded in the fire, the effect on the agents and their equipment was devastating.

Zach knew modern night vision and infrared devices were equipped with automatic shut-off, "auto-gated" mechanisms. These circuits were meant to protect the sensitive tubes from sudden bursts of light. And that's just what happened to the CBP equipment.

The human brain suffered a similar condition. While Zach's surprise, combined with the 3-sided fire pit, didn't throw any shrapnel, the agents were still disabled. It was if they had been hit with a flashbang grenade of massive proportions.

Blinded, stumbling, and deaf, the border patrol team was completely dazed, none of them noticing Zach sliding out from his hide and running like hell toward the valley below.

He was a good 70 yards behind them, moving as quickly as possible through the rough terrain. He broke out onto the flat valley floor, the smoother ground allowing the lanky Texan to take advantage of his stride.

That's when Zach spotted the three official-looking SUVs sitting alongside the path. He could clearly hear one of the radios through the otherwise calm, desert night.

With a grunt, the ranger detoured toward the government vehicles, hoping all of the agents had made for the canyon. Sure enough, he found the three SUVs idling unattended.

Zach couldn't help but grin as he opened the first vehicle's door. He studied the radio for a moment under the dome light's glow and then pushed a quick series of buttons. He depressed the microphone's talk button and wedged the device between the seat and center console, careful to keep the unit transmitting.

With the keys still in the ignition and the broadcasting radio blocking the primary communications channel, Zach closed and locked the door.

The ranger did the same on the other two green and white patrol units and then spirited away toward the Mexican border. It would take a while before the CBP boys figured out why their personal radios were no longer working. Unless they had spare keys in their wallets, it would be even longer before they were mobile.

Running hard now, eating up the distance across the level basin floor, Zach hoped he would never meet the federal agents he'd just left behind. He was sure they would shoot him on sight and leave his carcass for the buzzards. "Some people have no sense of humor about this shit," he whispered between breaths.

The Texas lawman, now turned criminal, slowly made his way across the desolate landscape that was northern Mexico, eventually arriving at a two-lane, blacktop highway that the map identified as Carretera Federal 2.

Zach began walking east, staying to the edge, ready to hide in the rocks if headlights appeared ahead or behind.

There was little population in this part of Chihuahua, the arid climate and volcanic rock supporting only the occasional ranch or small village. Still, the ranger knew that the U.S. Border Patrol occasionally worked with the Mexican authorities. By now, the American agents he'd left behind would be over the shock and awe of the encounter in the canyon. They would be steaming pissed and clawing for payback. Calling in the Policía Federal would be about their only recourse, short of invading a foreign country.

The thought of spending time in a Mexican prison wasn't at the top of Zach's bucket list.

So the ranger kept to the side of the road, scurrying to hide whenever the rare car or truck appeared in the distance. Highway 2 in this part of the world was never a busy artery. Given the early hour, the roadway was all but abandoned.

Were it not for the speed limit signs posted in kilometers and the occasional "No Rebase" warning drivers not to pass, Zach noted no difference between this road and the typical U.S. state highway.

Just after 3 AM, he approached a bridge crossing a small, dry creek bed. A sign declared the structure was Puente El Venado.

Zach left the roadway and climbed down the embankment, cautious of snakes or other wildlife that might have found the manmade structure attractive.

After a quick search with his flashlight, the Texan found a suitable rock and made himself as comfortable as possible.

He passed the time nibbling on a power bar, drawing water from his CamelBak, and admiring the impressive field of stars that illuminated the Mexican night.

At 5 AM, he recognized the whine of a truck engine coming from the east. The vehicle did a U-turn and then stopped right on the bridge. Zach heard a door being opened.

"Ranger Bass, I presume," boomed BB's voice over the railing. "Welcome to Mexico."

"You know if this doesn't go well, your career with the rangers is over," BB stated with a matter of fact tone.

Zach didn't respond for a bit, his attention seemingly focused on the passing Mexican countryside as they drove east.

"Yes, I know," Zach eventually sighed. "What's really troubling is that I'm not bothered by that nearly as much as I should be. I hate to admit it, but being a ranger hasn't always been a good fit for me."

The older man grunted, "That's probably why you're a good lawman. If you liked the job … if it was a perfect match, then I'd say something was seriously wrong inside your head."

The comment surprised Zach. Somewhere along the line, he'd developed a sense that all of the other rangers loved their jobs and wouldn't think of doing anything else. His peers had seemed to develop something more than professional dedication or loyalty to the cause of law and order. It was almost as if they had found the perfect mesh between God's desire and nature's design.

BB took the younger man's lack of response as a signal to expound. "I lost my wife early. Miss Lily succumbed to breast cancer. God rest her soul. She was 51, and I watched her die a horrible, painful death. That fucking disease took everything away from her, and it did it slow and mean. I lost my faith, watching her wither in agony and melt away to nothing. She'd been a God fearing woman all her life. Never harmed a soul and touched anyone who came close with her kindness and love. She didn't deserve to go out that way."

Zach was a little surprised at BB's openness. "I'm sorry to hear that. I knew she had passed on some years before we met, but I never heard any of the details."

"I hit the bottle pretty damn hard…. Tequila became my best compadre. My captain was a patient man. He tried to give me time to straighten things out, but I'd already started sliding down a pretty slippery slope. When I eventually did return to duty, I was a bitter son of a bitch who didn't give a fuck about anything or anybody. That's a dangerous combination for a big hombre who carries a gun and a badge."

The younger ranger had seen it before. The ranks of law enforcement had more than their fair share of disgruntled officers who, for whatever reason, had gotten sideways with the world. The occurrences of spousal abuse, alcoholism, and suicide were all much higher among those in this line of work. Opinions regarding the causes of such things were as varied as the recommended treatments for them.

The conversation was interrupted by a slow-moving truck struggling to climb a grade. After BB had safely managed to pass, he continued with a monotone voice. "I answered a call in Marathon one night. According to the dispatcher, a deputy had cornered a suspected bank robber and was requesting backup. By the time I got there, the suspect was fighting with the officer, both of them rolling around on the ground, throwing punches and kicking for all they were worth. What was even more troubling was the fact that the officer on the scene was getting whooped."

With his eyebrows arching skyward, Zach asked, "What happened?"

BB frowned in pain, the memory obviously unpleasant. "I jumped in, of course. One of my kind was getting his ass kicked. I tore into the suspect and damned near beat that poor bastard into his grave … almost killed him. He lost an eye, use of his left arm, six teeth, and never walked again without a limp."

Zach threw a glance at BB when the narration paused, but the older man wasn't in the cab of the pickup anymore – at least not mentally.

"Problem was, the suspect wasn't the bank robber. He was a close match to the description and driving a similar car. Some of the senior officers thought the poor bastard deserved it, but times were changing. People didn't want tough cops anymore. Everyone was throwing around phrases like civil rights and excessive use of force. My captain gave me a choice. Stay and face potential charges, or resign and get on with life. I resigned."

"How did you end up living in Mexico?" Zach asked, trying to tie the story together.

BB grunted, "For a while, I didn't think my captain was going to be able to keep Austin off my ass. There was all kind of talk, folks speculating that charges were going to be filed against me. So I decided to spend a little time exploring Mexico. I took the grand tour of every cantina from Juarez to Reynosa. The tequila was cheap, the señoritas friendly, and no one cared if I was Santa Claus, the Easter Bunny, or a washed up Texas Ranger."

Again, traffic required all of BB's attention. Zach knew they still had some distance to travel, so he let his friend come to it when he was ready.

"We're about 30 minutes from the ranch," BB finally stated. "My place isn't much, but it's mine. The cost of living down here is next to nothing, and I'm only 20 minutes from Texas if I want to go back."

Zach wanted to hear the end of the story. "So what changed, BB? How come you didn't end up with a failed liver or beaten and left lying in the gutter somewhere?"

The old ranger grinned, "Isabelle."

"Isabelle?"

"Queen Isabelle…. Or at least, that's what I call her. She was a waitress in some run-down cantina. Hell, I can't even remember the name of the dump. I was there one night when a handful of punks started giving her a rough time. They made a circle and were shoving her back and forth, making it clear she was going to be part of their entertainment that evening – like it or not."

"And?"

BB's answer was matter of fact. "And I changed their minds."

Zach grunted at the casual response but didn't doubt the story for a second. *I'd rather slap Satan across the face than go hand-to-hand with BB in a bar fight*, he figured.

The old-school lawman continued, "I went back into the place the next few evenings, but they seemed to have lost their desire to frequent that establishment. Izzy and I got to talking. Her family owned some land up in the mountains but couldn't afford to do anything with it. I had a small retirement from the rangers and a little money saved back. So, we moved in and started raising horses, a few head of cattle, and a nice, big garden. She convinced me to cut way back on my vices, and we've been together ever since."

The veteran ranger was soon guiding the pickup onto a lane that was little more than a dirt path. The old truck bounced and bumped, kicking up a small rooster tail of sand and dust as they meandered upwards into the Carmen Sierras.

Zach felt his ears pop at about 4,000 feet. The air cooled as the foliage outside the pickup began to change drastically. White Oak clogged the draws and box canyons, the steeper slopes taken over by juniper. "The locals call this La Frontera," BB announced. "I call it damn fine country. Kind of reminds you of the Davis Mountains back home, don't it?"

The young ranger had to agree.

The ranch consisted of two adobe buildings, the one with a thatch roof housing the barnyard animals, the one with a tin crown being the main house. The fences and corral were a weave of mesquite limbs, none bigger than Zach's wrist. A Latino woman was standing in the doorway.

"My queen," BB laughed as he exited the truck. "The ruler of all she sees before her."

As BB completed the introductions in Spanglish, Zach studied the woman that would be his hostess for the day.

She was younger than BB, probably by 15 years, but it was difficult to tell exactly. Isabelle was obviously tough as nails and a woman who wasn't afraid to put in a hard day's work followed by a warm night's comfort. It was also clear that she adored the ex-ranger.

Zach sensed Izzy was immediately suspicious of his presence, and he couldn't blame her. The ranger was sure she grasped the unspoken truth that he was about to draw her man into something dangerous, and she didn't like it. More than once, she looked at the cuts from San Antonio, still visible on BB's head, and grimaced.

There were two younger vaqueros from a neighboring spread that helped manage the livestock.

"You'll find a hammock behind the barn," BB announced after watching Zach yawn. "Have a couple of Isabelle's cheese and egg burritos, and then go catch some shuteye. Most afternoons there's a good breeze blowing down the mountain, and those two old oaks will keep the sun off of you until at least mid-afternoon."

Despite the urgency of his quest, Zach's hike through New Mexico and encounter with the authorities had worn the ranger thin. "I think I'll take you up on that."

Chapter 13

It was the most wonderful smell. Zach's eyes fluttered open, the aroma drifting past the hammock and pulling him from the depths of slumber.

For a moment, the ranger didn't know where he was – a sure sign he'd managed at least a few cycles of REM sleep.

Next came a bit of confusion as he struggled to swing out of the hammock. Finally managing to get his feet on the ground before his ass, he checked his boots for scorpions and other desert critters, and then stood to stretch.

The breeze brought him that appetizing fragrance again. Someone was cooking meat over mesquite. His stomach rumbled a thunderous approval.

The meal was simple and one of the best the Texan could remember. Thin strips of steak cooked over an open fire of mesquite bricks. Small ears of corn dipped in homemade, extra salty butter, and a cold blonde ale called Baja that was served with orange peels floating in the glass.

Zach was embarrassed at how much food he was shoving into his pie hole, but couldn't stop himself. BB and Izzy seemed gratified that their guest was gorging himself on their fare.

After everyone had finished eating, BB motioned for Zach to join him in the barn. Glancing left and right to verify no one was around, he lifted a thick, wooden pallet from the floor and swept away an inch of loose sand, exposing a heavy, metal slab buried in the earth. "My gun safe," the lawman-turned-rancher announced.

BB produced a key, uncapped the protected lock, and opened the weighty door. Reaching inside, he pulled out two bundles, each wrapped in a spongy oilcloth. A few moments later, Zach was holding an AR15 rifle, complete with holographic optic and mounted flashlight. "Where did you get this?"

"From time to time, I've cleaned up a few bad apples here and there – kind of helping out the local authorities. If the criminals happen to have a well-maintained firearm in their possession, I consider it to be a finder's fee."

Reaching again into the cache, BB produced a couple of gym bags stuffed with magazines, each filled to the brim with 5.56 NATO ammunition. Zach whistled, "Expecting trouble?"

"A man never knows in this country, Ranger Bass."

Zach grinned, "Understood."

Twenty minutes later, both men exited the corral with smiles on their faces. Zach had expected BB to provide some firepower, but nothing like the old ranger had delivered. "Tomorrow morning, we'll pack up, and on the way stop by a certain canyon I know to zero these weapons," the host announced. "After that, we'll go hunting."

"That would be good," Zach nodded. "That would be very good."

The two rangers left BB's ranch shortly after daybreak. Once out of sight of the vaqueros, they stopped to test and zero their weapons.

While Zach was adjusting his red dot, BB began to outline their trip. "You know we're going to have to be extremely careful. With a civil war going on, we're going to have to avoid the bigger towns. That might take a while."

"You're the expert," Zach replied. "My Spanish isn't even that strong."

BB laughed, raising the AK47 to his shoulder and snapping three rounds that nearly cut a small barrel cactus in half. "Let me guess, you know the basic phrases, like 'How much is the tequila,' and 'Put your hands up, or I'll shoot your sorry ass.'"

It was Ranger Bass's turn to chuckle, popping a double tap into a plate-sized rock 100 meters out. "Something like that."

Wiping a quick cleaning rag through their barrels, BB became serious. "Why, Zach? I mean, I can understand a man having a strong sense of right and wrong. I can even sympathize with your wanting to catch the one that got away or to catch the bastard who shot up that gorgeous partner of yours. But you're throwing everything away on this little adventure of ours, and before I put my salty, old hide on the line, I'd like to know why."

Nodding, Zach understood where the older man was coming from. It was time to be honest. "Because I fucked up, that's why. I made a huge mistake over in Syria, and all of this suffering and death is resting on my shoulders."

It was obvious BB was trying to grasp what the younger man was saying, but it just wouldn't come. "I'm sorry to be a senile, ancient fool, but you're going to have to paint this picture nice and pretty for me. I don't *comprende*."

"There is a man we know only as Ghost. He was the mastermind behind all the shit the republic went through over in Syria. He was behind the counterfeiting … and the highjacking … and Buck's death. I had him, BB…. I had my cuffs on his wrists and his ass in my pocket, and I let him go. I'm convinced he's behind all this shit that's going down around us."

"You're 'convinced'? You're not sure?"

Zach shook his head as he began checking magazines. "Are we ever sure? I can tell you that I'm about as positive on this as any case I've ever bird-dogged. It's Ghost, all right. His fingerprints and DNA are all over this, and I'm not going to let him get away again."

BB took some time to study his new partner, almost as if he was trying to make up his mind. Finally, he said, "I'll be the first to plead guilty that sometimes a lawman has to trust his gut. Still, you're putting a lot more on the line here than just one ranger's career. That weapon you're holding can do a lot of damage to the people of both Mexico and Texas. Are you sure you're willing to risk an international brouhaha?"

Zach's face became taut, his eyes on fire. "A lot of the death and suffering we're seeing on the nightly news is my doing. I feel the weight of it on my shoulders. I can see a parade of dead faces in my sleep. Those Marines. All of the Mexicans in body bags. Gus. There is no shortage of people whose lives have been fucked up. I've got to end this. I've got to make it right."

The old man nodded. He knew exactly what Zach was going through. "That's why you asked me to help," he whispered. "And that is why you knew I would agree."

"You've been there, BB. I thought you … of all the capable men I know … I thought you would understand."

The elder lawman glanced back up the mountain, toward Queen Isabelle. Finally, he nodded, "One riot, one ranger. One civil war – two rangers. Makes sense to me. I'm in, Zach. With you all the way."

A few minutes later, the duo was driving west, the old pickup making good time across the blacktop surface of the two-lane highway. "We've got about an hour of smooth road, and then things are going to get a little bit more vigorous. We'll have to cut off the highway and do a little back road navigation to avoid the sizable towns and cities. All said, if our engine don't quit, and the creek don't rise, we should be in Tampico by sunrise."

"Works for me."

"And when we get there? I'm kind of assuming we're not traveling across Mexico with all this illegal firepower just to do a little duck hunting. Do you have a plan?"

Zach nodded, but there was a slight hesitation. "I've got some inside information that indicates we should visit the marina in Tampico. Ghost is being sponsored by the head of the Gulf Cartel, an hombre known as El General. I've heard he's hanging out in Tampico. Even if that tip doesn't play out, I'm hoping a bull that big leaves a trail as it crosses the pasture."

"They usually do," BB grunted. "Besides, I did a little bounty hunting for the Tampico Chief of Police a while back. Tracked down a couple of very nasty banditos and delivered them alive … mostly. If we come up empty, he might be able to point our noses in the right direction."

"That's why you're earning the big money on this trip, BB," Zach teased. "It's not what you know, but who you know – right?"

"Big money, my ass," the old man spat. "That'll be the day."

The country that passed outside Zach's window wasn't much different from his native West Texas. Neither were the people.

Sure, most of the automobiles they saw would have benefited from a trip to the car wash. Nearly all of them had seen better days. The mountains seemed a little less sharp and pointed. It was almost as if the land was an elderly man whose body was no longer as cut or defined due to time and a life of hard labor. Still, there was a raw beauty to the countryside, a comfort that comes from stability, a gratitude earned from years of providing.

The duo passed through tiny hamlets and villages, avoiding the metropolitan areas and the suburbs for fear of bumbling into the local authorities, or worse yet, the civil war.

As they had traveled across central Mexico, Zach had noticed a large segment of the population didn't possess all that much pigmentation in their skin. It dawned on him that he could be traveling through southern Europe given the color of people's flesh. He remarked as much to BB.

"I thought I'd stand out down here like a sore thumb," Zach noted. "Yet a lot of the locals I'm seeing have a fairer complexion than I do. Just goes to show you, a man can't believe everything he sees on TV."

"That's a common misconception," BB replied. "There are just as many mixed-blood people in Mexico as there are in Texas. Don't worry; we won't stand out unless you start flirting with a señorita. She'd pick up on your bad Spanish and northern accent in a heartbeat."

Chuckling, Zach promised his new partner that wouldn't be a problem. At least not on the trip down to Tampico.

As they continued, the young ranger realized it was more than just the people that left an impression of the old world. The architecture carried a sense of age as well.

While the territory outside the truck was comprised of modest communities, the buildings were constructed with softer curves and caught the afternoon sunlight in a different way. There was a simplistic nature in their form and function, be it an humble abode or the mayor's office.

Basic pastels consumed the color scheme with only one exception – the churches.

It was clear the local folk took their spirituality seriously. In every town and burg, it was always the church's steeple that first appeared on the horizon. Rarely, did another structure rival the chapel's size, and never was there a challenger to the gemstone-like colors that exploded from the stained glass windows.

Then there were the people themselves.

BB's truck required a fuel stop, and while Zach couldn't remember the name of the town, the genuine friendliness of the place had stuck with the ranger. The people didn't smile and nod to get tourist money; their greetings and interactions were heartfelt efforts to make the traveler feel at ease.

Twice they stopped at a roadside cantina to fill their human tanks, and again, Zach sensed a deep level of gratification in everyone from the señorita who served their food to the young busboys who cleared their plates.

By sundown, Zach had reached a comfort with his surroundings that extended far beyond familiarity or the repetition of seeing the same basic scene outside of the pickup's cab, mile after mile. He decided that he liked the culture they were driving through, and it gave him another dimension of righteousness to their cause.

He admired the friendly, unassuming people they encountered. He respected their lifestyle and knew they deserved better than to be slaughtered in a civil war or to be dominated by ruthless criminals.

"We're going to do a good deed if we kill these men," he said out loud, surprising BB.

Recovering, the old ranger responded, "Was there ever any doubt about that?"

Zach grinned, "No, I suppose not. Still, I feel better about it. It's as if these people we're passing by want us to succeed. They want us to win, and I think we're going to need all the support we can get."

By the time the two rangers were pulling into the outskirts of Tampico, it was difficult to tell the duo from the locals.

Zach's three days' worth of stubble did a lot to hide his lighter completion and served to make the rogue lawman look like anything but a traveling gringo tourist.

It was hard to estimate when BB had last shaved, his salt and pepper stubble providing a grizzled accent against his sun-darkened, leathery skin.

There were plenty of men who looked like they'd just ridden into town after spending the day on horseback. Other than their height, the two rangers could easily pass for a pair of charros, in town to bust a bronc at the local rodeo.

Given the information passed along by the general at Fort Hood, Zach didn't want to waste a second and asked BB to pilot them to the local marina.

While Tampico was a large city, the fleet of local pleasure boats was a bit disappointing.

Zach had visited the huge facilities along the Texas coast, places like Clear Lake, the Galveston Yacht Basin, Port Aransas, and others. There he'd found mammoth yachts by the dozens, some well over 100 feet in length and worthy of the most discriminating taste.

Even the sports fishermen had been impressive vessels, their tall bridges and stout outriggers catching the eye of a land-loving cowboy like Zach.

Instead of a fleet of glittering, white pleasure craft stretching off into the distance, they found a short section of finger piers, most of which were empty. The few boats that were docked hardly seemed fit for a man of El General's wealth and reported taste.

"I don't see but a handful of boats here that could safely handle you and me, let alone a drug lord and his security detachment. Are you sure we're in the right place?" BB quipped.

"There's only one marina listed in Tampico," Zach replied, now disappointed. "I guess our man isn't here."

"Maybe he's left town?"

Zach had thought about his partner's question. There was a possibility Vincent had flown the coop, but the ranger doubted it. "He was born and grew up here. My read on the man is that when the going gets rough, he'll want to stay on familiar ground. The Gulf Cartel supposedly owns this burg from skyscraper to sewer pipe. I think he's here; we just have to find him."

BB shrugged, "It's not like we have anyplace else to go. Let's get something to eat and think this through."

The older ranger had worked in the area and knew of a place to grab some coffee and a couple of sausage and egg tortillas.

Despite taking turns driving and catnapping throughout the night, the warm food made Zach's eyes heavy. "I need to get out and walk for a bit," he announced.

"Good idea. Wouldn't hurt to get the blood flowing from my ass to my brain."

There was a city park not far away, a place where BB felt like the truck, and its arsenal within, would be safe from prying eyes. As the two men stretched their legs, Zach asked, "So if you were one of the most powerful drug kings in the world, where would you hang your hat in this one-horse town?"

"Well now that's the $64 question, is it not?"

"Normally I would assume this guy would be surrounded by luxury digs of the highest quality. From what I read though, El General is one smart cookie. He's been the first of the major crime bosses to put together a super-cartel of sorts. He managed a ceasefire and has run this latest scheme like a maestro conducting an orchestra. I would think he would be wise enough not to flaunt his ass around town while there's an all-out war brewing, especially one that his name written all over it."

BB tilted his head, "So you're saying we should start by searching the slums?"

The question made Zach grin. "No, I don't think we need to go to that extreme just yet. Tampico is a lot bigger place than I imagined. I had it in my head that we would just drive around, looking for a bunch of gangsters riding around in black SUVs and follow them back to the criminal mastermind's lair."

"Should we go visit my friend the cop?"

The ranger had already considered contacting BB's acquaintance, finally concluding that would be their last resort. Conducting a successful business transaction with a bounty hunter didn't preclude the local officers from being on someone's payroll. "It's not time yet. We just got here."

With their circulation somewhat restored, they left the park and headed toward downtown. Zach had a thought, "If there was a civil war brewing in Texas, what would you be doing?"

BB pondered the question for a moment before answering, "I'd stock up on beans, bullets, and whiskey."

"Exactly," Zach said. "No matter where El General is going to ride out the storm, he'd need a goodly amount of supplies for his security detail and business entourage. It takes a lot of grub to feed 8-10 beefy bodyguards, a couple of señoritas, and a handful of middle management types. Maybe we should be checking the local grocery stores and seeing if anyone has noticed a bunch of heavily-armed guys buying several tons of food and tequila."

"I'd think he'd also need access to good communications as well. If your snitch was right, and El General is hoping to pull off a coup, he would want to stay in touch with the boys. After all, he has to be able to issue orders if he wants to overthrow a government."

Grunting, Zach nodded his agreement. "He'll also want a back door … an escape route. One thing I learned about chasing Ghost all over the Middle East – the man always had a Plan B that is damn near as good as the first choice."

"Airport?" BB pondered. "A hacienda near a waiting plane?"

Zach nodded, "Or a hotel suite close to the runways. Still, that would expose the man to a lot of eyeballs. I wonder if there's any way to find a list of all of the private airstrips around Tampico?"

"What we need is some local expertise," BB said. "Let's go visit my friend."

Still having his doubts, Zach disagreed. "Let's drive around a bit more, and let me think this through. We've only been in town a few hours."

"Suit yourself," BB shrugged. "I promised my Izzy that I'd get her a surprise from the big city. You care if we stop up here so I can get my shopping out of the way?"

"No problem. It will give me some time to think."

The pickup managed a few turns that brought them into an area of shops, sidewalk cafes, and other businesses that obviously catered to Tampico's upscale residents. After finding a parking spot, BB said, "I'll be back in a few minutes. Keep an eye on that cargo in the back, would ya?"

"Sure. Take your time and get her something extra special."

Zach watched his friend walk away, the ranger's mind weighing the positives and negatives in visiting the local cops. After 10 minutes, he'd decided they didn't have much choice, the marina being a wild goose chase.

The ranger's analysis was suddenly interrupted by a stunningly beautiful woman strolling down the sidewalk, a brawny, rather antisocial-looking fellow at her side. Her skin tone was remarkable, with unusual features and a body that drew the Texan's eye.

There was something more ... something familiar about her.

A lightning bolt of realization shot through Zach's mind. He knew that girl! He'd seen her picture! It was the missing woman Gus had been hunting, one of Cheyenne's co-borrowers at Trustline.

The ranger's hand reached for the door handle, his first instinct to rush up to the woman and launch an interrogation right there on the sidewalk. He then paused, reason entering back into his road-weary brain.

Zach's eyes never left her sexy, little swagger as she casually strolled down the street, occasionally stopping to gawk in a window or scan an advertisement. The Texan tried to remember her name, but he couldn't. He did remember Gus and the image of the El Paso cop's body lying in the street with half of his head missing. "Payback," he hissed.

Three blocks away, the ranger spied BB's gangly stride heading back, a small paper bag in his hand. Zach jumped out of the truck and began stepping briskly to meet his friend halfway.

The moment the senior lawman spotted Zach hurrying his direction, he instantly knew something was up and paused, not sure what to do.

Trying to keep a discreet eye on the wandering woman while explaining his discovery to his friend, Zach and BB kept their own leisurely pace through the shops and markets.

"I'll go back and get the truck," BB said after the debriefing was finished. "You follow them on foot, and I'll be close by. Try to stay where you can see her and me at the same time."

Zach wasn't sure. "Maybe we should snatch her right now. I'm sure we could convince her to tell us where El General is holed up."

"Maybe. Maybe not," the older man countered. "That's some serious cartel muscle keeping an eye on her, and besides, what's that hostage syndrome where the victim becomes attached to the kidnappers?"

"The Stockholm Syndrome," Zach answered, his eyes never leaving the short head of dark hair now about a block ahead of them.

"Let's just follow and hope they lead us back to the nest. I'll keep the truck parallel on that side street. When you see that they're finished with their little shopping excursion, come running."

Nodding his agreement, Zach moved on while BB rushed to retrieve the pickup.

The little Miss continued browsing for another hour, most of the time spent in a boutique that specialized in beachwear. Her cartel escort never wandered away from the store's entrance.

Her spree made it easy for BB to keep in sight, a parking spot opening up less than half of a block away. When she finally emerged, Zach realized that she was done for the day.

In addition to the two packages under Mr. Muscle's arm, there was an extra briskness in her step, a subliminal message that the day's fun was over, and it was time to head back. *But back where?*

The two subjects reversed direction, a tactic that made sense to their watchers. Their car was no doubt parked at the other end of the area, where the shopping had begun.

Zach heard BB start the old pickup's engine as the woman sashayed right past him, so close he could smell her hair. For a fleeting moment, he hoped she hadn't smelled him.

Then the chase was on, BB rolling along at a snail's pace on the side street, Zach subtly trying to keep up without being noticed. Six blocks later, the suspects cut off the main drag, right toward the spot where BB was idling. Mr. No-neck produced a key fob and pressed the button, the lights of a blue SUV blinking as the doors unlocked.

Zach was just jumping in the cab when the woman and her driver pulled away from the curb. He was relieved that BB held back, even happier that traffic was nearly non-existent.

It quickly became clear that BB had tailed a suspect or two in his day. Zach had to admit the old ranger was good – damn good.

Only occasionally was their truck in the SUV's rearview mirror, and then only for a short period of a block or less. BB spent most of the journey one street over, sometimes behind, sometimes ahead of the unaware cartel chauffeur.

"They're heading toward the river," BB noted, cutting hard to make the traffic light at a cross street. "Maybe your sources weren't so full of shit after all."

They entered an industrial section of town, the lack of automobiles making it difficult for BB to remain unseen.

Zach couldn't figure it out, the area they were travelling almost the exact opposite of where he thought El General's lair would be housed. At one point, the ranger was worried they had been spotted and were being led into an ambush.

"This doesn't look like the sort of place where an ultra-wealthy drug lord would hang his hat," Zach noted. "Matter of fact, it looks damn dangerous."

Pointing to the burned out shell of what had once been an enormous warehouse, both of the lawmen shook their heads in concern.

The sole remaining wall of blackened concrete blocks was leaning heavily as if about to collapse. BB wondered why the last windstorm hadn't already toppled the death trap. Zach pondered if the spooky looking skeleton was a harbinger of what was to come. Both of them were relieved when the pickup passed through without being crushed.

The scenery didn't improve much as they followed the cartel SUV further in. It was obviously a district that had seen better days, a relic from an era where ships had been the preferred method of moving cargo. Now, over the road trucks hauled most freight, and the local real estate market had suffered badly. Again, Zach wondered why Vincent would have picked this section of town.

It all became crystal clear after another block, a bend in the road allowing the two rangers vantage to see the enormous outline of a yacht tied alongside the river.

"That's it," BB said, pointing with his head. "That's about the biggest damn boat around and a private ship to boot. I think we've found your man."

The younger lawman had to agree. "Don't take a chance on them spotting our tail. We know where they're going now. Besides, the closer they get to home, the more diligent the driver will be."

BB cut down the next street, turning off and then parking as soon as the blue SUV was out of sight. "What now, Ranger?"

Shaking his head, Zach responded, "We need to get a closer look at that boat. Let's wait a bit until the dust settles and then go exploring."

Vincent stood with Ghost, the two masterminds studying a map.

"Is it time to announce our new capital?" El General asked.

Ghost turned to the large television and seemed to be studying the ongoing newscast streaming out of Mexico City. "President Salinas is nowhere to be found," he began. "Probably hiding with his private guard at some remote villa. The capital and Tijuana are in chaos with rioters roaming the streets. There have been two uprisings at the border refugee camp and sporadic skirmishes among the military, police, and cartel armies all over the country. Yes, Jefe, I believe it is time."

Vincent didn't react immediately, a sly smile creeping across his face at the realization that his dream was coming to fruition.

"We want to start with the television and radio station in Tampico first. Have your people start broadcasting what I've scripted. Reynosa is next … and then Monterrey. Are the warehouses full?"

"Yes, my men have been unloading truckloads of rice, beans, and other essentials for over two weeks. There are over 1,000 tons of foodstuffs ready to receive the tide of refugees."

Ghost nodded his approval, "And the antidote?"

Again, Vincent delivered the positive news. "Yes. Our kitchen below the mortuary has been making about three pounds a day. My staff believes we'll be able to immunize at least one million people by tomorrow. They'll keep producing until I order otherwise." .

The terrorist seemed satisfied, "Then it's time to untie this vessel and head out to sea. I would estimate that we should be able to return in 5-7 days, depending on Mexico City's reaction."

"No," El General replied firmly. "I've decided to change that part of the plan."

If he was surprised, Ghost didn't show it. "May I ask why?"

Vincent paced for a few steps while he considered his response. "Because I feel that we can do a better job of managing the revolution from here. We can react faster if something goes wrong, and there may be situations where my presence might make the difference."

"You are also putting yourself at great risk," Ghost responded in a neutral tone. "While this vessel is well protected, the military still has assets that can reach her, and thus you. Are you sure about this decision?"

"Yes," Vincent answered. "I am certain."

Ghost shrugged, "You are the boss, El General."

"I will go and issue the orders to take control of the television and radio station. I will also have the couriers deliver the next internet video. Will you join me for dinner this evening?"

"Of course," Ghost replied. "It is always an honor."

Vincent pivoted to leave, his co-conspirator studying every aspect of his employer's body language as he exited the room.

"They're all the same," he whispered once alone. "They all feel they are invincible. He doesn't want to be close by to keep control of his men, he wants to be here to relish in the glory."

Ghost let his mind wander for a moment, images of Vincent waving to the cheering crowds from the steps at Tampico's City Hall, drug lord turned savior. "I hope it works for you," he continued. "As long as you keep paying me, I will say your name in my prayers to Allah."

Chapter 14

Zach and BB didn't have any trouble finding a good spot to scout the massive yacht. The industrial section surrounding *Rose*'s mooring was full of two and three-story warehouses, old factories, and only a few low-rise office buildings.

Adding to his list of committed felonies, Zach made quick work of the rusty padlock securing the tallest structure within ten blocks. According to BB and his better grasp of Spanish, the immense and bare building had been a warehouse for sugar and cotton decades ago.

The interior was completely void of contents, the far-reaching concrete floors covered with nothing more than a thick layer of dust.

It took the two rangers just over five minutes of searching to find a stairwell leading to the roof where long ago air conditioning and dehumidifying equipment once existed. After climbing the iron rungs and pushing open the hatch, Zach and BB found themselves on a flat, tar roof that was thick with pigeon and seagull droppings.

"The things I do to maintain the rule of law," BB complained, looking at the carpet of bird shit that was about to soil his boots.

Zach advanced slowly toward the edge, fully aware that El General probably had his own lookouts and scouts deployed on and around his yacht.

The younger ranger returned a few moments later, "This is the perfect spot, but we need some sort of cover. Any ideas?"

BB scanned around the level, featureless rooftop and shrugged. "Got a pigeon suit?"

"Funny. Seriously, if either of us gets close to the edge, we're bound to be spotted. We need some sort of camouflage."

Again looking at his now-soiled boots, BB said, "What we need is a butt load of newspaper for this bird cage."

Ignoring his partner's complaining, Zach decided that maybe they didn't have the perfect location and began scouting around for a better spot. It was then that he had an idea.

"We need big cardboard boxes and some spray paint," he announced.

"Huh?"

"You heard me, old man. Do you know where there's a moving company hereabouts?"

BB tilted his head in bewilderment. "No, but that shouldn't be too hard to find. Mind drawing this *old man* another picture?"

"Come on, I'll show you instead."

By the time the third package was delivered to media outlets throughout Mexico, the news editors and anchormen had come to expect the unexpected. This latest edition of El General's studio-quality production didn't disappoint.

The now-familiar face of the handsome, young actor appeared, sitting behind the same desk but with a different suit and tie.

"As I predicted just a few days ago, our nation is racked with strife and conflict. Powerful men in Mexico City are attempting to take control of Mexico by any means, and they will stop at nothing to fulfill their unwavering desire to control all of our lives."

The image then changed, a panning view of hundreds of desperate faces staring at the camera from behind a barbwire fence. "Our brothers and sisters are being held in pens like cattle and pigs, their effort to escape tyranny resulting in internment."

Back to the announcer, "But there is hope, my countrymen. Powerful men among us still have freedom in their hearts and maintain the will to fight."

A map of Mexico then filled the screen, "As of today, the cities denoted on this map are hereby declared safe zones. Some of our nation's greatest patriots have stockpiled food and medical supplies to feed those desperately trying to escape the violence that consumes the land. All citizens are welcome to join us. All will be fed and provided shelter."

Then came a picture showing rows of dead bodies, the few living among the corpses wearing the now-familiar Haz-Mat suits so commonly seen throughout Mexico. "In addition to providing safety, freedom, and the essentials of life, these great benefactors have taken possession of a large supply of vaccine that will protect one and all from the plague unleashed by the traitors. This medicine was being hoarded by the very people you elected to our government. They intended to keep it for themselves, but now it has been liberated. Come. Join us. Enjoy the safety and health every citizen of our great nation deserves."

The video ended with the map of Mexico returning to fill the screen.

In Tampico and a few other large cities, cartel enforcers arrived at the television and radio stations that provided millions with their daily information. Within an hour, the airwaves were filled with not only Vincent's message of propaganda but also trusted commentators and anchormen reinforcing the story as presented. The fact that men with automatic weapons were just off camera or microphone remained unknown to the average man in the street.

Ghost watched it all from *Rose*'s media center without comment or emotion.

Finally, when the news began to cycle, he stood to leave. "Now the game begins in earnest," he whispered.

An hour later, the two rangers returned to the warehouse – a large cardboard box, two cans of spray paint, and three furnace vents in their hands.

"Thank God for home improvement stores," Zach snipped. "One-stop shopping for the undercover policeman."

Ranger Bass quickly set about assembling his contraption, which consisted of painting the unfolded box a metallic gray and then gluing the metal grillwork to the outside. "It's not perfect, but in low light and from a distance, it should pass as a rooftop air conditioner."

To "age" his pretend HVAC system, Zach scraped up some dust from the floor and threw it on the still-damp paint.

The rangers again made for the warehouse's stairwell, eventually exiting onto the roof. Zach lifted his invention over his head and began slowly making his way toward the edge of the structure.

BB grunted, watching the younger man duck walk bit by bit, slowly advancing toward a spot where he could observe the yacht below.

It took the young ranger almost 30 minutes to advance just a few yards, Zach wary of someone below noticing the movement. Finally, he was in position and studying El General's vessel through a small cutout while using a pair of binoculars BB had brought along in the truck.

"I gotta hand it to ya, Zach. That's the damndest ghillie suit I've ever seen," BB said from the stairwell.

It was hot inside the box, and the ranger had to remain on his knees, but he had an excellent view of El General's yacht and the surrounding area.

It quickly became obvious that a frontal assault was out of the question.

At both ends of the concrete pier were men with automatic weapons and cover. Zach counted three more shooters idling in the doorway of the warehouse directly in front of *La Rosa Roja*.

Movement on the sundeck drew Zach's focus.

The woman he'd spotted shopping in town appeared, now resplendent in a formal gown. Immediately behind her, approached the same man he'd spotted at the steakhouse in San Antonio – Vincent.

A flash of disappointment streaked through Zach's mind when Ghost failed to follow.

The ranger watched as another man arrived, a pair of wine glasses in his hands. "I wonder if you know Vincent was shopping around in Texas trying to buy my girlfriend," the Texan whispered to the hostage. "I wonder if Chey was going to be your replacement or competitor."

Zach continued to observe as the couple sipped their wine while standing at the rail and observing the river beyond. "At least, I've got the kingpin," he grunted. "Ghost is probably out delivering the plague to an orphanage. I'm sure he'll be back in time for dinner."

On cue, another figure entered into the magnified circles of Zach's vision. It was Ghost.

"You son of a bitch," Zach hissed, his first thought being to rush down to the truck, grab his rifle, and rain volleys of hot lead down on his nemesis. "I knew you were behind all this. I knew this entire bag of shit had your stink all over it."

Ghost had brought his own wine and soon joined his hosts at the rail. "Now aren't you just one, big, happy, narcotic-supplying, plague-producing, dysfunctional family," Zach growled. "Isn't the view from your mega-yacht lovely this evening? I wonder how the poor people onshore are doing out there thanks to your influence. I am curious if watching your nation's children gunned down in a crossfire is your evening's entertainment?"

The ranger wanted Ghost more than anything he could ever remember. Watching the casual wine sipping made his heart race with fury as adrenaline surged through his veins. His only respite came when he recalled how it felt as his fists slammed into the terrorist's face during their brawl in Istanbul. "I wonder how long it took before you could eat without pain, bitch."

Zach forced himself to turn away, his mind churning to formulate a workable plan of attack.

El General had chosen his hiding spot well, Zach eventually admitted. It would take a small army to overcome the ring of security that surrounded the floating keep.

Perhaps an airmobile assault team could leverage the element of surprise and board the boat, but they would suffer extensive causalities in the effort.

Armor could pierce the defenses, but by the time the large, noisy machines could approach, Zach was sure Vincent would be motoring at high speed out to the open sea.

Zach wondered about a waterborne assault, the ranger having read about the U.S. Navy Seals practicing such tactics. But he didn't have a SEAL team on speed dial and doubted if President Clifton would answer his call.

He could snipe Ghost and Vincent from his current position, the 500-yard shot doable, even with the small caliber rifles he and BB had brought along. That, however, was a suicide mission. It wouldn't take a ballistics technician to figure out where the shots had originated, and Zach was sure El General's men would turn the warehouse into a deathtrap in less than a minute.

"I've got to hand it to you, Ghost. You've picked one hell of a spot to ride out the looming war and pandemic."

Zach retreated back to the stairwell and soon joined BB, who was keeping a lookout below.

After listening to the younger man's report, BB nodded toward a building down the street and said, "Something's going on in that other warehouse as well. A semi pulled up while you were on the roof, and a bunch of cartel thugs starting unloaded the cargo. The place is full of pallets and boxes. I think we've found El General's stash house."

Zach studied BB's discovery for a bit, finally turning and admitting, "I can't figure out a way to get at them. That fucking boat is built like a battleship, and no doubt it's twice as fast. Even if we could muster enough firepower to shoot our way through their defenses, Vincent and Ghost would be motoring off to the deep blue yonder before we could even get aboard."

"And who knows how many shooters he has on the yacht," BB added. "Even if we did somehow manage to board her, that might be the same as jumping from the frying pan into the fire."

A feeling of helplessness flooded Zach's mind. He'd finally tracked down the men responsible for so much death and destruction, and yet they were unreachable – as if they were on another planet.

BB sensed his partner's dwindling mindset. "You haven't slept much the last few days. Let's go someplace comfortable and quiet where we can think this thing through. You know our friend El General isn't going anywhere... at least not for the moment. Besides, I need to give Izzy a call. She's probably going loco with worry, and I could use a beer."

Zach initial reaction to BB's remarks was anger. Didn't the old coot realize what was at stake? He wanted a beer? To call his lady? No wonder the rangers had pushed him out.

A cool head soon returned to Zach's shoulders. It dawned on the ranger that rushing in half-cocked had played no small role in the current shit storm. They'd made sound decisions so far, and luck had been on their side. Was taking a few minutes to develop a strategy sage or lazy?

In the end, he couldn't argue the older man's wisdom. Besides, every minute they spent in the area infested with Vincent's private army increased the odds of the two lawmen being discovered.

"Okay, BB. I get it. Let's go find someplace to think this through. But not too far ... and not for too long. I don't want our kingfish swimming away."

They found a small, run-down cantina less than a mile away from Vincent's floating fortress. Inside, a small radio played Corrido music while a handful of patrons stared into their drinks.

As the two lawmen pulled back the antique art deco chairs at a corner table, a middle-aged woman appeared to take their order. "Dos Coronas, por favor," BB smiled.

As they waited for their refreshments, BB pulled out his cell phone and punched in Izzy's number. "We only get cell service on clear days, but at least, I can leave her a message."

The weather must have been good up north, BB's call answered after only a few rings. The old ranger's face brightened with a huge smile when he heard Isabelle's voice.

Zach decided to give his friend some privacy. Besides, he was too keyed up to sit and sip a brew. Taking his beer from the server, he wandered outside using the excuse that he wanted to keep an eye on the truck.

Leaning against the pickup and noting the setting sun, the ranger thought about the man he'd recruited to join him on what was an extremely dangerous quest. BB moved to a different rhythm than most of the lawmen Zach had worked with before. There were times when the man was pure genius, coming up with creative solutions and showing a degree of preparedness that was impressive.

Other events had left Zach frustrated as hell.

Zach had learned a long time ago to distance his reasoning in any complex situation and look at things from a broader perspective. It had helped him solve numerous crimes.

His mind ventured to a place where he watched from afar, like an angel floating above BB and himself, watching their activities with a third party's perspective. After a few minutes of recounting their adventure, the ranger had to chuckle.

An old joke summed up the view from the heavens. A young bull and an old bull were standing on a hill, peering down at a herd of cows. "Let's run down there and service one of them," the young bull suggested.

"Let's *walk* down and service them all," countered the old bull.

The humor, tasty beer, and beautiful sky helped Zach regain the perspective of a professional lawman. He was able to push aside at least a portion of the gut-felt hatred for Ghost that had been controlling his thoughts.

Guilt, coupled with a rage derived from failure, had been driving his actions as of late. That might be acceptable when dealing with bank robbers and child molesters, but Zach knew he was pursuing an entirely different level of criminal brainpower.

Most crooks were just plain stupid. Ignorant not only of social values and lacking conscience but low on the scale of human intellect. He remembered the showdown with Tusk, recalled thinking that the man probably couldn't count. In reality, that most likely wasn't far from the truth.

Ghost and El General, however, were completely different animals. Both men demonstrated notoriety that wouldn't have been possible without extremely high IQs. That intelligence, combined with a streak of ruthlessness had paved the road to their ascent to power. They were the most dangerous adversaries he'd ever faced, and if he didn't start using his brain over brawn, they would win.

The ranger's thoughts returned to BB, wondering if the older, more-experienced lawman had realized all of this from the beginning. "Maybe I should do what BB is doing," he thought. "Maybe there's method to his madness."

Zach had purchased a no-contract cell phone while shopping for the box and paint. He hadn't known why at the time, but the advertisement for "Free Calls To Texas and The United States," had drawn his eye.

He pulled the older model flip phone from his pocket and completed the setup in less than a minute. From memory, he dialed Cheyenne's number.

The busy model didn't answer, which wasn't unusual. In a way, Zach was relieved to hear her voicemail. He hadn't been sure what he was going to say.

He started to put the phone away but then dialed Sam. She answered on the second ring.

"Ranger Temple," his partner's voice chimed.

"Hey."

"Zachariah Bass, where in the hell are you? And don't you dare spin some lie that you're in the mountains hiking."

"I don't want to tell you where I'm at. And believe me, you don't want to know."

"Zach? Are you okay?" she responded, the worry genuine and thick in her voice.

"Yes, I'm just peachy. I'm enjoying a cold brew and looking at a beautiful sunset," he answered honestly.

Her sigh of relief sounded across the international connection loud and clear. "Well, that's good, I suppose. What are you doing? Can you tell me that at least?"

"No."

Sam's famous temper got the better of her concerns over his wellbeing. "Well … then why did you call me?"

Chuckling, Zach again was forthright. "To be blunt, I'm not sure why. I guess I was worried about your leg. How are you doing?"

"Bullshit!" she barked, but there wasn't much ire behind it. "Seriously, Zach, what's going on? I'm your partner, damn it. The entire world has gone to hell in a handbasket, and you leave me a message that you're going off on some fucking pilgrimage into the mountains. I've been worried sick about you."

There it was. The last part. Somehow, that made Zach feel better. He now knew why he'd called.

"I'm sorry, Sam. I really am. I just had to go do this by myself. There wasn't any other way."

"Asshole," she snapped, but then immediately regretted it. "But I forgive you … I think … I guess…. Hell, this sucks Zach. I am glad you called, though. I was about to write you off."

The ranger grinned again, not believing she would ever give up on her partner. "Yeah, I'm good for the moment. Let me ask you something – do you know how to disable a boat?"

"Huh?"

"I've got to figure out a good way to keep a boat … a big boat … from moving. I don't think I can sneak on board and remove the distributor cap," he chuckled, trying to lighten the mood somewhat. "So how in the hell would you go about something like that?"

There was a silence on the other end, making Zach think that Sam was looking up the number for the nearest insane asylum. Finally, she responded, "Just shoot a hole in the hull and sink it," she answered.

"It has a steel hull, and I would have to shoot about a million holes for it to sink. It's a big boat – really a ship."

"Blow up the engines," she suggested.

"I can't get on board … at least not without a battalion of Marines helping me out, and I'm a little short on assault troops and explosives at the moment."

Sam was tiring of the game, "Shit, Zach! How in the hell would I know? I've only ever been on a boat one time, and that ended up a disaster. My dad took me fishing when I was a girl, and somehow I managed to get the dock line tangled up in the propeller. We were powerless, drifting around for an hour before somebody towed us in."

Light bulbs flashed and the ideas began to spark. "That's it! You're a genius, Sam! I have to go. I'll call you in a few days … I hope."

"Ranger Zachariah Bass, what on God's green earth are you talking about? Don't you hang up on me, damn it! Zach? Are you there?"

Sam looked at the disconnected cell phone, the wrath of hell's fire beaming from her eyes. It passed quickly, though, replaced with sadness. "Please, be safe, Zach. Please."

The lady ranger started to return the phone to her pocket but didn't. Instead, she glanced at a business card lying on the coffee table and picked it up.

Sam contemplated calling the number, her mind whirling with a cyclone of stress, concern for her partner, and fear for her country. Texas wasn't weathering the storm that was lashing its southern neighbor very well, and it looked like the violence was heading north.

The economic impact alone was staggering. With closed borders on all sides, international trade had come to a standstill.

Protests had turned into riots and widespread civil unrest in Dallas, San Antonio, and Houston. El Paso had a massive march scheduled for the following day.

International outrage monopolized its own percentage of the headlines. President Clifton seemed to be outmaneuvering Simmons in the diplomatic blame-game. Somehow, the republic had ended up holding the bio-weapon development bag, and a lot of people across the globe made it clear they wanted nothing to do with such a "rogue" nation.

Mexico, before the government had fallen apart, was threatening to file charges in the International Courts in The Hague, Netherlands. There were legal firms in Dallas and Austin working on class action lawsuits on behalf of those who had lost family or livestock due to the plague.

Just that morning, Sam had watched a news report out of Brownsville, the segment droning on and on about how many workers were calling in sick, afraid to leave their homes because of the epidemic.

Sam eyed the business card again, in full realization of the consequences if she made the call, and it didn't go well. Then again, her partner was clearly in danger, and the republic was teetering on the edge of a very, very deep abyss.

"What the hell," she whispered, punching the numbers onto the screen.

After the first ring, she almost hung up, barely fighting off the urge.

On the second ring, her thumb was hovering again.

"Foot Hood," sounded a male voice. "How many I direct your call?"

"General Hopkins, please."

"One moment."

This time, a female voice answered, all business. "General Hopkins's office. State the nature of your call, please."

"This is Ranger Samantha Temple. I need to speak with the general, please. It is a matter of national security."

"Hold one moment, please."

Sam almost hung up again, a ball of fear trying to crawl from her stomach into her throat. It was almost two minutes before the general's familiar voice came on the line.

"Ranger Temple, I hope you are well."

"Thank you, General," Sam replied, trying to keep her tone professional. "Sir, I need to speak with you, and time is of the essence. Do you have a few moments?"

There was a pause, Sam bracing for rejection and perhaps even a scolding. "I do, Ranger Temple, but not over an unsecured line. Is there any chance you could visit me here on the base? My duties require that I remain here for the foreseeable future."

Glancing at her always-ready crutch, Sam responded, "Yes, sir. I can be there in about an hour if that is acceptable."

"Of course," the military man warmly replied. "I will leave word at the gate. It's always a pleasure to assist the republic's law enforcement officers. Will Ranger Bass be accompanying you?"

"Ranger Bass is the reason for my visit, General. But we can discuss the details in an hour."

"Agreed. See you shortly, Ranger."

Chapter 15

After disconnecting with Sam, Zach remained outside for a few more minutes, mulling over the plan born of his partner's childhood experience.

Tipping back his beer, he ventured back inside and found BB engrossed in a Mexican newscast, a deep frown directing the old ranger's brow. "Your friends on the yacht are some very bad men, Ranger Bass. They have managed to stir up the biggest pot of shit I've ever seen."

"Told you."

BB grunted, "I should have taken your words more to heart. Anyway, I've been thinking this through, and my suggestion is still the same – let's go talk to my friend, the chief of police."

Zach nodded his agreement, but there was more to it. "I think we should pay him a visit, but the conversation I'm envisioning probably isn't what you are thinking."

"Go on," BB said, his eyebrows arching in anticipation.

For the next 30 minutes, the two lawmen hashed and rehashed Zach's plan. The younger ranger knew BB was onboard when instead of a second beer, the old timer ordered two cups of coffee.

Sipping the steaming cups of java, BB's face flashed with inspiration. Waving over the waitress, the old ranger produced a handful of pesos from his pocket while exchanging a string of Spanish that Zach had trouble following.

Eventually, after three rounds of negotiation, BB handed the woman a handful of bills and then stood. Motioning Zach to follow, he enlightened his partner, "Come on, we're going to become high-tech crime fighters."

The barmaid led them to a grungy back office and pointed toward a new-looking computer residing on the cluttered desk. "Gracias," BB responded, and then sat down in front of the monitor.

Zach was stunned as the old timer's fingers began pecking on the keyboard. After a bit, a blueprint of Vincent's boat was displayed on the screen. "I found an old listing at a yacht brokerage," the weathered lawman explained with pride. "I figured that purchasing that big-ass boat was like buying a house, and the broker would have pictures and a layout."

"That's brilliant, BB. Can you print that shit out?"

"Sure 'nuff."

The nearby printer began humming and clanking as paper slid in and poured out with various pictures, drawings, and information about *La Rosa*. Zach paid special attention to the location of the propellers.

As the duo returned to their table, BB glanced at his watch and said, "If we're going to pull this off, we'd better get moving. There's a lot of work to be done."

It was just getting dark when they finally left the cantina and headed for the shopping district where they'd first picked up Vincent's scent.

Two hours later, they were parked outside the sugar and cotton warehouse. "I want to wait until at least midnight before we make our move," Zach said. "I'll take the first watch if you want to get some sleep."

"I thought you'd never ask," BB replied, reaching down to recline his seat while pulling his hat low over his eyes. "Wake me in an hour."

"Will do."

Sam drove like a demon to Fort Hood.

As before, the security procedures were thoroughly obnoxious.

She had just pulled into the denoted "Authorized Visitors Only" parking spot when she spied General Hopkins marching across the well-manicured lawn. He was making a beeline for her car.

After a quick greeting and handshake, the senior officer surprised Sam by suggesting they take a walk.

"I'm not walking so well, sir," Sam answered, pointing toward her crutch.

"There is a nice shady bench not far from here, Ranger. I think I have a pretty good idea why you've come to visit, and I think it would be best if we had our conversation outside."

Sam loved a good mystery novel, would even admit to receiving some twisted sense of enjoyment when working a particularly difficult murder. Today, however, she wasn't in the mood for cloak and dagger adventures.

"Sir, I feel an extreme sense of urgency about this matter. I would appreciate it if...."

The general raised his hand to stop her mid-sentence. "Zach called you right before you called me. He's in Mexico."

Sam was stunned. "How did…. Are you…."

The general motioned for Sam to start hobbling along with her crutch. She wanted answers and saw little alternative than to do as the man wished. After they had rounded the corner and entered a small, park-like setting, he began. "Your phone and Ranger Bass's cell were placed on a watch list after you last visited this facility. We take our security very seriously, Ranger Temple. It is standard procedure for us to monitor the communications of anyone who is the recipient of classified information."

Immediately furious, Sam snapped, "Are you watching me take a shower, too?"

"No, Ranger Temple. While we could do that, most people don't divulge secrets while bathing. It really upsets you to know that we were eavesdropping, doesn't it?"

"Yes. It most certainly does," she replied forcefully.

"So now you know the primary reason for our multiple layers of secrecy and demand for discretion. The feelings you are experiencing at this moment are common to practically anyone who becomes aware of our capabilities. Even I was shocked when the program was first launched. That's one of the main reasons why we must keep it so closely guarded."

The lady ranger had to admit, he had a valid point. "I bet you know a lot of secrets, General."

"Our equipment hears a lot of secrets, Ranger. Unless it is a matter of national security, no human becomes involved. A computer listened to your conversation with Ranger Bass to make sure neither of you was discussing privileged information. Short of that, it wouldn't have mattered if you and your partner were discussing robbing a bank or killing a man who cut you off in traffic, we wouldn't get involved. Crime is none of our business. We only breach our citizens' right to privacy if they are placing the republic directly in danger or planning to sabotage our military capabilities."

"And non-citizens? How much information do your machines gather from those outside of Texas?"

"That's classified and irrelevant to our discussion, Ranger Temple."

Sam nodded. "I understand, sir. Besides, you've already passed along the primary reason for my visit by telling me Zach is in Mexico. Can you tell me where he is by any chance?"

Hopkins nodded, "Yes, he's in Tampico, along the riverfront. I assume you would like the exact address?"

Again, she was amazed. "You can track someone's location that closely? That is very scary, sir."

The general looked left and right as if he were trying to verify that no one was paying them any attention. Reaching into his breast pocket, he pulled out a small slip of paper and handed it to Sam.

"Your partner could use some help, Ranger Temple. I suggest you get in touch with the man on that note."

Sam glanced down and saw some map coordinates above the name, "Captain Billy Riddell, ROTMC," and a phone number. She recognized the area code as south-central Texas.

Hopkins noted the confusion on her face. "Captain Riddell was the officer in charge of the training platoon that was ambushed near Langtry. As a matter of fact, I've taken the liberty of contacting him already. He's expecting your call."

Sam started to ask for more, but General Hopkins stood, making it clear their discussion was over. With a firm smile, he added, "I'm sorry to cut our visit short, Ranger Temple, but I have pressing matters to attend to. Thank you for stopping by."

Then he was stepping away, leaving Sam clutching the name of a Republic of Texas Marine and little else.

After exchanging catnaps, Zach and BB began preparing for their nocturnal activities.

Grumbling about having to wade through the bottom of a birdcage, BB climbed to the roof to make sure nothing was new along the pier. Zach began changing clothes.

The ranger had purchased a set of swimming trunks during their shopping spree, as well as some additional dark clothing and a set of flippers. After trying on his nautical attire, the Texan then set about darkening his face and hands with a mixture of Vaseline and charcoal. It was the best camo paint he could come up with on short notice.

Next, he inflated a dark blue floatation device, just like a vacationer would find drifting atop the pools at the seaside resorts on the tourist side of town. His knife, a waterproof flashlight, and a pair of goggles rounded out the Texan's kit.

Then, he hefted a length of steel cable, the sturdy strand about the size of Zach's little finger. He'd purchased 50 feet of the stout line, which weighed just over 150 pounds. The pool-raft would hold a full-sized adult; he prayed it would keep the coil afloat as well.

The ranger used duct tape to secure the cable to the raft, and then he was ready.

BB returned, quickly informing Zach that all appeared quiet around the yacht. "Looks like everyone but the lookout has turned in for the night. There's one guy with a shoulder-fired weapon walking around the deck, three more blocking each end of the dock. I'm sure there are more, but I couldn't see them."

"Okay, let's get this over with."

The duo made their way to the riverside, Zach estimating the yacht was just over 400 yards downstream. Peering down into the water, the Texan couldn't help but shiver. BB noticed his hesitation.

"I don't blame you for having second thoughts," BB teased. "Who knows what's lurking in that murky water? That's got to be worse than the bird scat on top of the warehouse."

Flashing his friend a pained expression, Zach countered, "Oh, thanks for that, BB. What a wonderful thing to say about now. "

"What?" BB replied with feigned remorse. "That's not why you were stalling?"

"No," Zach said. "I don't swim all that well."

Before BB could mutter an apology, Zach was descending a ladder. The elder lawman watched as his partner lowered himself into the dark waters. "Lower down the float," Zach hissed, still clutching the ladder. "This fucking water is a lot colder than I thought it would be."

The senior lawman did as he was told, grunting with the weight of the attached cable. Zach accepted the pool toy without comment. "See you downstream," the voice called from the water. And then the ranger shoved off, his darkened face and arms barely visible as the river took him toward El General's floating palace.

Zach soon found the current wasn't very strong, and after a few minutes, his body started to adjust to the chill.

While he'd been spying on Ghost and company from his rooftop perch, Zach had noticed some children swimming on the opposite bank. Despite BB's comment about the water quality and unknown composition, the ranger figured it couldn't be all that deadly if parents were letting their kids get wet – if they were aware of any unseen threat.

In less than 15 minutes, Zach was nearly even with the bow of Vincent's yacht, the impressive superstructure rising like a skyscraper above the Texan's head.

He dropped lower into the water, leaving nothing above the surface but his hands grasping the plastic float, and his mouth and nose grasping for air. If someone on the deck above did spot the mini-raft drifting by, he was counting on it looking like just another piece of trash floating down the river.

Kicking silently under the surface, Zach propelled himself toward the massive hull, finally letting the river take over when he was close enough to reach out and touch the side.

With the nearly black background of the water, his skin and clothing darkened, he prayed the lookout didn't have night vision and wasn't an overly observant fellow. As the seconds passed, the ranger waited for the beam of a flashlight to illuminate his trespass. He was pretty sure illumination would be quickly followed by gunfire if he was discovered, and there was no place to go, hide, or retreat.

No challenge or bullets came from above.

It seemed like it took forever to float the length of Vincent's pleasure barge. After raising his head just long enough to sneak a quick glance, Zach observed that the stern of the huge vessel was finally approaching.

Just as he passed the rearmost part of the ship, Zach kicked hard for the dock, his flipper-equipped feet struggling to move the mass of his own body and the raft. If he was to have any chance of pulling this off, he couldn't drift too far past *La Rosa*.

The glow of a cigarette caused the Texas to freeze, his head floating less than a yard away from a sentry's feet. The Texan stopped breathing, making no more noise than a church mouse pissing on a rug.

Moving only his eyes, Zach spotted one of Vincent's bodyguards standing on the yacht's rear platform while enjoying a smoke. If the man had any night vision and peered down, the ranger would quickly find out how the fish felt while being shot in a barrel.

The guard flicked his butt into the river, the small cherry landing less than two inches from Zach's nose. With his nicotine craving satisfied, the man pivoted and disappeared into *Rosa*'s water garage.

Zach reverted to kicking hard for the pier, his legs burning like fire from the effort. By the time he finally reached up and grabbed onto the concrete wall, he realized he'd floated far past the point where he'd hoped to make landfall.

The blueprint BB had found online told the ranger that the propellers were eight feet below the surface. According to the brokerage, they were massive blades, six feet in diameter, each powered by a 1500-horsepower diesel engine.

Using the pier to pull himself back against the current, Zach finally managed to recover from his overshooting the mark, and tied off the pool float to the concrete wall of the dock.

He next pulled his knife and began carefully cutting away the tape securing the cable.

With a firm grasp of one end, he let gravity uncoil the heavy, steel line as it fell to the bottom. If he let go of his end, or the cable snagged onto something, his swim would all be for naught.

He checked the back deck where the guard had been smoking, finding the fiberglass platform void of any patrols. Pulling down his goggles and taking a deep breath, Zach kicked hard for *La Rosa's* stern.

Between the weight of the cable and fighting the current, the ranger thought he'd made a huge mistake. Despite pumping his legs as hard as possible, he wasn't making any progress.

Visions of Gus and Buck surged into his mind, raising his rage and bolstering his determination. Zach channeled the anger to his aching legs and kicked with longer, harder strokes.

He finally reached the underside of the platform where he discovered a handhold and silently raised his head out of the water.

The fiberglass extension had been added to *Rosa*'s steel hull, the shipyards in Germany knowing that their wealthy clients wanted to swim, scuba, and have access to jets skis and launches. It was also a godsend for Zach, as he drew air into his lungs without worrying about being spotted from above.

With his oxygen replenished, the ranger pulled out his flashlight, refilled his lungs once more, and dove under the surface.

Again, the current fought his progress, the Texan trying to dive down while holding his position relevant to the hull above.

With the inky black waters limiting visibility to just a few feet, and knowing the massive vessel was above him, Zach began to feel a coffin-like sense of claustrophobia. Despite his flashlight, the world seemed to be pressing in on his body and mind, his brain demanding that he surface and draw air.

It took all of Zach's will to keep going, fighting the waves of hysteria that crashed against his soul. Down he went into the black hole, ignoring the internal voices that he stop this foolishness. He felt like a truck was sitting on his chest, struggling to control his weak, unresponsive limbs.

Finally, the huge bronze blade of a propeller showed in the tiny circle of his flashlight. Then another, and, at last, the tire-sized, bullet-shaped nose of the hub.

The ranger didn't waste a second, looping the cable in and out, weaving it between the blades. He had to kick hard to go deeper, but could let his natural buoyancy pull him up.

His lungs were burning by the time he'd finished the port propeller, but he didn't think he could make the journey back down a second time … or ever again.

With a nearly super-human effort, the Texan kicked hard for the starboard propeller and again began entangling the cable within its massive blades.

Air had never tasted so good when he finally managed the surface. Zach didn't care if the guards could hear his breathing.

After drinking precious oxygen into his lungs, the ranger felt a sense of euphoria fill his core. He'd done it! He'd disabled Vincent's primary escape route, crippled a multi-million dollar yacht with $40 worth of cable and a couple of pool toys.

The joy was short-lived, however. He still had to get out of the river and find BB. If he missed the exit point, he could easily be washed out to sea.

Wouldn't that suck, he thought, watching the shoreline pass. *Here I pull off a stunt worthy of a Navy SEAL, and then I drown because I couldn't get back to land.*

The thought, along with the fact that he seemed to be moving faster and away from shore, caused Zach to start swimming overhand, his hands making gentle splashing noises as the ranger started to gain against the river's flow.

He finally managed the pier, grasping onto to a wooden pillar and catching his breath.

Relieved, fatigued to a point beyond where his body had ever been, Zach spied a ladder extending down into the river from above. It would save him having to pull his soaked frame up the vertical wall.

Zach was on the third rung when the gun barrel pressed into his forehead. "Hola, amigo. Out for a swim this evening?" a low voice from the pier growled.

The ranger's exhausted mind wanted desperately to recall his Spanish, but it just wouldn't come. Somehow, he realized that the first word of English out of his mouth would ruin any reasonable excuse he could conjure. "Hola, Señor. I fell in."

Loud laughter filled the otherwise quiet evening as the pistol's hammer cocked. "And you just happen to have painted your face before falling into the river, Señor."

It was a statement, not a question.

"I got a little drunk and fell overboard. That's not face paint; it's mud from the river."

"I don't believe you. You are lying to me, and so I am going to kill you."

Zach clenched, waiting for the hammer to drop, wondering how far his body would drift before being discovered – if ever.

A string of angry Spanish came from behind the gunman, Zach picking out enough words to know the man about to blow his head off was being called stupid. "The jefe will want him alive. El General will demand to know what he was doing in the river."

Yeah! Zach's mind raced. *Don't shoot me just yet. Let Vincent torture my ass for a while before you spread my brains all over Central Mexico.*

The conversation continued on the pier, Zach using the delay to plot his next move.

Finally, the gunman stepped back, waving his pistol and ordering the ranger to continue his ascent up the ladder.

There were two of them, burley gents for certain. *That figures*, Zach thought, calculating his chances of overpowering the two thugs. *Not many employment opportunities for wimpy dudes in the cartel security game.*

One had what appeared to be an MP5 sub machinegun. The other was holding a Glock pistol that had been pressed against the ranger's forehead until a moment before.

When Zach finally stepped onto the pier, the beam of a flashlight hit him in the eyes. "Ahh! A tall gringo. What are you doing in our river?"

"I told you. My family and I are down here on vacation. We rented a boat upstream, and I fell overboard."

The interrogator stepped closer, tilting his head as he stared at the dark goo covering Zach's face and arms, then shining the light up and down the ranger's frame.

"You fell overboard with flippers on, Señor? I think this is bullshit."

Damn it, Zach thought. *I should have kicked these fuckers off in the river.*

Another conversation in Spanish ensued, the two lookouts obviously disagreeing about what to do next. Zach squinted, trying to regain his night vision after the assault from the flashlight while translating the string of obscenities flying between his two new friends. The ranger spotted a shadow rising behind the two gunmen. A hand appeared over the pistol holder's mouth as his back arched forward. BB had arrived.

Still half-blind, Zach threw himself at the other man, reaching for anything he could get. He managed the fellow's shoulders and jerked his head forward with as much force as the Texan could muster.

The ranger's forehead smashed into the man's nose with a crushing blow, muffling his half-breath scream. Zach coiled for another strike but stopped when BB's knife was buried to the hilt in the gunman's throat. Only the sound of a wet gurgle escaped.

Two splashes sounded a moment later, both of the cartel goons "sleeping with the fishes." BB hefted the MP5, whispering, "I don't have one of these in my gun safe. Nice."

Zach, still breathing hard, simply muttered, "Thanks."

The sun was rising just as the two lawmen made it back to the pickup. "I need a shower. A hot one. A cup of coffee, and about three fingers of quality bourbon," Zach stated as they drove off.

"I take it you managed to find the ship's propellers?" BB teased.

"Yes, and God help me if I ever have to do something like that again. Once was plenty for this land lover. That sucked."

They drove to a cheap hotel, BB paying in pesos and answering all of the clerk's questions in passable Spanish. "I'm going to go find us some coffee and bourbon. Don't use all the hot water. I'll be back in 30 minutes."

"You can skip the whiskey," Zach countered. "Now that my nerves are crawling back inside my skin, I'll settle for some breakfast."

"Done."

Zach couldn't remember hot water ever feeling so good. Despite the dingy room, nasty bathtub, and the cheapest soap he'd ever seen, the ranger scrubbed and washed every inch of his body and hair at least three times.

He was just buttoning his shirt when BB returned, steaming cups of coffee and a bag of sugary, Mexican donuts in his hands.

Zach relaxed with the java and breakfast while BB took his turn purging two days of travel and work off his carcass. When the seasoned ranger finally reappeared, Zach suggested, "Let's go visit your friend at police headquarters before someone notices two missing guards."

They drove to the city management complex. BB was surprised how much security was in place until Zach reminded him of the fact that Mexico was in the middle of a civil war. "I guess that makes sense," BB admitted.

Twenty minutes later, they were shown into the chief's office, the Mexican cop acting like BB was his best friend who'd just returned from the dead.

Zach, too, received a warm, friendly greeting after BB introduced his traveling companion as a Texas Ranger.

"I'm working with Ranger Bass in much the same capacity that I worked with you," BB explained. "He hired me to help him track down a suspect, and we've found our man right here in Tampico."

Evidently, BB's old buddy thought the ranger was in for a bit of "la mordida," or "the pinch," as bribes and graft were commonly called. With Texas dollar signs in his smiling eyes, the chief said, "How can I help you apprehend this desperado?"

"Oh, no, no, my friend," BB smiled back. "We're here as a professional courtesy. You see, Ranger Bass has called in a team of Special Forces from the Texas military. They should be arriving before noon, and I wanted to warn you that they would be operating nearby."

"Tejas military? Here? In Tampico?" questioned the now-troubled cop. "This is allowed by my government?"

"Yes, we have approval from Mexico City," Zach lied. "You're welcome to call your superiors and verify this."

The chief was suddenly unhappy, but also appeared not to know exactly what to do about it. Finally, the frustrated man decided to call the mayor. While he was dialing, Zach and BB were heading for the door. "Thank you," both of them mumbled as they reached the exit. "See you soon."

"Let's get the hell out of Dodge before he has us arrested," BB said, hurrying down the hall.

"Right behind you, partner. I'll bet you a good steak dinner that he's really calling Vincent."

"I'm tempted to take you up on that. Knowing that corrupt old bastard, he's sitting down there right now trying to figure out how he can make a profit with his newfound knowledge."

The two rangers pulled out of the parking lot without incident, heading directly for the warehouse and their makeshift HVAC hide.

Twenty minutes later, Zach was wishing BB had accepted the wager.

Men were rushing all over, the anthill of activity both on and around Vincent's yacht, some trying to carry large boxes of supplies up the gangplank at the same time as others were trying to exit. The number of sentries had been tripled.

Zach could see Ghost was still aboard, as well as the female hostage from Texas. Vincent was hustling here and there, trying to direct traffic and issue orders, but, in reality, making things worse. The ranger had to chuckle when he saw the crime lord's eyes often scanning the sky as if he was looking for the helicopters that would deliver death from above.

"It won't be long now," Zach grinned.

Another 20 minutes had passed before El General decided he'd dillydallied enough. Strings of harsh orders were barked up and down the pier, resulting in several of the guards rushing to man the heavy dock lines that secured La Rosa to the bank.

Zach heard the powerful diesel engines crank, puffs of black smoke rising from under the yacht's stern. The gangplank was pulled aboard, a man wearing the whites of a ship's captain supervising the final steps before casting off.

Through his binoculars, Zach watched the vessel's master jog up a flight of stairs and into what the Texan assumed was the bridge. The engines revved as La Rosa's bow began to drift out into the river. Again, the throttle was applied to the big diesels, this time followed by a sickening screech of metal against metal.

Dense clouds of black smoke now boiled from the exhausts, but La Rosa didn't move.

Panic ensued aboard the boat, the captain reappearing and shouting for the dock lines to be reattached before his now-dead vessel drifted too far out into the current. Men were scrambling fore and aft, lines and rope arching through the air.

Vincent and Ghost arrived on the deck just as La Rosa was being pulled back toward the shore, at least 20 men straining to tug the huge yacht back to her mooring.

It was obvious that the ship's owner wasn't happy with her skipper. Zach watched Vincent's hand gestures and body language, wondering if the captain was going to be executed right on the spot. The woman from Texas inserted herself between El General and the captain, trying to calm the situation down.

The captain shrugged his shoulders, pointed toward the engine room, and seemed to be begging for mercy. Ghost stood beside his boss, taking it all in without the slightest reaction.

While he would have loved to stay and watch the show, Zach had to retreat from his cardboard hide and prepare for the next act of the drama.

The ranger rushed down the stairs and through the warehouse, finding his partner waiting in the idling pickup. "I'd give them 20 minutes tops," Zach said while climbing into the cab.

"We'll be ready," BB responded, an almost evil gleam of anticipation in the older ranger's eyes.

They drove a few hundred yards further along the riverbank, coming to rest next to an empty lot of waist-high weeds and trash.

The lot had been selected for three reasons, all of which were critical. First of all, it was a mere 600 yards from the now-disabled *La Rosa*.

Secondly, the overgrowth provided excellent cover.

Finally, it was less than two blocks from a major roadway.

The duo rushed to pull their weapons and magazines from the pickup's locked toolbox, each ranger checking the actions of his respective firearms. Then without a word, both moved into the overgrowth and headed for the river's bank.

Zach had been wrong about how long it would take Vincent to activate plan B. It was closer to 40 minutes before the steady thump-thump-thump of an approaching helicopter reached the duo's ears.

"I knew he'd have a copter waiting close by," Zach bragged. "No way a guy like that buys a boat with a helipad without having all the accessories. I bet the paint job even matches."

"We're about to find out," BB replied, finding a tree trunk size of driftwood to brace his weapon.

The helicopter came in low from the west, following the river less than 500 feet off the ground. As the two rangers shouldered their weapons, the pilot made a slow, looping turn for his approach.

Zach's rifle was a bit more accurate than BB's AK, but the older lawman's bullets carried more punch. "Steady," BB said, keeping the bubbled glass in his sights. "Nail that bastard when he's about 10 feet off the deck."

The ambushers waited, watching as the bird's nose flared upwards to check its approach. The pilot then started bringing her down slowly, hovering directly above *La Rosa's* flat landing area.

Flicking off his safety, Zach fired.

Striking a man at 600 yards with an AR15 was doable, but very difficult. Hitting a target the size of a helicopter wasn't all that hard.

Both of the rangers starting firing as fast as they could reset the trigger and pull again, arching round after round at the descending aircraft.

The bird's smooth, steady descent suddenly changed – the airframe tilting, jerking, and then holding steady as each ranger kept up a steady stream of anti-aircraft fire.

Zach wanted to knock the bird down and watch a fiery ball of flame envelope *La Rosa* after the crash, but that wasn't in the cards. Instead, the pilot attempted to increase his altitude just as smoke started pouring from the aircraft's turbine engine.

"He's trying to get away," BB shouted over the constant roar of their weapons.

Both rangers locked back empty at almost the same moment. Slamming home a couple of fresh magazines, the two lawmen returned to their assault within seconds.

The pilot was fighting for control now, the copter spinning and wobbling directly above *La Rosa*. Out of the corner of his eye, Zach noticed tiny figures running across the deck.

Flames, adding their sense of doom to the thicker column of black smoke, appeared as the two Texans continued throwing a relentless maelstrom of lead at the stricken bird.

The aircraft tilted sharply and banked hard toward the center of the river.

The helicopter struck the surface on its right side, the still-spinning rotors throwing up a curtain of water and mist as they slammed into the river.

Zach watched as the fuselage did a cartwheel across the surface, and then a red and white fireball erupted as burning gasoline was thrown 50 feet into the air.

"We gotta get the fuck out of here," BB snapped. "They'll be coming ... and coming hard."

While he would have loved to stay and watch the death throes of Vincent's flying limo, Zach knew his partner was right.

The two bushwhackers hustled for the pickup, scrambling into the cab with their weapons – just in case Vincent's bloodhounds responded a little faster than anticipated.

BB threw the transmission into gear and they were off, throwing up a cloud of dust, speeding toward the main road as fast as the aged V8 would take them. Less than two minutes later, they were merging into traffic and slowing down. There wasn't any sign of pursuit.

Once the two lawmen were comfortable that El General's boys weren't on their tails, BB turned back toward the river. "If your read on Vincent is accurate, he'll be going loco about now. He'll want to get as far away from here as he can get."

Zach nodded, keeping his eye on their surroundings. "He's down to one option – evading by car. Let's get to work on our funnel."

During the rooftop scouting and tours of the area, Zach had noted a significant tactical oversight by the man everyone claimed to be a "General."

While the river provided a means of escape and limited 180 degrees of access to his position, it also had the reverse effect of limiting the number of routes available for sneaking away. Without a boat, the water suddenly was like a prison's wall, and thus El General's enemy.

Then there was the industrial area where Vincent had chosen to moor his yacht. It was an isolated part of town, designed for interior square footage, not motor-traffic. There were only two streets in and out, and Zach planned to reduce that number by half.

BB drove to the burned out hulk they'd passed on the way in. When they'd first noticed the lone, still-standing wall and labeled it a deathtrap, neither ranger had known how accurate their prophecy would be.

After backing the truck into position, BB hopped out and grabbed a lengthy section of cord from the pickup's bed. "Been a while since I roped a steer this big," he grinned at his partner. "Sure hope this little scheme works."

Stepping toward the dilapidated structure, the old ranger began spinning the lasso with a broad, circular motion of his arm.

The noose shot through the air, arching high and falling perfectly over a piece of rebar 20 feet above. BB tightened the line and then made a quick knot on a second length of rope to make sure they had plenty of space.

While BB connected the "extension cord," to the lassoed building, Zach was tying it off to the truck's trailer hitch.

Back in the pickup, BB glanced at the younger man and said, "I always wanted to pull the bars off a jail cell and set my gang of outlaws free. I guess this will have to do."

BB gently rolled the truck forward until the rope was tight and then gave the V8 a boot's worth of gas. The back tires kicked up a plume of dirt and sand as they spun. For a moment, it looked like the old wall was far sturdier than either ranger had predicted.

Cutting the wheel right and left in short jabs, BB caused the back end of the pickup to swing back and forth. Rubber barked as the wall began to topple.

Zach watched in the side mirror as they began to roll forward, a child-like grin crossing the ranger's face when the three-story monolith of brick and concrete came crashing down. A huge cloud of debris billowed into the air as a rumbling thunder rolled through the area.

Waving the dust from their faces, the two Texans exited the truck to inspect their handiwork.

They found the narrow street blocked by a four-foot high wall of crumbled block, jagged rebar, and piles upon mounds of brick and concrete.

"That was fun," Zach coughed, the dust sticking in his throat.

"No shit. That was worth the trip just by itself," BB grinned.

Now Vincent had only one way in or out, and the rangers were going to be waiting for him.

Chapter 16

El General had been suspicious when the Tampico Chief of Police had called, claiming the Texas Rangers were in town. While he had his doubts about the cop and his information, there was no need to panic. After consulting with Ghost, it had been decided that moving their base of operations was sage.

Vincent had even been willing to accept the captain's excuse that an old dock line had somehow managed to foul *La Rosa's* propellers. While his famous temper had boiled over the incident, he was worldly enough to know that no amount of planning and preparation could overcome simple bad luck.

"Call in the helicopter," he'd ordered. "We'll go to the alternative plan."

While the crew and security forces scrambled to pack and prepare to abandon ship, El General had remained calm – at least as compared to some of his more notable outbursts. The captain was still alive, preparing to send a diver over the side to check on the propellers.

The drug lord knew something was terribly wrong when bullets started striking his freedom bird. Perhaps the chief hadn't been completely full of shit.

With his mind racing to figure out how the Texas Rangers had found his lair, Vincent still had alternatives – *La Rosa's* 22-foot speedboat being the next option.

While his men hustled to take up defensive positions and prepare to engage the Texas Special Forces that were surely on their way, El General went about packing an overnight bag and instructing Weekend to do the same. They would ride *La Rosa's* launch to the open water of the Gulf and then motor south to safety.

As his most trusted bodyguard toted their bags, Vincent and Weekend navigated the passageways that led to the yacht's water garage and the waiting powerboat.

One deck above the "toy shed," El General could hear the powerful outboard motors rumbling through the bulkhead. Turning to Weekend, he said, "Someone is finally thinking ahead and warming the engines," trying to steady his own nerves. "Given everything else that has gone wrong today, I should give them a raise."

They came to the hatch leading to the garage just as the engine noise increased its pitch.

Opening the watertight door, Vincent was stunned to see the speedboat accelerating away from *La Rose*, Ghost at the helm, waving goodbye from behind the wheel.

"Shoot him!" El General screamed at the bodyguard. "Kill him!"

It was too late, the launch coming up on plane and blasting across the surface of the river, fading quickly into the distance.

Weekend and the protector braced for Vincent's volcano of fury to erupt, but the explosion never came. Instead, the now frightened cartel boss said, "Get the cars packed and ready to go. Right now. We'll drive out of here."

Turning to give one last glance at the tiny white dot of Ghost's stolen vessel, El General hissed, "When I find you, your death will be very slow and agonizing, my friend. You will regret this treachery with every fiber of your being, so help me God."

For the first time since she'd met Vincent, Weekend detected fear in his voice. He'd always been so confident and self-assured.

She didn't really understand the fast-moving events of the morning, nor did she grasp the political aspirations of the man who treated her like the world's most pampered prisoner.

She could clearly see, however, the first flashes of insecurity and self-doubt, and that made her smile. Obviously, El General was in trouble, and she would welcome watching the mighty fall.

Zach touched the wires again and listened to the engine crank while his boot stomped on the gas. He'd never hotwired a vehicle before, but the old delivery van they'd spotted had been manufactured years before computer chips had made grand theft auto a high-tech crime.

Looking up at BB, he said, "I don't think it's going to start. What now?"

The old ranger knew their streak of good luck couldn't last forever. "I suppose I could block the road with the pickup, but they'll probably just ram right through. We need something heavy and wide to block their egress."

Zach glanced around, looking for something, anything, he could use as a roadblock. The van had been the perfect solution, but now its ancient motor wasn't going to cooperate. "Can we tow this beast?"

Glancing back and forth between his pickup and the heavy truck, BB tried to judge the distance. One of the front tires was flat on the bigger truck, but they only had to move it a few blocks. "Can't hurt to try," he finally shrugged. "I don't see another building we can pull over."

The two lawmen scrambled to connect the ropes, Zach taking the job of trying to steer the lifeless wreck. "Make sure you put it in neutral," BB advised, climbing into his pickup's cab.

Again, the back tires smoked as BB gave the Detroit V8 the gas.

Sitting in the cab of the delivery truck, Zach felt the frame move a little, then some more, and then the ancient workhorse was rolling. "Yeah! Go BB! Go!"

It took all of the Texan's considerable strength to turn the unassisted wheel, the flat rubber and lack of power steering making the sweat pop on his brow. But they were rolling.

Once the heavy van was on pavement, the ranger's task became a little easier. After a few minutes, and a couple of muscle straining corners, he was cutting the wheel hard to turn their mobile roadblock sideways across the pavement.

"We did it!" he yelled, climbing down from the cab. "Now we've got their sorry asses pinned. Let's get ready for a little turkey shoot."

BB pulled the truck into a back alley and out of sight – just in case things went wrong and they needed their own escape pod.

The two rangers then hustled to pocket the rest of their ammunition and weapons.

Zach took the north side of the road, BB the south with the van between them. The younger lawman chose what had once been the offices of a factory, the frame of a window providing an excellent field of fire while the heavy block wall would protect him from incoming lead.

BB's ambush hide was a waist-high mound of dirt that somehow had been deposited in an empty lot. The more experienced ranger always liked being able to move during a gunfight, and the open spaces surrounding the dirt mound gave him a lot of options.

After 20 minutes, Zach began to worry that Vincent had found another way out of their trap. At 30 minutes, he fought a strong urge to leave his post and go check on the activity around the yacht.

"What the fuck are they doing?" he yelled across the street to his partner.

"It's that little lady he's got on his arm," BB shouted back. "Don't you know it always takes women forever to pack?"

Zach appreciated the older man's use of humor to relieve stress. It was another 10 minutes before the two lawmen finally heard the sound of approaching engines.

Ducking low behind his cover, the ranger checked his spare mags for the Nth time and flicked the safety off of the carbine. His job was to take out the lead vehicle. BB would pepper the rear-most unit so they could pin anything between. It was to be the classic ambush.

Four SUVs came roaring up the street, their speed indicating that Zach wasn't the only one who thought things were taking too long.

Just as the rangers expected, the convoy stopped well short of the blocking delivery van.

Zach and BB had anticipated such a move, selecting their positions perfectly. Centering the red dot on the point vehicle's radiator, the ranger began firing as fast as he could pull the trigger.

Sparks and puffs of splintering metal announced he was on target, round after round tearing into the SUV's engine compartment.

The driver did what he was trained to do, hitting the gas in an attempt to steer through the kill zone. Problem was, there wasn't any place for him to go.

As the lead unit passed his position, Zach sent another series of lead pills into the doors and windows before turning his attention to the second target in line.

BB was pelting the rear guard of the cartel parade, slamming the heavier, Russian caliber bullets into the motor and front wheels. That driver decided to try and back out of the hailstorm of death, squealing the tires in reverse while attempting to execute some sort of fancy spinning turn.

The maneuver did nothing but expose the sides and rear to BB's relentless barrage. Evidently, the old lawman had managed to kill the thug behind the wheel because the SUV kept moving in reverse, eventually going off the road and slamming into a utility pole with bumper-crushing force.

The cartel shooters weren't amateurs. Within seconds, they realized the trap, many of the henchmen probably having pulled similar ambushes at some point in their criminal careers. Concluding they couldn't drive out of the kill zone, they decided to attempt escape on foot.

Doors were flying open on three of the four SUVs, men appearing with guns drawn as they scrambled for some sort of cover. Zach began to hear, feel, and see incoming fire pointed in his direction.

The ranger ignored the shooters, his attention drawn to the third vehicle. It remained idling in the street, its occupants seemingly uneager to hop out and join the building firefight.

"That's where Vincent and Ghost are riding," the ranger whispered. "Gotcha."

Zach centered on number three and began nailing the black Chevy as fast as his finger could work the trigger. After putting at least 10 rounds into the engine bay, he then moved his aim up to the windshield. That was his first indication that something was wrong.

The glass should have cracked, puffed, and splintered like the other escorts, but this one was different. Shot after shot impacted the glass in front of the driver, but no holes appeared. The ranger adjusted his aim and went for the passenger door window, and was shocked to see the same results.

"Bulletproof glass?" he hissed. "Bullshit. That crap is only in the movies."

The ranger dropped his aim again, putting the door's dark paint behind the red dot. While holes did appear, it was obvious that he was striking some sort of enhanced material.

Now Zach was beginning to worry. At least eight cartel enforcers had escaped their SUVs, the ranger assuming they would continue to run for their lives. But would they?

Deciding Vincent's armored ride wasn't going anywhere, Zach began sweeping for the bodyguards.

It saved his life.

Around the corner of a building the assassins came, spreading out in a skirmish line and firing on full automatic.

Zach ducked just as concrete and mortar shrapnel exploded all around his head, dozens of incoming rounds peppering his position. The goons hadn't been running away; they'd been regrouping.

While he kept his head down, Zach could hear the heavy pop, pop, pop of BB's Kalashnikov hammering away from across the street. To the ranger's ear, it sounded like the old timer was having his own issues.

Zach chanced rising up and sending four quick shots at the approaching gunmen, sure he wasn't going to hit anything, but hoping he'd at least slow them down. He was surprised at how close they had managed to advance already.

Evidently, his move pissed Vincent's boys off, another avalanche of hot lead slamming into the spot where Zach had just been. Larger chunks of brick rained down on the ranger's head, the block walls only able to absorb so much punishment.

"Time to retreat," he announced, knowing that the white hats had probably just lost their best chance at catching Ghost and El General. Now, his thoughts turned to surviving the encounter.

Leaping to his feet, Zach snap-fired a few rounds and darted through the old factory. He'd scouted the place briefly and knew there was a loading dock at the far end.

He was halfway across the junk-strewn main space when the cartel gunmen announced they too had entered the premises, unleashing a thunderous, sweeping spray that chased the ranger's retreat.

Zach dived behind a pile of old scrap iron, bullets pinging and popping all around the pile of debris. The volume of fire was so intense; he thought the walls might collapse from the vibrations and impact.

The men pursuing the ranger were pretty good. While their marksmanship left him uninspired, they were skilled enough to keep one of their four weapons firing at all times, never taking off the pressure while reloading.

They continued to advance, walking upright and blasting away. Zach knew he had to chance exposure, finally lifting his head, taking an extra half a second, and centering his optic on a man's chest.

Two 5.56 NATO rounds tore into the thug's sternum at just over 3,200 feet per second, the long, tublar body tumbling as they struck flesh, ripping and tearing ribs, lungs, and muscles before exiting out the already-dead man's back.

Zach hit the deck and rolled as another blizzard of pain launched in his direction. In a single motion, the Texan spun around, stood to his feet, and scurried half bent at the waist, trying to keep the garbage heap between the hunters and his carcass.

The ranger harbored a dim hope that seeing their comrade cut nearly in half would slow his pursuers down was quickly diminished. The cartel enforcers came harder now, seemingly motivated by their friend's demise.

Zach took the opportunity to slam home a fresh magazine as he ran, zigging and cutting through the rusting hulks of whatever machinery was left behind. Vincent's hellhounds were breathing hot on his heels.

The ranger managed the back of the building, pulling hard on a metal door. Fresh air and bright sunlight met Zach as he rushed out into the street, but that was no consolation. There wasn't any place to hide. No cover.

His brain began screaming for the Texan to run like hell, to put distance between himself and the chasers. Some instinct overrode his survival voice, taking no more than a microsecond to realize he'd be gunned down less than 50 feet from the exit.

Zach began walking backward, his weapon on his shoulder, aimed at the door that had just banged shut behind him. He had a little surprise for the first guy who stuck out his head.

The door flew open, the ranger's finger pulling the trigger instantly. No one came out. "Nice," Zach whispered. "They must have watched old Westerns, too."

Now, he was stepping backward as fast as he could. Distance was life. If he could just make the corner.

Again, the door opened; this time, a hunk of metal flew out. Zach pelted it with two shots before he realized it wasn't a body. Then they came in a rush.

How all three managed to squeeze through the door, shooting at the same time, defied physics and was a mystery Zach didn't stick around to solve – he was too busy running.

He could feel the rounds snapping by his head as he made the edge of the factory, the building's façade erupting as at least a dozen rounds chased the fleeing lawman.

Zach hadn't managed more than 10 steps when he realized another SUV was parked ahead, men with weapons pouring out of the doors.

I am so fucked, he thought, trying to get his carbine to aim at what he assumed was cartel reinforcements. No wonder Vincent hadn't scrambled to get out of the kill box – he knew help was on the way.

Pinned between the two groups, Zach finally managed to center the red dot as he skidded to a halt. His finger was putting pressure on the trigger when something flashed familiar … a head of long, dark hair. He knew that hair.

Sam's face came into his mind just as the new arrivals launched a salvo of their own, all four of the riflemen unloading at the men behind Zach.

Surprised, the cartel hunters stumbled, fell, and danced death's jig as Sam's associates engaged with withering accuracy.

Zach, regaining his composure, jogged up to his partner with a look that indicated he was trying to decide if she were a hallucination or not.

"About time you got here," he spouted with a sly grin. "I had resigned myself to dealing with these assholes all by myself."

Sam's fists flew to her hips at the audacious greeting. "Why … you…. From where I stand, Ranger Bass, you were about to get sliced and diced all by yourself. And you are not welcome … asshole."

A man appeared beside the two rangers, tan, fit … his demeanor carrying an air of authority. While his Hawaiian print shirt and golf shorts made him look like a tourist, Zach's mind said, "military."

"Zach, meet Captain Billy Riddell, Republic of Texas Marines."

The two men nodded, a battlefield obviously not the place for handshakes and the exchange of business cards.

"Captain Riddell was in charge of the training that day at Langtry. He and his men took some of their accrued leave for a short vacation in Mexico. I came along to see if I could help," Sam explained.

The ranger had a million questions for his partner, but the sound of gunshots a few blocks over stopped the interrogation. "BB!" Zach barked, cursing himself for forgetting his partner.

The ranger started to run in the direction of the gunfire, but Sam put out her hand to stop him. Riddell explained, "My gunny sergeant and a few more of our boys are helping your partner, Ranger. No need to be concerned."

Zach's eyes darted back and forth between his partner and the Marine officer. "It's okay," Sam reassured. "They were chasing down a couple of stragglers. BB is just fine."

Nodding with relief, a vision of the third, bulletproof SUV popped into Zach's mind. "Vincent!" he snapped, again commanding his legs to move.

"Where was he?" Sam asked, holding him back.

"He's in the third car of the convoy. We disabled three, but El General's ride was up-armored."

"There were only three vehicles in the kill zone, sir," the Marine reported.

Zach looked at Sam with wide eyes, urgency in his voice, "Come on! He's headed back to the yacht. We can't let Ghost and that asshole get away!"

Somehow, they all squeezed into the rental unit, gun barrels and Sam's crutch pointing every which direction.

As they drove toward *La Rosa's* mooring, Zach spotted BB standing next to his pickup, shooting the shit with a bunch of what appeared to be tourists armed with M4 carbines. The captain had his men jumping into action in a second.

They all rushed to *La Rosa*, Vincent's dinged, but still-functioning Chevy Suburban sitting at the foot of the gangplank.

Two men appeared at the top of the yacht's rail, their weapons spraying at the Marines as the brave young assaulters spread out and then began to concentrate their return fire. One of the cartel defenders went down, the other choosing to retreat.

Up the gangplank rushed the Marines, pouring onto *La Rosa's* main deck and establishing a beachhead in seconds. BB didn't want to be left out and was soon scurrying to keep up.

Sam, with her crutch under one hand and a .45 pistol in the other, started to follow. "What the hell do you think you're doing?" Zach asked.

"I flew all the way down here to end this thing. I intend to see it cleaned up … personally."

Zach could see she wasn't going to be denied, and given the fact that she'd just saved his life, decided to stay back and cover his partner as Sam limped up the incline of the ramp.

The Marines were spreading out now, four 2-man teams moving with well-coordinated, disciplined movements as their captain shouted orders and gunny made damn sure they were followed.

"Clear," came a voice, another echoing further down, "Clear on the bridge."

"Head for the lowest deck," Zach advised. "There's a swim platform down there... maybe Vincent's going to try and scuba to freedom."

Shots rang out as another Cartel bodyguard tried to defend the ship. He didn't last long.

It seemed to be taking hours to sweep the massive vessel, the Marines not wanting to leave any threat to their rear. Zach hung back with Sam, the lady ranger doing her best to keep up despite a gimpy limb.

While he would have never said it aloud, Zach was impressed with her determination. Finally, the main decks and superstructure were cleared.

As the captain was dispatching a team to the engine spaces and another to the forward stores, a single shot rang out from the stern of the ship.

The gunny did a quick headcount, turning to his commander and saying, "Not one of ours."

Everyone rushed toward the solo gunshot.

Zach was envisioning finding Vincent dead, the ranger guessing that the cartel honcho would kill himself before being captured. It then occurred that perhaps there was only one scuba tank aboard, and Ghost had done Texas a favor and killed the drug lord himself.

The two lead Marines burst into the water garage, closely followed by Zach and the rest of the boarding party.

There was Vincent, his body draped in an awkward position over the seat of a jet ski. There was blood soaking the back of his shirt, leaking from a crater in the back of his skull. Weekend was standing, staring blankly at the dead man's face, a smoking pistol at her side.

Zach walked up and gently removed the weapon from her limp grip. He could hear her whispering, "You son of a bitch, you son of a bitch," over and over again.

Zach took her chin and made eye contact, "Where is Ghost? Where is the other man?"

She actually laughed, an evil tinkle echoing off the hull. "He betrayed this fucker when the helicopter went down. He stole the launch over an hour ago."

Looking out the open bay of the water garage, Zach scanned for any sign of the escaping terrorist. He knew it was hopeless. Ghost was long gone.

Sam stepped up beside her partner as if to help him search the horizon. When Zach finally looked down, it was clear he was feeling beaten. "I can't believe that guy got away … again. What in the hell does it take to catch that madman?"

"We'll get him, Zach; I promise. He just got lucky is all. We'll get him."

Sam and her Marines had flown down on a private plane, courtesy of a grieving father who had lost a son in the massacre.

As she and Zach prepared to head back to Texas with their rescuers, BB was helping himself to the crème de la crème of the cartel weapons, as well as a few bottles from *La Rosa's* well-stocked liquor cabinets.

Sam sat down by Weekend, draped her arm around her shoulder and said, "You should start packing. We've got room enough on the plane for you and a couple of bags."

The young lady shook her head, "No, I'm going to stay. I've been spying on Vincent for over a year now. I know where a lot of his skeletons are buried, as well as the passwords to a few of his offshore accounts. I even know where he's stashed the antidote for the plague. I'm going to stay right here and help fix some of the damage he's done."

Zach was a bit taken aback by the tiny woman's declaration, her words and attitude not matching her age or physical appearance whatsoever.

For 20 minutes, the two rangers tried to talk her out of such a high-minded scheme. "How are you going to manage this by yourself? Even if you have access to Vincent's ill-gotten gains, the organization's lieutenants are going to step in and take over. They always do." Sam reasoned.

"Either that or one of the competing cartels will invade and try to take over his territory. They're not going to want you hanging around."

Weekend was polite but firm. "Thank you both for your concern, but no, my mind is made up. I can do this."

About then *La Rosa's* captain returned, along with two of his non-combatant crew. It took them a while to explain how they had abandoned ship, escaping to hide ashore during all of the shooting. The sailor immediately rushed into Weekend's arms.

Zach and Sam exchanged looks, the two officers realizing that Weekend had been having an affair with the yacht's master. After the emotional reunion, she turned to one of the crewmen and said, "Follow me, please."

Exchanging shrugs, the two rangers decided to follow, curious what the suddenly aggressive woman had planned.

They soon arrived at *La Rosa's* extensive media room. "I want to make a video and upload it to all of the cartel's social media accounts," Weekend stated.

The crewman hustled to execute her wishes, flipping a few switches and then aiming a tripod-mounted camera. Weekend produced her cell phone and ordered, "There is a picture of Vincent on here. I want it to be clearly shown."

The rangers watched fascinated as the yacht's tech downloaded an image that showed El General was clearly dead. Then, after straightening her hair and taking a deep breath, Weekend moved to stand in front of the camera.

"My name is Leticia Gabriela Diaz. The man known as El General is dead. I killed him for what he has done to Mexico and her wonderful people. By common law, I was his wife and now claim my rightful ownership of his estate. I am going to do my best to repair the damage he inflicted, starting with the distribution of the antidote for the plague and identifying where this terrible weapon was being manufactured."

Sam and Zach stood stunned as she continued, her words striking in their honesty, her message powered by the truth.

A short time later, the Marines were ready to head out, the plane waiting to ferry them back to Texas.

Zach and BB shook hands, the two lawmen having established a bond shared by men who had fought side by side and survived. "Promise you and Ranger Temple will come visit Queen Izzy and me after the border reopens," the old lawman said.

"If you'll cook some more of that steak, we're in," Zach grinned.

After hugging Sam, BB pivoted without another word and strolled to his pickup. He waved again while driving off, a tarp covering the mound of booty riding in the bed.

"Let's get going, Ranger," Sam said. "There's going to be one hell of a lot of work patching things back together again, and I've got a feeling Major Putnam is going to be looking for both of us."

Zach nodded, scanning *La Rosa* one last time. "It was a hell of a vacation while it lasted. We should come back next year and do it again."

Epilogue

Cheyenne's eyes twinkled in the candlelight, their rich hue enhancing what had already been a memorable evening.

Their dinner had been perfect, from the savory cuisine to the romantic ambiance of the restaurant's atmosphere. Certain he had kept his promise and arranged a special date for his special lady, Zach's mood was light-hearted and carefree.

He couldn't help but admire the vision she created, the ranger finding it difficult to look at anything else in the room. Chey's company could make any man feel special, and it was more than her raw beauty. There was a wholesome energy in the woman, a force that projected warmth and honesty.

Finally, he managed to break her spell, reaching in his jacket pocket and producing a slip of paper. "I borrowed some money out of my retirement account with the republic," he said. "I want you to pay off that loan with Trustline. You can make the regular monthly payments back to me."

"Oh, Zach," she replied with a knowing smile while pushing the offered check away. "You don't have to do that."

"I want to," he reassured her with sincerity. "Besides, there's nothing the law can do to help, and I don't want to see you harmed in any way. I'd arrest those crooks at that bank in a heartbeat, but given the lack of regulations or consumer protection, my hands are tied. This is the only way out."

"You're so sweet, but seriously, that problem has already been solved. Everything's fine," the beauty responded, flipping her hair over her shoulder and flashing a "cat that ate the canary" smile.

"Huh? What are you talking about?"

"While you were gallivanting around Mexico, I decided to take matters into my own hands. I mean, after all, Mr. Carson had been taken out of the picture, and I figured it would take Trustline a bit to regroup. I knew though, that it wouldn't be long before they followed through on their threats to ruin my reputation online and thought I would just give them a dose of their own medicine," Chey explained. Pausing for effect, she sipped her wine before continuing. "I started posting what was happening on social media and everywhere else I could think of. A few of my friends got on board, and within a day, the whole thing went viral. There were almost a million people online saying that they would never do business with that bank again. A bunch of others said they had checking accounts and were going to close them out and move to a new bank."

Zach was puzzled by the whole thing. "Still, if you don't pay that loan, they're going to ruin your life."

Chey shook her head, "Trustline called me the next day and apologized for the entire affair. They promised that everyone's loans and accounts would be audited for irregularities and then cleaned up, and that they were firing the men responsible for the entire fiasco. They've even asked if I would be interested in being their spokesperson for a new series of television commercials that would help repair their reputation."

Rubbing his chin, Zach had to smile. "Social justice," he whispered.

"What?"

"Social justice…. Maybe those who want a smaller government are right. Maybe we don't need all those complex laws and government agencies. Perhaps social justice will take care of problems like this for us."

Shrugging her shoulders, Chey made it clear she had more important matters on her mind. "Take me home, cowboy," she whispered in a sultry tone. "It's time I rewarded my hero."

THE END

Made in the USA
San Bernardino, CA
12 March 2016